SALVAGING TRUTH

HUNTERS & SEEKERS

BOOK 1

BY JOANNE JAYTANIE

This book is a work of fiction. The characters, places and events in this story are fictional. Any similarities to real people, places, or events are not intentional and purely the result of coincidence.
Copyright © 2019 by Joanne Jaytanie
Formatting by Self-Publishing Services, LLC
Cover by Tell-Tale Book Covers
All rights reserved. No part of this book may be reproduced, scanned, redistributed or transmitted in any form or by any means, print, electronic, mechanical, photocopying, recording, or otherwise, without prior written permission of the author.

Dedication

To my editor extraordinaire—Ruth Ross. I'm beyond grateful for your unwavering support of me. When I thought about scrapping this story, you pulled me through to the other end. I am forever in your debt.

For my husband, Ralph, and daughter, Julie. Thank you both for your time and expertise with regards to the Navy and Coast Guard. You are always there to answer my unending lists of questions and to fact-check my stories' details.

Acknowledgements

Author Photo by Samantha Panzera
Edits With a Touch of Grace
Self-Publishing Services, LLC

Table of Contents

Chapter One 1
Chapter Two 3
Chapter Three 8
Chapter Four 15
Chapter Five 21
Chapter Six 28
Chapter Seven 36
Chapter Eight 44
Chapter Nine 51
Chapter Ten 59
Chapter Eleven 64
Chapter Twelve 71
Chapter Thirteen 78
Chapter Fourteen 83
Chapter Fifteen 88
Chapter Sixteen 94
Chapter Seventeen 101
Chapter Eighteen 107
Chapter Nineteen 113
Chapter Twenty 119
Chapter Twenty-One 126
Chapter Twenty-Two 135
Chapter Twenty-Three 143
Chapter Twenty-Four 149
Chapter Twenty-Five 157
Chapter Twenty-Six 161
Chapter Twenty-Seven 167
Chapter Twenty-Eight 176
Chapter Twenty-Nine 183

Chapter Thirty	189
Chapter Thirty-One	199
Chapter Thirty-Two	206
Chapter Thirty-Three	213
Chapter Thirty-Four	218
Chapter Thirty-Five	224
Chapter Thirty-Six	231
Chapter Thirty-Seven	239
Chapter Thirty-Eight	246
Chapter Thirty-Nine	253
Chapter Forty	260
Chapter Forty-One	264
About the Author	269

Chapter One

A buzz split the dark silence of Riley's room and jerked her away from fondling the chiseled backside of the magnificent hunk of a man lying next to her—in her dreams. She growled as her perfect scene of spectacular glutes melted away. Her semi-conscious mind replaced the scene with her mother walking into the room, reaching out for her. Her mom's icy fingertips slithered down one shoulder and Riley's eyes snapped open.

Half coherent, Riley groaned, rolled over, and reached out toward the nightstand. Her fingers brushed the phone causing the screen to light up. Her mother's cheery smile filled the screen as the phone slipped from her fingers and dropped to the floor.

"This better be life or death," Riley hissed.

Stretching out for the phone, she balanced herself with one hand extended to the floor, but she couldn't reach it before the buzzing started over.

"For the love of all that's good! A brilliant scientist and yet she can't tell time."

Snatching the blasted thing, she slumped back onto the bed and fumbled for the answer button.

"Mom, you do realize it's the middle of the night. You might be a night owl, but most of civilization is asleep this time of night. I told you I had to get up early tomorrow—well, today...." Riley stopped the rant when she realized she was talking to static. She ended the connection but noticed there was a message.

Riley dropped the phone back on the nightstand and snuggled back into bed. She rolled over to try and reclaim the ravishing male specimen attached to that exquisite ass. But Mr. Beefcake had disappeared right along with whatever chance she had of sleeping.

She sighed, grabbed her phone, and clicked on her voicemail.

"Riley, it's Mom."

Mom was breathing hard and there was a high, terrified pitch to her voice. "Our ship—" A loudspeaker in the background squawked to life and drowned out her voice. "My research, it's—" Static drowned out mom's voice. "Riley, don't let them get my research."

"Claudia, we must go *now*!" cried a male voice in the background. "Get to the lifeboats. Oh, shit! No, we can't go that way. The water—" Static.

Riley wasn't sure who was talking to Mom, maybe one of her numerous assistants?

She couldn't be sure with all the noise in the background. Riley bolted out of bed and started pacing the floor, her phone crammed to her ear.

"I love you, Riley." Her mother panted between words, sounding as if she was running as she spoke.

The phone went dead.

Chapter Two

A few short hours ago the marina was deserted, except for Dagger and a couple of snoring Harbor Seals sunning themselves on the dock. Now the marina was bustling with people.

"Hey, Dagger. You're down here early, even for you. What's up?" Kaleb asked. He grabbed a handful of diving gear from the pull cart on the dock and handed it to his partner.

Dagger took the well-worn dry suit, nearly-new top-of-the-line swim fins, along with towels and dry clothes, and stacked them alongside a pile of items he'd already loaded into the thirty-five-foot inboard runabout. They purchased this specific motorboat for its speed, maneuverability, and the diver's platform off the stern.

"We got a new contract early this morning. I agreed to head out first thing. The San Diego Police requested inspection and video of a research ship," Dagger Eastin said, never missing a beat in his loading process.

"Nice! Why didn't you text me or Stone?" Kaleb asked.

"Like I said, it was early."

"You forwarded the damned office phone to your cell again, didn't you?"

Dagger frowned at Kaleb. "Hello—new business. If we don't get our company into the black in the next six months, we're gonna be in deep shit."

"I feel like a broken record. The three of us are *partners*. Which means it's all our asses on the line. We're doing all we can do, Dagger. Maybe we should've gone back to Washington to homeport the business."

"I know you'd prefer to head back home, but we agreed to go into business together. For Stone, you, and me to pull our weight throughout the year, San Diego is the ideal place. This is a warm water port. The only time we need to pull the boat out of the water is for maintenance. It saves us a load of money not to pull it out every winter and place it in dry storage. You have to admit we have better coverage of the west coast and a greater ability to bring in more business."

"Yeah, I know, but it sure is more expensive to operate a business here. Either way, it won't make a hill of beans if you don't take some time off and sleep every now and then."

"I'll sleep when the business is solid."

Kaleb shook his head. "And I always thought it was the military that made you rigid. Shit, you are one bull-headed SOB."

Dagger threw kisses at Kaleb. "I love you, too," he said between smacking sounds.

"Holy hell, knock it off. It's too early for this crap." Kaleb snapped. "Which one of us do you want to go with you?"

"Neither."

"No way. You know better. You might be one bad-ass diver, but no one dives alone." Kaleb clenched his hands into fists so tightly his knuckles turned white. "I'm going to get my gear."

"No, you're not." Dagger grabbed Kaleb by the arm, stopping him. "You and Stone are staying here, I need you on point.

"I'm only going there to get some video and an initial feel for what we are dealing with. I won't be down for long. The place will be crawling with Coast Guard. There'll be plenty of eyes on me. I don't need you babysitting me. What we do need is another *paying* gig. Helping your friend's sister was a nice thing to do, don't get me wrong. But the electric company won't take a feel-good story for payment."

"Cute, Dagger—and yeah, you do need a babysitter. If you show up and the Coast Guard isn't on site, you radio back and we'll come out to cover you. I mean it," Kaleb said, challenging his partner's glare. "No one, not even hot-shot Dagger Eastin dives alone. And if we find out you did…well, trust me, you don't want to go there."

"Yes, mommy. I'll behave." Not waiting for a comeback, he changed subjects and barked orders at Kaleb. "Send Stone a text. Get him up to speed. Make sure you find another contract today—

preferably one that *makes* us some money. No more donating time until our bills are paid if you want to keep the lights on and not have to bunk at the shop."

"Slave driver. You really know how to ruin a great morning." Kaleb tossed Dagger the rest of his gear. "Anything else, Mom?"

"That's it." Dagger secured his equipment and started the engine. "Oh, for shit's sake. Who was the last douche to take this thing out? The tank is half empty. What's the rule?"

"You take it, you fill it—Don't give me that look. It wasn't me this time. I had my fill of your ranting last time. I'll let Stone know he was a bad boy."

"Fat lotta good that does me now." Dagger shook his head in disappointment. He hated playing the heavy; but if he didn't do it, no one would. "Grab the bow line. I gotta haul ass over to the fuel dock before the queue gets too long."

Kaleb tossed the ropes into the runabout as Dagger started backing the vessel out of their slip. "Remember, Dagger. No diving if the Coast Guard isn't on site. Don't forget. I gotta couple buddies I can contact," he threatened. "Don't think I won't damn well know if you're giving me the brush off. Make sure to shoot us a text when you get on site or I just might have to drop in on you."

Dagger waved at Kaleb without glancing at him and roared off toward the fuel dock.

****

Deep blue ocean stretched out before Dagger. In the distance he could make out the white hulls of two Coast Guard cutters. The sea shimmered in the early morning light.

Dagger pulled the handset from its cradle.

"US Coast Guard Cutter Chinook, this is motor vessel Salvage Hunter approximately one hundred and fifty yards out. We've been contracted by SDPD to assist in the investigation. Over." Dagger was home on the water. A sizzle of anticipation shot through him.

"Roger, Salvage Hunter. This is Chinook. Hold tight while we confirm your status. Divers in the water. Over." The man's voice commanded.

"Roger, Salvage Hunter standing by. Out."

Dagger cut his engines. Figuring it would take them some time, he stripped down and pulled on his dry suit and checked his gear. The ocean didn't allow second chances. One faulty gauge or leaky hose could mean your death.

"Salvage Hunter, identity and authorization confirmed. Be advised we still have divers in the water. Over."

"Roger, Chinook. Requesting status of investigation. Over."

"No survivors found. We have retrieved sixteen bodies. Crew manifest states a total of nineteen, including crew and research team. Over."

"Were life boats put into the water? Over."

"We found one life boat among the floating wreckage. My men believe it broke loose when the ship sank. Last night the weather was driving rain. My guess is the life boat wasn't tied down properly. The other three boats are still stowed on the ship's deck. Over."

"Roger. Has the vessel been searched for survivors? Over."

"Confirmed, none found. Over."

"Request approach to begin investigation. Over."

"Approach granted; stop at sixty yards out on starboard side. Out."

Dagger hung up the handheld and started the engines. He moved into position and cut his engines as instructed, leaving the requested distance from the Coast Guard's ship, and dropped anchor. He went up to the deck to raise the diving flag, then stopped and grabbed his phone to text his partners:

> Coast Guard Cutter Chinook and a second ship on site. Starting diving operation. Will contact when heading back.

He hit send and locked the phone in the safe; not knowing exactly who might board his vessel.

Dagger headed topside, with an Alpha dive flag under one arm and a red buoy in his other hand. The red buoy was the universal sign of a claimed salvage site. He ran the Alpha dive flag up the flagstaff perched on the roof of the forward cabin. Moving to the stern of the runabout, he dropped the diving platform, sat down, and pulled on his dive hoodie and neck seal. He slid his MK3 knife into the neoprene holster and attached a spear gun to the back of his hips, right below his tanks. Before getting wet, he triple-checked his breathing equipment.

He slipped into the water, grabbed the buoy and the five-pound weight equipped with a retractable line, and swam toward the wreck.

When he was over the site, he attached the clip on the line to the bottom of the buoy and released the buoy. He headed down to the wreck where he'd drop the weight on the ocean floor.

The water was calm and a clear lapis color. A few feet under, Dagger swam by two Coast Guard divers and gave them a thumbs-up. The blue of the ocean darkened with every foot he descended. He switched on his light as the blue bled into a colorless gray. The dark outline of the eighty-five-foot research ship came into view. Pulling out his video camera he switched on the attached high-powered, compact light and started filming. He approached slowly, making sure to include everything.

The ship had come to rest on its port side at approximately a thirty-degree angle. While upright vessels were the easiest to work on, he couldn't ask for a much better scenario. He thought of the contract they closed last week. The ship had settled on its deck, with the stern embedded into the ocean floor. He silently laughed as he recalled Stone's colorful tirade over trying to move around inside without wanting to spew his lunch.

Dagger swam to the stern and then around to the port side, recording the scene. He glided through the water using his fins as little as possible to avoid disturbing the bottom.

Everything appeared intact until he reached the front third of the ship. A large ragged horizontal gouge ran a good nine feet along the side of the metal-hulled ship. It looked as though an object sliced the hull. What could have done this?

Dagger squinted and zoomed in closer. The gash showed no signs of paint transfer, and the edges of the ripped hull were bent inward and scorched. He slowed his breathing and filmed even more slowly.

After Dagger was satisfied he'd recorded all the details on the outside of the vessel, he moved inside. He painstakingly moved through room by room, documenting everything.

As the Coast Guard said, he found no bodies on board and no signs of a struggle. Aside from the expected turmoil due to the inrush of water, the inside appeared normal, or as normal as a sunken ship could look sitting at a thirty-degree angle. He finished his inspection and headed for the surface.

Chapter Three

After her mother's mysterious call, Riley spent the next four hours on the phone trying to track down Wayne Samuels, the CEO of Sheridan and her mom's boss. She paced the floor and went through gallons of coffee as she made non-stop attempts to reach Samuels. Her stomach churned, the coffee alternately threatening to spew its way to the surface or burn straight through her stomach wall. Having no success reaching Wayne and unable to wait any longer, Riley jumped in her SUV and headed for Sheridan Enterprises.

As she approached Sheridan Enterprises, the flag flying was at half-staff. Her vision misted as she fought back tears.

More than five hours had passed since Riley first listened to the voicemail. She pulled into the first open spot and killed her engine. Clutching the steering wheel with both hands, she dropped her head against it, closed her eyes, and struggled to steady her breathing as she replayed her mother's call over and over in her mind.

Her mom was a seasoned diver and an excellent swimmer. Riley was sure she would be found—she just had to be.

Riley couldn't begin to fathom how she would live if Mom wasn't a phone call away.

There was a sharp rap on the window, making her jump. Wayne Samuels stood next to her door, arms crossed and staring down at her.

"Wayne, you scared the life out of me," Riley said as she rolled down her window.

"What are you doing here, Riley? Didn't my assistant assure you I'd keep you updated? There's no news and I have a million things to do today. Our missing research vessel has left me with an unending list. The insurance company has already contacted the office. How the hell did they find out already? What are you doing here, don't you have classes?"

She put her hand on the door handle, but Wayne refused to move out of the way. "Mom is not only your employee, she's your friend. You don't seem too upset about her disappearance."

He sucked in a breath and sighed heavily as he let it out. "Of course I'm upset. You're right, she is my friend. But she's not the only one missing, nor my only friend on board." He tried to appear sympathetic, but it didn't quite reach his eyes. "There are eighteen other employees missing and eighteen families demanding information. And that's to say nothing about the media firestorm this accident will cause for the company." Wayne finally stepped back from her car.

Riley changed her mind; Wayne sounded plenty upset…about all the work that just landed on his desk. How could he be so self-centered?

"Now, tell me what exactly is being done." Riley demanded.

"All the appropriate steps have been taken." Wayne assured her. "The Coast Guard has been notified of the missing ship and the search is underway. We're doing everything possible to locate the ship. There's nothing here for you to do. Go teach your classes."

"I have no intention of teaching today. My mother is on your missing ship. My assistant is filling in for me. I intend to remain here until I have answers."

"I told you—" His body stiffened as he leaned closer with a warning glower.

Refusing to let him intimidate her, she lifted her chin and glared back at him.

"I heard you," she snapped.

"Well, hell…fine. I don't have the time to argue with you any longer. I'm on the way to my office. Let's go." He turned and walked away at a brisk clip, leaving Riley hurrying to catch up.

"Hold the elevator," Samuels bellowed, as his heels snapped smartly across the gleaming marble floor of the spacious lobby. He stepped directly into the center of the elevator, forcing people towards the walls.

The doors closed directly behind Riley as she rushed in after him.

"Morning, Mr. Samuels," Kathy, his secretary, greeted him as they exited the elevator. "Good morning, Ms. Rawlings." Kathy handed Samuels a cup of coffee and cocked her eyebrows in Riley's direction in a silent question.

Riley shook her head. Her stomach was still churning. Now it felt like a volcano ready to erupt. What she wouldn't give for a fistful of antacids.

"I'm so sorry about your mother's ship. I'm sure she'll be fine, just fine." Kathy reached out and patted Riley on her arm. "Mr. Eastin arrived early," Kathy said. "He's waiting in your office."

Samuels threw his secretary a smoldering glare. "What have I told you about allowing people in my office unattended?" Samuels snapped.

"I didn't think it would be a problem. He asked where he could sit to make phone calls. I thought he might like some privacy."

Samuels ignored Kathy as he opened the door to his office. Riley followed. An imposing man sat in one of the high-backed guest chairs, head down, typing away on his tablet. His sable hair appeared nearly black, a riot of wavy layers, tight on the sides and back, longer and almost curly on top.

"Eastin," Samuels said.

The man looked up, his magnetic topaz-colored eyes skimming over Samuels and locking onto Riley's. "Hope you don't mind. My day started at the crack of dawn. I finished my prior work early and decided to come straight here rather than return to my office." His gaze never wavered. "You look like your mother."

"Dagger Eastin, this is Riley Rawlings," Samuels said as he walked to his desk and sat in his chair. "We're planning on hiring Mr. Eastin's company as our investigators for our missing research vessel."

"Are you referring to the sunken vessel the Coast Guard is currently involved with?" Dagger asked.

"Yes," Samuels said.

"Then I'm afraid my company will have to pass on your offer."

"Excuse me. Aren't you a salvage and investigation company?" Samuels frowned.

"We are, yes. However, we've already been contracted by San Diego Police Department to assist them in this investigation."

"What! Why is the SDPD already involved? Whatever caused our ship to sink, it was an accident."

"Standard operating procedure requires the Coast Guard to submit an incident report. The Coast Guard is cooperating with the SDPD on this investigation," Dagger said. "I've been given the authority to fill you in on the current status. By the time I arrived, the Coast Guard pulled sixteen bodies from the water. All eight of the crew and eight of the research team."

Riley gasped.

"Your mother was not among them. At this point, there are three unaccounted for, Dr. Rawlings and the remaining two of her team. I took extensive video of the wreckage. After we're finished here, I'll be heading back to my office to study the video."

"But it was an accident, there's no need for a criminal investigation," Samuels said.

"Multiple deaths demand a careful investigation. It's premature and inappropriate for me to comment on the ongoing investigation," Dagger said.

"I need answers. Now. I've a board to report to and eighteen families to update. I'm certain this company isn't liable in any way for this tragic accident, but we need to know the details."

Riley tore her stare from Dagger and nearly snarled at Samuels. There was the man she knew. All about the bottom line. In the DNA lottery, he entirely missed the sympathy gene.

"There's nothing more I can tell you at this time. Perhaps you should contact the SDPD if you'd like additional information," Dagger said.

"If you've nothing more you can tell me, I have much to do," Samuels said, dismissing him.

"Good day, Mr. Samuels. Ms. Rawlings." Dagger gave her a slight nod. He stood and left the room.

Wayne Samuels ignored her and went about his work. Realizing she wasn't going to get any more information from him, Riley jumped up, and raced after Dagger.

Dagger stepped into the elevator and the doors started to shut. "Mr. Eastin…" Riley called.

Dagger shoved his hand in between the doors and pulled them open. "Ms. Rawlings, what can I do for you?"

Riley joined him in the elevator. "First, call me Riley. I'll go nuts if I can't help in some way with my mom's search. I know you can't say anything…I get it. But I must do something. Anything to help... I have to find my mom."

"Ms.—I mean Riley. I don't make it a habit to involve civilians. I'm sure Mr. Samuels—"

"No, he won't keep me in the loop," Riley interrupted. "I had to follow him to get the bits of information I did. I promise I can help."

As they pulled into the parking lot at the docks on Shelter Island, Riley was surprised. "Your office is down here?"

"You seem shocked. I am a salvage diver as well as a private investigator."

"That's not what surprises me. I'm down here quite often. The university owns a covered slip about five docks down. I'm just amazed I've never seen you or your company before."

"I see. We're a small company with big plans. One of us is here often, but the other two are out on the water; we also start early. We contract work all up and down the coast."

Dagger walked her down to the office, the old boat rental and repair building. The rough-cut barn board siding looked new, cared for. Up near the peak of the roof was a large wooden sign painted white with carved out letters trimmed in a metallic gold and painted navy blue—Hunters & Seekers. Riley stood on the dock, gazing up at the sign.

"You don't like our sign?" Dagger asked in an accusing tone.

"What? No—I mean—yes. I like your sign. I just can't believe I haven't noticed it before."

"Don't beat yourself up. We only installed it two weeks ago."

"Interesting name," Riley said.

"We're salvage divers and private investigators. Welcome to Hunters and Seekers, or as we often say, the boatshed." Dagger opened the door for her.

They were greeted by a booming, deep male voice.

"Bullshit! I know I didn't leave it out. I put it away the last time I used it."

"Hell you did! If so, it'd be where it was supposed to be now, wouldn't it, numbnuts?"

"I can't even leave you two alone for a morning without you tearing the place apart?" Dagger broke into the argument. "Children, we have a guest. Could you please *try* and act like adults?"

The two men stopped and turned toward the new voice, but it

wasn't Dagger they stared at. Like bird dogs on point, they both stood stock still and aimed at Riley; like a quail, she froze in the spotlights of their eyes.

"Riley Rawlings, meet my knucklehead partners, Kaleb LaSalle and Stone Garrison."

"Nice to meet you, Kaleb and Stone," she said, hoping she sounded unintimidated. The two men were as handsome as Dagger.

Kaleb was the first to offer his hand. "Nice to meet you, Riley. How can we help?" He gave Dagger an assessing glance, as if he wondered if she was a client or friend.

"My mother, Claudia, was...rather, *is* the lead scientist on Sheridan's research vessel. I heard you were involved with the investigation, and I'm hoping to be of some help." She bit her tongue, forcing back the overwhelming need to break down and start bawling. She needed to get hold of herself. She could fall apart when she was in the safety of her own home. She bit harder, pushing the anguish away and replacing it with physical pain.

Stone ran to the closest chair, swept up the stack of papers and files, turned a complete circle and dumped them on a desk. Kaleb grabbed a towel and tried to wipe the stains off the chair. When that failed, he snatched a throw pillow from the sofa and put it over the stains, as though she was too much a lady to lower herself by sitting on a smudge. Both men gestured for her to sit. Riley hid her smile; the comic relief was a blessing. She didn't want to insult the men she'd just met, so she moved to the chair, and placing the pillow back on the couch, took a seat.

Dagger settled one hip on a desk, one hand on his thigh, the other hand resting on his wrist. "You two are acting like a couple of kids who got caught hosting a kegger while their parents were out. I warned you. We're not in the service anymore. When our door opens you never know who might step in. Could be a pretty new client." He gave Riley a quick wink and she felt her cheeks warm.

"Don't give it a thought. Believe me, I hear much worse on a daily basis. I teach university students. You wouldn't believe their vocabulary," Riley said. "Am I to understand you were all in the military?"

"Navy, retired, ma'am," Kaleb answered, suppressing a salute.

"Were you all divers?"

"Actually, we're all SEALs."

"I see. Quite the elite group. No wonder Wayne would want to hire a new company. I'm sure your track record is stellar."

Dagger acknowledged her comment with a cock of his head and lopsided grin. Then he refocused on his partners. "What did you two lose now?"

"Umm, no big deal. We just misplaced the checkbook momentarily; it's not in the safe, but it's here somewhere," Stone said.

Dagger glared at the two of them. "I swear to God, if you lost our checkbook again, I'm going to make you go to the bank and explain to them why we have to open a new account for the third time in one month."

"Don't sweat it," Kaleb said. "I never took it out of the office. I used it to pay the water bill, then I...oh, *shit*." He went over to the sitting area, pulled the cushions off the sofa, and ran his massive hands in the crease where the back met the seat. "Found it!" he said with childish glee.

"Right, Mister-I-put-it-back-in-the-safe." Stone snorted.

"Stone, from now on you are in charge of the checkbook. Lock it in your top drawer," Dagger said.

Stone grinned and snatched the checkbook out of Kaleb's hand with lightning speed. Kaleb pouted like a five-year-old.

"You may find this difficult to believe, but we always have each other's back," Dagger said to Riley.

"If we didn't kill 'em first," Kaleb said with a laugh.

Riley smiled. "I can see that. I would swear the three of you are brothers."

"We are," Stone said. "Not by blood, but brothers all the same."

"Now that we've made such a professional first impression, let's get to work." Dagger grimaced. "Did you get a security team out to the site?"

"Called them right after I hung up with you. The first shift arrived shortly after you left. They are on an eight-hour rotation. They'll stay on site until they hear from us," Kaleb said.

"Expecting trouble?" Riley asked.

Chapter Four

Dagger paced the length of the boatshed. He turned and refocused on Riley. "We're always expecting trouble. When you're sitting on a salvage site you run the risk of treasure hunters, pirates, or possibly in this case, someone looking for a story," Dagger said. "I don't want anyone snooping around, and the SDPD pays us to keep the site secure for the sake of the evidence chain should the case go to court," Dagger said.

"I put down a deposit for the salvage vessel. It's finishing up on another contract. The captain said he needed to haul the vessel into port and get it serviced. They will head out our way the end of next week. He'll let us know when they're a day out. Companies like ours are keeping him hopping, so he says," Stone said.

"Great. Thanks, Stone." Dagger walked over to his desk and plugged a video recorder into the computer. A large screen lowered from the ceiling near the sitting area. He started the video and all eyes were glued to the screen. "Okay, here is what I found this morning."

The video began as Dagger approached the ship.

"I checked the weather report for last night," Kaleb said. "It was no picnic out there. Wind gusts were thirty-nine to forty-six miles per hour, the waves averaged eighteen to twenty-five feet. They had lots of spray and driving rain."

"Check that out," Stone said and pointed up at the screen. "Life boats are still on board. The vessel must've gone down fast."

Kaleb elbowed Stone in the ribs, motioning toward Riley who was biting her lip and studying her fingernails.

"I'm sorry, Riley. I don't mean to be insensitive," Stone said.

"It's fine, Stone, really. A little shocking to see the actual shipwreck, but I must come to terms with this somehow. I want to help, so handle this case like you would any other."

Stone looked at Kaleb and the two glanced at one another and then to Dagger. Dagger gave a shrug and cocked his head to one side. "We'll do the best job we can for everyone involved, especially our client, SDPD. To do a thorough job, we have to walk this step-by-step and leave nothing out."

The video circled the hull, starting at the stern and moving forward to the bow of the vessel. The large ragged horizontal gouge came into view. The close-up of the gash showed scorching around the entire length of the gouge.

"Is that what I think it is?" Kaleb asked.

"It appears to be continuous burn marks," Stone said. "Which indicates some type of explosive."

"You think someone planted explosives on the hull of the research ship and blasted it open?" Riley asked.

"Either that or something ran into the ship and blew up," Dagger said. "See the way the edges turn inside?" He paused the video and pointed at the hole in the side of hull. "That's a classic example of explosives placed on the outside, in a pattern that's referred to as a shaped charge. Meaning the explosives were shaped to focus in a certain pattern."

"An explosion wouldn't go unheard. It should've alerted everyone on board. They would've had time to send an SOS. They should've been able to get off the ship. So, what happened?" Riley asked.

"I don't know—yet," Dagger said.

"Look," Kaleb pointed to an empty boat lift. "They did get one life boat in the water."

"You're right, Kaleb, and the Coast Guard located the life boat among the floating wreckage. They inspected the lift. Said it'd been stowed wrong and the boat must've torn free either during the storm or as the research vessel went down. No one was on board."

"Kinda feels off," Stone said as he studied the scene.

"How so?" Dagger asked.

"Yes, it was blustery. Even so, Riley's question is valid. No one thought to send out an SOS. The ship went down so quickly no one had time to deploy the life boats? These people weren't your average party boat people with no idea what they were doing. They were marine scientists, a seasoned crew. I can't put my finger on it, it just feels off."

"There's a missing part to this puzzle and we're going to find that piece," Dagger said. "And if the ship was deliberately sunk, there are at least nineteen possible motives."

"I don't understand. How did you come to that conclusion?" Riley asked.

"There were nineteen people aboard the ship. Any one of those nineteen could be the reason why. It could also be insurance fraud, or some other arcane reason; but it begins to look intentional," Kaleb said.

Riley nodded as she pulled her phone out and clicked open the call history. "Mom called me at two-twenty-seven AM."

"You spoke to your mom before the ship went down?" Dagger asked.

"Yeah, I mean, no: I couldn't get to my phone in time and she left me a voice message. Didn't Wayne tell you? I left him at least half-a-dozen voice messages. I thought my messages are what prompted him to call you and the Coast Guard."

"He told me one of the people on the ship had a family member call him, but he neglected to mention it was you," Dagger said.

"May I borrow your phone and upload your mom's message?" Kaleb asked.

She hesitated, not wanting to let go of what could very well be her mother's last message to her. Finally, she handed it to him and he set to work, tapping away on the screen.

"Don't worry. I'll only record the one message and you will still have the original," he gave her a reassuring smile.

Dagger rolled out a whiteboard. He made two columns, one with time and the other with corresponding actions. "Does everything look correct so far?" he asked.

Riley nodded.

"Kaleb, play the message." Dagger tapped the marker on his hand. "Let's focus on the sounds in the background."

Kaleb started the message.

"Riley, it's Mom. Our ship—" A loudspeaker in the background squawked to life and drowned out her voice. "My research, it's—" Static drowned out Mom's voice. "Riley, don't let them get my research."

"Claudia, we must go *now*!" cried a male voice in the background. "Get to the lifeboats. Oh, shit! No, we can't go that way. The water—" Static.

"I love you, Riley." The line went dead.

A few seconds later, Dagger made a cut motion across his throat. "Riley, do you recognize the man's voice?"

Riley's heart felt heavy and her pulse quickened as the sound of her mother's voice filled the room.

"He sounds familiar, but I'm not certain. It sounded like one of Mom's assistants. But she goes through so many," Riley said.

"Even though the boat was sinking, your mother mentioned her research before anything else. It must have been very important to her," Stone said.

"Mom doesn't panic. She must have believed the ship was in real danger of sinking for her to call me…and for her to choose to tell me about her research instead of taking care of her people? There's something vitally important about that research."

"Do you know what she is working on?" Stone asked.

"Not really. I know it has some relationship to algae. She kept it to herself."

"Is that normal for her?" Dagger asked.

"Actually, no. This was a first. We normally discuss our projects at length."

"Not to be a Debbie-downer," Kaleb said. "But how do you know for certain this is the only project she kept from you?"

Riley ran her hands through her hair, pulling it away from her face. Was Kaleb right? How did she know for certain this was her mother's only secret research? Her mother never said she only had *one* personal project.

"You're certain her research is the reason she was out there?" Stone asked.

"Not the main reason. The research ship belonged to Sheridan Enterprises. She was working, and her assistants were with her. Mom was frequently involved in several projects at one time, around six or seven, maybe more. I had dinner with her the night before she left, and she told me she and her team would be working on a variety of projects on the ship, but she intended to spend her free time focused on her research project."

"Stone, Kaleb, did either of you pick up what was said over the loudspeaker?"

They shook their heads. "Hold on," Kaleb said. "Let me edit out the voices." A few seconds later he hit a key.

"Man the life boats. This is not a drill," said the staticky voice on the loudspeaker in the recording.

"They got notice to get off the ship," Stone said.

"Yeah, but the water was already coming in. Did you hear the guy in the background who mentions 'the water?'" Kaleb asked.

"Yeah, good chance they had a couple of minutes before they were notified to abandon ship. Even so, Riley's mom already knew something was going on. She phoned Riley before her assistant entered the room," Dagger said, as he made a note on the timeline showing water entering the boat. "Riley, how long was it until you phoned Samuels?"

"I was in shock. I tried Mom's phone three or four times until I got my wits about me and phoned Wayne."

"So, maybe ten minutes after you got the message?"

"No more. Except it took me over fifteen minutes of disconnecting and redialing Wayne before I decided to leave my first message."

Dagger made another note on the whiteboard. "Kaleb what time was her last call made to Samuels?"

"Zero-four-forty-two," Kaleb said. "Hold on a second." He typed away, his brow furrowing as he worked. "That's what I thought," he said, half under his breath as he sat back in his seat.

"Want to share with the class?" Stone asked.

Kaleb looked at them with a sly grin. "Earlier, I emailed my buddy who works in communications for the Coast Guard. I told him we hooked this contract and wanted any information he could give us. He sent me a response. He said they got a call came from Wayne Samuels at zero-seven-ten reporting they had a possible missing ship."

Dagger scanned around the room, then turned and marked the time on the board. He made a second mark at seven-twenty.

"At zero-seven-twenty Samuels contacted me. I bugged out and was in route to our objective in less than thirty minutes."

"Wait a minute," Riley leapt from her chair and went up to the board. "I left my last message at 4:42. However, I told him in my first message there was trouble with the research ship. I explicitly told him to contact the Coast Guard. I knew I should have done it myself, except I didn't want him blowing up at me and telling me it wasn't my place, or that I was overreacting—as if. He must have heard his phone ring. Mom said he's never without it, never. Which means there's a gap of three hours before Samuels decided to act. Just what was he doing *for three hours* before he contacted the Coast Guard?"

"Maybe Samuels had other calls he needed to make," Stone said and rubbed his eyebrow.

Riley could tell by his tone that even *he* didn't believe what he was saying.

"Nonsense," she said. "Contacting the Coast Guard with an SOS is priority—you know it, and so does Wayne."

"All right. I made the note on our timeline. We'll make sure to inform the SDPD regarding the three-hour lag. Let's move on," Dagger said.

They listened to the audio of the phone call a few more times. Not gleaning anything more, they returned to the video.

"Stop, right there!" Riley jumped up and moved closer to the screen. "There's my mom's stateroom."

"You're certain?" Dagger asked.

"Yes. Go back a few seconds please, Kaleb. Stop—right there." She pointed to a small yellow spot on the video. "See the yellow thing floating in the head? It's my mom's yellow sweater, she never goes on a ship without it, she loves that sweater. Did you search her room, including all drawers and closets?" Riley turned to study Dagger.

"I didn't have the time to search every room."

"Yeah, especially since he was diving *alone*," Kaleb said.

"I've got to get on the ship and search her stateroom. Mom is always good under pressure. She may have left a clue about her plans or her whereabouts for me. I need to see it for myself. She would have tried to tell me how to find her."

Chapter Five

Dagger looked at his two partners hoping for reassurance or a lifeline. Naturally Riley was emotionally involved. He should've given this situation more thought before involving her.

"I understand your longing to find your mother, Riley. But it's our job to locate the missing people and discover and preserve evidence; you are not authorized to be on the crime scene," Dagger said.

Riley paced the floor, her arms crossed and her finger tapping her chin. "I finally have something other than grief to occupy my brain. My mother lives her life on the water. Her body hasn't been found. She's still alive; I know it deep in my gut." She pinched the bridge of her nose and squeezed her eyes shut. "She and I are close; if she left clues about her escape and survival, I'd find them faster and easier than you would."

"OK, we'll let SDPD know that we are taking you to the boat as part of the investigation and that you'll be supervised. I guess it's as good a place as any to start," Dagger said. "Let's head out before we lose more light."

"About that," Kaleb said. "If we're going to have the report for our other contract done and sent today, Stone and I need the boat."

"Shit," Dagger said. "Think it's too late to rent a boat?"

"I have a way out to the site," Riley said.

"I suppose you could take me out there and be my lookout."

"Not that kind of a boat, champ." Riley smiled.

Dagger narrowed his eyes. "Just what kind of a *boat* are you talking about?"

"The university has a small submarine moored here. I'm in charge of it," Riley said.

"Really? So do you dive, Riley?" Dagger asked.

"I grew up on the water. My parents owned a diving school. I could swim before I could walk."

"How's your sign language?"

Better than yours, I bet, she signed.

"Great. Riley and I will go to the dive site. You guys take the boat."

****

Riley punched in the security code and turned on the light. There in the halogen glow was a twenty-foot submarine with an eight-foot beam.

"Nice," Dagger said. "Tell me, how can a state university afford to purchase a submarine?"

"They didn't. We have some very rich, very influential alumni. They funded the purchase of the submarine for the Marine Biology department."

"What exactly do you do at the university?" Dagger quirked an eyebrow.

"I'm a Professor of Marine Biology."

"Sweet." Dagger grinned and nodded. "A sub would be a real benefit to our company…maybe one day," he sighed. "Shall we get on board?"

"Be my guest. I'll grab my gear. Go aboard, I'll be right there."

Riley finished stowing her gear and began the checklist in preparation to disembark. Dagger was in the co-pilot seat and assisted with the process.

"Coordinates are locked in. Once we clear the sea wall, I'll take it down to cruising depth. It shouldn't take long to reach the site."

"Yep. Those alumni must have deep pockets. If they ever want a cause, I'm available," Dagger chuckled.

****

A lone man stood two docks over. He watched through binoculars as the submarine headed for the sea wall. He pulled his phone from his back pocket and punched in a number.

"It's Eric."

"I know who you are. I've told you never to call me here," the man on the other end of the line hissed.

"Yeah, but you also told me to keep you updated and you didn't answer your damn cell. I thought you might like to know your girl, Riley, and Eastin just left the docks in the university's submarine."

"Are you following them?"

"That's why I contacted you."

"Follow them, you idiot! You keep a close eye on Riley. I don't want her giving us trouble."

"And what if she finds trouble?"

"Didn't you assure me the job was clean?"

"It is. That doesn't mean she can't stir up trouble."

"Did you manage to search Claudia's stateroom?"

"No. You just texted me the update four hours ago. I'm the best at what I do, but not even I can be in two places at once," Eric said.

"Then you better keep a very close eye on her. If Riley dives and searches her mother's stateroom, and there's anything to find, she'll find it."

"And what if I'm not sure if she found anything? Didn't you say Riley was the only person who could lead us to what you want?"

"Yes. But I'll have no use for her once I get what I'm looking for. She'll only be in the way at that point."

"What do you want me to do?"

"I want you to do what I hired you for. If Riley discovers anything, I want it. If you have even a tickle of a doubt, deal with her."

The line went dead.

"Prick. Your fee just doubled." Eric shoved the phone back in his pocket. He jumped into the power boat and headed for the wreck. He maintained a slow pace to allow enough distance between him and the sub, so he wouldn't be picked up by the submarine's sonar.

****

Riley dropped anchor when they had a clear line of sight to the wreck of the research ship. The sub's lights nearly lit up the entire boat. She had to admit, it shook her to see the ship on the video but staring out the porthole at the wreck made her nauseous.

It was now eleven hours since she last heard from her mother. Somewhere deep inside she knew each hour passing without word made it more and more likely she would never see her mom alive again. Her heart started to race, and she felt dizzy; she took in a big breath and held it for the count of five before slowly exhaling.

"Are you all right?" Dagger asked, reaching out and gently touching her shoulder.

Riley froze under Dagger's touch. "Yes. I'm fine. I just haven't eaten anything today."

"Why didn't you say something? You can't dive if your blood sugar is low. Hold on." Dagger pulled his rucksack off the floor and dug through it. "Here." He handed her a protein bar and a bottle of electrolyte water.

"I'm fine," Riley insisted.

"I'm not taking you inside that ship until you eat and drink." He dropped into a seat.

"Thank you." She unwrapped the bar and forced down a couple bites. She guzzled the water to quell her stomach's rebellion.

Slipping on his dry suit, Dagger said, "I'll lead the way. We go straight to the stateroom you saw the sweater in and search it. If everything goes okay and there's still time, we'll investigate the other rooms."

The pressurized chamber would only fit one person at a time. Dagger went first and waited for Riley. She exited the sub and gave him a thumbs-up.

They switched on their head lamps and swam to the ship. Riley stayed directly behind Dagger. She'd dived her entire life, but being inside of a sunken ship wasn't something she had much experience with. It was an eerie, cold feeling, particularly knowing her mom may have spent her last hours here.

Dagger pointed to the open hatch on his left and swam inside, Riley behind. The minute she entered the stateroom a warmth flowed through her, as though her mother was treading water right by her side. She swam over to the head and found the sweater caught on the sink faucets and carefully pulled it free. She held the sweater tightly, then placed it in her hip bag.

****

Dagger pulled out his camera and recorded Riley. He watched as Riley untangled her mother's sweater, hugged it for a few seconds, and then delicately placed it in her bag. So far, she seemed to be holding up, but he was waiting for the severity of today's events to hit her.

She searched each drawer in the head and placed a few other items inside her bag. Riley was on the last drawer of her mother's stateroom when a metallic bang rang through the ship. Her hand halted mid reach, her head snapped up, eyes wide, seeking Dagger's. He lifted his index finger to his mouthpiece, motioning for her to stay quiet. They slowly kicked their fins to remain in place, listening. Another sound echoed through the wreck, a scratching sound, like something or someone rubbed metal against the bulkhead.

Dagger's gaze shifted to Riley and he could see that she, too, heard the second sound. He motioned for Riley to come close. *It might be a Coast Guard diver, but just to be safe, be quiet and stay glued to me,* he signed.

Could it be someone from the security firm you hired?

He shook his head and told her the divers attached to the security team wouldn't be diving until tomorrow.

He was certain they weren't alone.

Dagger pulled out his spear gun and motioned for Riley to stay put. He peeked out into the passageway and seeing no one, shot out of the stateroom and swam toward the sound. Riley followed. He scowled when he turned and found her directly behind him and again told her to wait.

He swam up the companionway and checked the next deck. Nothing. Turning, he saw Riley, and furiously signed for her to go back. She shook her head. Giving up on her, he sprang out the hatch and immediately realized the cost of the distraction. Something small and fast, trailing a line of tiny bubbles, entered his peripheral vision just as Riley followed him through the hatch.

Dagger whipped around and kicked his fins with all his strength, as he lunged toward Riley. He barreled into her with enough force that both of them almost made it to safety. But at the last second, he jerked as pain coursed up his calf, where a crimson cloud was blossoming through the water. A spear had shot right through his calf.

Pushing them both farther out of the line of fire, Dagger watched as the blood from his leg permeated the area. Riley pulled out a dark blouse of her mother's from her bag and wrapped it tightly around his calf. Between the shirt and the salt water, the water around his lower body changed from a deep red to light pink.

He motioned for her to remain behind the bulkhead as he reached for her bag and pulled out what looked like pajama bottoms.

Dagger pushed his open palm toward her, reinforcing his message to stay put. He moved close to the bulkhead and listened. No lights, no sound.

He waved the pajamas out the hatch. A split second later, a

spear shot past, through the pajamas and ripped them out of his hands.

Shit.

Dagger motioned for Riley to turn back and swim away from the hatch as he followed, guarding their rear. She torpedoed through the passageway, swim fins never slowing.

She reached the end of the passageway in a couple minutes and headed up the companionway for the hatch. He grabbed her foot, pulling her back, before she exited onto the main deck. She looked at him and he shook his head. Instead, he took the gamble and moved out onto the main deck. No spears whizzed by.

He motioned for Riley to follow, and they swam as quickly and as closely to the deck as possible until they reached the boat's gunwale. There they peeled off the ship and made a sharp right, propelling themselves back to the sub, Dagger still guarding her six.

Dagger entered the security code and the sub's chamber opened. She swam inside, closed the hatch, and started the process to empty the chamber of water as he waited outside the sub.

He might as well have painted a big red circle on his chest. He was a freaking target.

At long last the hatch opened and he plunged inside just as a spear and bubble trail shot past the opening. He pushed the lock button and waited impatiently as the water drained from the chamber and the hatch to the sub finally opened.

Riley was standing there stripped down to her long underwear. "Need help?"

"I got it," he said a little too tersely.

"No, you don't. You're bleeding everywhere."

"I'll live," he said, waving off her concern. "Our priority is to haul ass out of here. Another spear shot past as I entered the chamber. I'll pull the anchor, you get this bucket of bolts underway."

She ran forward and jumped into the pilot's seat. He hobbled over to the anchor and pushed the retract button. "Anchor's clear," he called to her over the engine.

"Okay, hold on." She engaged the forward thrusters.

Dagger limped over and dropped down into the co-pilot seat.

"Look." Riley pointed to their left.

There was a small beam of light. It swept over them once and then headed in their direction.

"He must have a diver propulsion device. He's heading right for us. The way my luck has gone today, I wouldn't put it past him to have a concussion grenade. Floor this thing."

Riley pushed the thrusters to the limit and slowly the light shrank into the distance. She kept the submarine submerged until they got within a half mile of the sea wall, then she surfaced and slowed the sub.

Dagger's phone beeped his partner's SOS. He pulled it out of his bag and checked his messages. He frowned before he thought to censor his face.

"What?" Riley asked.

"Nothing. It'll keep." He stuffed the phone back into his bag as he tried to come to terms with what he read.

"If it has to do with the wreck I want to know." Slowly the color drained from her features.

"I'll fill you in after we dock."

"I saw part of the message, along with my mother's name. Tell me what you know." Riley clenched her jaw.

He couldn't lie to her. He hated this. This news would break her heart.

"The Coast Guard found your mother, along with the last two students."

"She's dead, isn't she?" Riley stared straight ahead and held her body rigid, but there were tears welling in her eyes.

Dagger cautiously placed his hand on her shoulder. Riley's shoulder ratcheted up tighter.

"I'm so sorry, Riley."

Her gaze remained glued straight ahead. Abruptly, her resolve shattered, and her face crumpled, as tears slipped down her cheeks. Dagger had done this—he was responsible for breaking her heart.

Chapter Six

"C'mon, Dagger, lean on me," Riley said as Dagger fought to hold his own weight. "Bleeding out is not your best option here."

They both reached the boatshed door and Dagger attempted to stand on his own two feet. He gritted his teeth as another searing pain flooded his system and hissed a curse. Riley opened the door, only to find Kaleb and Stone waiting on the other side with a cart.

"Oh, hell no," Dagger said. "There's no damn way either of you are going to push me in that cart."

"Don't get your panties in a bunch, sweetie," Stone said. "We're here to load up the equipment."

"That's right." Kaleb grinned. "You're cheap and replaceable. Our equipment is expensive."

"I suppose I deserve that smart-ass remark," Dagger said.

"Yeah, you do. 'Bout time we get to dish it back," Stone said.

"That's right," Kaleb added. "I got a teenager ready to step into your position with one phone call."

"Sure you do, asshats," Dagger said with a growl. "Just get us out of here before I crush Riley or bleed out."

She gasped at his blood-soaked shoes. "We need to get you to the hospital."

"Nah, we got some fishing line back at our shack. I only fished with it once. Stone, dig through my tackle box; I'm sure there's a fishing hook you can use. No sense in opening a new one. Stone can sew Dagger back together in no time," Kaleb said. He took hold of the cart handles and rolled it in the direction of the sub.

Riley watched, slack-jawed, as Stone snatched Dagger's arm

from her. "Let's go, champ. I'll have you all fixed up in a jiff."

"Wait!" cried Riley. "I'm taking Dagger to the ER. I'm not going to be responsible for his leg getting gangrene and falling off."

"No worries. I do this all the time, and we still have all our parts," Stone said.

Dagger bit his tongue. He knew exactly what his buddies were up to, and it was working. The longer they could keep up the charade, the longer they kept Riley's mind off the loss of her mother.

"If you really want to help, grab the door," Stone said, as they approached the boatshed.

Nearly running to keep up, Riley pleaded, "Stone, Dagger—be reasonable. My vehicle is right over there." She pointed to the parking area. "We can be at the hospital in minutes."

They walked into the boatshed and Stone dropped Dagger into the closest chair. "I can have this done in seconds. Could you drag a chair over here and help Dagger get his leg on it?"

Riley's normal golden-bronze complexion was quickly turning a shade of sickly green. Her head swiveled from him to Stone. Dagger got the impression if Stone didn't stop his deception immediately, he wouldn't be Stone's only patient.

"Riley, you're looking a bit peaked. Why don't you grab another chair and take a rest? Stone's a doctor. He knows what he's doing—trust me." Dagger gave Riley a warm smile.

Stone dropped his stack of medical supplies on the desk next to Dagger. "I was a doctor in my first life. But I got bored, so I joined the Navy Medical Corps and went to work with the SEALs. I got out right around the time Dagger did. Moved on to this." He cocked his head and looked around the boatshed. "I think I'm here to stay. Guess you could say, I'm one of those guys who lives for the thrill."

"Being a doctor wasn't exciting enough for you?" Riley asked.

"It has its moments. But when you're an adrenaline junkie you want more than a few moments at a time." He grabbed a pair of pliers out of his medical bag.

"Hold on. Those look like regular pliers."

"They are. I left my forceps at home. Don't worry, I boiled them and doused them in alcohol."

"Are you *really* a doctor?"

"Sure I am! Now, come around to my other side and hold his leg down for me."

"I don't need anyone to hold me down. You know damn well I

don't," grumbled Dagger.

"Shit-on-a-shingle, Dagger. This looks pretty gnarly." Stone sputtered as he closely examined Dagger's wound. "This is gonna sting a smidge, so you'd better not kick me."

Riley grabbed Dagger's foot and held on, her eyes huge. Dagger's cussing was as colorful as Riley's face.

"Lucky for you, the spear just missed the arterial vein. Doesn't look like the bone is broken. You'll need to take it easy. With antibiotics and monitoring you should heal nicely. I won't have to amputate this time." Stone sent a sly grin in Riley's direction.

"Honey, I'm home." Kaleb came strolling in with an arm full of gear. "Thought you guys would be done by now. How long can it take to put a few stitches in a leg?"

"I would've been finished by now, but I decided I should clean it up a bit since Dagger is fond of his leg," Stone said. "You guys gonna tell us what in the hell happened down there?"

Stone applied a local and started stitching while Dagger told them what he and Riley discovered. As he started on the part about the other diver, Stone and Kaleb sat up straighter.

"Was he a treasure hunter?" Stone asked.

"Did you get a look at him?" Kaleb asked.

"No, he never got close enough. And I don't believe he was your run-of-the-mill treasure hunter. If he was, he would've left us alone after he chased us off the wreck. Instead he dogged us all the way back to the sub with the help of a diver propulsion device," Dagger said.

"Shit," Kaleb said. "So, you think his goal was more than treasure hunting."

"The question is, who does he work for? And oh yeah, what was he searching for?" Stone asked, as he tied off the last suture and sat up straight, pulling his shoulders back as he stretched. He grabbed a bandage and went to wrapping Dagger's leg.

"That's two questions, but I'll add a third: who was he trying to shoot?" Kaleb asked. "You said the spear appeared when Riley was entering the deck."

Dagger and his partners stared at Riley. She got the impression they thought she knew more about what was going on than they did.

"I wondered the same thing." Dagger moved his toes, trying to gage the pain. "Unfortunately, we don't have a clue. I'll give the Coasties and the SDPD a heads up. We need to inform our security team; they always need at least two divers in the water. No one dives alone until this is straightened out."

"Good idea—that means you, too, Dagger." Kaleb glared at him.

"Yes. And make sure you're armed. Keep an eye out for strangers, especially anyone watching or following any of us," Dagger said, turning to Riley. "Maybe it would be best if you stayed out of this and went back to the university."

"Forget it. I'm getting to the bottom of this. With or without your assistance," Riley said as she crossed her arms tightly across her chest.

Dagger glanced at each of his partners for help and got shoulder shrugs. "You could get yourself killed—" he raised his hand before she could protest. "But...I know there's no stopping you. In the meantime, no going out on your own."

Riley stared into space as the guys ran through the day's events step by painful step. Her heart raced, and she began to shiver as cold seeped through her. If only she'd answered her mother's call right away.

"Riley, you've been put through the wringer. Kaleb will take you home, you need to get some rest."

"No. I don't want to go home. I can't be alone right now."

"When was the last time you slept?" Stone asked.

"I won't be able to sleep. What I want is for someone to explain to me what happened to my mother. Why is she dead? Where did they find her? And why did it take so long to locate her? Why would somebody shoot at us?" Riley bit her upper lip. Her hands clenched into fists. The cords of her neck pulsed. Like a train leaving the station, it started slowly and increased until she dissolved into sobs. The more she tried to control the outburst, the harder her tears fell.

Dagger reached out and laid a hand over one of her cold fists. "You're exhausted, Riley, both emotionally and physically. You won't be any good to anyone, especially yourself, if you don't recharge." The haunted, lonely look on her face gave Dagger pause. "How about one of the guys drives us both over to your place? I'll keep you company. I don't think anyone will bother you, but it doesn't hurt to be proactive."

"I can't ask you to spend your entire night at my place. You're injured, and you need your rest to heal."

"Believe me, I can rest anywhere. A sleeping bag, a spare sofa or even an overstuffed chair would work just fine."

She lifted her head and looked at Dagger. Her thick black eyelashes sparkled with the diamonds of tears. "I have a guest room. With a real bed, pillows, and blankets. I would certainly appreciate it, but I don't want to impose."

"You're not imposing, I'm offering. Since we still have no idea what happened on the ship. For your safety, I don't think you should be alone. It's been a long, draining day. I'm afraid tomorrow will be a repeat. Let's call it done and we'll all meet back here first thing in the morning."

****

The next morning, Riley woke to the sweet aroma of fresh coffee. She sat up and looked around the room. The picture of her mother on her bedside table and the last twenty-four hours slammed through her mind like a movie in fast forward. She covered her eyes with her hands, trying to block out the horror, lest she cry again.

She'd spent half the night crying and thought by now her tears would be utterly dried up. She felt the wetness on her hands. Riley pulled them away, rubbed them on her blanket and shook her head. There was plenty of time to cry. Ahead were days, months, and years to grieve. She would have the rest of her life to mourn her mother and was positive she would do so with each passing day. Now was the time to focus. To find out why Mom died. She threw her covers back and stumbled into the shower.

****

"Good morning, I was just about to come wake you up," Dagger said as she entered the kitchen.

"Hope you like eggs and bacon. Kinda figured you must, since that's what I found in the refrigerator." He put the plate on the table and motioned for her to start eating. "Take a seat and eat them while they're hot. Take anything in your coffee?"

Riley opened the refrigerator and grabbed the cream before sitting down. "You didn't have to do all this, thank you." Her stomach churned and heaved in protest. The last thing she wanted to do was eat anything.

"I know you don't feel like eating, but your system needs fuel to keep going."

"How's your leg?" She stirred her coffee, stalling.

"Surprisingly well. A cat nap or two will do that. I spoke with

Kaleb and Stone. They have a few things they are going to check out. It's important we search your mom's house. Are you feeling up to the trip?"

"Yes. I want to help. I want to be involved in figuring out what happened." She saw a hesitant look in Dagger's eyes. "I know what you're going to say. We've already had this discussion."

"I was hoping a good night's sleep would change your mind." Dagger frowned.

"Try to understand, this is something I must be involved in. I realize you're the expert, but I promise I'll listen to you and follow your lead."

Dagger shook his head. "Like I said last night, you shouldn't be left alone. I planned on hiring a bodyguard for you."

She held her breath hoping he understood how she was feeling.

"If you promise to follow my instructions and let my team take the lead, we'll give it a try. The guys dropped off your car this morning. There's a change of plans. Kaleb, Stone, and I decided we could cover more ground if we split up. They brought the stuff you gathered in your mother's stateroom. The SDPD will allow you to keep what you found. They requested an itemized list and will contact you if they decide they need something. I thought you would want to go through this before we head out today."

Riley pulled off the box lid. The smell of the ocean floated out of the box. Her mother was a creature of habit; Riley had seen these same items so many times before. She reached in and delicately picked up the yellow sweater.

"The guys did the best they could with your mom's sweater. They didn't wash it, but they laid it out to dry overnight."

She rubbed the sweater between her thumb and forefinger feeling the gritty salt from the ocean. Grief threatened to drown her again, but she fought back the tide of tears. She wouldn't fall apart in front of this man any more. It would only confirm his suspicion she'd be a liability if he included her in the search.

She set the sweater down on the table and went through the other personal items in the box. "There are no USBs here. Mom always backed up her research on USBs. I thought it strange when I was searching her stateroom."

"Not finding one doesn't mean she didn't have one. The USB could've been lost to the sea," Dagger said.

Riley frowned and picked up the sweater. She started to fold it up when something caught her eye. There was a small tag sewn along the seam of the sleeve. She gathered up the sweater and studied the tag; it contained two words sewn into it with green thread; *home starfish*.

"Searching my mother's house has moved to the top of the list."

"What does *home starfish* refer to?" Dagger asked.

"A secret hiding place that only Mom and I know about."

"Good. Let's head out."

****

Eric sat in his car a block away from Riley's. "They just arrived at Claudia's house. Do you want me to kill them at the first opportunity?" He hated having to report his every step to this pompous windbag.

"Since you missed your chance at the wreck, let's see how this will play out. You still aren't sure she found anything."

"She's got a box full of something. I bet the box is full of her mom's stuff," Eric said. "Why else would she keep it with her?"

"Fine. Retrieve the box at your first opportunity. I've been giving it some thought. I'm still not sure Claudia told Riley anything of value to me. Which means she's currently of little threat. What I do know is that Riley and Claudia were close. She could prove an asset by stumbling onto a much-needed lead."

"You said she could be trouble."

"I know what I said. So far you have nothing. We need to locate that research. And, if anyone knows where Claudia hid her formula, it would be Riley. As of now, it's your job to keep a close eye on her."

"I can get rid of her if you change your mind—all you have to do is say the word."

"I'll let you know if or when we need it done."

The line went dead, and Eric scowled at his phone.

This job was quickly becoming a pain in his ass. Some days there wasn't enough money in the world to put up with the arrogant bastards who hired him. Today was one of those days. Hell, shooting his current client would be better than being paid a penny.

Eric tossed the phone into the passenger seat and started the car. He pulled away from the curb, turned the corner, and parked. He wanted to make sure he was far enough away that Dagger wouldn't notice him. These guys weren't his average dumbass marks. He'd done his homework and knew he was dealing with ex-special ops.

At least it gave him a challenge to look forward to; they would keep him on his toes. Maybe his current arrogant client could be balanced out after all…with the money he'd get paid for completing the job and the opportunity to kill a SEAL.

He walked down the alley and in the direction of Claudia's neighbor's house but steered clear of Claudia's. Eric had staked out the neighbor's house and knew they were out of town. He hadn't yet had the chance to search Claudia's. So he'd let Riley do the heavy lifting, and then he would take his turn.

Eric walked up the sidewalk surveying his surroundings. Just to be sure, he rang the bell. Hearing no voices or shuffling about from inside, he pulled out his lock pick kit and made quick work of the lock. The residents' state-of-the-art alarm system was not set.

Eric couldn't count the number of times he'd experienced this same scenario. Why waste the money if you weren't going to use the damn system? Just made it easier for guys like him.

Making sure to keep clear of the windows, he moved cautiously to the far side of the house and located a bedroom with the best view of Claudia's house. He opened his briefcase and pulled out the binoculars. Without disturbing the blinds, he stood near the edge of the window and surveyed his target and the surrounding neighborhood.

Dagger and Riley were moving around in Claudia's house. He couldn't see what they were doing. Even so, instinct told him they were there to search her mom's house, and he knew this could take a while.

He found himself a chair, pulled it to the corner of the window, and using the blinds as camouflage, he settled in for a long surveillance. He wanted to get a good look at what they were up to but thought better of it. He couldn't get sloppy while dealing with an ex-SEAL and he couldn't afford to blow his cover. Assholes or not, this contract paid damn good money.

Chapter Seven

Riley walked to the antique buffet in her mother's dining room. She pulled out the side drawer, placed it on the floor, and reached inside. She shimmied loose the side panel and reached in and slid her hand behind the adjacent panel.

"I've got something. I think it's an envelope," Riley said.

She opened it and pulled out a slip of paper with a small key taped to the bottom.

"It's a Power of Attorney for a safe deposit box," Riley said.

"Did you know about this box?" Dagger asked.

"No, but it must be important for Mom to have hid it in our special place. We need to check it out."

The bank officer led them to the vault. She stuck the bank key into one of the boxes and then placed Riley's below. "You may use one of the small cubicles if you'd like," the officer said as she turned and left the vault.

Riley pulled the box free and walked over to the nearest cubicle. Dagger stood over her, blocking any wandering eyes. She sorted through the box and found her mom's will, deed to her house, and some other legal documents. She pulled out an amber-colored medicine bottle; something slid around inside the bottle, but it wasn't pills. She opened the bottle and dumped a small white stone onto her palm. On the stone were the letters: "*OG EHER*" written in green ink.

She looked up from the stone into Dagger's questioning expression. "This is Mom's handwriting, and she always used green ink for corrections in her notebooks."

"Do you know what those letters spell?"

Riley rolled the stone around in her hand. "No—wait. This stone is from my grandparents' place. The last time my mother and I were there together was after my grandmother's funeral. I'd taken off work for a few days to help my mom pack up their house. Granddad passed a few years earlier and Grandma had never recovered from his loss.

"We took a break on our last day and walked on the beach for hours. I found this stone. I loved its smoothness and roundness. It looked so out of place on the beach, as if it'd fallen from a child's bag of marbles. I handed the stone to my mom. She slid it into her jeans pocket and said she would always keep it as a reminder of all the happy times we spent at Grandma's and Grandpa's together."

"Did she always carry it with her?"

"No. Last time I saw the stone, it was sitting in the crystal bowl where she stored her rings on her dresser. There weren't any letters on it then."

"Are you sure?"

"Yes. I picked it up and rolled it around in my hand remembering my grandparents. I didn't see these letters."

"Was it the night before she left, when you said you had dinner there?"

"Now that you mention it—no. It was about a month before. Mom sent me to her room to get something—that's when I saw the stone. Even so, there must be a reason she put this in the safe deposit box."

"The stone is a souvenir of a special memory the two of you shared. She might have put it there just so it didn't get lost or ten other reasons that have nothing to do with her research." Dagger rubbed at the side of his jaw. "Do you know if she ever told anyone about the stone or what it meant?"

"She didn't. She told me that day it would be a cherished memory between the two of us. The stone would remind her of all the past holidays and summers we spent at Grandma's as a family." Riley handed Dagger the stone. "Then wouldn't it make sense if she was hiding something—like her research—something she didn't want anyone else knowing, that she might leave a clue only I would understand?"

"You know your mother. It's as good a starting place as any,"

Dagger said, as he examined the stone. "This might be the first piece of the puzzle." He handed the stone back to Riley and she slipped it into her pocket.

****

Riley paused and stared at the pile of papers. She'd found something. Dagger watched as her eyebrows scaled up her forehead. He waited a heartbeat, then two—trying not to put any further pressure on her. Finally, she reached down, pulled an envelope out of the box, and gingerly placed it on the table. There was something other than a letter inside, evident by the large bump in one end of the envelope. They were both transfixed by the legal-sized, cream-colored envelope, with one word hand written on the front – *Riley*.

Riley ran both hands up and down her jeans and bit her bottom lip.

"Do you want me to open it?" he asked, as he pulled his pocket knife out and placed it on the table.

She shook her head and stared at the envelope as if it might jump up and bite her. She reached out and lightly ran her fingertips over the bump. Riley picked up the pocket knife and she gently opened the envelope.

There was a folded piece of cream stationary along with another item. Riley tilted the envelope to one side and poured the loose object out. The object was a packet made from tissue paper about two inches square and securely taped together. Setting the packet on the table, she again picked up the pocket knife and sliced the tape. Inside the tissue paper was a diamond ring.

"This is Mom's engagement ring," Riley whispered. "I asked her where her ring was the night before she left. When she picked up her wine glass during dinner, I noticed she wasn't wearing it. She has worn that ring every day for the last forty years. I asked her what happened to her ring, where it was, and she told me she put it away for safe keeping, but she'd been vague and changed the subject when I pressed her for reasons why."

"Did she leave it behind every time she went out to sea?"

"No. This was the first time I know of."

Dagger could feel heat from her stare.

"She knew…she knew there was going to be trouble. Mom would never have taken off her ring unless she was certain they were headed for trouble."

"Read the letter, maybe she explained why she locked up her

ring."

Riley pulled out the cream stationary and unfolded it. Dagger watched as she slipped into her own world, miles away from him and this room. Riley began to read the letter aloud:

"*My Sweet Riley,*

"*Before anything else, I need you to know you are the most important thing in my life. You, Riley, are my heart, my reason for getting up each morning and moving forward. You come before everything in my life, including my work and my research.*

"*You're reading this letter, which means you found it in my safe deposit box and I am no longer a part of this world. I left my will in the box; everything now belongs to you. The house, the money, all my assets, and all my research. Read over my contract with Sheridan Enterprises carefully. Give them only what we agreed to and nothing more. Use my lawyer, she knows everything and can be of great help.*

"*As you are aware, I have been working on several research projects. One project I shared with no one, not even you, my darling daughter. I mentioned this project to you but gave you no details. It was not because I didn't trust you. I trust you with all I am. I did it to keep you safe.*

"*This has been a life-long project of mine, the basis of which was laid long before I went to work for anyone. I've finally drawn my conclusions, worked out the formula for this research, and have documented everything. These findings could change a major industry as we know it today—for the good. You will not locate this information in my usual storage, nor did I leave it here. I have come to fear that some bank officers have been bribed or threatened by those who want my research. For the past month or more I am certain I've been followed. I dare say I believe there is a plant inside the company, or possibly within my team, but I have yet to discover whom.*

"*Riley, the information I have will make an immense, world-wide impact, and there are people out there who stand to lose a fortune if this research comes to light.*

"*You must be very careful. Trust no one; tell no one about this letter. I can't tell you where you can locate my research for fear this letter may fall into the wrong hands.*

"*Remember your childhood and all the wonderful games we played. Growing up causes one to forget the magical possibilities life can hold. Be true to yourself. Open your heart to the wonder of love. There is someone special out there just for you. Your dad and I will watch over you. Live life, Riley. Please don't hide inside your work.*

"*With all my love,
Mom*"

Dagger watched as a multitude of expressions played across

Riley's features. It started with excruciating sorrow and changed to confusion, anger, and finally love, as her lips turned up ever so slightly. But when she eventually looked over at him, she appeared as confused as he felt.

"It's clear your mom loved you more than life itself. She trusted you completely, Riley. To her, your safety was her priority," Dagger said. "Do you have any idea what she was talking about?"

"I know her lawyer. And I know Mom thought I worked too much. But I have no idea where she might have hidden her research or the formula."

Dagger's phone rang and he pulled it from his pocket. "What's up? Really? We'll be right there." Dagger slid his phone back into his pocket and looked over at Riley. "Stone wants us back at the office. They've got some new information, they say it's important."

"Did he tell you what?" Riley shoved the contents of the safe deposit box into her purse.

"No. He said it's something we will want to see right away. Grab your stuff."

****

"What new information did you find?" asked Dagger, as he held the door open for Riley to enter.

"We've been studying your video," Kaleb said. "Check this out. Start it up, Stone."

Stone started the video and everyone focused on the screen.

"Now watch closely as you get to the engine room," Kaleb said.

"What exactly are we supposed to be looking at?" Dagger asked.

"Freeze it right there." Kaleb walked up to the screen and pointed at one spot. "Enlarge that, Stone. Can you see it?"

"Give me a clue...oh, wait."

"See there?" Kaleb pointed to the spot again. "Those two tiny bubbles in the engine room?"

Riley and Dagger stared at the spot where Kaleb had pointed out. "Are those air bubbles? It's blurry," Dagger said.

"I've been over and over this video and I'm sure they are."

"What do the bubbles mean?" Riley asked.

"There could've been a malfunction," Kaleb said. "Or someone could have tampered with the equipment. It's something, and it's out of place. We won't know for sure if this means anything unless we get back down there and inspect the area and entire engine room."

"With you and Riley getting attacked, the safest way is for the three of us to go together," Stone said.

"I agree," Dagger said. "Let's get all our gear together and we'll head down."

"I'm going with you," Riley said.

"No, you're not. You don't know what we are looking for. If someone is trying to drive off investigators into the wreck, it's too dangerous. We were hired for this assignment," Dagger said.

She took in a deep breath as though she was going to argue. He readied himself to stand his ground but was saved by the bell when her phone beeped. She pulled her phone out of her bag, looked at the screen and frowned. "Darn it. I've got to go. This is my first experience serving on a Ph.D. student's committee, and today is the culmination of five years of work. She defends her dissertation today. I *have* to be there."

"You're not going on your own," Dagger said.

"I'm on it," Kaleb said as he grabbed his phone and entered a number.

"On what?" Riley asked as she glanced at each of the men.

"He'll be here in seven minutes," Kaleb said.

"Who?" Riley asked in sharp tone. Dagger could tell she was slightly agitated.

"We have a security company on stand-by. They're good at their job, all ex-marines. One of the guys will be following you to the campus and making sure you arrive safely," Dagger said.

"Do you really think—" Riley started.

"Yes," all three men answered.

Riley shook her head and shoved her phone back into her handbag. She pulled out all the paperwork she and Dagger had discovered in the safe deposit box. "I don't want to take Mom's papers to the University. I won't be able to keep an eye on them." She pulled her mom's ring from her bag and placed it on her right hand.

"No problem," Stone said. "We can lock them in our safe."

"That would be great, thanks." Riley handed the paperwork to Stone. "Do you really think someone might be following me?"

"We're going to err on the side of caution. That means you'll either have one of us or a bodyguard with you until we sort this out," Dagger said.

"Now I'm concerned."

"About what?" Dagger asked.

"I didn't put the sweater and the rest of Mom's things I found on the ship in my safe. I left them on the kitchen table."

"Shit. That was just as much my fault as yours. We were in a hurry. I'll head over to your place and make sure everything is locked in your safe."

"You might as well take these and keep everything in one place," Stone said, as he handed Claudia's papers to Dagger.

Riley dug out a key ring and handed two of the keys to Dagger. "I really appreciate this. Thanks, Dagger. My safe is in my office. This is the key for my safe and here's the house key. I've got a spare."

"I'll take everything over and then I'll come back to here to catch up on few things. Send me a text when you're leaving the campus and I'll meet you at your place," Dagger said.

"Ride's here," Kaleb said.

Riley smiled at the three men and rushed out.

The phone rang and Dagger picked it up.

"Eastin, do you have any new information?" Wayne Samuels asked.

Dagger put the call on speaker. "Good afternoon, Mr. Samuels. As I explained to you earlier, we're working for SDPD. Any information I might've acquired I can't give to you without permission."

"I assume you have men watching the site," Samuels said.

"We do, sir. Rest assured no one will pillage your ship."

"I need to tell my board something. They want that boat back. We've not heard anything."

"I'm sorry Mr. Samuels. I've told you all I can. I suggest you call the SDPD and speak with the lead detective."

"Fine. I'll get what I need from someone else." Samuels hung up on him.

"What the hell? He knows damn well we can't give out any information. Strange, I wonder who he thinks is going to tell him what's going on," Stone said.

"I noticed you didn't offer any information about Riley and what we've discovered." Kaleb dropped down onto the sofa and took a bite out of an apple.

"Like I said. We can't give him our information," Dagger said.

"He knows we can't give him anything. So why does he keep calling us?" Kaleb asked. "He's a smart man. He should be calling SDPD and getting updates from them."

"You're right, Kaleb. He knows how this process works. He wants to keep tabs on us," Dagger said. "He's hoping we'll slip up and tell him something. I think he knows more than he's letting on. Maybe he already knows how his ship sank."

"But we *are* going to keep digging. Even though it's not what the SDPD hired us for," Stone said, even though he already knew the answer. "You do realize if we do this it's on our own dime."

Dagger shrugged. "We don't have to run it through the business. I can stay on it on my own time."

"Hell, no. I didn't say we weren't staying on. I'm just saying we'll have to cover the expenses," Stone said.

"I'm in," Kaleb said.

"We're all in," Stone said.

"Besides guarding the site and the wreck, our SDPD contract includes discovery of why the research vessel sank, bringing the vessel up to the surface, and towing it into port." Dagger said. "I say, if we happen to stumble on who and why the ship sank—that's a win-win." Dagger crossed his arms and rubbed his chin. "I'm very interested in finding out whether that ship sank intentionally, and if so, who did it? With all those explosion marks on it, something's hinky there. I think we ought to figure that out no matter who we are or aren't working for."

"You've got a good point," Stone said.

"And I'll be damned if some yahoo is going to take a shot at one of us and get off scott-free," Kaleb said.

Chapter Eight

Dagger entered Riley's house and walked into her office. As he pulled the papers out of his back pocket, the safe key slipped from between the pages. Bending over to pick it, he heard a sound behind him. Before he could react, something slammed into the back of his skull.

Dagger slumped to the floor like a puppet cut from its strings. "Not as quick as you thought you were, are you?" Eric leaned down and checked Dagger's pulse. "Yeah, you're still alive and breathing. You wouldn't be if it were up to me. At least you'll have a bitch of a headache when you wake up." Eric picked up the sheets of paper Dagger dropped on the floor. "Aha! Looks like you saved me some time. You brought the will to me. Good. I spent too damn much time searching Claudia's and finding nothing." He took one last look at the unconscious man, turned, and walked out of the room.

****

Riley was surprised to see Dagger's car in her driveway. It'd been hours since he left the shop, and she thought he would've dropped the papers off right away. She noticed there wasn't a single light on inside, nor was the porch light on.

In the dark, she attempted to locate the front door's keyhole and vowed to have a motion-triggered light installed on the garage, or at least put a small flashlight on her key chain. She unlocked the front door and switched on the lights in the living room.

"Dagger? Are you still here? Where are you?" She dumped her stuff in the chair by the door and started to search the house. She switched on the light to her office. It took her mind a second to catch up with what her eyes were seeing. "Dagger!"

She ran to him and dropped to her knees.

He was lying on his side next to the desk. A dark reddish-brown spot encircled his head. She felt his neck for a pulse and finally exhaled when she detected the beat—but it was weak.

Riley pulled her hand away; her fingers were coated in blood. She ran her fingers through his hair and discovered the gash still oozing blood.

She ran to the bathroom and grabbed a handful of towels, then gently rolled Dagger over and placed them under the wound. She called 9-1-1 and then called Stone.

"Stone, this is Riley. I found Dagger—"

"So, where's he been hiding? He left us to do all the work," Stone said.

"I just got home. I found him in my office. Stone, he's unconscious and has a head wound." On the other end of the line, it sounded like Stone stood up so forcefully his chair hit the floor.

"Hang up and call 9-1-1. We'll be right there."

"I already did. The 9-1-1 operator was pleased when I told her I needed to hang up and call you. I'll call you back when I know which hospital they're taking him to."

"Hell you will. We're getting in the car now. We'll be there in minutes."

A 1965 silver-blue Mustang squealed around the corner just as the medics were rolling an immobilized Dagger out on a stretcher. The Mustang came to a screeching halt a few yards from the back of the ambulance. Stone and Kaleb jumped out of the car and ran towards the medics.

"How is he?" Stone asked.

"He's holding his own but he hasn't come to yet," one of the medics said. "We need to get him to the hospital as quickly as possible. He's lost a lot of blood."

"We'll be right behind you," Kaleb said. He turned and looked at Riley.

"Don't even start," Riley said. "I'm going to the hospital. It's my fault Dagger got hurt and I'm not going to sit around and wait to hear what happened."

"Don't be silly, Riley. This wasn't your fault. If you insist on coming, you can ride with us," Kaleb said.

****

The three of them paced the waiting room. They took turns getting coffee and pestering the nurses. The minutes crept slowly by, turning into an hour and then two. The doors to the ICU swung open and the doctor who admitted Dagger walked through.

"How's he doing, doc?" Stone asked.

"He's a tough one. He took a good blow to the head," the doctor said. "It took us some time to stabilize him; his blood pressure was of some concern. Most likely due to the amount of blood he lost. Mr. Eastin's a lucky guy. The x-rays showed no signs of a skull fracture. I stitched up his scalp and he's on intravenous fluids. He has a mild concussion, but he should make a full recovery within a few days."

"Do you think Dagger might have slipped and hit his head on the desk in Riley's office?" Stone asked.

"No. He was hit near the top of his head with something large and solid," the doctor said. "The wound is much too high for it to be caused by a slip and fall."

"So you're saying he was attacked in my house, while doing me a favor?" Riley asked. Guilt filled her. If she had only taken the time to put away her mother's things, none of this would've happened.

"What I'm saying is Mr. Eastin was hit from behind in a way that makes it unlikely he fell and hit his head."

"But there are no signs of intracranial bleeding?" Stone asked.

"None. He's still unconscious and he will probably remain so at least throughout the night. We'll monitor him closely."

"When will he wake up?" Riley asked.

"It's difficult to say. But if I were a betting man, I'd say within the next twelve to twenty-four hours."

"And if he doesn't, his brain could start swelling," Stone said.

"It might. I don't think it will. But if he doesn't come around sometime tomorrow, we will do more tests on him. His admittance form shows no contacts for family."

"Stone and I are the closest thing to family Dagger has," Kaleb said.

"I see. And you?" the doctor asked as he nodded in Riley's direction.

"I'm, ummm," she stuttered.

"Riley's a very good friend of Dagger's," Kaleb said.

They stood in silence waiting for the doctor to continue. "Well, then…would you like to see him now?" the doctor asked.

"Yes, please," Riley said.

They followed the doctor through the swinging doors and into the ICU.

"I thought it best we keep him in intensive care for the night. We have someone watching his monitors closely."

"Can we stay with him through the night?" Kaleb asked.

"You can stay for an hour or so. After that, I think it would be best if you all go home and get some rest."

"We can't just leave him alone," Riley said.

"I understand your concern, but we can't have you all here in the ICU. Let me see what I can do, I'll speak with the charge nurse. Dagger is currently stable. If she's okay with it, I'll have him moved to the room closest to the ICU and allow one person to stay through the night. I suggest you rotate and the other two go home. I'll be back in to examine Mr. Eastin after I complete my rounds." The doctor nodded and quietly left the room.

"Hell of a way to find out we're on the right track," Kaleb said.

"What do you mean?" Riley asked.

"It's a pretty safe bet if the ship sinking was connected to someone else on board or had nothing to do with Claudia, then no one would've broken into your home and attacked Dagger."

"I'll take the night watch," Stone said. He pulled his keys out of his pocket and tossed them to Kaleb. "You take Riley home. Search her house inside and out. See if you can find any clues. Riley, you pack whatever you need for the next few days and return to the office with Kaleb where we can protect you." He gave her a stern look, as if he were scolding his sister. "It's not safe for you to be at your home alone. You two go get some rest and come back in the morning."

"We have a state-of-the-art security system," Kaleb said. "Not even a mouse can get through undetected. You'll be safe at the boatshed with me."

"Fine. We'll be back in six hours," Riley said. The two men glowered at her. "Give it up guys. I'm coming back. It's my fault Dagger's here." She walked over and placed her hand over Dagger's. "Rest now. Tomorrow we expect to see you awake and healthy."

****

"Do you have any idea who might've attacked Dagger?" Riley asked. She looked over at Kaleb who seemed deep in thought, staring out the Mustang's windshield.

"No, and I have a suspicious feeling we don't know all the players either. I suspect you have a better idea than me."

"I don't understand."

"Okay. This is what we know. We were hired by SDPD to secure Sheridan's research vessel, gather evidence, and bring it back to home port. It's secured, and we'll be towing it back soon, where we'll release it to the SDPD. Samuels contacted us today. He wanted information. He said the board wants their ship back," Kaleb said.

"He didn't ask if you knew how the ship sank?"

"Let's just say he was pissed off that we wouldn't tell him anything."

"Did he ask if you have any idea how my mother and the rest of those people died?" She was stunned.

"That wasn't his priority. He didn't give us any information, but we do know that an explosion of some kind brought down that ship."

"How often do one of you get attacked while on a contract?"

"We've had our share of run-ins," Kaleb said.

"Do you think the person who attacked Dagger is somehow connected to the person who chased us off the wreck?"

"I don't believe in coincidences. But at this point we have no evidence one way or the other."

"What's your gut feeling?" Riley asked.

"Based on my past experiences. It's more likely than not the two situations are somehow connected. You know Samuels better than us. Is he capable of hiring someone like that?"

"Wayne Samuels is a shrewd, tightfisted megalomaniac who is more than capable of going to extremes to protect his interests. His first priority is to his company. He wants that vessel back because it's in his own best interests. It appears he isn't anxious for SDPD or anyone else to know how his ship sank. I don't trust the man—never have." Riley's thought of Samuels. If he were standing in front of her at this moment she'd spit in his smug face, or at least slap for all she was worth.

Kaleb glanced over at her. "You don't believe discovering what happened on the ship that night, how all those lives were lost, is Samuels' priority?"

Riley's eyebrows pinched together as she frowned and shook her head.

"If that's true, then he's going to have a rude awakening. SDPD is still on the case, but even though our contract is done with SDPD when the vessel reaches the dock, we won't stop investigating until we know how those people died," Kaleb said.

"Wayne's concerned about the bottom line. I don't believe he cares about helping me, or any of the families involved. There's a definite conflict of interest here—in my opinion," Riley said. "I'm determined to find out how my mother and all the others aboard died. As soon as your contract with SDPD is closed—I want to hire Hunters and Seekers."

"Believe me, Riley. We're already on the job."

****

A warm, tingly sensation ran through Dagger's hand and up his arm. Somewhere far off in the distance he thought he could hear Riley calling to him.

He tried to walk in the direction of her voice. Each time he attempted to take a step, he found his legs sunk deeper in a sea of melted caramel. The more he fought to move toward her, the deeper he sank. Exhausted, he gave up and slipped back into the sea.

"Did you have a nice nap?" Kaleb stood at the side of Dagger's bed. "We were starting to think you were going to leave us with all the work." Cocking an eyebrow, Kaleb reached down next to Dagger and grabbed a white remote.

Wait; that's not what it was. Dagger's mind was hazy and his throat dry. He tried to reply but couldn't seem to push out a sound.

"Take it easy," Stone said, from the other side of the bed.

Dagger must have looked as disoriented as he felt.

"You got a pretty good whack on the back of your head and you lost a good deal of blood. You're in the hospital, Dagger. Just be still. The doctor is on his way." Stone patted his arm.

An older man in a white doctor's coat walked into the room. "Good to have you back, Mr. Eastin," the doctor said. "Let me take a look at you."

Dagger tried to recall what had happened. How long had he been out? Shit, his head felt like it was in the grip of a shark's jaw. He reached up and felt the bandage around his head.

"You're going to have a nasty headache for a couple days," the doctor said.

"You went to Riley's to return her mom's papers yesterday afternoon. Someone snuck up behind you, which I find barely believable, and clocked you. You've been out for over twenty-four hours. It's a little after eight in the evening," Kaleb said. "The doc was getting a little concerned about your long nap, but we told him you were just trying to get out of all the hard work."

The doctor patted his arm. "Your throat is probably feeling dry. You've been on IV's for a while. Here, take a sip of water…slowly now, not too much…good. You're a lucky man, your skull wasn't fractured."

"I always said you were a hard-headed S.O.B.," Stone said with a relieved laugh.

"You're a funny guy," Dagger croaked. His throat felt like sandpaper.

"I'll have the nurse give you something for the pain. We'll discuss our next step later. Rest now."

His partners patted his shoulder and walked out with the doctor. Dagger emptied the small cup of water. He was disappointed Riley was nowhere around. He was certain he'd heard her calling to him. Must've been wishful thinking he thought, slipping back off to sleep.

Chapter Nine

"Good morning," Riley said.

Dagger turned his head slowly and with great pain toward the sound of her voice. "Morning?" He croaked the word, sounding like a bullfrog.

Rising from the chair, she walked up to his bed. "Yes. It's morning. How are you feeling?"

"Like someone smashed me in the head with a rock."

"Close. It was one of my awards. He grabbed it off my bookshelf and knocked you out."

She wrapped both her hands around his. Her warmth trickled up his arm and spread throughout his body. A foggy memory tried to bubble to the surface. He didn't reach for it. Instead he relaxed and relished the feel of her hand in his.

"Should I call for the nurse?"

"No." Dagger smiled up at her. Riley remained silent, her espresso-colored eyes shimmering with uncertainty.

"We're all happy you're alive."

"Stone and Kaleb said they'd be here soon. The doc said I'm getting discharged today."

"I know. I'm here to take you home."

"I don't want to put you to any trouble. I'm sure I won't be leaving for a few hours. I'll wait for the guys."

"They won't be back until late this afternoon. They went out to the ship."

"Without me?" He attempted to sit up, but Riley held him down.

"The doctor told them you are not to dive for at least a week."

"Oh, for shit's sake. It's just a damn bump on the head."

"It's more than a bump on your head. Stone said you would be unreasonable about this. He also assured the doctor that he and Kaleb would make sure you would—in his words, 'be yanked out of the water if you waded in any deeper than your ankles.'"

Dagger's silent scowl was his only answer.

"Stone also said to tell you, he and your other *partner* are more than capable of investigating a dive site without your assistance. And that you would be responsible for managing the office for the next week."

"Okay. You can stop torturing me now. I got the picture," he grumbled.

"Good. Now if you're done feeling sorry for yourself, you can sit up, slowly." She backed away from his bedside.

In one quick motion Dagger sat up and swung his legs off the bed. The room tilted and began to spin. His throat burned from bile, and he broke out in a cold sweat.

"What in the hell are you doing?" Riley carefully lifted his legs back onto the bed.

"What? You said you're here to spring me from this joint. I'm ready to be sprung."

"First, you ignored what I said. You need to take things slowly, which I'm beginning to realize is not in your wheel-house. Second, the doctor said you were not to move out of this bed until he sees you."

"Fantastic. Where is he?"

"Why? You have a hot date?"

"As a matter of fact, I want to meet the guy who bopped me."

****

Dagger sat in the passenger seat of Riley's Subaru with his arms crossed. He was not impressed with the parameters of his release. The doctor insisted he not be left alone for the next two days.

What a complete pain in the ass.

On top of that, his partners were tied up on the project that he'd been looking forward to exploring. With the two of them diving, he'd be nothing but a burden to poor Riley, who'd have to watch over his sorry ass. The tightness in his chest increased. It felt like every damn muscle in his body was as taut as a stretched rubber band.

"Dammit, Riley. I can find someone else to keep an eye on me. For that matter, I'm a grown man, and I'm sure I can handle this situation on my own. You can't convince me you want to waste your weekend babysitting me." His words were little more than a growl.

She cocked an eyebrow at him. He had to give her credit. Most people went running and screaming when he used that tone. Instead she just smirked, as if he'd made a joke.

"No can do, sport. I promised Kaleb and Stone I would not let you out of my sight. Besides, I have no plans for the weekend. Is the turn coming up?"

"Yeah—next road on the right," he grumbled. "It's the last house at the end of the road."

"I'm surprised," Riley said, as she pulled into the driveway of a rustic house sitting on the water's edge.

"Why? Did you think I lived in a tent, or maybe a cave?"

"I pictured you in a posh townhouse or apartment. Some place with little maintenance. From the road this looks like a quaint cabin, until you get closer and realize it's a large house. This is lovely and has a lot of character. Your view is spectacular."

"Wait one second. My brain isn't that scrambled. I believe you both insulted and complimented me. Thank you—I think."

Her warm laugh made him grin. "Okay, champ. Let me help you inside and you can show me where to put my stuff."

"Really. I can walk all on my own. Believe it or not, I mastered that feat over thirty-eight years ago."

"I know you can walk. I'll just be right beside you in case you get dizzy. The doctor said—"

"Yeah, I know. Falling down is a very bad thing." He rubbed a hand over his eyes.

This is not my idea of bringing a woman home, he thought. *What the hell am I thinking—now I really am losing it.*

"Dagger? Dagger."

He nearly jumped as he realized Riley stood only inches from him in the open car door. Hell, the last thing he needed was to lose time, or for that matter, to even think about Riley in any capacity other than professional.

"You okay? You look confused. Maybe I should call the doctor."

"I'm fine. My mind was wandering." He slowly got out of the car as she studied him. "Come on, I'll give you the five-cent tour and show you the guest room."

****

Riley was astonished at the cabin. It was masculine and tastefully decorated. The décor was high-quality and reflected the tranquility of the sea, all done in shades of blues, greens, and browns. The main living area was open and airy with enormous windows filling the wall. A large sliding door opened to a slate and brick patio that ran the length of the house. The upper floor walkway overlooked the downstairs, reminding her of an oversized loft. The upstairs held a large den; but even with the enormous desk, the room looked more like a library to her. There was an extensive workout area, two guest bedrooms, and a bathroom.

"Dagger, your place is lovely."

He wrinkled his nose. "Not exactly the reaction I was going for."

"Sorry. What I mean is, it's very masculine."

He looked drained to her. His face was ashen.

"Why don't you take a nap. You don't want to overdo it on your first day," she said.

"I want to wait until I hear from the guys. I need to know what they found out on their dive. Yesterday they told me about the scene at your house. The papers never reached the safe. I got bushwhacked before I got the chance to lock them up."

"Don't worry about those," Riley said. "I've contacted Mom's attorney. They're hand-delivering a copy of the will to me tomorrow and I kept my mother's letter with me. None of Mom's things I left on the kitchen table were touched. So stop worrying. Go take a nap, I'll wake you as soon as the guys make contact. I promise."

Riley's phone vibrated in her pocket. She pulled it free and looked at the screen. It was Kaleb.

"Hey, Riley. How's our boy?" Kaleb asked.

"Cranky. He's resting now. The trip home from the hospital tired him out." She looked out the window and noticed dusk had fallen. "Did you find anything?"

"Yeah, we did. We thought we'd pick up some dinner and head out to you."

"Sounds good. We'll be waiting."

Riley walked out of the guest bedroom and looked down into the main room. They'd forgotten to leave any lights on. The dusky sky was scattered with bluish-grey clouds. The two-story enormous windows facing the water were illuminated by the last rays of the sun reflecting off the ocean, giving the interior a mysterious glow. As her sight adjusted, her surroundings came into clearer focus.

She was descending the stairs when the door to Dagger's room opened. He switched on the main light and she squinted from the brightness; her footing missed a stair. She fell forward expecting to land face first on the hardwood floor. Instead she was scooped out of midair and landed against the safe warmth and hardness of Dagger's chest.

"Shit. I'm so sorry I nearly blinded you. Are you okay?" he asked, still cradling her against him.

"You shouldn't have caught me like that. Did you hurt yourself?" she asked.

"I'm not worried about me. You almost broke your neck."

Riley frowned up at him. "I'm fine—you caught me."

The sound of waves breaking against the rocks rippled through the house. Dagger gradually set her down. "Someone's here. That was the doorbell."

"I was on my way down to wake you. It's Stone and Kaleb." He headed for the door.

"No. You—go sit down. I'll let them in," Riley scowled him.

He rolled his eyes and kept walking.

"Dagger! I mean it. You're supposed to take it easy. And the last time I checked the definition of those words, I don't recall that catching someone out of midair was a permitted activity."

Dagger turned back and smiled at her. His pale, topaz-brown eyes sparkled like champagne. He rubbed one hand over his chin. He sported more than a five o'clock shadow and it suited him.

"All right. I'll go sit." He sighed as he moved to the oversized chair and flopped down. "The last thing I want is to have you three ganging up on me and sticking me back in the hospital."

She waited for Dagger to settle himself and put his feet up on the footrest. He raised an eyebrow and made a haughty, sweeping motion with his hands as if to say, "carry on." Images of a king bestowing his treasures on his flock flashed through her mind.

He must have been a real handful as a child, she thought.

The insistent sound of the doorbell pulled Riley from her thoughts and she opened the door.

"Finally. This stuff is getting heavy," Kaleb said, as he walked inside with armloads of takeout food and headed to the kitchen table.

"He can be such a baby," Stone said. He followed Kaleb in

carrying an enormous box. "Okay if I set this down on the coffee table?"

Dagger nodded.

Before closing the door, Riley took a step outside and looked around.

"Where are you going?" Kaleb asked.

"No one else is with you?" she asked.

"No. Just us—why?" A confused look crossed Kaleb's features.

"You brought enough food for ten people for three days."

"I wanted Thai and Stone wanted Mexican. We weren't sure what you would like to eat, so we picked up Italian and a few salads. And of course, we wanted beer and figured you'd rather drink wine. Sorry buddy, no alcohol for you for the next week. Doctor's orders."

"I won't have to cook all weekend," she said, laughing.

"I wouldn't bet on it," Dagger said. "They can put away a lot of food."

Kaleb headed back for his third plateful, as Stone pulled out his laptop and set it up.

"We confirmed our initial thoughts," Stone said.

"Which ones?" Dagger asked.

"There was a leak in the system." Kaleb said, as he set his heaping plate on the table, reached into his pocket, and handed Stone a USB. Stone plugged it into the computer. "Check out this first picture," Kaleb said, between bites of food.

The picture was of a long black object, that ran the length of the frame. On one end there was a wide silver band with bolts sticking out of it. Circles, about the size and color of dimes, dotted the object. Riley noticed the concentration of the dimes appeared greatest around the silver band.

"We inspected the entire engine room. Everything was maintained in tip-top condition. Everything except the piping coming out of the engine and going into the engine exhaust system." Stone pointed at the silver band.

"Son. Of. A. Bitch." Dagger articulated each word as he examined the picture. "Hell if you weren't right, Kaleb. The flanges on the piping were loose."

"What does that mean? What happens if those flanges are loose?" Riley asked.

"That pipe carries carbon monoxide. A leak would make

everyone disoriented. An accumulation could kill," Dagger said.

"Maybe it happened during the accident," Riley said. "Or someone could've been working on the pipes right before the ship started to sink."

All the men focused on her like she had two heads. Their intensity made her mouth go dry.

"Anything's possible." Stone broke the silence.

"Yeah, but what's more likely is someone loosened those flanges on purpose. It would take some time for the entire ship of people to get exposed to the carbon monoxide gas. The storm the vessel was caught in during the night would've forced everyone into their cabins, or at the very least, inside the ship. The perfect storm to poison people. No one would spot the loose flanges, because no one would be doing maintenance, unless it was an immediate threat to the safety of the crew or ship. Their focus would be on getting the ship through the storm. The leaking CO gas would have time to seep throughout the entire ship's interior," Kaleb said.

"That's not what happened." Riley leaned back in her chair, putting more space between her and Kaleb. "It can't be. You're saying, not only was my mother killed, but someone on board did it? You think it could've been one of her team? It's unthinkable." Riley shook her head vigorously.

"You've believed from virtually the beginning that something wasn't right that night," Dagger said.

"But not being murdered by the hand of a person she worked closely with."

"They're on a ship, out to sea. The engine room was meticulous. The engineer would have noticed the flange had it been loosened before they left port. Someone on that ship loosened those flanges." Dagger pointed out.

Dagger was right. Had the flange been loose early on, someone would have noticed. She knew it deep in her heart. Nevertheless, hearing it said out loud…someone her mother called a friend might have gassed her and a shipload of innocent people.

For what? Was it just for some damn formula? Just greed?

The more Riley thought about it, the sicker she got. "What about the gouge in the front of the hull?"

"We're still working on that," Stone said. "Dagger was right. We investigated the gouge up close. Neither Kaleb nor I could locate even one fleck of paint transfer."

"I'm proposing that everyone on board was affected by the CO gas. They were either dead, or their ability to think was impaired before the ship sank," Dagger said.

"So now what do we do?" Stone asked. "Do we pass our findings along to SDPD?"

"No. Not yet," Kaleb said.

"Kaleb's right. We keep our findings between the four of us for the time being. We continue investigating and we watch," Dagger said. "When we write up our final report to SDPD we'll have to include our working theories. But we have a little time before we get to that point."

"My mother wasn't dead before the ship went down. She was on the phone, leaving me a message. Why didn't she get to a life boat?" Riley demanded.

"Kaleb, play Claudia's message."

The cabin filled with Claudia Rawlings last words—once, twice, three times.

"How does she sound to you, Riley? Does she seem off?" Dagger asked.

"No. She sounds fine. She…she sounds tired, not quite as sharp. But it was two in the morning."

"Didn't you tell us your mother stayed up late as a matter of habit?" Stone asked.

"She does…did. It doesn't mean she wasn't tired."

"True. But listen to her enunciation. Her slight slur. Was it normal for her to slur when she was up late?"

Riley's emotional dam broke wide open. She shook violently from head to toe.

Chapter Ten

"Riley, you've been out here for hours. You'll freeze if you stay out much longer," Stone said, as he stepped out onto the back patio. He wrapped a blanket around her. "Kaleb and I had to hog-tie Dagger to keep him from coming out here. He's one stubborn jackass, even when he's injured. Why don't you come inside? You'll put Dagger's worries at ease, and Kaleb will make you one of his famous hot buttered rums."

When she didn't look up at him, he squatted down in front of her.

"I know this situation is difficult. If it's too painful, we can leave you out of the investigation until we have some answers."

She turned her head slowly and locked on to Stone's eyes. "Are you sure we can find the answer?"

"I think so. Riley, we're good private investigators. Let us do our job. Between us, the Coast Guard, and the SDPD, we'll make sure to get whoever did this—and we'll keep you safe."

"And have you solved every case?"

"Every single time. Before you even ask—this time is no different."

"Then let's get back to it," Riley said.

Stone slid the glass door open and followed Riley into the house.

"Kaleb put those bartending skills of yours to work. Riley is chilled clean through and I promised her one of your hot buttered rums."

"You got it. All around. Oops, sorry. Not for you, buddy,"

Kaleb said, grinning at Dagger.

"I've spent most of the afternoon reading over my mother's letter," she said. "Most of it is pretty straightforward; except there's one sentence that doesn't seem to fit."

"Which sentence?" Dagger asked.

"Remember your childhood and all the wonderful games we played."

"Why don't you think it fits?" Kaleb asked.

"It doesn't fit the context of the letter. Childhood games have nothing to do with the rest of the letter. Nonetheless, this sentence tugged at me. Why would she bother to put that in there if it didn't mean something? We played games when I was a young girl, but nothing out of the ordinary. I decided to make a list of every game we played, to see if it would help me figure it out."

"And?" Dagger asked, when she remained quiet for a minute too long.

"And they're all just regular games, nothing special. Except for one—"

The guys straightened up in their seats, shifting a bit. No one said a word. They didn't want Riley to lose her train of thought.

"My mom loved hiding little treasures for me to find, like a scavenger hunt. She would give me a note containing a clue, and I would have to find the hidden treasure. It was never easy. The first note led to a second, then a third, and so on until I finally found my treasure. We played the game until I graduated from college. Even my graduation gift was part of a scavenger hunt. I solved twelve different clues before I found the keys to my first car."

"You think your mom has left behind a scavenger hunt for you to follow to the formula?" Dagger asked.

"I do, without a doubt. How else could she be sure that only I would be able to find her research?"

"How can you be absolutely positive there's not another possibility?" Dagger asked.

"I wasn't at first. I went back to her letter and read and re-read it." She pulled the letter from her jeans pocket. "Then it finally dawned on me—I'm already playing the game. I've solved her first three clues."

The guys looked at her like she had six arms and two heads.

"Don't you see? The first clue was Mom's yellow sweater, with the tag that read—*home starfish*. The second clue was the hiding spot in the buffet, and the third the safe deposit box which contained the white stone, which read: OG EHRE. Now, the scrambled letters on the stone are obvious." She reached into the pocket of her sweater and pulled out the small white stone. "You were right, Dagger. She left clues only I would understand—*OG EHRE*. She told me—*GO HERE*. The next clue has to be at my grandparents' house. Mom and I found this stone at my grandparents' house—where I'm guessing we find our next clue."

"Okay," Stone said. He nodded and rubbed his fingers down the outer edge of his eyebrow. "It makes sense up to this point. Where's your grandparents' house?"

"Washington State. In the Puget Sound, on San Juan Island," she said.

"What if she was using the stone to represent something much broader, like a beach in general?" Stone asked.

"I know how my mother thin—thought. She wasn't a general type of a person. She was a research scientist." Riley looked down at the letter in her hands. "It makes me wonder…if Mom is putting us on a scavenger hunt for her research, who is she hiding her formula from?" Riley asked.

"It could be a number of entities, couldn't it?" Dagger asked. "She told you only to give Sheridan Enterprises what was agreed on. So could it be them? Our government? Somebody else's government?"

"Hell, it could even be an entire industry." Kaleb said.

"Could it be from the university she left behind?" Stone asked. "Based on what you've told us, she's worked on this research for years. Maybe someone at the university feels it belongs to them?"

"It's not the university," Riley said. She held her hand up before the guys could start to argue with her. "It's not. Yes, Mom did leave her teaching position at the university to go to Sheridan. But she didn't truly *leave* the university. She held regular seminars there. She did workshops. All her assistants are past or present students. Regardless, I need to follow her next clue. I've looked at plane tickets. I could fly out on Wednesday."

"Hold on. You aren't going alone. I'll go with you," Dagger said.

"You can't travel, Dagger," Stone said.

"The doc said to lay low for the next three days. I'll follow his orders. Tuesday, I have a follow-up appointment. I'll make sure to get the all-clear from the doc, then we can fly out."

"And just who is going to man the office?" Kaleb asked.

"One of you two bozos. I have complete faith in you."

Kaleb and Stone gave him a fierce glare.

"Lest you forget, we have a research ship to bring up and tow back to the harbor," Kaleb said.

"It doesn't take two of you to captain the salvage tugboat and tow barge. The reason we hire this particular vessel is because of the dedicated crew. All they need is one guy to be the captain." Dagger said. "One of you tends the shop, the other oversees the ship. Problem solved."

"I call the ship," the two guys yelled in unison.

Riley giggled.

Dagger sighed. "Can you two boys work this out or do you want to arm wrestle for it?"

"Best two out of three?" Stone cleared a section of the kitchen table off.

Kaleb laughed as he flopped down into a chair. "You're on."

****

"What time is the last ferry?" Riley asked as they waited at the baggage claim at Sea-Tac Airport. They were unable to catch a flight together until late Thursday and she was anxious to get to her grandparents.

Dagger pulled out his phone and clicked on the Washington State Department of Transportation, or WSDOT. "Eight twenty-five. And as it takes over an hour and thirty minutes to drive to Anacortes, we're not going to make it to the ferry on time. I have a better idea. What do you say we rent a boat out of Anacortes?"

"Not happening, champ. You promised your doctor you would stay out of the water for another *six* days." Riley placed her hands on her hips. "By my count, you have to stay out of the water until Monday."

"I'll be *on* the water, not *in* it. Same as if we take the ferry."

"It's not the same. If you're piloting a boat, there's a good chance you'll have to get into the water at some point." With her hands still firmly planted on her hips, she leaned closer and glared up at Dagger.

"Only up to my calves."

"Dagger." She stiffened and squinted at him, trying for her best *tough* look.

"Is that your best serious look?" Dagger chuckled, and she had the urge to shake him, like a mother correcting her child. Instead, she crossed her arms and shook her head.

"Option three. We could charter a seaplane or helicopter," he said.

"How about we stick to the plan, it's not a big deal that we can't make the ferry," Riley said attempting to take her own advice. "We're not in a huge rush. Let's go stand in the line for our rental car, have dinner in Seattle, and after dinner we drive to Anacortes and stay overnight. We can catch the first ferry out in the morning."

"First ferry is at four fifteen in the morning," Dagger said giving her a half-smile.

"Holy mother of…why in the world would someone want to take a ferry that early?" She feigned a shiver. "Okay, we'll get up, have breakfast, and catch a ferry around nine."

The more he thought about Riley's plan, the more he liked it. This way they would spend more time together. Lately Dagger looked forward to spending time with her, but if he didn't keep himself in check, he might find himself in deep waters. He had to keep reminding himself that Riley was a client—and completely off-limits.

"Dagger? What do you think?"

"Huh—yeah, sounds like a plan."

****

"Have you figured out where they're going?" Eric sat in a chair a few baggage carousels away from Dagger and Riley as he spoke into his phone.

"No idea," the man on the line said. "Riley and her parents travelled around before settling. I know they spent time in the Seattle area. How the hell am I supposed to know where they're headed? You're the damned one tailing them. Why do I even pay you?"

Jackass, how I hate this man. "You can't track their itinerary?" Eric knew his anger was showing.

"I could, if there was one to track. The only thing I can locate is the flight you just arrived on. Don't lose them and don't get spotted, I'm paying you good money to find out what Riley knows. Call me when you have something."

Chapter Eleven

"I enjoyed riding the ferry," Dagger said as they joined the masses on the auto deck and disembarked the boat.

The Puget Sound sparkled like a mirror ball in the morning light, with calm seas and clear skies. He and Riley had picked up coffee in the ferry's galley and sat on the sun deck at the bow of the boat.

"My grandparents' place is on the outskirts of Friday Harbor."

"How long has it been since you've seen their place?" Dagger asked.

"When I went with Mom and packed my grandparent's house up a little over two years ago. We used to visit every summer and most winters. Neither of us could bring ourselves to visit since they died. A couple weeks before Mom—left, she asked me if I was interested in spending some time on the island this summer. I told her I'd let her know when she got back." Riley sniffed and dabbed at the corner of one eye.

"I'm sorry, Riley. I shouldn't have asked."

"Don't be silly. I've got to work through my emotions. It's more difficult than I thought it would be after all this time. Nonetheless I can't break down every time I'm asked a question or see something reminding me of my grandparents."

"Stop being so hard on yourself. You're still reeling from the loss of your mother. You've experienced a lot of loss in a short period of time. Do you have any other family?"

"Just an aunt. My dad's older half-sister. She'll be landing in San Diego today. She's going over to the funeral home to make all the arrangements."

"I'm kinda surprised you didn't want to stay home to be there when your aunt arrived."

"We're not close. I haven't seen Aunt Fran since my dad's funeral, over nineteen years ago."

He gave her an odd look. "Mind if I ask why she's the one planning the funeral?"

"A few months after Dad died, Mom told me if the time came when someone would have to identify her body, she didn't want it to be me. She fell apart when dad died. I was the one who organized everything. I made all the arrangements to bring Dad's body home from Oahu and planned his funeral. She felt terrible about it and didn't want to put me through the process once again. She made me promise I would let Aunt Fran take care of everything.

"Mom and Aunt Fran kept in touch. Mom visited her several times. My aunt will organize as much as she can now and then return home. Aunt Fran plans to return and finalize all the details once Mom's body is released from the coroner. I have to tell you, it's been both a blessing and a heartache to stick to my promise."

"She wanted to protect you."

"I know."

"Mind if I ask how you lost your father? He must have been fairly young." Dagger started the SUV and headed out of town.

"Much too young and still so full of life. It was an accident. We were living in San Diego and a few months after Dad sold the dive school in Oahu, he got a call from the new owners. They offered to pay to get him back out to Oahu to help them with the business. He and one of the new partners were killed in a float plane. They were returning from a meeting on Hawaii, flying back to Oahu when their plane crashed."

"How awful. And such a shame you lost both of your parents to something that is such a part of your life—the ocean. I'm truly sorry, Riley."

"You know in a strange way, losing Dad to the sea has brought me solace. I feel him with me when I'm in the water."

"I understand your feeling," Dagger said. "I lost a few friends to the sea during my years in the SEALs."

Her grandparents' house sat at the far end of San Juan Island, hidden from view by a grouping of Douglas fir and pines that were common on the island. The trees stood over one hundred feet tall in most places. She pointed out the concealed driveway to Dagger. As they broke through the trees, she embraced the familiar feeling of serenity, even after all this time.

The two-story craftsman-style house was painted a cool green and butter yellow with pure white trim and accents. Large lavender bushes edged the wrap-around porch. The house sat upon a slight incline that provided them with a panoramic view of the Puget Sound. A pristine acre of grass ran all the way down to the beach. The beach was a mixture of sand and rock and was dotted with Pacific madrones along the water line.

As if to welcome her back, a pod of orcas frolicked in the Sound, breeching and spraying water out their blowholes.

"Wow. This is paradise," Dagger said.

"It is. Whenever I'm here it feels like the weight of the world slips away."

"The house and yard look well kept."

"Yes, there's a caretaker. After my grandmother died, my mom kept him on." She paused.

"Does he live on the grounds?"

"Last I heard, Mr. Ford and his family moved into the place next door."

Dagger glanced around in confusion.

"I don't see any neighbors."

"When you're on the beach you can see a couple houses. I called Mr. Ford to let him know we were on our way here. I told him we would only be staying a day or two, but he insisted on stocking the kitchen."

They walked up the front steps and Riley unlocked the door and turned off the alarm system.

"I thought you and your mom packed up the house?"

"We did. It took us days to pack up Grandma's and Grandpa's clothes and personal items, streamline the kitchen, and clean up the boatshed. We left most of the furniture and a few of their favorite things. You wouldn't have believed all the stuff they'd accumulated. We decided we wanted to keep the feel of my grandparents, that's why we left their furniture."

"When you live in the same house for forty plus years, I'm sure you collect a lot of things." Dagger walked over to the teak sideboard sitting under one of the large picture windows and picked up a photograph. "Is this you and your family?"

"Yes, it was taken a few months before we lost Dad. That's him." She pointed at the man with his hands on her shoulders. "There's Mom, Grandma, and Grandpa."

"It's beautiful. Maybe you should take it with you."

"I have the same picture hanging in my bedroom. Dad framed it for me and gave it to me for my birthday." Riley felt wetness fill her eyes. She shook her head and turned toward the windows. "Want to take a walk on the beach?"

****

The aroma of fresh ground coffee, bacon, and cinnamon wafted into his bedroom. Dagger yawned and stretched his arms over his head as his stomach growled. He hopped out of bed and headed downstairs.

"Something smells delicious," he said, walking into the kitchen. Dagger thought Riley was the perfect petite package, with curves in all the right places. Her smile could out-shine a thousand stars. Hell, her frown was sexy, too.

Riley peeked over her shoulder at him as she pulled a pan of cinnamon rolls from the oven. "Morning. You're just in time," she said.

"Be still my heart. It's been years since I've eaten homemade cinnamon rolls. You must have gotten up at the crack of dawn to make these." Dagger rubbed his palms together.

"I'd love to take the credit for them, but all I did was stick the pan in the oven. Mrs. Ford stopped by and brought these, along with baking directions. She wanted to say hello and welcome me back. I told her about Mom. She broke down." Riley placed the rolls on the table. "Grab yourself some coffee and have a seat. I'll pull the quiche out of the oven. I did make the bacon, cheese, and mushroom quiche."

Dagger noticed she didn't dwell on her conversation with Mrs. Ford.

"I'm surprised I didn't hear the doorbell or voices." It wasn't like him not to wake when there were sounds, especially in a new place.

"I was walking on the beach when I ran into her. She saw me on her way to the house and met me with the rolls."

"Couldn't sleep?"

"Only for a few hours. Then the nightmares started."

"I can sympathize. Coming back here, coupled with what

happened to your mother is a lot to deal with," Dagger said. "When you were on the beach, did you come up with any thoughts regarding the next clue?"

"I've thought about it all morning. My plan is to stay with the game theme. My grandparents collected tons of games that we'd all play. I'm going to try to find our next clue in the games. If that doesn't pan out, I'll search the house, every nook and cranny, and hope I come up with something."

"I'm not going to be much help, although I can move things around."

"I'm sure you need to touch base with the guys. Doesn't the salvage tug arrive today?"

"It does. And they are still arguing about who would pilot it, even though Stone was the clear winner at arm wrestling. Will I be in your way if I set up my computer in the living room?"

She smiled. "Feel free to set up your office anywhere. I'll move you if you're in my way."

****

Dagger was finding it difficult to concentrate as his attention kept shifting to what Riley was doing. She had meticulously examined each piece of the multitude of board games and hadn't found a clue. She'd moved from room to room, pulling out drawers, looking under the beds, and scouring the closets.

Dagger skyped with Kaleb and Stone, tracking the process of raising the research vessel. They'd run into a few issues, which slowed them down. To make matters worse, they were running against the clock as an impending storm was on the horizon. If they couldn't get the ship up in the next five hours, they'd have to wait until the storm passed. That meant more money spent for their security team and tug rental. It also meant any evidence still left inside the research vessel could be washed away and destroyed by the storm. With nothing left to do once they hung up, Dagger walked out to the porch.

Riley rocked in the rocking chair, head resting on the chair back, eyes closed. The notebook lay open next to her rocker, covered in notes and doodles. "I haven't found anything."

Dagger sat in the empty rocker next to her.

"Maybe this is a wild goose chase. What if my theory is wrong?" She opened her eyes and glanced over at him.

"Don't second guess yourself, Riley. You know your mother

and her thought process. Stick with your gut." He reached out and wrapped his hand around hers, interlacing their fingers. "What is your gut telling you?"

She looked down at his hand but didn't make a move to pull away.

"I can't come up with any other options. I still believe Mom set up a scavenger hunt."

"Then we stay the course. She had to make it difficult. Otherwise anyone would be able to figure it out—right?"

****

Riley gazed at the clock next to her bed for the tenth time in the past twenty minutes. She was mentally exhausted, yet her mind refused to shut down and let her rest. She closed her eyes and willed herself to sleep.

Crreeeak...

She sat up ramrod straight and listened in the darkness. She strained to hear any other sound out of place.

The crickets and frogs chirruped. Off in the distance a red fox cried out—exactly like a woman screaming. Then a scraping sound...so close.

The crickets and frogs abruptly stopped.

She held her breath, one, two, three, heartbeats.

The chirruping returned.

Slipping both legs out from under her covers, she placed her feet on the floor as soundlessly as possible. Slowly shifting her weight, she stood up and tiptoed to the door. She crept out of her room and headed for the stairs where she stopped and listened.

It was a moonless night, and she couldn't see more than a few feet, but growing up in this house she felt comfortable moving in the near blinding darkness.

She moved onto the first stair and stopped. Making sure of her footing she skipped the next stair knowing it would squeak and gracefully landed on the one below. All the while keeping her hands away from the shaky banister that her dad had promised to fix years ago. She continued down the remining stairs, stepping only on the solid treads. She moved toward the front door. The security system wasn't active. Had she set it before bed? She couldn't remember. Cracking the door open she slipped out into the night.

Out of nowhere, a massive hand covered her mouth and an arm wrapped around her waist. She tried to scream, but the man yanked her back and knocked the wind from her lungs.

Chapter Twelve

Riley fought for her next breath. She reached for the steel grip encircling her waist and pulled at the muscular arm with all her worth. She squirmed against the imposing body holding her in place, battling, as spurts of adrenaline coursed through her. Abruptly she was pulled off her feet. His hot breath washed her neck.

"Riley, stop. Stop struggling. You're safe. It's me," Dagger whispered into her ear. "Shh. It's okay, but be quiet." Dagger removed his hand from her mouth and lowered her to the porch. "Someone is here."

"Where?" she whispered.

"I'm not sure. It's too damn dark out here. I thought I heard something downstairs. I got up to check the alarm and I saw a quick flash of light outside the front window. The door was ajar. They were prowling around the house. I think they headed for the beach. I was on my way after them when I heard you. Did you set the alarm tonight?"

"I can't remember. Do you think they were in the house and turned off the alarm?" A shiver started at the top of Riley's head and shot down through her toes. Someone had been in the house and that someone was still out there.

"They made it inside and either the alarm wasn't set, or they bypassed it. I'm sure they left the house. I did a quick search before heading outside. You go back in. Keep the lights off and stay away from the windows, in case whoever it is has night goggles. I'm going to take a quick look around. Lock the door. I've still got your key."

"No. What if they have a gun?"

"I'll be careful. Please, go inside."

She nodded and slipped back in through the door, locking it behind her.

Riley sat on the floor and leaned against the sofa. She couldn't hear a sound. It was eerily quiet.

The door opened and closed. She stiffened.

"Riley, it's me. Where are you?"

"On the floor, by the sofa," she whispered.

"Stay put."

Dagger pulled down all the blinds, throwing the house into an even deeper darkness. A click sounded and one of the table lamps turned on.

"I didn't mean to frighten you, but I needed to stop you before you left the porch, to keep you from stepping out into the clear. If you're sneaking around someone's property at night, there's a fairly decent chance you're going to come armed. And we don't know if they found all they were after when they broke into your house, so I think it's fair to assume they're dangerous—says the guy with the lump on his skull."

"Did you get a look at the intruder?"

"Only briefly as he moved through the yard."

"It was a man?"

"Pretty certain, and he moved like he knew what he was doing."

"Who would be out here? Was it a robber? The place is usually empty. Maybe he's been here before, cased it, and planned to rob it. We might've surprised him by being here."

"Possibly."

"You don't think so?"

"I'm not one to believe in coincidences."

Riley stood up and headed into dining room. "I'm getting us a brandy. Maybe two."

She set two snifters and a bottle of brandy on the coffee table. She peeled off the seal and filled each of the snifters over half full.

"Why do you doubt it was a robber?" she asked.

Dagger pulled a gun from his back and placed it on the table. He sat on the sofa next to her and leaned down, pulled up his pant leg and removed a serious-looking knife from a calf holster.

"I see you brought weapons with you. Were you expecting trouble?"

"I'm always expecting trouble and I always travel prepared."

He picked up the snifter and took a long sip. "Who knows you were coming here?"

"Mr. and Mrs. Ford."

"Anyone else?"

"No."

"You didn't call the university and tell your boss, maybe a friend?"

"No. I'm on personal leave. Wait—are you saying you think we were followed to the island?"

"That was my first thought."

"Why?"

"My best guess, I think someone believes you know where your mother hid her research."

"What now? Have we scared them off?"

"Yes. And, we keep looking. But if we're being followed, we must be vigilant. At least for the time being, we have the upper hand. Make sure not to text, call, or tell anyone what we're doing."

"Okay, what about Kaleb and Stone? Shouldn't we keep them in the loop?"

"We will. We have our own code for just these circumstances. I'll let them know what's happened." He pulled out his phone and typed a quick message.

"What did you tell them?"

"Weather is terrible at our next destination. Change of venue in the works. Searching for sunshine."

She crinkled her nose. "And what exactly does that mean?"

"We've got a tail, everything's fine. Plan on leaving in the next few days. Will keep an eye out for our shadow."

Dagger's phone beeped. He read the text out loud. "Guess we'll stay home, hate bad weather. Let us know if you need foul weather gear. We can ship it overnight." Dagger nodded with approval. "Which translates to: we'll stay put for now, keep us updated. Let us know if you need backup. We can be there tomorrow."

Riley sat quietly as she inspected the brandy in her snifter.

"What's wrong?" he asked.

"I was just thinking it must be a wonderful thing to have such close friends. You share a code, they have your back, and they're there for you at any time."

"I never gave it much thought. We are lucky. We shared some pretty rough times while we served. Don't get me wrong. It's not only about the bad times. We've also been there for one another through the good times. We don't by any means take each other for granted," he said. "What about you? You must have friends you can count on?"

"I have friends. Lots of friends. Most of them are from work. I'm sure they would help me if I asked. I wouldn't say they'd drop everything at a moment's notice for me. I'm sure if I needed something reasonable, they would help. But I doubt any one of them would come running if I was in danger or being stalked."

"You might be surprised." Dagger put his arm around her and rubber her shoulder.

"Thanks, Dagger. Right now I need to focus on finding that blasted clue. I don't know where else to look."

"It's only been two days. Something will spark your memory."

"I'm not as confident. I've studied my notes and I don't see any clues."

"What about the boathouse? You haven't searched there."

"Good idea. I'll start on it first thing in the morning."

Dagger yawned and rubbed his hand over his face. "We need to get some rest."

She headed for the stairs and stopped when she noticed he hadn't moved from the sofa. "I thought you said we *both* needed sleep."

"I did. From now on, I'm sleeping right here on the sofa."

****

Dagger continuously scrutinized the area as he and Riley headed down to the boathouse. So far, their intruder hadn't made a second appearance. Riley believed the incident was over. Not Dagger. The guy had to be desperate to take the chance he did last night. He knew the type of man. Hell, there were times, he was that type of man. And he wouldn't give up until he found what he was searching for. But whether this guy realized it or not, his biggest obstacle now was, Dagger. The asshat wasn't getting anywhere near Riley again.

She opened the boathouse door and stopped short. Dagger bumped into her, knocking her forward, he grabbed her to stop her fall. "Shit. I'm sorry. I was watching the beach. Why—" He stopped abruptly when he saw the answer for himself. The boathouse was packed with boxes stacked in rows, and indoor and outdoor furniture covering all the remaining floor space.

"Mom never arranged to have all the stuff we packed shipped to storage."

"She probably figured keeping it here was easier. Everything would be close if you needed something."

"I'm sure you're right." Riley blew out a long breath. "Let's search the boxes and look for board games. If you find any, let's stack them over here on the table." She pulled the table closer.

When they finally made it through the last box, Dagger said, "I count twenty-seven games. Let's carry them up to the house and you can spread them out on the table."

Dagger watched Riley as she intently examined each game. She would check each game's box, study the boards, and analyze every piece. Three hours later she'd investigated nineteen games and Dagger felt a flicker of doubt. If they were on the wrong track, they might be here for days.

Riley pulled out Scrabble and opened the box. A smile spread across her features. "This was one of Mom's favorite games, she loved teaching me new words." Riley dumped the bag of letter tiles on the board, spreading the tiles out. "Look. There's a short green line on the edge of the bottom of the 'a.'" Her face lit up as if she'd found a million dollars.

"It looks like a green marker. Here's another green mark on the 'h' of this tile." Dagger's phone beeped and he pulled it from his pocket. A text from an unknown number lit up on his screen: *I'm watching you*. What in the hell? He frowned.

"Something wrong at work?" Riley had stopped what she was doing and stared at him.

"Um, yeah. Something's off with the salvage tug." He glanced at the screen again. Then he shoved it into his pocket in hopes that she wouldn't see the real message. Riley didn't need anything more on her plate. They examined every tile, pulling out the ones with green ink, until they were left with fourteen marked tiles.

"Deciphering these could take you some time. I think I'll take a walk to stretch my legs," Dagger said.

The text confirmed his itchy feeling—he'd felt like they were being watched. Someone was close by and they were good at surveillance. Dagger strolled the property line, casually watching for movement in the trees. An itch grew between his shoulder blades; he wondered if there was a target painted on his back. He'd nearly finished a second circuit when a man stepped out of the trees.

"Good afternoon, Dagger. How are you enjoying our island?" Mr. Ford asked.

"It's beautiful, I hope to come back some day."

"Good to hear. Is there something I can do for you? I noticed you've been out here a while."

"Have you seen anyone else around? Someone you don't know?"

"Now that you mention it, there have been a couple people by, which is kind of unusual. Generally, we only have an infrequent tourist every now and again. About an hour ago I caught sight of a woman walking back toward the park. I believe she's the same person who walked past earlier today. Are you expecting someone?"

"No. Just wondered how much traffic this area gets. You didn't happen to get a look at the woman, did you?"

Mr. Ford paused and then shook his head slowly. "Sorry, can't say I did. I was working on the lawn mower. Just happened to catch her out of the corner of my eye."

"Have a nice day," Dagger said.

Mr. Ford smiled and strolled away. Then he turned back. "I did notice a man on the beach the last couple days. I was going to go down and see if I could help him, if he came by again."

A tickle started on the back of Dagger's neck causing the hairs to stand on end. "No need. I ran into him earlier and helped him out." The last thing he wanted was for an innocent man to get caught up in all this. Mr. Ford nodded and smiled as he walked away.

"I did it," Riley said pointing at the tiles on the table as Dagger walked into the house. "I deciphered my mother's clue!"

"Hardgrave Chess?" He looked over at Riley. "Do you know what that means?"

"Stan Hardgrave bought my parents' diving school in Oahu. Our family chess set must be at the school. And I'll bet it contains the next clue. Dagger—I was right! She's leading me to her research."

"Then we must be very careful," Dagger said as he stared at each of the fourteen tiles marked with tiny green spots. "We have to be vigilant and make certain no one follows us." The target had just moved from him to Riley. She was the one, the only one, who could find her mother's research. A weird sensation overcame him. There was a tingling in his gut and he was having trouble swallowing. He was all that stood between Riley and the people who wanted Claudia Rawlings work.

Chapter Thirteen

While Riley was locking up the house, Dagger took the opportunity to check the rental vehicle for a tracker or bugs. He found a tracker attached to the passenger side fender. Their intruder must have planted the tracker the night he was discovered skulking around the house. Dagger went around the outside of the SUV one more time and then moved inside. He sat in the driver's seat and checked all the usual places; the center console, on the back side of the rear-view mirror, under the dashboard, in the glove box—nothing. But if he were in this guy's position, he would hedge his bets and attach a bug as well as the tracker.

He got out and moved to the backseat. He ran his hands under both front seats. Then he inspected the heating and air conditioning vent built into the back side of the center console. He ran his pinky finger between each of the vents and found what he was looking for.

****

Riley came out to the car carrying her bags. Dagger met her on the path.

"I found a bug and tracker in the rental," he whispered. Riley looked up at him, her eyes wide. "We'll leave the bug in the rental. I'll move the tracker when I find a better home for it. I need to put some clothes around the bug. As long as we speak in quiet tones, the bug will only pick up muffled sounds. Do you mind unpacking your suitcase and pulling out jeans and sweaters? I'll do the same. Hopefully we have enough items to secure them around the bug."

"No problem. Let me help you."

They moved everything directly behind the front seats and

stuffed their clothes securely around the backseat heater vent, anchoring everything with their two large suitcases.

"Make sure to act normal, don't say anything which might give our stalker any information. We need to come up with a plausible story, so we can misdirect him," Dagger said after they closed the back doors. Riley fidgeted with the door latch, worry etched her features. He covered her hand with his and she looked up. He gave her a quick wink. "Follow my lead," he said.

They got in the car and stayed quiet for a few minutes as they headed down the road in silence.

"Don't be so hard on yourself, Riley. It was a good idea, your mom leaving you information at your grandparents' house. Unfortunately, I think you should come to terms with putting it to bed. All you have now is the will and your memories." Dagger spoke in a slightly louder than normal tone.

"You're right, Dagger. I just thought maybe I'd find something. Even so, it did give me a chance to go through everything at the house and send some cherished things home. I'll come back here soon and sell the items I don't want to keep." Riley followed suit and spoke loudly enough to be heard through the bug.

They moved at a crawl loading onto the ferry. Dagger leaned over and whispered into Riley's ear. "I'm going to place the tracker on another vehicle after we load. You stay put until I come around and help you out."

The instant Dagger put the vehicle in park, he was out the door. His phone vibrated and lit up. He'd left it in the cup holder between the front seats. Riley looked at the phone, and slowly her eyebrows drew together as she read; *I know what you're up to.*

What was that about, she wondered, biting her bottom lip.

Dagger pulled the tracker off his SUV and waited for the people in his immediate vicinity to leave their vehicles and climb the stairs to the upper decks. He'd picked his target while loading, the pickup truck directly in front of them had out of state plates. Crouching down, as if he were tying his shoe, he attached the tracker to the underside of the rear bumper. That would confuse their shadow, at least for a little while.

"Are we good?" Riley asked, pulling herself together as she stepped out of the SUV.

"Yup." Dagger nodded in the direction of the pickup.

"I'm impressed. I didn't even notice you move it. Your phone beeped a minute ago."

Dagger grabbed the phone, pushed the power button, furrowed his eyebrows and scowled.

"Problem?" Riley asked.

"No," Dagger said as he shoved his phone into his pocket. "I spoke with Kaleb earlier. I told the guys we're being followed, and they insisted on tracking us, on the slim chance we could get in trouble. This text is Kaleb's way of informing me he's completed the communication tracker."

As they climbed the stairs up to the passenger deck of the ferry, Dagger's phone beeped again. "Looks like our stay in Seattle will be short. We'll have just enough time to hightail it back to SeaTac airport and return our rental. Stone contacted a buddy who's a pilot. He said the pilot is flying a group out to the Hawaiian Islands late this afternoon. There are a couple seats with our names on them."

"I didn't pack for Oahu. I guess I'll have to pick up a few things when we get there."

"We'll both buy what we need when we get there. This plan gives us a better chance. By not returning to San Diego, our shadow won't find us as quickly."

"You really think we'll give our stalker the slip?" she asked.

"I think he's too good at what he does. The best we can hope for is that the tracker slows him down. Once he figures it out, his team will be monitoring trains, rental cars, planes, you name it. At least the private jet will give us a good head start."

****

Riley stepped off the plane into the tropical rain-drenched air of Oahu. She hadn't been back to the island in years. The luscious fragrance of plumeria burst open a flood of childhood memories. She shook her head, trying to clear her mind of the past. She didn't have time to reminisce or mourn. They were one step closer to locating her mother's research and fully aware their endeavor would soon be tracked—unless someone was already hot on their trail.

"I think it's safer to take a taxi than rent a car," she said, as Dagger stepped out behind her.

"Absolutely. Taking the private jet gave us a head start on whoever is following us. Let's not lose the advantage now," Dagger said as he hailed a cab.

On the ride to the dive school, Dagger scanned the road behind them. Their taxi dropped them off at the edge of the beach. Its radiant, cream-colored sand was a stark contrast to the sapphire-blue ocean. As much as she loved home, San Diego didn't compare to Oahu.

"Never can get enough of this view," Dagger said, echoing her thoughts. "Good looking shop, too." He nodded to the building located a few yards away.

"The new owners have done a lot of work, though I guess I shouldn't call them the new owners anymore since they've owned the business for over nineteen years."

"Did you ever meet the new owners?"

"No. I was in my senior year at high school and I was much too busy, or so I thought." Riley came to a dead stop.

Dagger gave her a questioning look.

"It just occurred to me, I've no idea if the original buyers still own the business or if they sold it."

"Wouldn't your mom mention the business being sold?"

"Not necessarily. We were both numb for a long while. It took everything I had to keep focused on my education. As the years passed, we each became wrapped up in our current lives. It was easier to leave the pain and loss of the past in the past. It's only the last few years we could reminisce about our lives with Dad. I do know her research vessel worked out of the Hawaiian Islands every now and then, but she never mentioned visiting the school or the old neighborhood."

"No time like the present to meet the owners of the business your family started."

Dagger pulled the door, and without breaking her stride, Riley lifted her head high and willed her body through the doorway.

The shop was full of milling people, and there was a long line at the far side waiting at the register.

A gentleman who looked to be in his early sixties was answering customers' questions and directing people. A woman around the same age ran the register along with a younger girl, who was typing on a computer at the counter at the far side of the shop. Yet another man was fitting wet suits and equipment, but Riley didn't recognize any of them.

"Welcome!" The older gentleman greeted them, his arm outstretched. He smiled and shook Dagger's hand, and then turned to Riley. "What can I—" He stopped and a smile lit up his face. "Riley? Riley Rawlings?"

"Have we met?"

"No. At least not in person, except I'd know you anywhere. I'm Stan. Your parents blessed me with this perfect piece of paradise…what is it now? Going on twenty years, I think. What brings you here? Is your mother with you? It's been a few months since we've enjoyed Claudia's company."

"My mother visited?"

"Yes. Not in the beginning mind you. The loss of Mark was a tragedy. I lost two friends that day, your dad and my business partner. Claudia was a mess. I tried to keep in touch, only she was beyond comforting."

Stan caught the attention of the woman working the register. "We sent her an invitation to our wedding. Honey come over and meet Mark and Claudia's girl." She smiled and waved. "The young lady over there registering students is our daughter, Jill. I don't know what we will do when she heads to the mainland for college next year." Stan smiled at his daughter. "As I was saying, we sent an invite, just to let Claudia know what was going on in our lives. Imagine my surprise when I looked out into the crowd and saw Claudia's bright smile."

Stan's wife approached the group. She reached out to grasp Riley's hand. "Hello, Riley! I'm Estelle. Is Claudia with you?" Estelle looked past them toward the door. "It's been over five months. She promised me next time she was here we'd take a shopping trip over to the Big Island, a girl's weekend." She shot her husband a smile.

"No. No, she's not." Riley heard Dagger say.

Chapter Fourteen

Dagger recognized the instant every muscle in Riley's body went rigid. He wrapped his arm around her, cupping her shoulder. He smiled at the couple and reached out to shake their hands.

"Nice to meet you both. I'm Dagger Eastin, a friend of Riley's."

"We're so happy to meet you, Dagger," Estelle said. "Claudia always keeps us up-to-date with Riley's life. We know you've become a well-known marine biologist. Your mother is so proud of you! Like mother, like daughter. It's like we've been there every step of the way. Claudia is the sister I never had," Estelle continued. "I've missed her. Is she on a project? Will she be arriving later? I hope so, I've missed her."

Each word Estelle spoke ratcheted Riley's anxiety more. Dagger pulled her in closer and rubbed her shoulder. Knowing she was fighting to maintain her cool, he took the lead.

"Would you mind if we go somewhere more private?" Dagger asked Stan.

"Of course not, let's go back to the lounge," Stan said.

They walked into the lounge and Stan shut the door. Estelle sat down in a rattan chair, and Stan sat beside her.

Riley reached for Dagger's hand, and they sat together on the loveseat.

"Is everything all right with Claudia?" Stan asked.

"There was an accident," Dagger started.

"What happened?" Estelle asked, putting her hands over her mouth.

"Claudia was on a science vessel fifteen days ago when her ship sank. There were no survivors," Dagger said.

"No. That's impossible. I just spoke with her less than a month ago." Estelle shook her head. She broke into sobs.

Stan hugged Estelle, his eyes brimming with tears. Riley's face contorted in agony. She clenched her teeth, determined to dam up her emotions. Dagger reached for her and pulled her into his arms. She crumpled against his chest and wept silently.

"We've had a long couple of days. Maybe it's best to continue this discussion tomorrow," Dagger said. "I'm going to take Riley to our hotel. May we return tomorrow?"

"Yes. Please do," Stan said over Estelle's shoulder.

****

Riley hadn't uttered a word. She walked zombie-like as Dagger led her out of the school and into the taxi. She remained unresponsive as they checked into a hotel and went to their room.

He'd tried to book two rooms, but with the short notice and the time of year, the hotel manager informed him he was lucky they had one. On the upside, it wasn't a basic room. Thanks to Kaleb and his connections they had a suite with two bedrooms, a main sitting area, and a kitchenette.

Dagger thought this was perfect, especially considering Riley's current state of mind. Frankly, he was more than a little concerned. Although he'd only known Riley for two weeks, she'd never seemed as grief-stricken as she was now. The woman he knew was a fighter, a problem-solver, and a glass-half-full kinda girl.

But everyone had their breaking point.

He led Riley into her room and sat her on the bed, removed her shoes, and examined the intricate way she'd put her hair up. One at a time he removed each of the hair pins, allowing her thick, silky, cocoa-bean strands to flow through his hands. Dagger pulled back a blanket and tucked Riley in.

"I'm in the other bedroom right over there if you need me," he said.

Her glassy, deep brown eyes focused on him for a heartbeat, before she rolled away and faced the wall.

Getting her a glass of water, he placed it on her nightstand and made his way out of her room, leaving her door open a few inches. He told himself he did it in case she woke in the night and was confused about her surroundings, but he knew he left the door cracked open for his own peace of mind—to keep an eye on her and keep her safe throughout the night.

Dagger walked out onto the balcony. He looked out at the calm turquoise ocean, and the ever-present need to be on the water tugged at him.

The sidewalks below were humming with activity. For an instant, he caught a glimpse of a woman's shimmering coal-black mane floating by. He rubbed his eyes and refocused, but as quickly as the woman appeared, she vanished.

"Get a grip, man. You know damn well that couldn't possibly be her."

****

"What do you have?" The man asked as he answered his phone.

"Not one thing. It's like they disappeared from the face of the earth," Eric said.

"We both know that's a crock of horseshit. They're just better than you," he snapped.

"Best watch your tone with me if you want to continue this arrangement," Eric grumbled. "I checked all modes of transportation. They must still be here somewhere."

"Seems to me they can hide better than you can find," the man hissed back. "Did you check the security tapes at the airport?"

"I told you, they didn't fly anywhere. Their names aren't on any manifest."

"What about a private plane?"

"I can't access those flight plans," Eric said.

"You can't, or you don't know how? Stop wasting my time and find someone who can locate them—now."

Eric hung up and slammed down his phone. Dialing another number, he fantasized about slamming the dickwads head into the table.

"Eric, what do you want? I'm still at the university. Dr. Bender is staying late," Neal whispered.

"What's the problem? Keeping Bender in the dark is old hat for you. By the way, how'd you know it was me?"

"Your name came up on my screen."

"You dumbass. Take it off your phone, you shithead. The last thing I want is to have my name flash up on your phone screen."

"And put what? It would look more suspicious if I was answering an unknown number. I never do that."

"The morons I have to work with," Eric said. "Make up a

name—shit, list it as your momma, I don't give a damn. Just take my name off your phone—now."

"Did you need something, or did you only call to bitch?" Neal asked.

'Bout time the prick developed a backbone, Eric thought. "Pull today's security tapes from SeaTac. You're looking for that diver and the girl. I need to know where they went, immediately."

"You've got to be kidding…"

"Don't start with me. You do, and you'll find me showing up at your office. You've got the connections, now get it done. I'll be waiting."

****

What had he gotten himself into? Neal thought, staring at his phone. He was beginning to think he wasn't built to be a spy, no matter how much he was getting paid. He nearly had a stroke when he was aboard the research vessel. Eric failed to mention the ship was already sinking. He'd turned on Eric, telling him he'd never agreed to any physical involvement. His only job was to gather any pertinent information and serve as the conduit.

Neal replayed the chaotic scene on the ship over and over in his mind. Claudia was stunned to see him standing in the doorway of her cabin. She'd been on the phone when he entered. Most likely she was saying goodbye to her daughter. God—had she told Riley it was him? He didn't think she did, only he wasn't certain. There was far too much noise, and the ship bobbing furiously between the massive waves, making it sound like the hull was going to bust apart.

He'd thrown up in a trash can before reaching Claudia's room. She'd questioned him as to how he got on board the ship. He'd told her he'd explain everything once they were safe. Neal vividly recalled his heart beating so hard he'd thought it would rip open his chest. His hands had been so sweaty, it took him three tries to get the damn syringe into her neck. Thank God she was in front of him and never saw it coming. Still, he was remorseful. He liked Claudia. She treated him like a friend when she was at the university. He shook his head.

"Hell of a way to repay her," Neal muttered.

"You say something?" Dr. Bender asked as he walked out of his office.

"I said goodnight."

"Goodnight, Neal. You're not staying? It's getting late."

"I have a few more items to check off my to-do list. I'll be leaving soon. See you in the morning, sir."

Neal stayed late to search the airport's security video. It took two hours, but he finally found what he was looking for.

"I've located them," Neal whispered in his phone to Eric. He knew there was no one in the office; nevertheless, he wasn't taking any chances. He liked what he did, and the last thing he wanted was to land in prison. "They boarded a private plane heading to the Hawaiian Islands."

"Where the bloody hell are they going?" Eric asked.

"It came to me while I was investigating. Claudia went to the Hawaiian Islands often. That's where she and her family lived before they came to the mainland. They owned a diving school and shop on Oahu."

"I'm on my way to SeaTac. Book me on the next flight out. Text me with all the information." Eric hung up before Neal could get another word out.

Neal stared at the phone. When did he become that dickhead's secretary? Shaking his head, he opened his personal laptop again and searched for a flight. Uh-oh. Dickhead was going to be super pissed when he found out there wasn't another flight until tomorrow. Neal sighed; he just wanted to get the crazy man out of town as quickly as humanly possible.

Chapter Fifteen

A shaft of light pierced the gap between the heavy curtains. Lying on his back, Dagger threw his arm over his eyes. Something warm was pushed up against his side. He turned his head and found Riley curled up next to him. Except for the guy who tried to smash his brain in, which *really* didn't count. Because Dagger knew the asshole was there—he'd just realized it a second too late…So, this was a first. No one ever snuck up on him, let alone get right next to him. It felt good having a warm body to wake up to. It'd been a very long time since a woman shared his bed. He reached over and grabbed his phone. Holy crap, it couldn't be eight. He never slept past six, and even six was sleeping in. He set his phone back on the nightstand and felt her stir.

"Good morning," he said.

"Morning," Riley said with a yawn. "I'm sorry I made myself comfortable. I woke up in the middle of the night and couldn't stay alone in a strange place. I want you to know that's highly unlike me. I live alone. I don't depend on anyone."

"No need to apologize. You've been dealing with an immense amount of emotional trauma."

She had shed her clothes during the night and was dressed only in a flimsy cropped top and shorts. She blushed as his eyes skimmed down her body. He wondered if the heat sizzling through his veins and scorching him clear up to his face showed.

"I made a complete fool of myself at the shop. I don't know if I can even face Stan and Estelle again." She dropped her gaze. Was she embarrassed, or did she feel the same heat?

"You didn't make a fool of yourself, Riley. You witnessed your mother's close friend experience fresh shock and grief. It would've been difficult for anyone."

"I feel like I break down in front of you on a daily basis. You must think me a real idiot. If I were you, I'd be looking to get as far away as possible from me and my hot mess." She rolled away from him and got out of bed.

"You feel that way because of the situation. We've spent the last two weeks together. You have no one else. Maybe in a way—you trust me."

"Of course I trust you. Do you think I'd ask you and the guys to help me find my mother's killer and her formula if I didn't?"

"Good. Then trust me when I say you didn't make a fool of yourself. You are a daughter grieving for her mother. The two of you shared a close bond. And by Estelle's and Stan's reactions, Claudia meant a great deal to them, too."

"It's all changing today. I've cried myself dry." Riley pulled her shoulders back and stood taller. "It's time to move forward. The priority now is to straighten out this entire mess. So mom didn't tell me everything. I didn't tell her everything, either. Still, I find it odd she'd become such good friends with Stan and Estelle without me knowing."

****

"I'm so sorry about last night," Estelle said, as Stan escorted Riley and Dagger into the lounge. "I was stunned and broken-hearted for the loss of Claudia. I didn't even have the decency to tell you how unbelievably sorry I am." Estelle wrapped her arms tightly around Riley. "You were her world, Riley. 'The moon and the stars all rolled into one perfect package, that's my Riley girl,' Claudia would say whenever she was singing your praises."

"She did?" Riley asked. She pulled back to look into Estelle's face. Over Estelle's shoulder, Dagger gave her his familiar wink. Riley smiled at him and Estelle. "Thank you, Estelle. Your words mean a great deal to me."

"I feel so badly about the way I acted." Estelle shook her head and dropped her gaze to the floor. "I should have thought about you first. I hope you'll forgive me. I'd love to get to know you."

"There's nothing to forgive. You lost a good friend, and you shouldn't feel guilty for expressing your grief. I'd love to get to know you and your family better, too."

"Mom, will lunch be ready soon? I'm starved," Jill burst

through the door, and blushed at finding two people she didn't know.

"Yes, dear. This is Riley Rawlings and Dagger Eastin. Remember I told you they would be joining us for lunch?"

"Oh—yes. Nice to meet you both. I'm sorry about your mom. Claudia was a wonderful woman. I loved spending time with her."

"Thank you, Jill. It's nice to meet you."

"Everyone grab a seat, lunch is ready," Estelle said.

"Can I assume you didn't come here solely to inform us of your mother's passing? Particularly since you weren't aware of our friendship," Stan said. He stood up and circled the table refilling everyone's glasses.

Riley smiled. Dagger could tell she wasn't certain what to say.

"You're correct, Stan," Dagger said. "For you and your family's safety we can't give you all the details, but we're following up on a lead Claudia left."

"And that's what led you to us," Estelle said with a nostalgic smile. "Leave it to Claudia. No matter what life had in store, she was always thinking three steps ahead."

"By any chance did she give anything to any of you for safekeeping?" Riley asked.

"No, nothing," Estelle said.

"Would you mind if we take a look around the shop after lunch?" Riley asked.

"Be our guest. Anything you need—just ask," Stan said.

"If anyone asks why we were here, or if we were looking for something, tell them we came out to inform you of Claudia's passing," Dagger said.

Everyone looked at Jill.

"I got it," she said. "My lips are sealed."

After lunch Stan, Estelle, and Jill went into the shop. Stan sent his employee out for his lunch break, and when there was a lull in customers, Dagger and Riley slipped quietly into the store.

"There are so many memories here," Riley said, as she slowly moved around the store. "Even with all the upgrades Stan and Estelle did."

"This wall of photos is impressive," Dagger said. The photos ran the entire length of the shop.

"Wow. I can't believe they kept this going. Dad started this photo wall. This picture was taken the day they opened the shop."

Riley pointed up at the only framed photo on the wall. "I must have heard the story hundreds of times."

"I see you found opening day," Stan said, walking up behind her. The photo had been taken in front of the shop and was a picture of Riley, her mom, and dad all smiling.

"You framed it," Riley said. "Dad taped it to the side of his old cash register."

"That's where I found it. We thought it should be framed and displayed," Stan said. "It's this shop's history. We want to always remember. Nostalgic, I know. But it's important to us."

"Are you saying you've kept every photo ever posted up on this wall?" Dagger asked.

"Every single one. We're going to have to add another wall soon." Stan chuckled and left them to help a customer.

Riley glanced over at Dagger and caught him smiling at her.

"What?" she asked.

"You were a cute teenager who grew up into a stunning and caring woman. Your dad would've been proud," Dagger said.

"Thank you." Riley blushed.

Dagger laughed and threw his arm casually around Riley's shoulders.

"I love this wall," Jill said as she walked up to them.

"Me too," Riley said. "So, what did you do when my mom visited?"

"Mostly we'd go diving or take walks along the beach. We spent the nights playing board games and laughing." Jill smiled. "Chess was our favorite. And it was even more special playing with the set of chess pieces you and your mom collected and painted."

Riley's eyes lit up. "Mom left the game here?"

"Yes. The last time she visited. She always brought the game with her and took home when she left. But the last time she visited she asked if she could leave it. She said she wasn't going straight home and she was afraid the game would get lost or damaged. The games are in the back. Come on, let me show you."

Jill led them to the back area and storage closet.

"There," Jill said, pointing toward a plastic bin at the top.

"Here let me get that," Dagger said.

"I need to get back. Oh, by the way, Claudia stapled a picture of the two of you inside the box holding the pieces. She said it was one of her favorites and didn't want it getting lost on the wall."

Riley pulled out the chess board and saw the wooden box. It had been so much a part of her life growing up. She opened the box and began placing all the pieces in their spots.

"These are wonderful," Dagger said. He picked up a piece and studied it. Placed it back on the board and picked up another. "Are all the shells local?"

"Yes. Mom and I collected each one of them during our diving adventures. We hand painted every piece."

After she placed the last piece on the board, they both glanced over it.

"The queen," they said in unison.

"She's missing," Riley said as she inspected the inside of the larger plastic box.

She glanced at the picture stapled into the inside of the wooden box and carefully pulled it free. On the back of the picture were four words written in green ink; *The Queen's back home.*

"Look," she said, turning the picture for Dagger to see.

"This was taken on board our boat right before we made our last dive together. It's a rock formation next to some coral reefs. That's where Mom found the shell we made into the queen."

****

"Good morning," Riley said, as she and Dagger walked into the dive shop. "We brought pastries and coffee. I hear these are the best pastries on the island."

Stan's eyes lit up. He rubbed his palms together, licked his lips, and grabbed a donut. "I heard you found what you were looking for yesterday," Stan said, wiping sugar flecks from his lips.

"We did. We'd like to go for a dive," Riley said, brushing the powdered sugar from her hands.

A half hour later, Riley and Dagger were heading for the site. Dagger's phone buzzed. He pulled it from his back pocket. The name "Fred" displayed.

"It's my team," he said. "They are calling through our scrambled secure line."

"Fred?" Riley's eyebrows drew together.

"Yeah. Don't ask. It's Kaleb's sense of humor. We go along with him," Dagger said. "What's up?"

"You guys enjoying your fun in the sun?" Kaleb asked.

"Yeah. We've been lounging on the beach, drinking mai tais."

Riley heard Kaleb chuckle. "Thought you should know, we got

another call from Samuels this morning."

"What'd he want?"

"He's still asking us what we found. What he really wanted was information on you and Riley. He wanted to know if you would swing over to his office."

"What'd you tell him?"

"I assumed your shadow has caught up to you, so I told him you and Riley went to the island to inform the owners of the dive shop about her mother's death, just like we agreed."

"Sounds like Samuels is still digging. If it is his guy following us, he'll be on the island soon, if he's not here already. I'd say he was hoping you'd lie about where we were, which would get him even more interested in what we're doing."

"That was my thinking. Have you seen your shadow?"

"Nope. We've been inside the shop most of the time." Dagger glanced over at Riley. "You and Stone deliver the research ship safe and sound?"

"As a baby."

"Did you take another look around before you released it?"

"Stone and I examined the ship from bow to stern, starboard to port. If we didn't find it, it wasn't there."

"Don't get too cocky. Thanks for the heads up." Dagger shove his phone into the small duffle bag he'd brought. "We knew the private plane would only slow them down."

"How do you mean?"

"All they need is a techie to hack the cameras at the airport. Eventually they will track us here."

"Are you saying you expected someone to find us here?"

"Let's put it this way. I hoped they wouldn't, however I knew there was a good possibility."

"We're not sure if they've found us, right?"

"Not one hundred percent. Not until today. Kaleb said Samuels called the office looking for us. He thought it best not to run the risk of lying to Samuels, so I'd say if it is his minion, it's highly likely we'll have a tail no later than tomorrow. We need to be careful. We don't want Stan and Estelle, or any other innocent bystander to get hurt."

Riley nodded. "Then the quicker we get down to that dive site, the better."

Chapter Sixteen

Riley and Dagger pulled on their swim fins as first light broke the horizon. They rechecked all the equipment, donned their air tanks, attached their mouth pieces to their masks, and sat on one side of the boat.

Giving each other a thumbs-up, they fell backwards into the ocean.

"I'd forgotten how great it is to dive here," Dagger said, as they treaded water. "The warm water feels like a heated swimming pool. I've dived in California waters for so long, I've gotten used to how cold the water stayed there."

"You sure you should go down?" Riley asked for sixth time since they left the hotel that morning. "I can do this alone. You could stay here and be the lookout."

"You're right about the lookout part. That's why I'm going down with you. It's not that deep and we won't be down long. I've stayed out of the water for longer than the doc insisted on. Let's go."

They spit into their masks and rubbed it with their fingers to keep the masks from fogging up. Then they rinsed the masks and pulled them securely into place.

"You take the lead, I'll be directly behind you," Dagger said.

Riley nodded. They put in their mouth pieces and headed down to the ocean bottom. It was a calm morning and the water below the surface was so clear, he could see the outline of the coral reef below them and scads of fish in a variety of colors.

Riley was a strong swimmer and ate up the distance rapidly.

When she reached the sandy ocean floor she stopped, barely moving the tips of her fins to keep from kicking up the fine sand and obscuring their view. Riley swam around to the back side of a large rock formation. A school of small bright blue fish with yellow fins and tails darted out from one of the openings between the rocks.

As they agreed, Dagger kept watch for other divers and sharks while Riley searched. She turned and looked at Dagger, her eyes sparkling as she pointed inside an opening in the rocks. About five inches inside he caught glimpse of something bright red. Riley reached for the object, but hastily pulled back as something with long bright white fangs shot out of the hole.

Dagger yanked her away from the opening and the moray eel slithered back into its home. Riley reached into her dive bag and pulled out her compact spade and unfolded it.

Dagger touched her shoulder and took the spade. He motioned for her to stay put. Then he moved slowly as he approached the hole with the spade. With blinding speed, the moray eel rocketed out and retreated just as quickly.

Pulling his MK3 knife out of the neoprene holster, he handed it to Riley and signed his plan. Riley nodded and repositioned herself slightly to his left. Using his fingers, he counted down from three, then he pushed the spade into the hole. The eel popped out and using the spade, Dagger distracted the eel as Riley slid the knife under the shell and scooped it clear of its nesting place. With the grace of a ballerina, Riley sprang for the shell, grabbed it and arched her body clear of the rock formation. They both backpedaled as fast as they could. The eel's jaws snapped open and closed as it slithered around the opening. Seconds later it retreated to the safety of its hole.

As they broke the surface of the water, they pulled their mouth pieces out and slid their masks off. While treading water near the boat, Riley examined the bright red, silver-dollar-sized shell. She held it out to Dagger. He turned it over and read the three words painted in green: *Go to Dad.*

"Do you know what she's telling you?" he asked.

"Yes. Dad's buried in the cemetery outside San Diego."

"Let's head back and return the gear. Then we can discuss our next step. I want to get back to the school as soon as we can, in case we're being watched."

"Have you seen anyone?"

"A couple divers were a few yards away from us the first time you approached the rock formation, no one else. But I *feel* like we're being watched—my skin's crawling," Dagger said as he scanned the water around them. "I don't want us being used as targets." He helped Riley into the boat first, tossed his fins in and quickly followed behind them.

"These waters are abundant with algae. If, like you said, her research revolved around algae, this would be a logical place to study it. Especially if she didn't want prying eyes," Dagger said.

"Funny you should mention the algae. I was thinking the same thing."

****

Dagger unlocked the door to their suite but stopped Riley with a touch to her shoulder. He shook his head and placed his index finger over his lips. She nodded and stood her ground. He stepped in and cleared each room before allowing her to enter.

It looked as though teenagers threw a wild party. Seat cushions covered the floor, the side tables in the main sitting area were turned over, and all the cupboards and drawers in the kitchenette were open and their contents were strewn all over the floor.

Riley gasped and headed for her bedroom.

"Wait," Dagger called, but in her fury, she didn't seem to hear him. He raced after her.

They gawked at the chaos. Every drawer in the room was dumped and scattered on the floor. The blankets and sheets were ripped from the bed and the mattress lay on the floor, its guts ripped open and scattered. Even the linings of her suitcases were cut free from their frames.

"You were right. I'm glad you insisted we get a delivery service to send my computer and briefcase back to Hunters and Seekers," she said, without turning toward Dagger.

"You didn't bring anything else with you that would give away any clues, did you?"

"Nope."

"What about the Scrabble tiles we found at your grandparent's home?"

"In my purse; Estelle had them when we were diving."

Dagger walked to his room, Riley trailing behind. The room was a near mirror image of hers.

"Did you bring anything important?" she asked, trying to see around his muscular build.

"Only my dive knife and pistol. They were on the boat with us."

"Now what? We need to wait twenty-four hours after diving before we fly. But our nemesis has found us."

"Believe me. He's no nemesis. I owe this jerk a beating and I always pay my debts. Besides, I already checked the flight schedules. Everything is full until late tomorrow. I got us on an evening flight. And before you ask, there's no pilot friend to hitch a ride with," Dagger replied in a low growl that made Riley shiver. He could be a very intimidating man. "He came, he saw, and he found nothing. With us both out of the suite, it was his opportunity to see what he could find here. He took a gamble and he lost. There's no need to go running with our tails between our legs. From my experience, he probably won't return. But he'll be watching us. I've had a feeling someone was keeping tabs on us all day."

"Do you believe the man works for Wayne?" Riley asked. "You said Wayne keeps calling Hunters and Seekers to scrounge for information regarding his vessel. If he knew Mom was working on her research project, maybe he believed it was the opportune time to acquire her research."

Riley pulled the queen from her pocket and rubbed it between her fingers. She turned it over and reread the three little words her mother had painted—*Go to Dad.* "The last time I dove on the formation was with my mom, the day before we left for the mainland. When we returned home, Dad surprised us with a lovely dinner and a gift for each of us. Mine was the picture of the three of us that I've treasured every day since. The framed one you saw at my house. He gave Mom a stunning antique hairclip." Riley gazed out the window. "I still remember the look on her face when she opened it. Dad told her it was to wear on her first day at the university. 'Pulling your hair back will make you look more like a professor,' he said." Riley looked up at Dagger. "He always told her she looked so young and beautiful, everyone would mistake her for a student."

"I thought your mother moved you to San Diego to work for Sheridan?" His eyes narrowed as confusion lined his features.

"No. We moved to San Diego because Mom was offered a position as a professor at the university. She went to work for Sheridan Enterprises during my fourth year of college. She enjoyed teaching, but research was in her blood."

"Which university did she teach for?"

"San Diego University, the same place I work."

"You really did follow in your mom's footprints."

"I guess I did."

"We'll fly out tomorrow and go to your dad's grave the next day," Dagger said.

"I'm going to take a shower." Riley headed for her room.

After she'd taken her shower and dressed, she decided this would be a good time to catch up on her emails. Opening her purse, she searched for her phone. It wasn't there.

The last time she remembered having it was while they were still at the shop. She must've left it in the chair where she'd been sitting before they cleaned the equipment after their dive.

"Oh, no. I left my phone in the lounge at the dive shop."

Riley walked out to the main room to tell Dagger, but he wasn't there. She walked up to his bedroom door and knocked softly. The door was slightly open.

"Dagger?" she called, hoping he would hear her.

His shower was running, so she found a piece of paper and left him a note. She picked up the room phone and ordered a taxi. She would have the driver wait while she ran in to get her phone. Grabbing her room key card, she headed for the shop.

Dusk had fallen, and lights were flicking on around the island. Riley waited for her taxi, but it never came. She decided to walk two blocks down to where the taxis often waited and catch one there.

"Excuse me. Do you think you could help me?" asked a male voice.

She turned and saw a man with aviator sunglasses and a ball cap with a team logo on it.

"I'm not from around here," the man said, trying to open a map as people swept by him on the sidewalk.

"Sure. Why don't we move out of the line of fire?" She smiled as they stepped out of the thoroughfare and moved closer to one of the store fronts. Riley walked behind him. He turned, continuing to fumble with his map.

"Would you mind if we step over here, before my map gets lost in the rush?" He stepped onto a garden path between the rows of stores. Tiki lamps sprinkled around the area served as the only source of light. Large bougainvillea shaded the path. Riley stepped beside the closest tiki lamp.

"Do you have a phone?" she asked. "I can show you an

application able to navigate for you."

"I left it in my hotel and I'm running late." He turned and held out the map to her. "I'd really appreciate if you could you show me how to get to the famous restaurant specializing in the local cuisine. I'm late and my friends are waiting."

"There's a few of those. What's the name?"

"I can't recall. I've a note in my pocket. Would you mind?" He shoved the map into her hands.

One moment she was looking at the map—the next the cold feel of steel was against her throat.

"Don't make a sound," the man breathed into her ear.

He yanked her off her feet and pulled her back behind the closest bougainvillea, into the dark shadows of the building.

A sudden chill raced through her body as a cold sweat rose on her skin. The banging of her pulse filled her ears.

"Where is it?" The man's voice was pitched low, threatening, full of danger, and didn't even sound like the lost man she was just talking with. The sharp edge of the knife against her throat blocked her ability to think.

"I don't have my purse with me. But I have a few dollars. They're yours. Take them."

He whipped her around and slammed her shoulder and side of her head against the concrete building; and stars filled her vision. Pain seared her face as he smashed her cheek against the building, crushing her chest into the wall.

She tried desperately to keep from hyperventilating as black spots dotted her vision.

"I don't want your damn money. Where's the formula?"

"I have no idea what you're talking about." Riley's mind blanked as terror set in.

He wrapped her long hair in his hand and yanked her head back. His whiskers poked her face, and his lips were pressed against her earlobe.

"Don't play dumb with me. Give me your mother's formula," he demanded.

"Hey! You there! Let her go this instant or I'll call the police," a woman's voice yelled.

"I'll get that formula," he said, his hot breath filling her ear. He threw her down.

She collapsed on the ground as the man fled.

"Miss, are you okay?" the woman asked. "I'll call the police."

"No. Call here, and ask for Dagger Eastin." Riley handed the woman her keycard.

Chapter Seventeen

Dagger ran down the nine flights of stairs and was out the door in seconds. He turned and began sprinting the same time he saw the flashing red lights of an emergency vehicle. He arrived in time to see the medics rolling Riley to the ambulance.

"How is she?" Dagger asked.

"You need to step back, sir," one of the medics said.

"Dagger, you made it," Riley's voice was a whisper.

"Of course. How are you feeling?" Dagger took Riley's hand.

"Like I just got hit with a two by four. I know I shouldn't have—"

"Don't worry about that now. Your health is the priority."

The shop owner who had called him tapped Dagger on the back. He turned toward the woman.

"The poor girl. I called the ambulance the instant that scum ran off. I hope she'll be okay."

"Thank you for helping her." Dagger smiled and shook the store owner's hand.

"It was terrible, simply terrible," the shop owner said. I looked out the window and saw—" The shop owner stopped abruptly and gestured toward the ambulance.

"Riley," Dagger told the shop owner.

"Riley stopped to help the man. He had a map, it looked like he was lost—the snake." The shop owner shook her head in distress. "Next thing I saw, they disappeared around the corner." She pointed in the direction of the shop. "There's a nice little walking path there with a few tiki lamps. Even so, I don't like my employees to take that path at night. You never know who might be out there. Anyway, something just felt off. I walked out the back door of the shop, to be sure Riley was safe. It was awful." The shop owner rubbed her hands up and down her arms. "That terrible man had pinned Riley against the wall. I yelled at him and said I was calling the police. He threw Riley down and her head hit the ground." Tears ran down the woman's cheeks.

Dagger took both her hands. "I can't thank you enough for helping Riley."

"If it's not too much of a bother, would you mind letting me know she's all right?"

"I will," Dagger promised.

"Sir, we need to get her to the hospital," the medic said.

"I'm going with her." Dagger hopped up into the ambulance. He took hold of Riley's hand. "You're going to be fine." He gave her hand a little squeeze.

"Thanks, Dagger," Riley slurred.

"The hospital doc instructed me to get pain meds on board. The meds seem to be kicking in," the medic said.

"I'll be right here when you wake up," Dagger reassured her. He gently moved Riley's hair away from the uninjured side of her face. Unable to stop himself, he ran his hand through her hair multiple times trying to convince himself that she was going to be okay.

They arrived at the hospital and a flurry of nurses took over.

"Let me show you to the waiting room," a male nurse said.

As they rolled Riley away, Dagger's hands balled up, his knuckles void of color. He clenched his jaw. If he ever found this guy, he would kill him.

He had no doubt Riley had been attacked by the douchebag who'd been following them. This was his fault. He'd told her this piece of shit wouldn't be a threat.

He paced the waiting room. His stomach was protesting the lack of food. It was going to be a long night. He wandered out into the hall looking for a vending machine. He found a row of machines for coffee, soda, and prefab food. He stood in front of them thinking about what could have happened to Riley and slammed his hand into the top of a machine. As the machine rattled, he reached into his pocket, pulled out a bill, and started to shove it into the coffee machine.

"I wouldn't do that if I were you," a man said. "That food might kill you before the ER could save you."

"I've had worse," Dagger said, turning around to see a man dressed in scrubs.

The man chuckled. "Probably so, but why don't you walk with me? There's a food truck right outside. The owner's an amazing cook."

"A friend of mine got brought in by ambulance a couple hours ago. I want to be here when the doctor comes out."

"I'm guessing I'm your man, Hubbard's the name. You're Dagger, right?"

"How—"

"Nurses know everything happening inside these walls," Dr. Hubbard said, interrupting him. "They shared a pretty good description of you."

"Is Riley going to be all right?"

"Given her head trauma, we performed an MRI to rule out any bleeding inside her skull."

Dagger grimaced.

"Not to worry. She has a concussion, but she will recover. I stitched up her forehead and wrapped up her ribs and wrist. She's lucky nothing was broken. With rest, she should be back to eighty percent in about a week. It will take about ten days for the concussion to completely heal."

"I know all about concussions. I just got over one."

"Well then, you should be an expert caregiver. I want to keep her here overnight. If things look good tomorrow, I'll discharge her."

"Can I see her tonight?"

"Only if you join me at the food truck." Dr. Hubbard smiled.

Dagger spent the night in Riley's room. He didn't want her waking to an empty room. The right side of her body suffered the most damage. The skin around her eye was puffy and red with tinges of purple starting to show. She was going to have a real shiner for a while. The doctor did a great job with her sutures, though. They ran neatly down half of her forehead. The good thing was—if you could call it a good thing—the wound was close to her hairline. It would be unnoticeable provided she let her long, satiny brown hair hang free. He lightly pushed her hair back and inspected the large, taped gauze covering her forehead.

"Dagger." Riley slurred in a sleepy voice.

"There you are." He ran his fingers though her hair once more, then he gently took her hand. "We've been so concerned about you. I texted the guys last night to let them know what happened. They were worried we needed more security and wanted to fly out immediately." He felt her stiffen. "Don't worry, I talked them down. I reminded them there were still thing to be done, and since I wasn't budging from the side of your bed, they should stay put."

"They agreed?"

"Not so much." He confessed. "They made me promise I would keep them updated on a regular basis."

There was a light knock on the door.

"Good morning. Excellent, I see our patient is awake," Dr. Hubbard said and smiled at Riley.

"Morning, doc. She just woke up."

"How are you feeling, Ms. Rawlings?"

"Like someone hit me with a steamroller, missed a spot, and backed over me. Even so, I'm glad to be here. Please call me Riley." She smiled and her hand flew to her mouth as her lip split open again.

Dagger winced.

"You're pretty banged up, Riley," Dr. Hubbard said. "Your right wrist is sprained, and you have stitches on the right side of your forehead. Your right eye may get blurry every now and then until it's fully healed. The tissue and bone of your left hip is completely bruised, as is your right ribcage. You suffered a concussion. An MRI was done to rule out bleeding inside your skull."

Dr. Hubbard glanced over at Dagger. "I see you never left last night."

"What gave me away?" Dagger asked.

The doctor chuckled and shook his head. "Mind if I ask how long have the two of you've been dating?"

Riley's previously pale face flushed bright pink.

"Oh, we're not—dating. Riley's a client."

"Is that what they're calling it these days?" The doctor chortled. His gaze jumped from Riley to Dagger. "The cafeteria is open for breakfast. It's not as good as the food truck but way better than the vending machines. Coffee's not bad. Go get yourself something to eat. I'm going to have the nurse take Riley for a follow-up MRI. Just to be safe. She'll be awhile."

Dagger sat at a table inside a glass-enclosed patio attached to the cafeteria sipping on his drink. He watched the people flow by until he caught sight of a woman with shoulder-length black hair and large sunglasses.

"Hell, no. It can't be." He jumped up and ran out after her just in time to see her get into a taxi.

She turned in his direction for only a second, but he was sure she had seen him, even though those over-sized sunglasses hid her coal-black gaze.

Her taxi sped off. Dagger froze, the absurdity of the situation scrambling his brain.

****

Dagger knocked on the door jamb of Riley's room. "Can I come in now?"

"Yes, we just finished," Dr. Hubbard said.

"You never told me when I'm being discharged." Riley said.

"There are a few more test results I should look over. If everything looks good, you'll be here for at least another day."

"But we have a flight home tomorrow night," she said.

"Don't worry about the flight, Riley. I'll reschedule it when Dr. Hubbard feels it's safe for you to fly," Dagger said.

"There's no hard and fast rule about flying when you have a concussion. However, there are many documented instances when the patient did decide to fly against doctor's advice. The result? Increased symptoms."

"Such as?" Dagger asked, before she'd the chance to make her stand.

"Nausea, dizziness, fatigue, lack of concentration, and headache, to name a few. A headache is a serious symptom, especially if it gets worse over time. It could be a sign you have bleeding inside your skull. Look, I know I'm throwing a lot at you; let's take this one step at a time. If you pass all your tests, then I'll discharge you."

"And we can fly home the next day?" she asked.

"I would advise you to stay put for at least the next two days."

She started to argue, but the doctor cut her off.

"Concussions are serious, Riley. You take it easy and get some rest. We'll talk again tomorrow." Doctor Hubbard patted her on the arm and left the room.

"I called for a taxi before I left the room. I waited, but it never came. I decided to walk a couple blocks to where the taxis wait. A guy in a ball cap and aviator sunglasses stopped and asked if I could help him with directions," Riley said.

"What did he look like?" Dagger asked.

"I couldn't really tell. I don't even remember if I saw the color of his hair. At the time, he just looked like an average lost tourist. We tried to get out of the flow of traffic, because he almost lost his map." Riley walked through the ordeal step-by-step.

"Riley, you're only what? All of five feet tall and weigh next to nothing? It wouldn't take a very big guy to pick you up."

"That's not what I mean. He didn't look threatening when I first saw him. He looked rather short." She heard Dagger's teeth grinding. "Stop," she said.

"What?" His word came out clipped.

"I know you're irritated. Your nostrils are flaring. You have a death grip on the arms of the chair, and you're about to rip them off. I told you, I was reckless. I'm sorry."

"I'm not mad at you, I'm mad at myself. You took a reasonable risk. But I'm certainly not upset at you for being attacked. For crying out loud, there were tons of people on the sidewalk. It takes a gutsy guy to snatch you out in the open."

"You believe it's the guy who's been following us, don't you?"

"No doubt. You don't?"

"At the time, I thought it was a mugging. Until he said, 'Give me your mother's formula.' Next thing I remember, I was waking up here."

Chapter Eighteen

"Now I understand why mom became so close to Stan and Estelle. They've treated us like family the past week. I hated saying goodbye tonight," Riley said, as she and Dagger walked along the moonlit beach.

"Yeah, they're pretty great people. There's still a mountain of food in the refrigerator in our suite," Dagger said. "I promised Stan I'd come back and dive with him later this year. Maybe you'd like to join us? After we find your mom's formula and put this thing to bed, that is."

"Sounds like fun. By the way, I'm glad you insisted we stay the week. I didn't realize how much I needed the rest. Dr. Hubbard was pleased today with my progress. He even gave me his blessing to fly home." She reached over and took his hand. A look of surprise swept over his face.

"Good. Because I booked our flight for tomorrow. You can spend a few days recouping, then we'll take up the hunt. Are we staying at your place, or mine?" Dagger asked.

"Maybe whoever was following us has given up. We haven't seen any sign of them since I was discharged." Dagger sent her a side glance. "Okay, your place is the one with all the bells and whistles when it comes to security. We'll stay there. But I don't need a few days to recoup."

He firmly took hold of her shoulders and turned her toward him. She looked up into his gaze. He slid his hands down her arms, took her hands into his warm palms, and stared directly into her eyes.

"Don't waste your energy, Riley. You're going to take it easy."

In the moonlight his eyes shimmered gold and the heat of his stare seared her. It took her a heartbeat to find her tongue.

"Fine, only a couple days. We start our search the day after tomorrow."

Dagger let go of her hands and tilted her chin up. He leaned down and tenderly kissed her. He pulled back and then closed the distance, reclaiming her lips. He ended the kiss but didn't straighten up. He ran a hand through her hair and studied her, as if committing her to memory. Then he smiled, took her hand, and continued their walk.

****

Trembling, Riley stood in the doorway of Dagger's room. He switched on his light within seconds, as if he'd sensed her presence.

"Another nightmare?" he asked.

She nodded.

He turned on his side, slid into the middle of his bed, and threw back the covers. He wore only a pair of pajama bottoms.

"Come here." He patted the spot next to him.

She climbed in, her back to him. "It's the same nightmare over and over. I just want it to stop."

"You're safe with me."

She closed her eyes and listened to Dagger's steady breathing. She scooted back a few more inches to soak up his warmth. He put his arm over her and drew her against him, softly resting his chin on the top of her head, and she relaxed knowing he was right—there was no safer place. Within minutes she dozed off.

Riley woke up alone in Dagger's bed. She yawned and stretched. As she walked into the main room, she found him on the balcony, lounging in the love seat with his feet propped up on the footstool as he talked on the phone. She poured herself a cup of coffee and stood in the kitchenette to drink it.

He turned, still talking on the phone, and gestured for her to join him. She tried to move around him to sit in the chair. His arm snaked out and pulled her down next to him, nearly spilling her coffee.

"We should arrive at San Diego International around nine tonight. Okay, we'll meet you outside the luggage carousels. Yes, we'll stay at Riley's tonight, so she can get all her things together. Tomorrow we'll move to my place. You'll need to search my place—the combinations are the same. I know I'll change them, Stone. I'll do it tomorrow when we're all there. See you at the airport." He ended the call.

"Do you feel like going down to the restaurant for breakfast, or would you rather stay up here?"

"I think I'd like to freshen up, then go out."

"Perfect. I already have a table for us on the garden patio. Reservation's in an hour."

He wrapped his arm around her shoulders, snuggling her close. They sat quietly enjoying their coffee and admiring the ocean view. Riley wondered what life would be like if she shared it with Dagger. Was he the kind of guy who would always be this attentive, or was he acting this way because of what happened to her? She'd seen many sides of him over the past few weeks, and although there were many, one trait remained the same. He was an honest man, someone you could rely on.

****

"How was your flight?" Stone asked as he took the suitcases from Dagger and put them in the trunk.

"No surprises," Dagger said. "Even better, no side effects."

"Good to hear."

"Is Kaleb at Riley's place?"

"Yeah, he searched it, inside and out, and is now standing guard. On a positive note, Riley, one of your neighbors kept a close eye on us."

"Mrs. Brown," Riley said with a giggle. "She means well."

When they pulled into Riley's driveway, Kaleb was leaning against the front door.

"Good to have you both home," Kaleb greeted them.

"Hawaii is great, but it's good to be back," Dagger said as Kaleb gave him a bear hug.

"Don't know if Stone told you, but Riley's house was broken into again. One of the window panes in the back door was shattered. No worries. I replaced it. We've got everything we need to set up a security system, Riley," Kaleb said. "Give us the green light and we'll have it in today."

"I never had to worry about my safety in this neighborhood. I guess that's all changed." Riley shook her head as she looked around. "You've got my blessing and thank you." She smiled and nodded at the three men.

"Does it look like anything's gone?" Dagger asked.

"Nope, although they left something behind." He pulled a cord from his pocket that ended with a tiny box. "Camera and recorder. I found a total of four; living room, bedroom, office, and kitchen. I cleaned the place up best I could. Sorry in advance if I put something in the wrong place. Looked like they were hunting for clues as to where you were while they planted the bugs."

"Someone bugged my house? My bedroom? That's down right creepy," she said.

"They turned your place upside down. Your closet doors were open and all your dresser drawers. They went through other drawers, too, and messed with your computer."

"Did they hack my computer? My student files are kept there."

"They didn't get into your system. The security on your computer held up." Kaleb said. "If you feel up to it, would you be willing to walk through the night of your assault? If not, it's okay. Dagger gave us the basic rundown; still it's always helpful to hear events firsthand."

****

Later that night, Riley lay in her bed, wide awake in the dark. She could hear Dagger pacing in the other room. Maybe he was pacing because it was a new place, or maybe the memories of being attacked here in her house haunted him.

She got out of bed and walked into the kitchen. The scotch bottle was sitting open on the counter; Dagger was pacing and drinking.

"Can't sleep?" she asked.

"Wound up. Every little noise has me investigating. If that sadistic bastard steps even one foot in your direction, he's as good as dead."

"I think moving to your house is best for everyone. You're familiar with the sounds around you."

"True. Although I've stood watch all over the world, and I can't ever recall being this jumpy. Kinda irritating me." He slugged back the last of his drink and grabbed the bottle to refill his tumbler.

Riley stepped closer and laid her hand on top of his. "This isn't going to help." She took his glass and placed it on the counter. Taking his hand, she led him from the kitchen, switching the lights out behind them.

"Is the new security system armed and all the doors and windows locked?" She asked.

"Of course," he answered. "The guys even tested it before they took off." She would swear he was slightly offended.

"Good. Then come with me."

She continued to lead him down the hall, leaving the blackness behind them. She walked into her room.

"I think you're on to something," he said. "I'm sure I'll be better able to sleep if I sit here, where I can keep an eye on you." He nodded at her overstuffed chair in the corner. "Got a footstool by any chance?"

"Are you serious?"

He looked at her with the innocence of a newborn baby.

"You're not sleeping in the stupid chair. You let me share your bed when I needed to. You are getting into mine and going to sleep. I know the sounds of my place. If I hear anything out of the ordinary, I'll let you know."

"Are you sure?" He didn't wait for Riley's response as he plopped down on the far side of her bed and yanked off both his boots.

"Of course. Let's get some sleep. We're going to need it."

Riley slid back into her bed as Dagger settled in. Even in the dark she could see him lying on his back and staring at the ceiling. She scooted over closer to him. He froze, not so much as breathing.

"It's okay, Dagger. Go to sleep."

He rolled over in her direction. She turned onto her other side, and he immediately pulled her into the curve of his body and wrapped his arm securely around her waist. "You know, I've only ever slept with you and one other person a lifetime ago."

"Somehow I don't believe that."

"No, really. I've never let my guard down enough to fall asleep with women."

Riley was stunned and honored by his confession, but also a bit jealous as she thought of the other woman. "Then thank you for trusting me," she said.

"Don't forget. You said you'd wake me if something wakes you."

"And I will."

"Thank you, Riley." He brushed a light kiss on the top of her head and nestled her to him.

His breath slowed and steadied. She listened for a few minutes until she knew he'd fallen asleep. Closing her eyes, she replayed the past two weeks. They had been full of deep heartache punctuated by such happy moments. When Dagger dropped into her life, it was spinning like a whirlwind, but he'd served as her sea anchor.

She was developing deep feelings for this man. She wondered what he thought of her. Did he see them as only friends, or something more? After all, this was the third time they'd shared the same bed. It was obvious he was at ease with her—he'd just told her as much; but did he feel more?

Logic told her no, or he would have at least *tried* to do more than kiss her. And he hadn't. Her head started to ache. She needed to push these frivolous thoughts to the back of her mind. There was a murderer to catch and her mother's lifelong research to recover.

Chapter Nineteen

As dawn broke, Riley and Dagger entered through the massive gates of the cemetery where her father was buried. She slowly drove the winding, one-lane road over the first hill. When she reached the crown of the second hill, she pulled her SUV over and parked. She opened the door to the backseat and retrieved a bouquet of flowers sitting in a tall cylinder-shaped vase.

"I've forgotten how beautiful it is here."

"I can see why you and your mother picked this place. The ocean view is spectacular."

Rising grief immobilized her. She would soon return here to lay her mother to rest beside her father. Dagger wrapped his arm around her. She inhaled deeply, breathing in the scent of him surrounding her. Riley's legs started to give way, but Dagger held her tight as she fought the urge to crumple to the ground. She remained sheltered by Dagger as they made their way to her father's grave.

Their shared headstone was a stunning, dark cobalt granite. The top half was carved into a perfect image of the sea with the sun setting into the water. Under the image, her father's name and birth and death dates were carved into the right side of the headstone. Underneath it said: "We miss you more with each setting sun. Forever in our hearts."

The left side of the stone held her mother's name and date of birth. The base of the stone extended out and held a carved vase holding a red hibiscus blossom.

Riley knelt next to the stone. "That's strange." She set her bouquet off to one side and stuck her finger into the vase. "We always bring cut flowers and a bottle of water to pour into the vase. But these flowers are not in water, they're in potting soil."

She reached into the vase with one hand, running her fingers deeper into the dirt until her entire hand was immersed in soil. She pulled the hibiscus out of the vase and scooped out the remaining soil.

"What're you doing?"

"I wonder if there's something in the dirt. I thought I'd pull the dirt out and plant the hibiscus in the ground in front of the stone, in case our shadow is around."

"Didn't you toss your diving bag into the back of your vehicle?" He turned and walked back to the SUV without waiting for her to answer. He quickly returned with her compact diving spade and handed it to her.

"Thanks. I forgot about my bag."

"I thought we'd be able to sell the story better, if it looked like we planned to move the plant." Dagger gave her a crooked smile.

"Good thought. Why don't you dig a small hole in front of my father's name and we'll transplant the hibiscus." She handed him back the spade and he squatted down beside her to dig the hole.

It took Dagger only one scoop to dig the hole, but he stayed beside her, watching her, and using his body as a wall to hide the vase from prying eyes. She handed Dagger the plant and he set it inside the hole, covered it with the potting soil, and leveled out the dirt.

Riley cleared all the dirt she could and reached inside the vase. She really wanted a flashlight, only she knew it would look fishy. Inside was a flat object that filled the vase. Delicately, she pushed on one side and it moved. She glanced over at Dagger. His eyes were glued to hers.

"Can you get it out?" he whispered.

"I think so."

She pushed harder on the side of the object within. Instantly it gave way. Her fingers brushed against something smooth. "It feels like a plastic bag. There's something small and thin inside, about the size of a business card." She slipped the bag into her pocket and put the flowers in the vase.

"Great job. Are you ready to stand up?"

He stood up and reached out for her. She placed her hand in his and stood. She laced her fingers with Dagger's and kissed the palm of her other hand and placed it on her father's gravestone. "Love you, Daddy."

She turned around and they walked back to the SUV. He held her car keys out to her.

"Would you mind driving?" she asked.

"Not at all." He walked her around to the passenger side, opened the door and waited for her to get situated, closing the door behind her. "Are you all right?" he asked, as he sat in the driver's seat.

"I will be."

He leaned into her and gave her a quick kiss on the lips. "To help you feel better."

His face was only inches from hers.

She smiled. "Thank you."

He ran his hand over her cheek, his touch as soft and gentle as the man it belonged to.

Neither of them spoke until they exited the cemetery. She pulled the clear, waterproof phone bag they'd found in the vase from her pocket. It held a thin, metal object the size of a business card.

"It's an SSD," she said in a soft voice.

Dagger glanced over.

"A solid-state drive—SSD. Dagger, we've found it! This must contain my mother's research."

****

"I suppose you wanted us here to help you figure out the next clue?" Kaleb asked, as Riley and Dagger entered the shop.

Kaleb was relaxing in his desk chair his feet propped on his desk. Stone was spread out on the sofa reading a medical magazine.

"I hate to be the one to burst your bubble," Dagger said.

"Yeah, ya do," Stone snickered, still reading his magazine.

"Okay, maybe not so much," Dagger said.

"Oh, for the love of—you three really are a bunch of brothers." Riley laughed. "What Dagger is trying to not tell you is…we found it."

"Found what?" Kaleb asked.

"We think we've found my mother's research." Riley pulled the bag containing the SSD card from her purse and put it in Kaleb's hand.

Stone threw his magazine down and hurried over to Kaleb's desk.

"We need your expert computer skills, Kaleb," Riley said.

"Have you tried to open it?" Kaleb asked.

"I thought it would be safer to wait for you to open it on the shop computer that isn't connected to the internet," Riley said.

"How long ago did you sweep the office for bugs?" Dagger asked.

"Just finished before you got here," Kaleb said.

"You did tell us our system has the most advanced buffer and virus detector on the web. I recall your exact words were 'hacking our system is more difficult than hacking the White House'—right?" Dagger asked.

"This will take me a little while. I want to prep an immediate backup and..." He looked up and watched as all three sets of eyes glazed over. "I can see I'm wasting my magic on the three of you. Take a seat, get a drink, whatever. Leave me be, and let me work on this."

"So, how'd you find it?" Stone asked.

While Kaleb did his thing, Dagger nabbed a couple of sodas and Riley gave Stone the details on their find.

"I'm ready," Kaleb eventually said. He slid the data card into the slot and waited for the information to pop up. Everyone moved over to Kaleb's desk.

One file after another popped onto the screen. Kaleb clicked on the first file. The screen filled with unreadable data.

"Don't tell us it's corrupted," Dagger said.

"Nope, encrypted. No surprise there."

"Can you break the code?" Riley asked.

"Of course I can, and if I can't, I know someone who can." Kaleb clicked through all the files to verify they were all encrypted. The last file he clicked on opened immediately. The title of the file read, *I knew you could do it. Congratulations, Riley.* "This one isn't encrypted, it looks personal. Would you like me to put it on a USB for you?"

"Yes, please. Would you mind printing it out, too?" she asked.

"It'd be my pleasure." Kaleb handed Riley the USB and a short stack of pages. "Let me see if I can break the code on the rest." His fingers flew over the keys like a world-famous pianist.

Riley got up and walked over to the sofa.

"We'll leave you to it," Dagger said to Riley.

"No, please. Sit with me. You too, Stone. If there's anything I need to read to you, this will save time."

The two men sat in the chairs across from her and waited.

Riley looked down at the printed pages. Her mom wrote about how proud she was of her not only for figuring out the clues, but for being the person she'd become. She told her how proud her dad would be. A couple of paragraphs down, her mom started talking about the clues, so Riley began reading aloud.

"As you know, only you, my darling, could decipher each clue and reach the end. For they were not only clues, they were pieces of our life—important pieces. I hope you took the time to understand every clue I used was to awaken a memory or impress upon you the significant things in life. I know it may sound strange coming from me, but there's more to life than your career.

"As for the items I left, the stone was to trigger your childhood memories of happy times and lead you home. We may no longer be there in body: nevertheless, our love will always be wrapped around you, especially there.

"The first place I sent you was to your grandparent's because I never want you to forget the importance of family. Your roots, our history, have molded you into the extraordinary woman you are.

"I put the clue in the Scrabble game to remind you of the hours we shared and the fun we had. From there, I led you back to your beginning, on the island of Oahu. You came into our lives and we cherished every day. From the day of your birth, we watched you grow and marveled in all you'd become. I hope you spent some time to get to know Stan, Estelle, and Jill. They're wonderful people and very dear friends. Keep them in your life, they will always be there for you.

"On the island you found my next clue, the queen. It broke my heart to leave it in the sea. Still, I knew deep in my soul you would retrieve her and keep her close. The queen represents the turning point in our lives, when we chose to leave our home on the island and begin anew in San Diego.

"Carefully consider each choice you make, Riley. Every choice alters your path, so be sure the walk is worth taking. Having someone walk with you will enrich your path.

"Lastly, I directed you back to your father. This is the most painful part of the hunt. It not only represents the death of your father, it serves to remind you that life comes in a full circle. This will happen much quicker than you think possible. Live life, love

deeply, and continue to be the best you possible.

"I'm sure you're enlisting the best computer guru you can find. He or she may be of help with my files later, but you are the only one who will be able to work out the password. Here are your last clues: Your first doll is still proudly displayed in the mini antique rocker in your room. What's her name? What was the first thing you told us you were going to be when you grew up?

"And remember: I will always love you!
Mom"

Chapter Twenty

"Are you okay, Riley?"

She hadn't noticed Dagger sitting next to her until he spoke. She looked up at him, her eyes filled with unshed tears. "I will be. Only my mom could create a scavenger hunt full of life lessons and choices."

"She must've been an amazing woman."

"She was."

"Holy hell," Kaleb said. "I'm not sure I'm going to be able to crack the password, let alone get to the encryption."

"I think I can be of some help," Riley said.

"You know the password?"

"Try, queen mermaid. Use different variants, with or without capitals or spaces."

The three men stared at her.

"What? Don't all little girls want to become a mermaid?"

"Err, Queen Mermaid?" Dagger snickered. "Are we still talking about you?"

"Queen is my doll's name." Riley put her hands on her hips and glared at him.

"I'm in." Kaleb said. "Your password broke the encryption. There's a ton of information on this card." He continued scrolling as they rejoined him. "This file contains many files labeled 'journals,' all arranged by date. These files over here are labeled 'studies and data.' And this last section just says 'formulas.'" He looked over at Riley. "She collected a massive amount of material."

"My mother was the epitome of a perfectionist who kept meticulous records. That's one of the things that made her the best researcher in her field."

"Where would you like to start?" asked Kaleb.

"Let's begin with the formulas. Go to the last entry and let's see what we have," Riley said.

Kaleb clicked on the file and it opened into letters, numbers, lines, and equations. He sent Stone and Riley questioning glance.

"Don't look at me," Stone said. "I'm a medical doctor, not a scientist. Riley's the only one with the knowledge and ability to figure this out."

"Mind?" Riley asked as she reached for the mouse.

"Go for it."

Dagger's phone beeped and he pulled it from his jeans pocket. He stared in disbelief at the screen blinking a code for a good seven seconds. "I gotta take this. I'll be right back." He felt like he was floating above the room, separated from his body, staring down at the action below.

"You okay, Dagger?" Stone called after him.

"Huh? Yeah, I'm great. I'll be back in a few." He gripped his phone as if it were the head of a deadly black mamba, walked to the door trying not to look spooked, and continued outside and down to the docks.

Alone, he stopped, stared at his screen again, and punched in his code.

"Hello, darling." The woman's voice was deep and breathy.

"Katarina?" Dagger asked in surprise. "What the bejeesus do you want and what scum of the earth gave you their cell phone in prison?"

"I'm not in prison."

"What do you mean, you're not in prison?" Dagger's blood pressure shot up and his collar started to choke him. "How—where are you? Have you been following me?"

"We'll have plenty of time to catch up. I need to see you."

"I'm a little tied up at the moment. Besides, why in the world would you think I'd want to be anywhere near you?"

"Darling, I'm an important person in your life; don't be coy, we both know you want to see me."

"You *were* an important person. I'm busy, Katarina. Go screw up somebody else's life. I have no time for your games."

"Don't you even think about hanging up on me. Not if you want your little wench to live to see another sunrise."

"I have no idea what you're talking about."

"Now who's playing games, Dagger? Not that I wouldn't love beating you once again. Sweetheart, she's really not your style. Four-ten, long, dark brown hair. Little, royal blue, short sleeve, snug-fitting top."

Dagger whipped around, surveying the marina.

"Don't bother, darling. You'll never find me. Meet me at our spot tomorrow evening at seven, and Riley will never know how close she came to death."

"Katarina—"

The line cut off. The one woman he never expected to see again had just dropped back into his life. "Bloody hell."

Dagger stood in the doorway of the boatshed and watched as Riley, Stone, and Kaleb worked with the files. He had to figure out how the hell he was going to meet with Katarina the following day. The strain on Riley was starting to show. But nothing would relieve the pressure until they could get the people responsible for this mess. With Katarina threatening Riley, he was sure Katarina was up to her neck in this; but he couldn't guess who she represented. Samuels? Herself? The Russians? All were possible.

"She's done it," Riley said seeing Dagger standing in the doorway. "It looks like Mom created a process to convert red algae's oil into a form of biofuel."

"I've heard about that research," Stone said. "But from what I've heard, nobody's been successful at the fuel conversion yet."

"That sounds like something worth killing for," Dagger said.

"I can see kidnapping her, however, killing the person with all the answers seems like piss-poor planning to me," Stone said. "Do you have any idea what the potential of this formula is? If Claudia introduced this into the world, it could revolutionize the fuel industry as we know it. Never mind make her, or anyone who owned it, a billionaire a number of times over."

Riley shook her head. "My mother never cared about money."

"I'm sorry, Riley. I didn't mean she was doing it for the money," Stone said.

"Looks like she has the sections grouped into research and personal journals. It's going to take me some time to go through all this information," Riley said.

"Why don't I give you an SSD with all the information? I'll set you up on Dagger's computer, our system is secure. You can take the time you need to try and make heads or tails of this information. But don't open these files anywhere but here. A halfway decent hacker can steal those files in the blink of an eye if you do, and you won't even see it coming," Kaleb said.

"Accessing the data within our system only is our best chance for keeping Claudia's research safe and under wraps. I will back up all your mom's data and save it off-site on our secured back up. No one can get in. If you agree, we'll place a hard copy in our state-of-the-art safe. It'd take an atomic bomb to break that baby open. You should place the original SSD in your safe deposit box."

"Thanks, Kaleb, that sounds good. I'll go through all the files later. Right now, I want to find out if there are any clues as to who Mom's killer is, or why she didn't want anybody, but especially her company, to have her research."

Riley had settled herself at Dagger's computer. She scrolled through the file names until she found her mother's last entry. She clicked on the last file and started to read.

"This was the night the ship went down." She pointed at the last save time. "Mom closed this file less than three hours before she called me. The last thing she wrote was 'The patent is pending. The patent holders are Claudia Rawlings and—'"

"You, Riley." Dagger finished the sentence reading over her shoulder. "It won't take much time for others to discover that fact. They only need her name to search for the existence of a pending patent."

"And that's going to put a big red bullseye on your back," Stone said.

Dagger threw him a dirty look.

Stone shrugged in answer. "Better to see it coming than to be blindsided."

"You're right, Stone. We need to tighten Riley's security," Dagger said.

Riley frowned, turned back to the screen and scrolled through her mother's notes. "Listen to this," Riley said, looking over a file of her mother's notes. "He's at it again," Riley began to read. "Anthony believes if he throws the weight of Premier Oil and Gas around enough times, I'll cave. There's no way I'd ever go to work for him and his company, and hell would freeze over before I gave him any of my algae biofuel research. I told him over a year ago to keep his bribes to himself." Riley raised an eyebrow. "It looks like we might have another player in this cat-and-mouse game."

"Who is Anthony and what is he to Claudia?" Kaleb asked.

"Anthony and my mother went through college and graduate school together. You might say they were friendly rivals. Mom and Anthony dated a few years after Dad passed away. At least that's what Anthony thought. Mom considered him a friend and colleague—someone she could enjoy a dinner with and discuss science. Until one night, when he proposed to her."

"What happened?" Kaleb asked.

"Let's just say it didn't end well. Mom tried to let him down gently. She tried to stay friends, but she'd wounded his pride. Anthony isn't the kind of man who can handle being turned down."

"Were they still friends afterwards?" Stone asked.

"In a way. They didn't go to dinner anymore. But they remained cordial at events."

"What does he do?" Dagger asked.

"Anthony Welby is the CEO of Premier Oil and Gas. He's quite cunning when it comes to business. He decided early on in his career to focus on building businesses rather than research and development," Riley said.

"Hold on, CEOs don't kill people, they buy them out or pressure them with threats of unemployment. Claudia doesn't seem particularly frightened in her journal, she just stated a fact and nothing more," Dagger said.

"So it sounds like he was after her research," Stone said.

"Anthony must have suspected she was working on something of interest to him. And, let's face it, if this could be a cheap substitute for fossil fuels, his fortune was at risk. Algae being made into biofuel could revolutionize the fuel industry. Man-made algae ponds could cultivate a new crop of algae every few weeks. Imagine if the world could cheaply produce biofuels. The right conversion method would mean you no longer need oil and gas for vehicles; it might also reduce the demand for natural gas. The world would become a cleaner, less polluted place, and fossil fuel would be history."

Riley returned to reading Claudia's journal. Kaleb got up and headed for the kitchen.

Dagger caught Stone's eye and tipped his head toward the kitchen. "We're going to get some coffee. Do you want anything, Riley?" Dagger asked.

"No thanks," she mumbled, never taking her eye from the

screen.

"What's up?" Stone asked as soon as they were out of earshot.

"You aren't going to believe who contacted me," Dagger said.

"I haven't a clue. But you looked like the devil was hot on your heels," Stone said.

"Katarina."

"What the holy hell?" Kaleb asked. Dagger scowled at him and made a jerking motion to stay quiet. "How did she get out of custody, and secondly—Jesus, it's been years. How in the world did she get your number and why?" Kaleb whispered.

"We do have a public business and my number isn't unlisted. Not that either matters. She sent me our old SOS code. I knew it was her the second I saw it. I thought I saw Kat twice while in Oahu, but I figured my mind was playing tricks on me. I think she's been tailing Riley and me since San Juan Island," Dagger said. "Mr. Ford mentioned seeing a woman walk by on the beach. She's not in prison. I have no idea how she got out and I don't want to know. She wants me to meet her tomorrow—and she knows about Claudia's research. I tried to blow her off, but then she threatened Riley. She described her and the blue top she's wearing."

Stone and Kaleb discreetly glanced over at Riley, sitting at Dagger's computer wearing a blue top. "Damn it all to hell. What are you going to tell Riley?" Stone asked.

"Nothing. And neither are the two of you. Tomorrow morning I'll tell her something important came up and I must handle it. I'll let her know you'll be picking her up, Stone, and bringing her back here. With any luck, she'll be so engrossed in her research she'll hardly notice my absence. Worst case, you or Kaleb will be taking her back to my place and staying with her. The stakes have risen tenfold with Katarina Petrin on the loose."

"I can't even wrap my head around this one." Stone shook his head "You need to tell Riley."

"Tell her what—that she's in more danger? I don't even know what the hell is going on." Dagger leaned on the counter and looked out the window over the docks.

"Dagger," Stone started.

"Don't start. Fine. I promise to tell Riley all about the meeting with Kat as soon as I know what Kat is up to," Dagger said.

He knew the promise of Riley was too good to be true. His life was about to implode, and the last thing he wanted was for her to be caught up in it. He needed her protected and as far away from Katarina as humanly possible.

"Dagger, you haven't been involved with *any* woman in six years. A blind monkey could tell Riley's something special," Kaleb said. "Don't blow it now."

"I know what I'm doing. Tomorrow morning I'll tell her we have a difficult client needing my attention. She doesn't need any more information. I'm trusting the two of you to guard her with your lives."

"You can't handle this alone, Dagger. You need backup," Stone said.

"No, I don't. You and Kaleb stay with Riley, no matter what."

"Don't worry about Riley. We'll take care of her as if she were our baby sister," Stone said. "But I'm telling you, Dagger, this is a mistake. We should be handling this situation as a team—and that includes Riley. Don't leave Riley in the dark."

Dagger wheeled around and stood almost nose-to-nose with Stone, who showed no sign of backing down.

"I'm not walking out on Riley. I'm keeping her safe," he snarled in a low menacing voice.

"Hey, listen. I'm no expert on women," Stone said. "But the way I see it, you're leaving her in the dark and not telling her about a direct threat to her life. If she finds out you're hiding something from her...She may find it unforgivable."

Chapter Twenty-One

"We made big strides today," Dagger said as he and Riley pulled out of the marina.

"I guess you're right. I finally know what my mom's lifelong research project entailed. But I would feel much better if we had a lead on her murderer and a way of eluding our stalker."

"We'll get one soon. I can feel it." He rubbed at the back of his neck and avoided Riley's gaze.

They pulled into Dagger's driveway, and he pressed the button to open the garage door. The lights in the garage turned on as they entered. The door started back down as soon as he parked his Range Rover.

"That's convenient," Riley said.

"It's times like these I'm glad I spent the extra money for the upgraded security." Dagger walked around to the passenger side and opened Riley's door. "Head on in. I'll grab your bags. The door will click open as soon as the motion and heat sensors finish their sweep."

Riley's eyes grew wide and round. She heard a click, and the door to the house cracked open.

"It's clear. Go ahead, I'll be right there." Dagger pulled his phone out and pushed the speed dial button.

"You two make it back okay?" Kaleb asked.

"Yep. Thanks for double-checking the system and getting the outside perimeter wired with motion detectors, Kaleb."

"Any time, you know that. So why the call? You could've said thanks tomorrow."

"I want you to do a complete search on Anthony Welby."

"Stone and I were thinking the same thing. It's already running. I can tell you one thing. From what I see so far, he's a ruthless bastard and will stop at nothing when it comes to business. On another note, you really think taking off and not telling Riley the truth is a prudent choice?"

"Don't you start. For now, I do. I gotta go, Riley's inside waiting on me."

"Call us if you need us. And Dagger, you better watch your ass tomorrow. Katarina's a leopard. Beautiful to look at, but she'll kill just for the sport of it."

"You're preaching to the choir, brother."

"I know. But pain and love can run deep. Don't forget all the shit she put you through."

"Not a chance in hell." Dagger hung up and stuffed his phone in his pocket as he walked in.

Riley sat in one of the overstuffed chairs with her feet up on the footstool. The chair was so large it practically swallowed her up. She sipped on a glass of water and stared out over the ocean.

"I'll take your things up to the guest bedroom."

"It's been a rough day. I'd love a glass of wine," she said.

"You were reading my mind."

He handed Riley a glass and dropped on the sofa beside her.

"Have you noticed our shadow?" she asked.

"I have a feeling he headed back into whatever hole he crawled out of."

Riley yawned and rubbed her eyes. "I should put an hour or two in on starting mom's list of associates."

"You're tired, Riley. Call it done for the night. Besides, you'll likely miss something in the state you're in." Dagger's hand rested on his lap, and Riley reached out and placed her hand over his.

"I don't think I've thanked you. I did mention it to the three of you, only you're different. I don't know what I would've done these past few weeks if you weren't here."

"You would've found a way. You're a strong woman."

"Maybe—but even a strong woman can shatter under emotional stress."

He cupped her chin in his hand. "Don't worry about doing this alone. I'll be there every step of the way."

Riley just smiled. He could see in her eyes she wanted to say something more. Instead, she got up and took her glass into the kitchen. "I'm beat. I'm going to head to bed. Goodnight, Dagger." She leaned down and kissed him on the cheek.

"Good night, Riley. Sleep well."

She walked up the stairs. He watched her out of the corner of his eye. He'd practically spilled his guts when she said she didn't know what she would do if she were alone. And then the kiss on his cheek. "Jackass," he mumbled. He must be doing a great job of playing the friend card.

Dagger sat in his favorite chair, took another swig of wine and cursed himself—for the second time. He'd almost blown it the night he'd brought her home from the hospital when she ended up in his bed—again. He'd come so close to telling her his true feelings. Except he couldn't—not yet. Riley was maneuvering through what was probably the most difficult time of her life. The last thing he wanted to do was scare her away by telling her his feelings. He needed to give her time to get through this nightmare and heal. He was terrified if she knew about his feelings for her, about his history with women, and his stellar way of screwing up his love-life, she'd hightail it and never look back.

What the hell was he thinking?

Kat was back. She was the expert at turning his world upside down, and once again she was forcing a showdown and threatening someone he cared about.

He felt relieved when Riley headed straight up to bed. He wanted to tell her she'd never be alone again. He would stay by her side forever. Should he tell Riley about Kat? No. The guys didn't know everything about Katarina. Riley was nothing like Kat. He couldn't pollute her life with his past garbage—he wouldn't. He needed to stick to his plan and make sure Riley and Katarina were never within sniper scope distance. He shook his head.

What on God's green earth was happening to him?

He'd never felt this way about any woman. There was a time he thought he did, but it was an illusion. Until the day Riley Rawlings walked into Samuels's office and flashed him that *you-don't-impress-me-in-the-least* look.

He shook his head. Yep, that's when he had turned into putty.

Dagger tried to distract himself with the news. He checked the time again. Riley went up to bed over two hours ago. Not being able to stand it any longer, he got up and went through the downstairs, checking the doors and windows. He wanted to stand out on the patio to fill his lungs with cool, clean ocean air. He resisted the urge. They were locked in for the night, and there was no good reason to tempt fate.

He heard Riley. It sounded as if she were having a bad dream or maybe just some fitful sleep. He put his glass in the dishwasher and turned it on. Then he walked from room to room and flipped off the light switches. He shed his clothes and slipped on his drawstring cotton pants and pulled on a clean t-shirt. He headed upstairs to secure the floor. Like a burglar in the night, he silently climbed the stairs two at a time. He inspected his office, den, workout room, and empty guest bedroom. In each room he checked the windows and examined every nook. He was on the last room when he heard Riley again. She moaned and whimpered like an injured child. He crept closer to her door and he peered in.

She was asleep with her blankets tangled around her legs and arms, as if she'd recently fought a battle with them. He slipped over to check that her window was locked.

As he turned to leave, she let out a quiet mew that nearly made him come undone. He moved the things from the chair and settled in. He didn't want her waking from a nightmare alone, in a strange environment. He told himself that once he was certain she was settled, he would return to his bedroom.

A cry woke Dagger with an adrenaline rush. The night sky was cloudy and the room was nearly pitch black. Riley sucked in a quick breath and curled up into a tiny ball.

Dagger brushed back a hair from her forehead, it was damp with sweat. "You're safe, Riley. It's me—Dagger."

Riley whimpered and then startled awake. "You're safe, Riley. No one will hurt you, I promise."

"Oh, Dagger. I was caught up in the most terrifying nightmare. I couldn't find my way out. I tried." She looked up at him.

He wanted to reach out for her, but he was afraid of scaring her away. So he slid up to the pillows, leaned against them and patted the bed. "Come here."

Riley hesitated for a nanosecond. Then she threw herself into his arms. He pulled her close and wrapped his arms around her. She was all warm curves and softness. Her long, deep brown hair always reminded him of the richest cocoa beans. He longed to run his hands through her hair. Instead, he lightly rested his chin over the top of her head and inhaled her scent of sunshine and tropical breeze.

"Why were you here?" she asked.

"When I came upstairs to secure the house, you were restless. I wanted to stay close so I could watch over you. I didn't want you waking up frightened in a strange place."

She put her hands around him. He could tell something was bothering her.

"Riley, tell me what's troubling you."

"Nothing, just the dream."

"I've come to know you slightly better than that. I know you're deflecting."

"I'm fine. Really."

He looked into her face. "Please tell me what's wrong. I can't help you if I don't know."

"That's just it—you can't help me." She dropped her gaze from his. "We're friends, right?"

"Of course we are. I'll always be your friend."

"There it is. Leave it alone, Dagger. You can't fix this."

"What are you talking about?"

"I'm talking about sharing the same bed and nothing more."

She glanced back up at him. He was totally confused. He thought they'd given each other comfort—like a bullet through the heart, the revelation threw him back.

"Are you saying you want *more* from me than friendship?" he asked.

"Yes…no…I mean…I want you to be in my life. So if friendship is what *you* want, then friends we will be," Riley said.

This time he closed the distance in one fluid movement and claimed her lips in a way she couldn't confuse with friendship. He kissed her thoroughly and completely.

His tongue played across the crease of her lips until she opened to him. He thrust his tongue deep inside her mouth and savored her. Her body melted into him. He took her with him as he leaned back against the pillows and slid her body over his. She sighed as he rubbed her satin-covered back.

She placed her hands on his jawline and kissed him again. Riley ran her hands slowly down his shoulders and softly dragged her palms over his erect nipples. Finding the edge of his t-shirt, she slipped her soft warm hands underneath.

What was he doing?

Yes, he wanted her, but tomorrow he would be heading off to deal with Katarina. Taking what they wanted now would make an even bigger mess of things. He couldn't do that. He wouldn't do that. He ran his hands down her arms.

"I thought..." She looked confused.

"I can't, Riley. Not now." Dagger gently lifted her off him and set her on the bed. Stopping this was one of the most difficult choices he'd ever made.

He reached over and tenderly moved her hair out of her face. She pulled the blankets up to her neck, shook her head, and shifted away from him. As he moved to leave, he looked back and saw her eyes brimming with unshed tears.

Had he just destroyed his chance with the only woman he wanted in his life? He turned and left the room, closing the door behind him. His hand was still gripping the doorknob when he heard her sob.

****

Riley laid in bed, staring at the ceiling. She'd tossed and turned the entire night. She'd cried and cursed Dagger Eastin. Her life was upside down and inside out. She wasn't sure she could pull herself through to the other side and come out whole.

She replayed last night over and over. At first she wasn't sure he wanted her. But the way he kissed her and held her made it clear he really wanted her, until he pushed her away and stabbed her in the heart.

Riley wanted to walk away. Leave it all behind. However, she needed Dagger to help find the answers and put the people that killed her mother behind bars. Only then could she turn her back on him. She'd shut off her emotions and soldier on.

As she descended the stairs, Dagger was standing with his back to her in the open doorway of the patio and talking on the phone.

"I got another damn text from her an hour ago. Yes, I know. I'm handling this—don't worry."

She was halfway across the main room when he turned. His eyes looked menacing while he listened to whoever was on the phone. As he spotted her, he smiled and waved her closer, as if the look on his face a moment before had been nothing but a figment of her imagination. She stayed where she was. The smile slipped from his face and he dropped his arm to his side.

"I've got to go," Dagger said, hanging up.

"Good morning, sleepy head. I thought you'd sleep longer." He took a step in her direction, and she answered with a small step back. He studied her with what looked like anguish. "I'm sorry, Riley. I would never intentionally hurt you."

But he had. They both knew it.

"I'm sorry I disturbed your call," she said.

"It's no big deal, but something's come up. Unfortunately, I can't take you with me, so I asked Stone to take you to Hunters and Seekers."

Uncertain what to do or say, she ran her hands through her hair. Now he was cutting her out, leaving her in the dark. Something was going on...something that reeked of another woman.

"Why?" It seemed to be the only word she could come up with.

"There's a problem with a client. I need to handle it personally."

She frowned. Problem client...Right.

The doorbell rang.

She turned from him and retreated up the stairs.

A crash rang through the house as something breakable hit the stone patio.

****

Dagger arrived in San Clemente several hours before his meeting with Katarina, knowing she'd already arrived. Kat's MO was to stake out a place early.

It'd been six years since he'd set foot anywhere near the San Clemente Pier. He and Kat would go there when they craved a quick get-away. Coming back here created a bitter taste in his mouth. He parked his Range Rover in a hotel lot, checked into his room, donned his ball cap and aviator sunglasses, and headed for the beach.

It was October, and the beach was still full of sightseers, surfers, joggers, volleyball games, and sun-worshipers. The scent of the salty ocean air mingled with suntan oil, hotdogs, pretzels, and sweat as he casually weaved around clusters of people and occupied beach towels. Nothing much had changed except the type of music blaring from smartphones and the amount of skin bared by even skimpier bathing suits.

Dagger walked the entire length of the beach and back at an easy pace. His only camouflage was his hat, glasses, and nonchalant attitude. With all the activity, it would be easy for a few lookouts to blend in. The agreement was to come alone, but Dagger knew better.

Kat had lied throughout their entire relationship. He had no illusions she would change now.

He sat on the hot sand and evaluated the meeting place—a bench a few yards from the pier. The wind whipped through, pulling at his clothes and ballcap. He yanked it down snugly on his head.

He sat soaking in the feel of his surroundings and discreetly scrutinized the beach goers. He'd yet to spot anyone looking out of place. Dagger was fairly comfortable no one else was scouting out the area, but he'd been wrong in the past. Committing the layout and flow of the beach to memory, he rose from his spot and headed down the beach.

"Nice to see you, Dagger. You look even sexier than the first time I met you. Getting assigned to you was one of the most fulfilling times in my life," Katarina said.

Katarina exuded sex and danger as she sauntered over. She casually turned and looked back down the beach. No doubt checking on her scouts. She was dressed in a bright red one-piece swim suit, cut to within an inch of her crotch and cut up high along the middle of each cheek in the back. She wore a very sheer black cover-up wrapped around her waist that somehow made her look more naked—which was probably its purpose. Her designer sunglasses hid her eyes.

Dagger wanted to spring off the bench and strangle her.

"Let me guess. You aren't planning on getting out of the spy business." He sat on one side of the bench, his legs stretched out in front of him and his hands clasped behind his head.

She shrugged. "You know me too well."

"Who are you working for, us or the Russians?"

"For whoever pays more."

"Do they know that, Kat?"

"They both think they control me."

"Is that all you care about—the money?"

"Dagger, money opens doors."

"When did you become so jaded?"

"This is who I've always been. You just refused to see it."

She was right, Dagger thought. Money and status were always her priorities. Once she'd told him she wasn't the best archaeologist because she loved what she did. She was the best because she loved the status. How did he ever think he loved this woman? Had it really been love? Or was what he had with Kat merely sexual obsession?

He experienced the same desire with Riley…but there was also something *more* with her.

"Let's get down to business, shall we," Kat said. "Rumor has it, you're in possession of Dr. Rawling's journals and formulas. I'm prepared to offer you a very handsome sum for them."

"I don't know who your source is, but I'd say you need a new one. Their information is way off base. I don't have the slightest idea where the journals and formulas are or if they even exist," Dagger said.

"You should give it some thought, Dagger. Either you can be rewarded with an amount of money you can't even begin to dream of and keep your little business in the black, or you could wake up one morning and find your business burned to the ground and your partners dead."

Dagger crossed his arms over his chest and shook his head. "All that training and that's the best you can do? I'm disappointed, Katarina."

"Don't piss me off, Dagger," she snarled. "If you thought my temper was bad six years ago, think again. I can hurt you so many ways now, you'll have no choice. You have two days to deliver the materials, or your lack of cooperation will be met with swift retaliation."

"Nothing will change between now and then, Kat. Keep your money and threats."

Kat turned and started to walk away from him. "You'd be astounded at how much your life can change in forty-eight hours. And I'm not talking about flowers and fairytales."

Chapter Twenty-Two

There was something warm and luscious draped over him; waking up would definitely spoil this dream. But eventually Dagger opened his eyes and discovered a sleeping Riley. Her head was resting on his chest, her arm hugged him. His fingers stroked her arm.

Had she been asleep in his bed when he fell into it right before dawn? He didn't know or care how or when she'd crawled in. For just a few minutes he'd block out all the other thoughts swirling in his mind and soaked in the scent of her hair and feel of her skin. He wanted desperately to wash away their last encounter. Dagger never wanted to hurt her.

Riley's breathing changed, but she remained still. As he looked down, he found her staring up at him. He bent closer, and she pulled away and sat up.

The haunted look he'd grown accustomed to was back.

"I'm sorry. I didn't realize you were coming back last night. I should've gone back up to the guest room," she said as she sat on the edge of bed. "What time is it?"

"It's eight-forty-five. I never sleep this late. I thought yesterday would never end," Dagger said.

"I can imagine. Dealing with *a problem client* must be draining."

He wanted to laugh. *Typhoon Katarina* was more on point. The way Riley said "problem client" made it clear she didn't believe him. It really shouldn't surprise him. She was an astute woman and very little got by her.

"Can I help?" she asked.

"Thanks, but no. Client privilege, you know how it goes." He wanted to believe she was his same Riley, only deep in the pit of his stomach he knew something had changed.

"Hey, Dagger." Kaleb banged on the bedroom door. "Get your lazy ass out of bed. Stone sent me a text. He has something and wants us to come in. I know you need your beauty sleep and all—"

Kaleb stopped in mid-sentence as the bedroom door swung wide open. Dagger stood in the doorway.

"Why don't you yell a little louder? I don't think the neighbor heard you," Dagger said.

Kaleb peered around Dagger and saw Riley sitting on the edge of the bed. He looked at Dagger and waggled his eyebrow. Dagger returned his partner's gesture by rolling his eyes and giving a quick headshake.

"Get it into gear. Stone took my vehicle last night, so I'm riding with the two of you."

Kaleb and Dagger sat out on the patio both on their third cup of coffee as they waited for Riley.

"Spill, bro. How'd your meeting with the She-devil go?" Kaleb asked.

"Katarina is marking her territory by threatening to kill us. She's always enjoyed these games. I just never thought I'd be on the opposite side," Dagger said. "She's given me forty-eight hours to get her the formula and research."

"How does she know you have it?"

"She doesn't. She's throwing out a wide net to see what she can catch."

"How do you know that for sure?"

"I know how she works."

Kaleb rolled his eyes in response.

"It's not the same. She snowed me regarding our relationship. But as far as working together, I know. Kat knows Riley is with us. She's playing the odds. It's gonna take some fancy foot work to figure out what's really going on as far as Katarina is concerned," Dagger said.

"You're saying we're not gonna shake her off?"

"Oh, hell no. Kat is a blood-sucker and she'll drain you slowly. Stay on your toes. You never know when she'll pop up."

"What are you going to tell Riley?"

"Nothing. And you and Stone aren't either. I don't want to make any more of a mess of this than I already have. We stick with the difficult client story."

"You got feelings for her, bro. This is only going to get messier."

The door opened and Riley stepped onto the deck, travel mug in hand. "Sorry to keep you boys waiting. I'm ready when you are."

"Morning, Riley," Stone said as she and the guys entered the office. "Sorry to ask you to come in so early. We received the results of the joint findings of the SDPD and Coast Guard investigation regarding the incident, and I thought we'd better go through it together."

Dagger could tell immediately by the sound of Stone's voice that the news wasn't good.

"What did the report say?" Dagger asked.

"They're officially calling it an accident," Stone said.

"What about the carbon monoxide?" Riley asked.

"And the gouge in the side of the hull?" Dagger asked.

"The official report is the ship ran into something, which caused the scorching and a leak in the piping. This allowed the CO to spread throughout the ventilation system, and rendered everyone on board unconscious," Kaleb said, as he read through the report.

"Bull shit," Dagger said. "The CO was leaking *way* before the ship sunk. Between the time of morning and the weather, the killer made sure everyone was down below, disoriented, and dying."

"Whoever did place the explosives was smart. They put them on the outside of the hull, which would cause the hull to be curled inward, imitating something hitting the boat," Kaleb said.

"Sounds to me like we have a cover up," Stone said.

"And based on this final report, it involves at least one person, probably in the Coast Guard," Dagger growled.

"Question is; do we track down the culprit, or do we continue deciphering Claudia's formula?" Kaleb asked.

"It's important to get your report findings into the hands of the powers that be," Riley said.

"We can't show our hand until we have all the facts," Dagger said.

"And all the players," Kaleb said.

Dagger threw Kaleb his *shut the hell up* look.

"The file is closed and sealed," Stone said.

"Which means what?" Riley asked.

"Which means the decision has been made and barring any new information there's nothing we can do to change the outcome," Dagger said.

"But we have the information," Riley said.

"We have suspicions and pieces of the puzzle," Dagger said. "We'll only have one chance to make this right. We need all the information before we go there."

"Yeah, that leads us to the second bit of wonderful news we received this morning," Stone said. "Samuels emailed us minutes after the accident report came in. He informed us that the research vessel will soon be in his company's possession. He said we're to steer clear of the ship. Hold on, there's more." Stone held his hand out palm up to stop his partners' comments. "Samuels also threatened to place a gag order on us if he even heard we were anywhere near his company or his ship. And if we violate the gag order, he'd make sure we never work for any company within the industry anywhere in the world."

"The lying sack of slimy shit has covered all his bases," Dagger said. "That could financially destroy us."

"Then we'd have all the time in the world for pro-bono work," Kaleb said, in an attempt to lighten the mood. He continued when he noticed it hadn't worked. "There is one good thing—he'll no longer be calling us." Kaleb gave them a crocodile smile.

"The douchebag," Dagger mumbled.

It wasn't even lunch time yet and his day had gone from Coast Guard fraud to financial ruin.

"I'd love to get my hands on the person or people they paid off," Stone said.

"Stand in line," Dagger said.

"And I've left the worse news until last," Stone said in a somber tone. "Riley, I'm really sorry to be the bearer of bad news. Your mother's body is being released to the funeral home today."

"At this point I don't trust anyone outside this building. I need to go to the coroner's office and verify their report and see the body and the photos for myself." Her voice was thick with emotion.

"I think you're right. I'll take you, Riley," Dagger said.

"Guys, I don't know if we'll be back today. Kaleb, keep working on Claudia's files." He pulled a jumpdrive out of his desk drawer and slipped it in his pocket. "We'll get a copy of the report and send it to you, Stone."

"No sense in putting this off. Let's get this over with." Riley raised her chin and gave the men a guarded smile.

****

Riley sat quietly the entire trip. Dagger parked his vehicle and walked around to her side. He opened the door and helped her out. As they headed into the Coroner's office, a possessive feeling overwhelmed him. He placed his arm around her shoulders and pulled her close, protecting her the best he could.

She didn't utter a word when the secretary asked who they were there to see. Dagger told the woman what they were there for. She told Riley how sorry she was for her loss and left to make the arrangements.

A few minutes later, a heavy-set older man got off the elevator and walked in their direction.

"Riley Rawlings?" he asked.

She looked at the older man with a blank expression. She cleared her throat. "Yes…I'm Riley."

"I'm told they verified your identity at the front desk," the man said, addressing them both.

Dagger slipped his arm from Riley's shoulder, reached down, and took her hand. She glanced up at him just long enough for him to catch the shimmer of tears in her eyes. She gripped Dagger's hand tightly and placed her other hand on his arm.

"How may I be of assistance?" the coroner asked.

Dagger gave her hand a reassuring squeeze.

"I would like a copy of your report, and I'd like to see your original photographs," Riley said.

"I've sent my report to SDPD and the Coast Guard. I'm sure they'll be sending you a copy."

"I don't want to wait. Please, I need closure from this loss. I'd like to see your report first hand."

The coroner studied her.

"I understand. You may see my report. Would you like to proceed alone, or would you rather your friend joined you?"

"I'd like Dagger to accompany me."

"As you wish." The coroner gave them a nod. "Follow me, please."

They followed him to the bank of elevators. He pushed the button for the basement. "I'm sorry it took us so long to release your mother's body. When foul play could be involved, these situations drag out, making it even more difficult on the loved one's family."

"We understand," Dagger said. "May I ask how the victims were identified?"

"We were able to use dental for many of the victims. However, due to the length of time some victims were in the water, DNA markers were our only option. This is another reason it took us longer to finish our work. We used DNA for your mother, Riley. It was an identical match."

"How did you make the comparison?" Dagger asked.

"One of Dr. Rawling's assistants was kind enough to bring a hair and toothbrush from your mother's desk drawer."

Dagger made a mental note to follow up on who acquired the items and how the chain of evidence was maintained. They stepped out into a bright white hallway. The smell of bleach and formaldehyde stung Dagger's nostrils.

The coroner stopped at a door. "This is one of our meeting rooms," the coroner said as he motioned them in. The room was full of a table and chairs. "I'll have you wait here. I'll be back shortly."

Minutes later he returned holding a large file. He placed it on the table. Dagger pulled the jump drive from his pocket. "We would appreciate if you could make a copy of the report."

Dagger could tell by the coroner's expression he was a bit put out. He gathered himself and reached for the jumpdrive.

"I'd be happy to," the coroner said in a clipped tone. He took a deep breath. "This will take some time. I'll be back."

Dagger waited. Riley would need to open her mother's file on her own.

Minutes ticked by as she stared at the file. Dagger was beginning to think she'd changed her mind.

"Would you prefer not to open the file? We can take the jumpdrive back to the office where Stone can read through it."

She turned and looked at him. Her face was white. He reached for her hands resting in her lap and found them ice cold. He covered them with his hand.

"I have to do this," she said so softly that, at first, he wasn't sure she'd said anything. "The reason we came here was to view the original file. We'll have no source of comparison to the electronic file if we don't go through with this."

She pulled one hand out from under his and gripped his hands tightly with the other. Her free hand rose to the table. She placed it on the corner of the file. Then she slipped her thumb under the cover and flipped the file open.

Riley stared at the head and shoulders of the woman in the picture. The length of time the body remained in the ocean was apparent. The sea life had badly distorted Claudia's features. Riley ran her finger around and around the image. She pulled her hand away and reached up to wipe her eye.

Her hand moved to the second picture of the woman's torso. Riley traced the image as if trying to commit it to memory. She was on her fourth time around, when her finger stopped. She released Dagger's hand and picked up the picture with both hands, examining the second picture closely.

The coroner walked in and handed Dagger the jumpdrive.

"Are these the only two photos? I expected to see full length photographs in an autopsy file." Riley stared up at the coroner.

The coroner looked down at the file. "You're correct. I removed a couple. One is full length and the other is a close-up of her chest."

"I'd like to see the photos."

"I thought I would spare your feelings," the coroner said, looking uncomfortable, his gaze alternating between her and Dagger.

"We need to see them all," Riley answered.

The coroner opened another file he'd carried in and pulled out the photos and handed them to her.

The door opened a few inches. "Excuse me, sir. The call you've been waiting for is on the phone," the woman from the front desk said. "Should I tell him you'll call back?"

"No. I'll speak with him now. If you'll excuse me." The coroner gave them a quick nod and left the room.

Riley placed the missing photos back into the file and once again scrutinized the pictures. Dagger realized he'd been holding his breath. What on earth was she looking at?

"This is not my mother," Riley stated in a low, quiet tone. She set the file on the table.

"What? How? The coroner assured us every precaution was taken."

"Look right here." Riley pointed to the upper part of the woman's left breast. She kept her voice low and in control. "What do you see?"

"Ah, nothing out of the ordinary. It's a breast," Dagger said.

"Do you see anything on her skin? Any birthmarks or tattoos?" she asked.

"No. There's nothing there, Riley."

"Exactly. This—is—not—Claudia—Rawlings. My mother has a tiny tattoo, right here." She pointed to her left breast, above the areola. "Four months ago, mom asked me to go to a tattoo shop with her. She placed a tiny arrow right here. It was about an inch long, a half inch tall. An arrow through her heart. The arrow was outlined in red and inside of the arrow, also in red ink, was a name—Mark. My father's name. She said she'd been missing him more and needed to have him close to her heart. I have no idea who this poor woman is. But I'm certain she is not my mother."

Dagger picked up the photo and held it close to his eyes. Nope, nothing. No tattoo, no birthmark, not even a scratch from the accident. He pulled out his phone and took a picture of each of the three photos, making sure the case file number and identification were clearly marked.

"I just need to be sure we have these photos—that they don't somehow go missing. We've seen enough," Dagger said. "Let's go. Keep your head down and act as if you've been overcome with grief. We're not telling anyone what you've discovered. Not until we can put all the pieces of this puzzle together."

Chapter Twenty-Three

Dagger and Riley walked slowly out of the building with Dagger's arm around her shoulders and Riley's hood pulled up over her head. Eyes down, Riley whispered, "Dagger she's alive! She must be." She wanted to scream or cry or jump up and down; a weight she had been carrying was gone, and her every pore was vibrating with hope and energy.

Dagger's arm tightened around her as he replied, "Slowly now. Wait until we get in the car and drive off." He shoved his phone into his pocket and opened her door. In the driver's seat he said, "Please, Riley, please don't get your hopes up. It's been weeks since her ship went down, and no one has heard from her. Anything could have happened by now. Let's take this one step at a time. I'm not saying Claudia isn't alive."

"I know my mother," Riley said. "Somehow she escaped and has gone to ground. She's trying to stay as far away from me as possible. Either to lead whoever is after her, far away from me, or to make them believe she really is dead."

"Riley, we need to walk through the possibilities calmly. We need a thorough look at what we know before we develop a plan. You know this, you're a scientist," Dagger replied as he pulled out of the parking lot.

Riley answered, "The scumbag in charge could have substituted another woman in her place, leaving everyone to believe she's dead while he searches for her."

"Or someone kidnapped her from the ship before it went down, or even retrieved her from the water prior to the Coast Guard showing up on site. After all, Wayne Samuels waited three hours before contacting the Coast Guard," Dagger said. He glanced over at her. "We could have just discovered why Samuels took so long to contact them. Maybe Claudia and her research were his first concerns."

"That's what I've been telling you," Riley remarked.

"It's a huge ocean, Riley. She could still be out there."

Dagger was concerned about her. She could read it all over his face, as plain as a neon sign flashing *danger, danger*. She reached over and lightly placed the palm of her hand on the side of his cheek.

"Don't worry so much. I realize my mother could very well be dead, but there's a chance she is still alive. If she is, we need to find her. I'm just thrilled Mom may have survived. At this point in time, it's a good day. The only thing we know for sure is, it wasn't my mother in those pictures. Who was it and how did she end up there? Was she somehow involved in this? Do you think someone is looking for her? She must have a family wondering where she is."

"She could be a Jane Doe. That would make the most sense. Or a body kept on ice until needed. But if she does have family, we'll make sure she's reunited with them. If she has none, we'll make sure she has a proper burial. For now, our complete focus is on figuring out who's behind all this, is your mom in hiding or has she been kidnapped, and if so, where is she being kept. My gut tells me Wayne Samuels is not the mastermind. I can't help feeling that Anthony Welby is somehow involved."

"Where are we going?" Riley asked.

"I texted the guys on my way out. Didn't give any details, just in case we're being monitored. I told them our new client has a change of plans."

"More of your code?" she asked.

"Yep. It means—*the shit has hit the fan*."

"And what exactly does that mean?"

"It's time to pull out the burner phones, weapons on your person at all times, and watch your ass," Dagger said.

"Fascinating that you have codes for this…life must be chaotic around you guys."

"Yeah, but we have a way of growing on you. At least I do, right?" Dagger waggled his eyebrows and flashed her his best sexy smile.

"What the hell happened?" Stone asked, as Dagger and Riley

walked in.

"It's not my mother," Riley said.

Stone narrowed his eyes and rubbed his hand over his forehead. Kaleb frowned and crossed his arms.

"Say again," Kaleb said.

"Get the marbles out of your ears, man. The woman said the woman in the morgue is not her mother. Kaleb, take this." Dagger tossed his phone to him. "I didn't want to send these photos. We are probably being electronically tracked."

Within seconds the photos were on the large screen.

"They verified identity?" Stone asked.

"DNA match to Claudia based on a toothbrush and hair brush. Came back a match," Dagger said.

"You're saying someone has access to a lab and can manipulate a lab tech," Stone said.

"Or that someone is a lab tech," Kaleb said.

"So how are you sure she's not your mom, Riley?" Stone asked.

Riley explained about her mom's tattoo.

"Whoever substituted this woman for Claudia was unaware of the tattoo. Which is logical based on its size, location, and it being newly acquired." Stone tapped his chin with his index finger as he studied the photos on the large screen.

Riley's phone vibrated. "It's Dr. Bender," she said, looking down at the screen.

"Who's Dr. Bender?" Dagger asked.

"He's the Provost and Vice President for Academic Affairs—my boss's boss." Riley had no clue why he'd be calling, but she answered it nonetheless. "Good afternoon, Dr. Bender. What can I do for you?"

"Riley, I'm sorry to bother you. Last we spoke I told you to take all the time you need to recover from the loss of Claudia. However, I must know if you're attending the event Saturday night?" Dr. Bender asked. "I'll be attending your mother's funeral, but I didn't want to bother you there."

"I'm sorry. What event?"

"Didn't you get the invitation? Oh, this is a disaster. My assistant assured me he'd sent it out."

"He probably did, sir. I haven't paid much attention to my mail lately."

"Yes, yes. I completely understand. With everything going on

I'm sure you forgot the Association of Marine Sciences is having their annual conference this week at the university and now the conference has dedicated its formal dinner event to honor your mother."

"I registered for the conference months ago. I wasn't sure if I was going to feel like attending, but if they are honoring Mom, I want to be there," Riley said.

"Riley, Claudia was a gift while she taught here and continued to support the university until the day she—I'm sorry. Anyway, many of her colleagues from the west coast will be in attendance. Scientists, CEOs, and representatives of education from throughout the country are attending. Everyone will be expecting to see you," Dr. Bender said.

"I'll be there, sir."

"Wonderful! And Riley, feel free to bring an escort. I'll have my assistant email you the details, just to make sure you have everything you need."

"Dr. Bender, if you don't leave now, you're going to be late," a man said in the background.

Riley bolted out of her chair, eyes wide and mouth agape. Her heart hammered and hands shook as she fought to keep the phone tight against her ear.

"Yes, I'll be right there. I'm sorry, Riley, I'm running late. Promise me I'll see you Saturday."

"I...I...Yes," she stammered. She placed her phone on the desk and looked up. All three men were staring at her. "I know who entered my mother's stateroom the night the ship went down."

"Who, Bender?" Kaleb asked.

"Did he threaten you?" Dagger asked.

"Wherever it is he wants you to go, you can't go alone." Stone said.

"It wasn't Dr. Bender. It was his assistant," Riley said.

"I'm trying to remember his name. Let's go to the university. He's there, and I want to question him," she said, her voice shaking.

"Whoa...Hold on there." Dagger reached the door and blocked it before Riley could turn the knob.

"We need to go."

Kaleb pulled the large whiteboard from its nesting place in the wall. There were many more details on the board from the last time she'd seen it. He snatched the marker and drew a line up from the spot reading "male voice in background," directly between "Claudia calls Riley" and "Claudia leaves her stateroom." He poised the marker.

"Have you remembered his name yet?" Kaleb asked.

"Ahhh, Nelson, Nick, no, umm, hold on. Neal—that's it. His assistant is Neal."

Kaleb wrote in Neal's name and added Dr. Bender and his official title to a list on the side of the graph.

"What's this?" she asked, pointing to the list.

"These are all the people you've interacted with since the day we started this board."

"Wayne Samuels, Samuels' assistant, Mr. Ford—my caretaker? Stan, Estelle, and Jill." The list went on. "You can't honestly believe Mr. Ford or Stan and his family have anything to do with my mother's disappearance?"

"We aren't saying everyone on this list is involved, Riley. It's our process of keeping track of all the moving parts," Dagger said. He'd stepped closer to her while she digested what she saw. "Come on, let's all take a seat and work through this before we talk to Neal." Dagger placed his hand on Riley's upper arm and led her to a seat.

"Start from the beginning and tell us everything Dr. Bender said," Stone said.

Riley reiterated the conversation.

"Sounds like Dr. Bender knows Claudia quite well," Stone said.

"Yes. Dr. Bender was the Executive Dean of Science and hired my mother. They've developed a friendship over the years and socialize now and again."

"Do you think your mother would have told Dr. Bender about her research and formula?" Kaleb asked.

"Not with any specifics or details. Besides, they're longtime friends. What purpose would Dr. Bender have to kidnap my mom and try to steal her formula?"

"The oldest one of all—money," Kaleb said. "I'll dig into his background and see what I can turn up. Stone, can you take Neal?"

"Sure can. Full dump?" Stone asked.

"Anything and everything. We need to find a motive," Kaleb said.

"It's convenient Bender suggested bringing an escort. I volunteer," Dagger said.

"The event is in three days and my mother's *funeral* is tomorrow. Even though I'm aware she will not be the one in the coffin, I still need to attend, to keep up appearances," Riley said.

Riley caught a brief glance between Stone and Kaleb and their knowing smirks. They could tell she held feelings for Dagger. She couldn't deal with her feelings now. She already had more than she could handle.

****

Dagger lounged on his patio with his feet up and a half-empty bottle of beer dangling in his hand. Anyone looking at him would see a relaxed man enjoying the afternoon in the sun, not a man who'd just gone into high alert.

His gaze swept over the entire yard and beach until he spotted her. Katarina leaned against a fir tree, one leg bent up, foot against the trunk. The instant his eyes met hers, his phone vibrated.

"Your forty-eight hours has passed," Katarina said. "If you'd like your little tart to *walk* into her mother's service tomorrow instead of laid out in a coffin right next to hers, meet me down the beach, next to the fallen trees."

"I'll be a few minutes. Riley's sleeping. If she wakes and I'm not here, she'll go looking for me and I don't want her interrupting us. I'll leave her a note," Dagger said.

"Ten minutes." The line disconnected.

CHAPTER TWENTY-FOUR

"Do you think this is a game?" Katarina asked, as Dagger approached her. "You must be out of practice. Your little plaything would be dead right now if not for my patience."

"We both know if you killed Riley, you'd never get what you want."

"Maybe. But if you keep testing me, I might kill her out of spite."

"And what would the person who hired you say?"

Dagger saw the sudden flash of fire in her eyes. Kat had always hated authority.

"That's of no concern to me. Your lackadaisical attitude is. If killing Riley doesn't move you, I could always pick off one of your boys; they'll only get in my way, after all, and Riley might be useful, at least for a while. Now then, do you have what I want or not?"

"I don't."

Kat straightened, and her hand slipped to her lower back as she reached for her gun.

"Hear me out. I don't have it because we haven't found it yet," Dagger said.

"I don't believe you. I was on San Juan Island. She found the research at her grandparent's house. Don't toy with me," Katarina said.

"No, we didn't. We packed up all of Claudia's things and brought them back, hoping to find something, but there was nothing there."

"And what about in Oahu?"

"We went there to notify the owners of the dive shop personally. They were good friends with Claudia. Again, Riley gathered up all her mother's belongings—still nothing."

Katarina stared like she was trying to get a read on him. She'd known him well when they were younger, and he'd never been good at lying. What it did do was teach him how to disguise his emotions and hide his feelings. She was on the defense and he the offense. Now, he waited.

"You know what this means. Until I get what I want or find out you're lying, you'll never know what corner I might be around. I want that information. And if my promise of killing Riley isn't enough initiative for you, I can convince the US spymasters you're a traitor—you know they won't hesitate to silence you for good." Katarina closed the distance and brought her mouth to Dagger's ear. "I'm watching you and Riley. You can't keep her tucked away forever. She's going to her mother's funeral tomorrow and then the memorial dinner. I can get my hands on her any time I want. I have to say, it would be my pleasure to inflict my newest torture techniques…just to watch her suffer. Don't forget it, Dagger. In the meantime, we'll be spending more quality time together." Kat squeezed his butt as she turned and kissed him on the mouth.

Dagger turned to walk away. He wasn't going to give her anything more, and he knew she wouldn't shoot him in the back—at least not yet.

"I mean it, Dagger, when I call, you come."

****

Riley sat up. She felt deeply uneasy. She looked out at the water and scanned the beach. Noticing movement at the tree line, she focused on the spot and saw Dagger walking with a woman with dark hair. The woman reached out and grabbed Dagger's shoulder. He turned toward her as she closed the distance between them.

The woman whispered in his ear, kissed him, and patted his butt…Was this his *difficult client?* If she was difficult, then easy was a live strip dancer. Whoever she was, their relationship wasn't professional—unless you thought all hired help welcomed being felt up. Dagger turned away and started back to the house. Riley pulled up the covers and turned away from the windows, but she couldn't stop seeing the view—over and over again.

****

Her mother's funeral was three days ago and Riley was still on an emotional rollercoaster. Attending that phony funeral turned out to be more difficult than Riley thought. The church hadn't been able to hold all the people who came to pay their respects. She'd shook hands and hugged until her arms were numb. She'd even cried real tears. The kind words, life stories, and grieving attendees overwhelmed Riley.

Despite his mysterious client, Riley was grateful when Dagger insisted they stay at his place yesterday. It gave her the needed time to rest and regenerate. She'd taken a nap and woke to find Stone there and Dagger gone. Stone told her Dagger had a last-minute meeting with those same difficult clients. Yet something about the way Stone handled himself needled her. He wasn't the easygoing, chatty man she'd come to know. He was quiet, even reserved. When Dagger returned, he seemed distant and aloof with her. Something had happened and neither man was going to tell her what. She pushed her feelings back into the dark places in her mind and readied herself for another ordeal. Tonight's event would no doubt be another phony funeral; how could she continue this charade?

****

"This is breathtaking," said Riley, as she and Dagger entered the ballroom. The mahogany floor was a deep reddish-brown with a flawless high gloss finish. Tables dotted the outer edge of the room and were covered with crisp white tablecloths; the chairs were high-back with black velvet upholstered cushions. The tall, glass centerpieces were cylindrical vases filled with water and a submersed red rose. White tealight candles floated on top. Crystal chandeliers glowed, giving the enormous room a warm, cozy feel.

"Breathtaking and gorgeous," Dagger replied, looking directly into Riley's eyes.

Riley wore a long, deep-purple evening gown with tightly-fitting long sleeves and a straight neckline meeting the sleeves at the shoulders. The dress fit as if it were custom made, flowing like honey over every curve and then flaring out at the bottom. The fabric shimmered as she moved.

Dagger had asked Riley why she didn't wear the typical black for mourning. She'd told him her mother always loved purple on her and this was her way of celebrating Claudia's life. Riley's hair was curled, and she'd pulled the sides and top back loosely, forming what looked like a square-knot on the back of her head, and letting the rest hang freely. The style accented her slim, pale bronze neck and artfully covered the scar on her forehead, which was healing nicely. Dangling diamond earrings were the only jewelry she wore.

Forget the event, he could watch her all night. No other woman even came close to her beauty.

"Stop looking at me like that. You're going to make me blush," Riley murmured.

"I'd like to see that. It would only add to your allure."

"You don't look so bad yourself. You wear that tuxedo like it was made for you." She gave him a quick up and down glance and flashed him a little smile.

Dagger was surprised at her interaction with him, considering the last few days had been strained between them. He'd play along. It gave him a chance to enjoy his time with her. "If we weren't here to honor your mother and look for leads, I'd carry you out this second."

She frowned slightly and looked away. Dagger wanted to kick himself. What the hell did he expect? Mixed signals had been the norm for a while now.

"Riley, you're here. Might I say, you look amazing. Your mother would be proud," said a tall, thin, older man impeccably dressed in a tuxedo.

"Good evening, Vice President. I'd like to introduce my escort, Dagger Eastin. Dagger, I'd like you to meet Dr. Kevin Bender. He is the Provost and Vice President for Academic Affairs at the university."

The two men shook hands and exchanged pleasantries.

"Come this way, there are some people waiting to meet you," urged Dr. Bender.

"Good evening, Riley," said a distinguished looking man.

He was well-built for his age, which Dagger guessed was early sixties. The man had salt-and-pepper hair, arranged in a pristine, high-fashion cut. He was dressed in a designer tuxedo, tailored especially for him, possibly one-of-a-kind based on the cut and fabric. Dagger figured the man's grooming and dress alone would pay one month's mortgage payment on his cabin.

"Riley, I'm sure you and—" Dr. Bender said.

"Good evening, Anthony. It's so good of you to take time from your demanding schedule to be here tonight. My mother would be honored."

"I wouldn't have missed it. I am sorry I've been remiss about contacting you and offering my condolences. Claudia was a wonderful woman and a huge influence on the marine biology community. She will be greatly missed. Who's your escort?" Anthony glanced at Dagger.

"Anthony Welby, meet Dagger Eastin," Riley said.

"Pleased to make your acquaintance," Dagger said.

"Dagger Eastin. Hmm. Where might I have heard your name before?" Anthony asked. Dagger got the distinct impression this man was sizing him up.

"My company was hired to find and retrieve the research vessel that sank with Dr. Rawlings aboard," Dagger said.

"Oh, yes. I was chatting with Wayne Samuels just the other day. He must have mentioned you by name. I called Wayne to offer my assistance. The loss of the ship was a tragedy, as was the devastating loss of Claudia. You know she meant a great deal to me."

"Thank you," Riley said.

"I won't keep you any longer, Riley," Anthony said. "There are many people I must see before the memorial begins. Please feel free to call me should you require anything." Anthony turned and walked away.

"What did you think of Anthony?" Riley whispered to him after the man left.

"I think he's pompous and full of himself, isn't he?"

"That about sums him up," she said with a laugh.

They spent the next hour talking to scholars, leading people in their fields, CEOs of conglomerates, the mayor of San Diego, several politicians, and some high-ranking military officers.

A tall man in a Navy dress uniform walked up and offered Riley his hand. "Good evening, Riley. I want you to know how sorry I am for the loss of your mother. She was not only a good friend, she was also a brilliant researcher and will be greatly missed."

"Thank you, Vice Admiral Morrison. It's an honor to have you in attendance tonight. This is my escort, Dagger Eastin."

Dagger snapped to attention. He may well be out of the military, but the military would never be out of him. "It's a pleasure to meet you, Vice Admiral," Dagger said and reached out to shake the man's hand. "I was on your ship a number of times during my career. It was always an honor."

"Yes. I remember you, Commander Eastin. You had an excellent salvage team. It was always a treat to have you on board.

It was what, a dozen times through the years, give or take, correct?"

"Yes, sir. Twelve times." Dagger was surprised the admiral remembered him.

"I hear you and two of your teammates now run a private salvage diving company."

"We do, sir. Please call us if we can ever be of service."

"I'll keep it in mind, Commander." He reached inside his double-breasted, dress blue jacket, and pulled out a card. "Take my card. If you ever need anything, don't hesitate to call on me. Do you happen to have a business card?"

Dagger reached into his jacket and pulled a card free. "Of course, sir, and thank you."

The evening was both torment and pride for Riley, who forced herself to look appropriately grieving at every turn.

Riley had continuously praised her mother since the first day he'd met her. Tonight, Dagger was learning that Riley herself had a notable career.

"I wasn't aware you are so well known in your field, too. Are you thinking of one day moving on from teaching and venturing into research?" Dagger asked her.

"I'm not well known, it's a small world I work in."

"Funny, most people's small worlds don't include mayors and rear admirals."

"They're my mother's friends, that's why they're here. They only know me because I'm her daughter. I'd love a glass of wine."

He wrapped her hand around his arm and walked her toward the bar. "Normally I would go get you a drink and bring it back, except I'm afraid you'd get swallowed up in another swarm of guests."

They had almost made it to the bar when Wayne Samuels stopped them. "Good evening, Riley. Eastin. This is a lovely turnout," Samuels said. "Your mother was a brilliant scientist. The world has lost someone who had the capacity to make a significant contribution."

"She made her mark. Others will remember her as one of the top marine biologists in the world, but I will simply remember her as my loving mother."

"Oh, of course." Samuels looked at Dagger. "No bad feelings, eh, Eastin? I'm sure we can do business in the future."

"Don't count on it. If you'll excuse us, we were on our way to the bar." Dagger didn't wait for a response from Samuels. He placed his hand over Riley's, whose hold on his upper arm was quickly becoming a death grip, and they walked away.

But before they could make it to the bar, another man stepped in front of them. "Good evening, Ms. Rawlings. My name is Neal, I'm Provost Bender's assistant. I wanted to show you and your escort to your table. We'll be sitting down to dine shortly."

Before he'd left the shop tonight, Dagger had played the recording of Claudia's phone message several times to memorize the voice of the man in the background. Riley hit the nail on the head; this was the guy. She behaved like a pro, smiling and nodding at Neal as he led them across the ballroom and up to the head table.

"Thank you, Neal," she said. "Your name sounds familiar. I believe my mother spoke of you."

"She did?" The tone of Neal's voice raised an octave. "She was a wonderful woman. I was her student assistant during her last year at the university." He beamed.

"That's right. She mentioned you a few times during our weekly phone calls."

"Here we are," Neal said, showing them their seats. "If there's anything you need, or anything I can do for you, please let me know." He nodded and walked away.

"Well done," Dagger bent down and whispered into her ear as he helped her into her chair.

"Thanks, I think," Riley said. "And the first thing I'm going to do when we get back to your place is soak in the hottest bath I can for an hour. With hope, some of the slime that's covering me will melt away." Riley's smile never faltered.

****

After dinner, Dr. Bender walked up to the microphone and read a touching speech outlining Claudia's contributions and special projects. He praised Claudia and Riley as her mother's daughter.

When the speeches finally ended, Dagger whispered, "Are you tired?"

"A little; still, I'd love to dance,' Riley said. "The bath can wait a little while longer."

Dagger rose and helped her from the chair and led her out to the dance floor. Most of the guests had stayed and were enjoying the dancing and conversation.

"I'd like to get another chance at Neal. He didn't act like a person who had a hand in her death," Riley said.

"Let's not push it. We need him to feel comfortable with you."

"But, Dagger, he's our only link to that night. I don't know how much longer I can wait."

"We'll make sure to talk with him soon."

Chapter Twenty-Five

"Thank you for seeing me on such short notice, Admiral Morrison," Dagger said as he stood in the doorway of the admiral's home. "I want you to know this isn't like me. I never had any intention of imposing on you. Unfortunately, I've found myself in a bit of a predicament."

"You're not imposing, son. Come on in and tell me what's going on," Admiral Morrison said.

The admiral walked Dagger through the house to a large glass-enclosed veranda full of plants and palm trees. A stone-lined pool filled one side, irregularly shaped, with two waterfalls. The admiral sat and Dagger followed suit.

"How can I help you, Dagger?"

"Well, sir, I've been retired from the Navy for two years now. I'm no longer in on the scuttlebutt and I need to know who's a good source and who isn't. When Riley explained to me that you and Claudia had been friends for years, I knew you were the person I needed to speak with."

The admiral stroked his chin and replied. "I see. You've got yourself into a heap of trouble and don't want the wrong people to know. Tell you what. Why don't you start from the beginning? Maybe I can help you find a course of action."

"It's not that I don't want to tell you. I just don't want to get you involved."

"Dagger, you're here because you want my help. Tell me your story and let me decide what I will and won't do."

"Have you heard of a marine archaeologist by the name of Katarina Petrin?" Dagger asked.

"Of course. There were rumors she was a sleeper agent for theSoviet Union. I heard she was jailed as a traitor and murdered by another inmate a few years back. Hold on..." The admiral sat up and eyed Dagger. "You were the officer she was engaged to. I knew there was something else about you I couldn't recall. As I remember, the military and CIA put you through the proverbial ringer, but nothing stuck," Morrison said.

"This probably sounds idiotic, but I knew nothing about her other identity," Dagger said.

"Well, son. You know what they say—love is blind."

"And makes you stupid," Dagger said.

The admiral chuckled. "I hope that wasn't why you retired. You're a good man and a great commander."

"You honor me. Thank you, sir. No, it wasn't why I retired. Although I was on the verge of retiring a time or two during the entire fiasco. Eventually I put in twenty-one years and decided I wanted to start my own company."

"Good for you. Let's circle back, shall we. Why are you here today, Dagger?"

"I'm here because recently I heard from her. She told me the government made her a deal four years ago. Apparently, she has an endless list of connections with Russian criminals, mafia, black-marketeers, you name it. Katarina told me she has the ability to retrieve the information others don't. She also said she's a private contractor and works for who she wants, when she wants. I've no idea if any of what she says is true. What I do know is she's after Claudia's research and has been dogging me for the past couple weeks. The research is potentially important to a lot of people and I've no idea if she's working for the Russians, Americans, or a private individual. I initially told her I wouldn't help her."

"Since you're here, I'm assuming she found a way to get to you."

"She did. She told me she could make it look like I was in cahoots with her all along. She says she has evidence to plant. Since what she was spewing was complete crap, I told her as much. It was at that point she threatened Riley's life. Admiral, I swear to you, I was never involved with Katarina in that manner back then or now. I knew nothing about her being a sleeper agent and would never turn my back on my country. But now that Riley's involved, I can't take the chance with her life."

"I see. You've no evidence to take to the police. You might be able to collect evidence and present your case to the authorities, but that would take time. If her claims are credible, or her evidence well-forged, you'd end up in the unforgiving hands of the CIA."

"Admiral, Katarina repeated her initial threat and told me if I went to the authorities, she would kill Riley. If you're willing, I'm hoping you might know someone who could verify Katarina's status. Find out exactly who she's working for."

"I've known Claudia and Riley for years, and I certainly don't want Claudia's daughter hurt. I've got a good friend I can contact who can check on Ms. Petrin's status. Before you even ask, he will be discreet and tell no one. We've had each other's backs for longer than I can recall. Let me go make a call."

"Thank you, Admiral."

"You're in luck," Morrison said as he walked back to Dagger. "My contact happened to be working on a Sunday. According to Katarina's handler, she hasn't gone to Russia in several months. She's been in the States and in London, but he hasn't heard from her in a few weeks."

"Katarina's working for someone," Dagger said. "I have no idea who. She only said one thing that I believe: she has no loyalty to anything but money, and this person or country is the highest bidder."

"You think they hired her with the intention of throwing you off your game?"

"That's what I'd do, or she could've been involved all along and is just now making her presence known." Dagger stood up to leave.

"Riley is still in danger, isn't she? This entire situation somehow revolves around her and her mom's research."

"Yes, it does. Don't worry. We're keeping her safe."

"Dagger, don't hesitate to contact me again. If there's anything I can do to keep Claudia's daughter safe, I'll do it. Either way, I would appreciate you touching base when this thing is over, just to let me know Riley's safe."

Dagger left the admiral's and stopped to get coffee. Sitting in his SUV, he pulled out his burner phone and pressed the button for the only saved number.

"What the hell, man. We're a team, we do things—as—a—

team. What possessed you to go rogue?"

"Thanks for your concern, Kaleb. I love you, too. I take it Riley's not around."

"No. She and Stone went out for a walk. Riley knows something is up. I have a sneaking suspicion she doesn't believe your 'difficult client' story. You're a real jackass, you know. You might've just screwed up the best thing you'll ever have. She keeps asking us where you went and why you went alone."

"What'd you tell her?"

"You had an emergency you needed to deal with, just like you said."

"Thanks, Kaleb."

"Don't make us run interference for you—with her or Katarina," Kaleb snapped. "You coming back to the office?"

"Not yet. I need to get a bead on Kat. I'm going to check out a couple people and places where she used to hang out."

"If you get into trouble, you damn well better call us."

"I'll be fine. You and Stone keep Riley safe."

"Yeah, about that…Riley says she's going back to teaching tomorrow. How do you want us to handle it?"

"Regardless of what we think, she's going to do what she wants. One of the two of you guards her at all times," Dagger said.

"She refuses to have one of us stay at the university with her," Kaleb said. "I've already contacted my buddy who owns the private personal security company. He's putting his best guys on her. They will meet us at the university tomorrow."

"No questions asked?" Dagger asked.

"Never. Just another contract for him," Kaleb said. "You'll be back tomorrow, right?"

"That's my plan."

"Good to know. By the way, I've been on the computer all day researching Katarina."

"And?" Dagger asked.

"Someone set up an intensive smoke screen. Says Katarina Petrin was killed while incarcerated. There's no more information anywhere, including the dark web. This smells like CIA. Gotta go. They're on the way in. You stay safe, or I'll kill you."

Chapter Twenty-Six

Riley stared up at the ceiling in Dagger's bedroom. Kaleb insisted she sleep downstairs, so he could hear her during the night. No one had heard from Dagger. At least that's what Kaleb told her. Even so, something gnawed at her. When she casually asked the guys if Dagger had a girlfriend, Kaleb had started to say something about a Ka—until Stone elbowed him in the ribs and Kaleb changed his story. She hadn't pushed the matter further, because they both clammed up and acted uncomfortable.

She'd thought something was starting between her and Dagger—was she wrong? The kisses between them had moved into the sizzling category, from her perspective. Now she felt like he was trying to distance himself from her. She was even more than a little agitated that he'd not explained his sudden absence.

Maybe the budding relationship was all in her mind. Was she staying in his house only because she'd hired him to do a job, or did he want to keep her safe? Riley moaned and rolled over. This entire idea that he had feelings for her was all in her head. She was only here because of Dagger's sense of responsibility.

She groaned and threw a pillow over her head. His scent permeated the pillow. If nothing else, she was sure he would explain when he returned—she hoped. She needed to quiet her thoughts and sleep. She was going back to the university in the morning and she needed to focus. She rolled on to her side and hugged his pillow.

****

"I want to thank you and Kaleb for keeping watch over me, and for making it possible for me to return to the university," Riley said as she and Stone got into his car.

"We don't want anything to happen to you, Riley. Not only because you're currently our mission, but because you mean a great deal to all of us, especially Dagger." Stone pulled out of the drive and headed for the university. An SUV pulled up behind them. "There's your bodyguard," Stone nodded to the sideview mirror. "He'll be shadowing you the entire time."

****

"Good morning. I'd like to see Dean Richards," Riley greeted the secretary. Dean Richards was Riley's boss.

"Good morning, Dr. Rawlings. It's so nice to see you. I'm so sorry about your mother," the secretary said. "The Dean is currently in a meeting. If you'd like to sit and wait, he shouldn't be much longer."

"Thank you," Riley took a seat and ran through her talking points.

A few minutes later, the door to the Dean's office opened and he bid a man good-bye.

"Riley, it's good to see you," Dean Richards said.

"I was hoping to get a few minutes of your time, sir."

"Certainly. After you."

She sat in the chair in front of his desk.

"What is it you'd like to discuss?" he asked.

"You've been very accommodating, and I want you to know how much I appreciate it. At this point though, I still have so much to deal with that I think it's unfair to the students if I were to return now. I realize you might have to fill my position."

"I had a meeting with Provost Bender yesterday. We both agreed to grant you leave for the reminder of the quarter. We'll keep the professor who is filling in for you until then."

Riley was speechless. She was positive she would be packing up her office today for good.

"Thank you, sir. This is more than I could've hoped for. Should I clean out my office?"

"I think we can manage with locking it up and awaiting your return. Take what you want for now, the rest will be safe. I do have one favor."

"Certainly."

"Would you mind spending a few hours with the substitute professor, just to see how she's doing and answer any questions she might have?"

"I'll be happy to help her any time she wants it."

****

Riley could no longer put off speaking with her mother's attorney. She squared her shoulders, picked up her office phone, and tapped in the numbers.

"Thank you for taking my call, Ms. Berry," Riley said, as she sat at her office desk, tapping her pencil on a pad of paper.

"Please call me Loreen, Riley. We've known each other for years. I've been wondering when I would hear from you. I expect you're overwhelmed, dealing with the death of Claudia. Don't forget, we need to go through her will and her other documents."

"I'm sorry for being a bit slow, but with everything..." She made a doodle of wild circles on the paper. "Actually, I do have a question with regards to my mother's documents."

"Any specific information you're looking for?"

"Did Mom leave you any documentation in relation to her employer?"

"I drafted an agreement between Sheridan Enterprises and Claudia, signed by both parties, prior to her accepting her position."

"What did it say?"

"Sheridan Enterprises agreed that any and all research Claudia started prior to her official start date with the company belonged solely to her. Along with a second document stipulating that she can use company facilities for her own research on her own time and still retain sole ownership of the research."

"And Wayne Samuels agreed to both?"

"Yes. He came down to my office and signed the contracts, both times."

"Were those the only two items?"

"That's everything."

"Thank you for your time, Loreen. I'll be by soon."

Riley shoved her notes in her pocket, locked her office door, and headed to the classroom to assist her replacement. At lunch time, she left her building and walked to the administration building. She smiled and nodded at the bodyguard who'd been following her all day.

She took the stairs up to the top floor, Dr. Bender's office. It exuded elegance and upper-crust style.

"Good afternoon. I was wondering if I might have a few

minutes with Dr. Bender's assistant?" Riley asked.

"I'm sorry. Neal's left for lunch. Is there something I can help you with?"

"Did he happen to tell you if he was leaving campus?"

"Neal stays on campus for lunch most days." The receptionist glanced at his computer. "He's probably on the walking trails now."

"Thank you." Riley caught the elevator and walked out to the trails.

"Would you mind giving me some space?" She turned and asked the guard. "I have a personal matter I need to discuss."

"No problem, Dr. Rawlings, I'll stay out of earshot, but I won't leave you alone; I'll keep you in my sights," the bodyguard said.

She'd walked for a bit on the main trail when she spotted Neal. Picking up her speed, she reached him. "Good afternoon, Neal."

He spun around in surprise and placed his hand on his chest. "Dr. Rawlings, you gave me a start."

"I'm terribly sorry, I thought you heard me coming."

"It's good to see you. Are you returning to campus?"

"Not just yet, Neal. Why were you on board my mother's research vessel?"

He spun around. "Pardon?"

"I have a recording of my mother's call when you entered her stateroom and told her she needed to leave."

"You must have me confused with someone else." Neal's face drained of color.

"I'll make you a deal. Tell me why and how you got involved in all this, and I won't take my recording to the police. I only want to know what happened to my mother."

Neal crumpled like a slowly deflating balloon. "I need to sit down." He fumbled over to the bench a few yards off the path and Riley followed. "I'll tell you what I know, if you promise not to tell Provost Bender."

"I promise," Riley replied.

"He has no idea what I've done. In spite of everything, I still love my job. I've worked for Provost Bender for three years now and I'd like to keep working for him. When Mr. White first contacted me, he explained that I'd be asked to acquire certain information from Dr. Bender's files or current projects."

"You spied on your boss and jeopardized the position you say you love?" Riley asked.

"I was naive." Neal paused as two runners approached them and passed by. "Mr. White promised he was going to offer Dr. Rawlings a position she could not refuse at his prestigious company. Mr. White made me a great offer to recruit her."

"Who's Mr. White?"

"I don't know him personally, he's a CEO who contacts me on a special phone." Neal fiddled with the zipper on his jacket. "Mr. White told me it was urgent. He had to see Dr. Rawlings and asked me to escort her off the boat directly to his office. A helicopter took me and Eric out to the ship, and we went to talk to Dr. Rawlings. But before I knew what was happening, Eric pulled out a syringe and injected her. I didn't know she'd be unconscious. You have to believe me, I would never hurt Dr. Rawlings."

"You helped him knock out my mother and kidnap her?" The pitch of Riley's voice rose in distress.

"I didn't have a choice. My mother is ill. She needs a nursing home and I can't afford it! They offered to cover all my mother's expenses forever, if I just helped them this one time."

"Tell me what happened next," she demanded.

"Dr. Rawlings was startled by my appearance. She wanted to know how I got on board. I told her I would explain everything after we were safe. Out of nowhere Eric materialized and injected her. He took Dr. Rawlings and told me to get up to the helicopter. As soon as I got on the helicopter, it took off. I screamed at the pilot to wait for them. He ignored me and flew me back to the airport."

"What happened to Eric and my mother?" she asked, finding it difficult to keep her anger reined in.

"I don't know. Since then, Eric called me a couple times to get information about you. I was afraid to ask him about that night. But my best guess is Eric threw your mother overboard." Neal's face was awash with tears. "You must believe me. I never would've gotten involved if I knew their ultimate plan was to kill Dr. Rawlings. What I told you the night of the memorial event was true; I thought of her as a friend. She got me the position with Dr. Bender."

Firecrackers exploded somewhere close to them. Riley heard people screaming and realized it wasn't firecrackers, it was gunshots. The next thing she knew, something knocked her to the ground, and she felt a razor-sharp pain in her arm.

"Neal, get down! Those are gunshots!" When he didn't react,

Riley pulled on his arm.

He slumped over and landed on top of Riley. A bright red splotch covered the left side of Neal's chest.

Chapter Twenty-Seven

"**H**oly hell," Kaleb said, jumping up from his desk like a sidewinder was slithering toward him.

"What?" Stone asked.

"We've got to get over to the university, pronto. Riley's bodyguard just texted me."

"What'd he say?" Stone asked.

"Shooting at campus. Dr. Rawlings involved. Come immediately." Kaleb read.

Minutes later, Stone and Kaleb were speeding in the direction of the university in Stone's Mustang.

"Anything more from the bodyguard?" Stone asked.

"Nothing. But the media is running rampant. Social sites are filling with students' posts," Kaleb said. "Currently the casualties are two; one with minor injuries and one killed."

Stone glanced over at his partner. "But the bodyguard didn't say Riley was hurt, just involved."

"Yeah, but he didn't say she wasn't," Kaleb pointed out. "And I'm just getting a damn busy signal…circuits must be overloaded."

Stone punched the gas pedal to the floor.

When they reached the university, police cars, fire engines, and news vans blocked their way. Kaleb jumped out of the Mustang and Stone looked for a place park the car. Kaleb made a beeline to a group of girls. They were all on their phones, taking selfies, interviewing each other, and chatting with anyone who stopped to listen.

"Excuse me, ladies. Can you tell me what all the excitement is about?" Kaleb asked and flashed them his friendliest smile. The entire group of girls fixated on him, their eyes as big as silver dollars and their smiles warm and welcoming.

"You haven't heard?" asked a cute little redhead wearing skin-tight jeans and a snug pink sweater.

Stone strolled up to join the group with his hands in his jeans pockets, looking relaxed like he was going to ask one of them to dance. Half of the girls were immediately drawn to him. "Afternoon, ladies. I see my buddy has already made your acquaintance."

"He has. You guys don't know what's going on?" the redhead asked.

"There was a shooting on the walking trails," a blue-eyed blonde said.

"A shooting? Is everyone okay?" Stone asked.

"No, two people got hurt," another girl said.

"We heard one person is dead," a fourth girl pipped in.

"That's awful," Stone said. "Doesn't look like we're going to make our meeting with the athletic director. He was interested in hiring us as assistant football coaches."

All the girls' faces lit up like it was Christmas morning and Stone and Kaleb were the gifts they were dying to unwrap.

"Really?" squealed the redhead, bouncing up and down on her toes. "Our sorority house is on the far side of the trails and the director's office is a short distance from the house. The police are kinda blocking the road, 'cause of the shooting and all...but we could get you close." She winked at Stone.

"We can't ask you to go out of your way," Kaleb said.

The blonde walked up to Kaleb and slid her arm through his. "You're not asking, we're offering. C'mon." The girl gave him a tug, and he took the cue.

The redhead grabbed Stone by the upper arm and snuggled up so close he could feel her underwire and everything it supported. "So, if you two decide to take the coaching positions, I guess we'll be seeing a lot of one another. I'm the head cheerleader. We practice the same time the team does." Her smile was blinding.

The group slowed as they approached a flurry of police activity.

"That's the building right over there," one of the girls said. "You might have a bit of trouble getting around the police."

"We'll be fine. Thanks for the escort," Stone said.

"Give me your phone?" The redhead asked Stone. The blonde stuck her hand out at Kaleb, who tried his best to look confused.

Stone patted himself down. "I seem to have left it in my car...why?"

"I wanted to give you my digits." She put her hands on her hips and pouted.

"Here, use this," one of her friends handed her a pen. The redhead took the pen and pushed Stone's sleeve up to his elbow. Bracing his arm close to her chest, she wrote out her number, name, and lastly a heart. Her blonde friend repeated the process on Kaleb's arm. "And don't worry if you forget to put it in your phone right away—that's a Sharpie. It won't come off for days," the blonde said, stroking Kaleb's arm.

"Sometimes even longer," another girl said.

Stone and Kaleb smiled and waved until the girls were nearly out of sight.

"So, old man, must be nice to know you still got it. That redhead was all over you. Sure you don't want me to take care of Riley? I'll bet the sorority will have a party tonight if you go back after our 'interview' and tell them you got the job," Kaleb said, a grin creasing his face from ear to ear.

"Funny. At least the redhead had good taste. Let's go find Riley before they change their mind and come looking for us," Stone replied, pulling his sleeve back down.

As they got closer to the murder site, the amount of people increased. Stone and Kaleb stopped near the yellow crime scene tape. They scrutinized the marked-off area. A body covered in a sheet was stretched out partially under a bench.

"I only see one body," Stone said.

"Let's hope to all that's good it's not Riley," Kaleb said.

"You two can stop right there. This is a crime scene. No civilians," said a police officer as he approached them.

"You don't understand. We've been hired by Dr. Rawlings for her protection." Kaleb flipped out his credentials.

"Says you. Stay right here. Don't move. And if you try to get any closer to the scene, I will have you escorted off the campus." The officer walked over to a group of police. Riley's bodyguard stepped out of the group and nodded at the officer who had confronted the guys. They shook hands and the bodyguard headed for Stone and Kaleb.

"I was with her, just like you instructed," the bodyguard said as he approached the guys. "She asked for a little space so that she could speak privately to somebody, but I stayed close. I still had eyes on her, I swear. Good thing the sergeant on scene is a buddy of mine. Come with me and I'll take you to her. She's right over there." The bodyguard pointed.

Stone's heart jumped into his throat when the guard pointed in the direction of the bench. "Is she okay?"

"She will be. She's in the middle of the group of people several yards past the bench," the bodyguard said.

"Thank you, Jesus," Stone mumbled to himself.

The two guys followed the bodyguard around the outside of the taped-off scene, passing by a couple officers standing guard. They walked over to the edge of a parking lot, where the large group was gathered.

"She's over here." The bodyguard lead them past the group in the direction of the ambulance. "They want to see Dr. Rawlings. She's family."

"She's been waiting for you two," the medic said.

Riley sat in the open doorway of the back of the ambulance. Her face was covered in dirt, she had a gash on her temple, and her clothes were covered with blood. A medic was bandaging her upper arm. Her opposite arm had a blood pressure cuff wrapped around it.

She looked up and sent them a tired smile. "Stone, Kaleb, I'm so happy you're here."

"Are you all right?" Stone asked.

"I think so. A bullet went through the meaty part of my arm. I didn't feel it happen right away. I hit the ground and then felt a sharp pain; I thought I fell on something as I hit the ground. I yelled for Neal to get down. When he didn't react, I grabbed him and pulled him down. But he was dead. I can't even process it. One minute we're sitting over there talking and the next instant, he's dead."

"Bender's Neal?" Kaleb asked.

"Yes." Riley stopped as a medic approached.

"We need to take you to the hospital and have the doctors look at that wound," the medic said.

"I'm a doctor," Stone said, as he pulled his medical ID card from his wallet. "I'll take her home and keep watch on her condition, if she agrees."

"Have they questioned you yet?" Kaleb asked.

"Yes," Riley said. "I told the detective that Neal and I were taking a walk together."

"Good," Kaleb said. "Did they tell you when you can leave?"

"They wrote down all my information. They told me I was free to go as soon as the medics cleared me," Riley said.

When they reached Dagger's place, Kaleb jumped out and did a quick search of the perimeter. He triggered the garage door open and Stone drove in. Stone and Riley waited in the Mustang as Kaleb cleared the house.

"I'm so fortunate you guys came into my life. I don't think I'd be alive now, if not for your support and education. Thank you," she said.

"I'd say all in a day's work, but you're kinda growing on us." Stone smiled. "Did they catch the shooter?"

"I don't think so," Riley said.

"Your bodyguard told us that Neal was the only person killed," Stone said.

Riley's eyes widened. "Do you think someone was waiting there to shoot Neal? The secretary at his office told me he spends most lunch breaks there."

"It's a possibility. Neal signed his own death warrant the day he agreed to work for—"

"Mr. White," she said.

"Who?" Kaleb asked as he walked up to her side of the car. Riley startled, not hearing him approach. "Sorry. Who's Mr. White?"

"Let's go in and settle into some comfortable chairs and I'll tell you everything Neal told me." She pulled a couple small sheets of paper out of her pocket. "Darn it. I forgot to tell you they gave me these prescriptions to fill. I think I'm going to want them tonight."

"Let me see them," Stone said. "Pain killers and muscle relaxers. There's some here. I brought them over for Dagger after the spear went through him. I found them in the kitchen cabinet today. I should have known he wouldn't take them. These are going to knock you out. Do you think you can tell us what happened before you take these?"

"I think so. Let's make it quick."

****

Dagger's phone vibrated in his pocket for the tenth time since he'd arrived in San Francisco. He pulled it out as he headed back to his vehicle and looked at the screen and saw *911 Hunters and*

Seekers displayed—their emergency signal.

He swore a long line of curse words as he waited for one of the guys to answer the phone.

"Where in the holy hell have you been?" Stone asked. "We were getting ready to send someone out to track you down. Last thing we need is another frigging emergency."

"I'm fine. What's going on?" Dagger asked.

"Yesterday morning I dropped Riley off at the university and her bodyguard took up his station. Yesterday afternoon there was a shooting on the campus."

"Son of a bitch! Tell me she wasn't shot?"

"I would be lying."

"Tell me she's okay?"

"She took a bullet to the upper arm. It went clean through but did some soft tissue damage. She was with Neal at the time. He was pronounced dead on the scene."

"Where was the bodyguard?"

"About twenty-feet away. Nobody can protect against a sniper. Look, I don't know if you're done trying to save Katarina from herself or not. Either way, you need to haul your ass back here—pronto."

"Don't be a dumbass. I wasn't trying to save her," Dagger snapped. "I'm in San Francisco. I went to the company where she was employed when we first met. I'll fill you in when I get back. Keep Riley safe, will you?"

****

Dagger pulled into his garage next to the Mustang. He jumped out of his Range Rover, leaving it to stop abruptly up against his workbench. He ran into the kitchen and found Stone and Kaleb working.

"Riley's sleeping. It's the best thing for her right now," Stone said before Dagger could get out a word.

"How is she?" Dagger whispered.

"She was running a slight temperature. It could be an infection. I gave her some meds and I'm hoping she'll sleep through the day. She should feel better tomorrow."

"What happened? Don't tell me she went to question Neal on her own."

"Of course not. Our bodyguard was with her. She asked the guard to give her space to speak with Neal privately," Kaleb said.

"Did Neal tell her anything?" Dagger asked, as Kaleb shoved a beer in his hand.

"Let's put it this way. He told her the version of the story he'd been fed," Kaleb said.

Dagger sat and listened as Kaleb repeated what Riley had told them.

"You're telling me Neal didn't know what was really gonna happen?"

"Just a pawn on the board," Kaleb said as he took a swig of beer.

"And now we have a new player," said Stone. "Assuming Eric is the sack of shit who's been shadowing you and who shot Neal, then we have to ask who this Mr. White might be?"

"No—did you already forget? We have two new players, Katarina and Mr. White," Dagger said. He filled the guys in on his last two days.

"Damn—we're gonna need a bigger whiteboard," Kaleb said.

"I'm hoping we're gonna stop finding new bad guys and gals. I didn't run into Katarina once while I was gone. I find it difficult to believe she didn't know where I was. So, it begs the question—what was more important?"

"You think this is two separate groups with different goals, or are they all working together?" Stone asked.

Dagger shook his head. "Honestly, I have no frigging idea."

****

The day bled into evening before they finished reviewing all their information.

"Katarina has always been short on patience. Best guess is we have a day, maybe two, before she's back in the picture," Dagger said.

"It's late. We're all tired. Let's call it a night and start back fresh tomorrow. We already have dibs on the two guest rooms. Guess that only leaves sharing a bed with Riley—again." Stone said giving Dagger a sideways glance.

"You can tell us to mind our own business, but we've always kept one another in the loop," Kaleb said. "So…just what the hell is your relationship with her?" Kaleb asked.

"Nothing's happened," Dagger said. He yanked the half-empty beer bottle out of Kaleb's hand and tossed it into the trash. Kaleb raised his hands in surrender.

"Don't be so defensive, bro," Stone said as he shoved his shoulder into Dagger's. "You know damn well that's not what Kaleb was asking."

"Yeah, I know. Guess I'm a little edgy…because I can't figure it out myself."

"We haven't seen you so smitten with a woman since Kat," Stone said.

"Smitten, really?" Dagger said as he rolled his eyes and shook his head.

"Stone's right. You got a way about you when Riley's around we haven't seen in over six years. But now Kat's back, and you were head over heels stupid about her."

"Thanks for the reminder, buddy." Dagger scrubbed his face with his hands, trying to erase the last thirty-six hours from him thoughts.

"Just don't be a jackass. If there's even the slightest chance you're going to bring Katarina back into your life, don't mess with Riley's head or heart," Stone said.

"What the hell!" Dagger dropped his hands and pinned Stone with his laser stare. "You really think I'm *that* much of a douchebag?" He crossed his arms over his chest.

"Thank God you're not going to bring that double-crossing, traitorous, ex-fiancée crazy bitch back into our lives," Kaleb said, twitching his head and shoulders.

"Tell me how you really feel," Dagger grunted.

"When are you going to tell Riley about Katarina?" Stone asked.

"I'll tell her…soon."

"Oooookay, just don't wait too long, 'cause she'll find out. Mark my words. It's that woman-thingy," Kaleb said.

"If the two of you are finished grilling me, I've been up for thirty-six hours and I'm beat." Dagger headed for his bedroom.

"She's a keeper." Kaleb jabbed Dagger in the arm as he walked by.

Riley was sound asleep on one side of the bed. She was curled into a ball, making her appear even smaller in his huge bed. Dagger went into the master bath and got in the shower, the cool water raining down on him.

Tomorrow was going to be difficult.

He prayed that the Katarina complication would not drive Riley away.

He toweled off and went back into the bedroom. He put on a fresh pair of cotton drawstring pants, slid into bed, and moved close to the sleeping Riley. She slept peacefully; but he could see the pain etched on her face. Was it physical or emotional? Dagger's last thought before drifting off was that he hoped he had not been the one who put the pain on Riley's face.

****

Riley woke the next morning surrounded by Dagger's muscular, warm body. Her injured arm was cradled in his hand. She was flooded by a sudden sense of relief and loss. How was it possible to experience both feelings at the same time?

Something was going on with Dagger. He'd distanced himself from her, both physically and emotionally. Something had happened, and he didn't want her to know about it. Did he have her best interests at heart?

Had someone asked that question nine days ago, she would've replied—definitely. At this point, she had no clue.

Their company was on financially shaky ground. Was Dagger the type of man who could be bought to save his company? Without knowing where they stood, she couldn't afford to become any more emotionally invested. If she did, it would cost her.

Dagger nuzzled her hair with his face and whispered, "We need to talk."

"Where did you go, Dagger? And how exactly does it keep me safe?"

"I—I can't give you any details now," he mumbled, his lips pressed against her head.

Dagger might not physically harm her, but she did know he would do anything to protect his business and his brothers—even at her expense. Money was a dominating bedfellow. Maybe he needed her as much as she needed him—but for different reasons.

Get a grip, Riley, she mentally scolded herself. *Two could play this game.*

Chapter Twenty-Eight

Riley and Dagger walked into Hunters and Seekers. Kaleb and Stone were standing at the whiteboard, deep in discussion. Kaleb was the first to notice them.

"This is a surprise," Kaleb said, nodding his head toward the door.

Stone turned. "Well. I don't see any new injuries." He made a big deal of looking both Dagger and Riley up and down.

"You're hilarious," Dagger said, punching Stone in the shoulder. "I know you're both still ticked off at me, and you certainly have every reason."

"Never mind the fact that we couldn't even reach you by phone," Kaleb added.

"I was a dickhead, and it won't happen again. I'm sor-r-ry." Dagger bowed at both Kaleb and Stone.

"Remember, you're the one always screaming about us being a team." Kaleb scowled at him. "It's looks to me like you and Riley worked it out. I suppose if she can forgive you, we can too—this time. Don't push your luck, Eastin," Kaleb said.

"We've examined this board for hours. Gone through every player. We can't find anything," Stone said.

Dagger noticed they'd left Katarina and any connection to her off the board. He was beginning to understand what they were telling him last night. This was getting sticky. They needed *all* the players on the board. He was going to have to deal with this, whether he was ready or not.

"Riley and I think our best course of action would be to confront Samuels to find out once and for all what his level of involvement is."

"I agree with you," Kaleb said. "When do you plan to do that?"

"Let's make sure we're all on the same page. Start from the beginning and work through everything we know."

The four of them spent the day updating the board. They filled every inch and then moved to the backside to compile all their collective information. Dagger got a couple dirty looks from his partners, but always when Riley wasn't looking.

"It's getting late. I'm going to call Wayne's office." Riley walked over to a desk and sat while she made the call.

"This is getting messy," Kaleb whispered to Dagger and Stone.

"I know. I need to deal with this."

"Soon," Stone said. Stone leaned in and pointing at the whiteboard whispered, "We're spinning our wheels without all the players on the board."

Riley walked over to them. "I just spoke with Wayne's secretary. She said he'll be leaving for the day within the hour."

"Let's catch him before he leaves," Dagger said.

It was late in the day and most of the faculty were already gone, leaving the parking lot sparsely populated. Dagger found a parking spot close to Samuels's vehicle.

"Here he comes." Riley pointed to the man crossing the street and heading in their direction.

Dagger nodded.

"Wayne, we want to speak with you," Riley said, as she jumped out of the Range Rover.

He looked thinner, sunken and haggard. Samuels spooked at the sight of them. "I have nothing more to tell you, Riley. You know everything I know."

"And we both know it's a complete lie. That wasn't my mother we buried. I saw the pictures. It wasn't her. Were you involved in her kidnapping? Is she still alive? Where is she?"

"I didn't kidnap anyone! It wasn't me," Samuels yelled at them and leaned in.

"We're going to the police with the information we've collected," Dagger said.

"If you don't want us telling them you orchestrated this entire travesty, this is your one opportunity to come clean," Riley said.

"I can't deal with the stress of this situation any longer." A sheen of sweat coated Samuels's cheeks and forehead. His gaze skittered from place to place, and he continually shifted his weight, from one leg to the other. "Yes, the ship was supposed to be sunk, but I was promised my people would have plenty of time to get to the life boats. Claudia wasn't supposed to be murdered, they only wanted her formula."

"Please, enlighten us. What exactly was the plan?" Dagger asked in a sarcastic tone.

"The plan was to kidnap her during the chaos. There were connections with some Russian spy. After Claudia gave up her information, they were going to make it look like she was kidnapped by the Russians. The spy was going to bring her home. That's what I was told. I promise you," Samuels said.

"What kind of person are you?" Riley asked. "How could you let someone sink your ship and endanger your employees?" Riley seethed.

Samuels straightened his back and glared into Riley's eyes. "A person who knew the industry was changing, even if the board didn't see it. I could make this company one of the largest in the industry. All we asked Claudia to do was hand over the *damn* formula."

"But she wouldn't, would she?" Riley met his hateful stare and answered with her own, not giving in one inch. "And due to the contract you signed prior to her employment, you had no legal standing to take it from her," Riley snarled.

"How did you know about her formula in the first place?" Dagger asked.

"I knew she'd been working on something groundbreaking. A few months ago, I went over to her house to speak with her about a project. The door was open, so I walked in just as she was coming down the hall. Her laptop sat open on the sofa. She walked over to it and shut it down, but she wasn't quick enough. I'd glanced at it on my way in the house and saw the words: algae as alternative energy."

Dagger caught a sudden movement to their right and a glint of silver barreling through the air.

"Down," he yelled, lunging for Riley. Snagging her by the waist, he turned to take the force of their fall as they hit the pavement.

Samuels fell a few feet away.

A blade was buried to the hilt straight through his neck. Blood oozed from the wound and Wayne was gasping for air. Riley shimmied out from under Dagger's belly and crawled to Samuels.

"Damnit, Riley. Stay down!" He shuffled after her.

"Wayne." Riley looked at him. His eyes were glassing over.

"I'm sorry, Riley." Samuels barely whispered between wet gasps. "Antho—" His breath rattled, and his jaw went slack. Blood collected under him as he bled out.

"Stay here, call 911," Dagger said.

Before Riley could utter a word, Dagger ran in the direction the knife had come. His anger fueled his pace. He spotted the assailant and closed in on the man as he crossed the campus. The assassin headed into the walking trails with Dagger in hot pursuit.

The assassin darted through the trees, zigzagging on and off the trails. When he was only a few yards ahead, Dagger leapt onto a concrete picnic table and propelled himself into mid-air. Dagger slammed into the assassin, seized his thigh but couldn't keep his grip. Both men sprawled on the ground.

The assailant struggled out from under Dagger, kicking his shoulder. They'd landed in the trees; rocks and limbs peppered the area. His adversary pulled a second knife from his ankle holder and sprang to his feet. Dagger jumped up at the same time, brandishing a large branch. He swung wildly from side to side, continually jabbing at his opponent to keep him from stabbing or throwing the knife. Dagger hit his mark and knocked the knife out of the assassin's hand.

They both scrambled for the knife. Dagger grabbed the branch, swung, and knocked his opponent off balance. The assassin stepped back, lost his footing, and slipped on a mossy rock. Dagger pounced on him and pinned him to the ground with the branch across his chest and arms.

"Who are you and who do you work for?" Dagger growled.

The man gave him a sardonic grin. "You can call me Eric. You're not as good as you think," he sneered.

"Seriously?" Dagger said. "You look a hell-of-a-lot like the shitbag who's been following me. Same build. You've a habit of playing with sharp objects, like knives and spear guns."

"I've been known to dive a time or two," Eric snarled.

"Where's Claudia Rawlings?"

"The scientist? Sinking her ship gave me a rush. Although,

since you mentioned the spear gun, shooting you with a spear was a close second."

"This is the end of the line, dickwad. Cops will be here shortly. You might as well tell me who you work for. And where the hell is Claudia?"

Eric heaved upward, pushing Dagger off balance. Dagger was forced to release the branch and tucked and rolled out of Eric's range. Eric grabbed his knife and caught Dagger's hip with the razor-sharp blade. Dagger rolled away, grabbed a large rock, and slammed it alongside Eric's head. For a split-second, Eric's eyes grew wide in surprise. Eric slumped on top of Dagger, his weight driving Dagger deep into the dirt.

"Dagger, where are you?" Riley yelled as she careened into the clearing.

Neither man moved.

"No—no—no—no—no!" She sobbed, falling to her knees. Her tears blinded her. She tried to push the killer off, but the he didn't budge. She recoiled when the man abruptly rolled off.

"Holy mother of hell. I feel like I got hammered flat," Dagger said.

"Dagger! I thought—I thought you were dead." Riley threw her arms around his neck and covered him with kisses.

"It would take a meaner bastard than Eric to take me out of the game."

Riley helped Dagger stand and he winced. As she reached around his waist, she clutched his injured hip. Her hand came away sticky and covered in blood. "You're injured."

"Eric got lucky."

"We need to get you to the hospital. You're bleeding."

"It's no big deal. Stone can stitch me up."

"You're going to the hospital. Who knows where his knife has been? You need a tetanus shot," Riley demanded.

"My tetanus shot is current."

"When?" Riley's dark gaze bore directly into his eyes; she looked like a fiery pixie trying to intimidate him.

"A while ago."

"Dagger Eastin, are you telling me you're afraid of a tiny needle, yet you have no problems with spears and knives?"

As they came out of the woods, a security guard stepped up to them and examined Dagger's wound.

"She's right, sir. Let Dr. Rawlings take you to the hospital. I've already radioed for the police. I'll secure the scene until they arrive. I'll let them know where you are. They're gonna want to talk to you."

"Thank you. Here's my contact information." Dagger handed the security guard his card.

"Thank you," Riley said to the guard.

"Dr. Rawlings, don't take this the wrong way, but you've never even been issued a parking ticket on campus. These past few days, you seem to be smack in the middle of the action. Maybe it's time to think about new friends."

"I don't know. I kinda enjoy the adventure."

"You know, the guard's right. You've been smack in the middle of all the action. I'd say that's a good sign we're getting close," Dagger said.

"There was no love lost between Wayne and me. Even so, I wish this never happened," Riley said as they walked away.

"When you play the game, you need to understand all the consequences," Dagger said.

Two hours later Dagger was sutured, given a tetanus shot, pain shot, and antibiotics. They were huddled in an exam room waiting for the police to arrive and the doctor to discharge him.

"I didn't hear what Samuels said, after he said he was sorry," Dagger said.

"Wayne said 'Antho—' that was all. If he was saying 'Anthony' then he was probably talking about Welby. I've even seen them together a time or two. I think we might have our first lead. I believe Anthony is somehow involved in all of this," Riley said.

"And Samuels mentioned a Russian spy," Dagger said. "I happen to know a Russian spy."

Riley spun around and gawked at Dagger. "What are you talking about? What Russian spy?"

"It's not as bad as it sounds. She wasn't a Russian spy when I first met her. I mean—she was, but I didn't know it. Her name is Katarina. She was a marine archaeologist. We first met when she was contracted to work with my team on a classified mission. I was the lead Navy salvage diver. Over the next few years we worked on a number of missions together."

"You're saying you were friends."

"Riley, I hadn't even spoken to her until a week ago when she sent me a text and demanded we meet. She knew about Claudia's research. She'd been tailing us throughout our entire hunt. I managed to stall her by telling her we haven't found the research yet."

"I see. This can't be a coincidence."

"Agreed. Someone hired her because they knew Kat and I have a history together. We need to figure out who hired her. We do that, and we're one step closer to finding your mother."

CHAPTER TWENTY-NINE

It was after midnight when the four finally made it to Dagger's house. They spread out on the furniture, exhausted and out of ideas.

"You have to come up with a way to keep stalling Katarina," Kaleb said.

"And how do you propose I do that?" Dagger asked.

"What if you tell Katarina we've found the formula, but we need time to decrypt Mom's code?" Riley asked.

"It could work," Kaleb said. "We can dress it up a bit, tomorrow."

"Good. Time to hit the racks," Dagger said. "You guys go upstairs and grab a bed. I'm sore and dirty. I'm going to catch a quick shower. Then I'll take the first watch."

"Are you sure?" Stone asked. "The two of you have been put through the ringer over the last few days."

"Try the last month," Kaleb said, as he climbed the stairs.

"I'm good. One of you can relieve me in four hours," Dagger said.

"Go get your shower," Riley said to Dagger. "I'll check the security and turn off the lights throughout the house."

Riley heard the guys already snoring with their lights still on. She crept up the stairs and stopped at the first room. Kaleb was still fully clothed and face down on the made bed. She switched off his light and closed his door. Stone had made it under the covers, but his arm was stretched out and laying on the nightstand. His hand rested on the base of the lamp; it looked as though he'd fallen asleep before he could even turn off his light. Riley smiled and switched off his light and closed the door. Dagger was spot on when he'd told her they could sleep anywhere. She went downstairs and shut off all the lights behind her.

Riley closed the door to Dagger's bedroom and heard the shower running. She glanced in the bathroom and admired Dagger's muscular physique through the frosted glass. Quietly, she pulled the door closed. She changed into her pajamas and slipped into the far side of the bed.

The shower shut off. She rolled onto her side, away from the bathroom and facing the windows. In case Dagger caught the windows reflection, she lowered her eyelids, so she'd appear she was already asleep.

The bathroom door opened, and she felt his presence the moment he entered the room. Riley mentally counted to five, then unable to keep from peeking, she opened her eyes barely a crack. Dagger stood inside his walk-in closet, a towel wrapped around his waist. Unexpectedly his towel dropped to the ground. Riley bit her tongue to keep from gasping. He was even more gorgeous then she had imagined, every muscle sculpted and defined. He tugged on his sleeping pants and Riley closed her eyes.

He moved around the room, but she didn't dare hazard a glance. Suddenly, she felt his hot breath on her forehead, followed by his warm lips.

"Sweet dreams, Riley," Dagger said softly. He ran his hand lightly down her arm as he drew away.

The door to the bedroom opened and closed. Riley rolled on to her back and stared at the ceiling. Dagger was a total mystery to her. Just when she thought she had him figured out, he threw her another curve.

Claudia stood in the doorway to her stateroom. Riley called out her name and rushed forward, but as she reached out to touch her mother's hand, water filled the corridor and pushed her mother away.

Riley swam toward Claudia and reached out again, only to be battered by another surge of freezing sea water exploding down the corridor. With each new wave, her mother was pushed further and further away until she disappeared.

Riley's cries broke the silence of the night.

"Riley, wake up. Please baby, wake up. It's only a nightmare. I have you."

She woke sobbing.

"You're safe. I have you. No one will hurt you," Dagger murmured into her ear. He gathered her up and drew her close to him, encircling her.

She embraced his warmth and heard his heartfelt words but sensed his fear.

He brushed her long hair back away from her face and kissed the top of her head. "That's better. It was just a nightmare. It can't hurt you. Shut it down and stay right here with me."

"I'm okay. I'm sorry I woke you." She took in long deep breaths to slow her racing heart.

"You didn't wake me, I was in the living room." He rocked her. She wasn't sure if it was for her or more to settle himself.

"When you cried out, you scared ten years off my life. At first I thought someone came into the room and attacked you, and I was the idiot who was dozing off in the chair. I came in and heard you whimpering in your sleep and thrashing around. Your pain felt real."

"I'm better now." She rubbed one hand up and down his arm.

"Do you want to talk about it?"

"I was on the research ship, trying to reach my mother. I could see her, only each time I went towards her, a massive wave of water flooded the corridor. I kept trying and trying to reach her. Each time the wave hit and pushed her further away until I couldn't see her anymore."

"Listen to me, Riley. I'll find Claudia and I'll bring her back to you. You have my word, I won't stop until I do."

Dagger's honest expression looked filled with devotion. To her surprise, he tenderly kissed each tear on her face, until his lips found hers. The kiss was sweet, passionate, and filled with hunger.

"Dagger, is everything alright?" Stone called from the staircase. Dagger pulled away and left the room.

"Hey, sleeping beauties. Time to get up. You don't want to miss this—Stone made us breakfast." Kaleb stood at their door.

"Morning." Riley yawned, as she opened the door and smiled at Kaleb. "Dagger will be right out. He said I used all the hot water and he had to wait for it to reheat. I told him you took the first shower, so it was your fault."

Kaleb's jaw dropped open and Riley gave him a soft poke with her elbow as she walked by.

Riley walked into the kitchen. "Smells wonderful, Stone. Anything I can help you with?"

"Sure, since you're asking, the coffee isn't made. I wouldn't let Kaleb near the coffee maker. Have you tasted the sludge he makes at the office? I'm pretty sure he filters it through tires." Stone's face screwed up and his whole body shivered.

"Come on, it's not bad. I follow the directions," Kaleb said.

Stone and Riley broke out in laughter.

"How'd you guys sleep?" Dagger asked. He stood in the middle of the main room checking his phone.

"Best sleep in a long time. Can we move in?" Kaleb gave him an alligator grin.

"My door's always open. Well, technically it's always locked. Anyhow, feel free to knock any time."

"Smartass. Did you forget who put in your security system?" Kaleb chuckled.

Stone pulled two quiches from the oven. He placed them on the table along with a huge bowl of fresh fruit and a plate of breakfast rolls.

"Looks great. Thanks, Stone," Dagger said as he joined the rest of the group at the table.

"Yeah, it does. Which restaurant did you order takeout from?" Kaleb teased.

"My Gran taught me how to make quiche and breakfast rolls when I was a kid. She used to say, 'Stone, if I teach you a few breakfast recipes, you'll have food for every meal.' She was a super woman."

"What's our plan for Katarina?" Dagger asked.

"We were discussing it earlier," Kaleb said. "We still think Riley's idea is the most plausible. In case Kat wants to take the formula and decipher it on her own, tell her Riley is the key to the code."

"You do realize it puts a big red bull's eye on Riley? I wouldn't put it past Kat to try kidnapping her," Dagger said.

"She won't get the chance. We keep doing what we've been doing and keep her with us, twenty-four seven," Kaleb said.

"With one major change; no more trips to the university,

Sheridan Enterprises, or anywhere else. We stay put here or at the shop," Stone said.

"The university is no longer a problem. Before the fiasco, I met with my Dean. He and Dr. Bender agreed to place me on leave for the reminder of the quarter," Riley replied.

The three men gawked at her. It was then she realized she'd failed to mention it to Dagger.

"Why the sudden change? You don't have to give up your teaching, Riley," Dagger said. "One way or the other, this mission is coming to an end. With luck, it'll be tied in a bow within the week."

"I know. I gave it a lot of thought. I need the time off to make some decisions about my future."

In unison, Stone and Kaleb's eyes shifted from her to Dagger. He took a bite of his roll and ignored them.

****

They were cleaning up the kitchen and joking around when Dagger's phone rang. He yanked it from his pocket and stared at the screen. "It's her."

"Put her on speaker," Stone said.

Dagger threw his partner a scathing look.

"Stone's right," Riley said. "We all need to hear—it is part of the mission."

"Katarina." Dagger put the call on speaker.

"That's no way to greet your fiancée," Katarina purred.

"*Ex*-fiancée. And this isn't a pleasure call," Dagger growled.

Riley's legs turned rubbery and she dropped into the nearest chair before they completely betrayed her. Fiancée?

"Did someone get up on the wrong side of the bed? Or is that little elf not giving you what you need?" Kat asked in a singsong voice.

Dagger gritted his teeth. Riley watched as his jaw flexed and unflexed. He didn't look in her direction.

The sound of their voices faded as Riley mentally put the pieces together. The reason why Dagger had backed off with his feelings was because his true love came back into his life. He found himself strapped between his love of Katarina and the love of his business. He couldn't alienate Riley because he couldn't afford the monetary loss to the business. Dagger's angry voice broke into Riley's mind. She refocused on what was happening.

"You want to play? I can play. Any chance you're missing a couple of major players who didn't come home last night? Don't count on seeing them tonight—or ever," Dagger bit out.

"I have no idea who you're talking about," Kat said, but the snarkiness had left her voice.

"Sure you do. One of them even mentioned you," Dagger replied.

"Those scumbags have no idea what the complete picture is or who I am." Now she sounded concerned and she'd made her first slip-up. Dagger waited her out.

"I want the formula today and don't even try and tell me you don't know where it is," Katarina hissed.

"Oh, we know where it is, all right. What we don't know is what it says. It's encrypted, and we've haven't got it all figured out yet..."

"We can do the work. Your only concern is to bring it to me."

"No, you won't be able to get it to work. We've discovered the key, but we need time to decipher the formula."

"Stop stalling, Eastin. Bring the key along with the formula or you're done."

"I won't do that. You see, the key is not a thing, it's a person—Riley's the key, and there's no way in hell you're getting your hands on her."

Katarina fumed, sputtered, and threatened. Dagger merely held the phone and waited her out. He knew her, and if he engaged Kat now, she would leave his life a burned-out mess.

"Bring the formula to the old industrial marina, along with the girl, tomorrow evening at six. Dagger, I'm done with your games. You do exactly as I say, or I won't only destroy your life and career. I'll kill your partners and that little tramp."

Riley stiffened. This woman was pure hate. What did Dagger even see in her?

"We're not meeting you anywhere until we're sure Riley won't be hurt."

"You seem to be under the notion you're calling the shots. And Dagger, if you don't come through with the formula, I will find a way to get my hands on your newest play toy first."

Chapter Thirty

Dagger stared at the phone in his hand. He inhaled a breath and looked over at Riley, who was staring straight at him. "It's not what you think. Yes, Katarina was once my fiancée. But we broke it off six years ago. I was telling you the truth when I said I hadn't seen or spoken to her until a week ago."

The three men collectively held their breath.

"This is about finding my mother, not my feelings. Step one complete. Where do we go from here?" Riley asked.

She wasn't about to expose her true feelings for all three of these men to bear witness. They'd grown close, but it didn't mean she was going to break down in front of them and call Dagger a liar. She took in a long, slow, breath and persevered. "And when this thing is done...and we get Katarina...I have first dibs on speaking with her alone. You know, girl time. I'm going to bitchslap that hussy while I explain to her how I truly enjoyed thinking my mother was dead."

Three sets of eyebrows shot northward.

"Well, remind me never to piss you off," Kaleb said.

"Count me in on what he said. Getting back to our current predicament...there's no way we can give them the formula tomorrow. We do, and we'll never know what happened to Riley's mother," Stone said.

"I think we should head to Hunters and Seekers, and work out a plan and fall back plan," Kaleb said.

****

Dagger stood at the whiteboard filling in the previously hidden parts of the timeline.

"So you're sure the first time you saw Katarina tailing you was on San Juan Island?" Stone asked.

"I didn't actually see her. We had the intruder in the house the night before. I'm sure it was Eric. The next day I received a text from an unknown number. It said: 'I'm watching you.' When I was out securing the property, I asked Mr. Ford, the caretaker, if he noticed anyone unusual. He mentioned seeing a woman walking down on the beach by the house, but he didn't get a good look at her," Dagger said. "I also received a second text on the ferry, when we left San Juan Island. It said: 'I know what you're up to'."

"Next time was in Oahu, right?" Kaleb asked.

"Yes. Twice. The first time I wasn't sure it was her. The second time I got out to the sidewalk quickly enough to see her getting into a taxi. That's when I was certain it was Katarina."

"After you got back, she made contact with you." Stone said, pointing to the coinciding spot on the board.

"That's right. She used our old contact code and I called. There were also a few times I had the sense of being watched. It felt like her." Dagger hesitated for a moment. "Our first face-to-face was in San Clemente. Katarina being who she is, she danced around when I questioned her. I'm certain she didn't tell me the truth about who she worked for. She said she'd heard rumors that we were in possession of Dr. Rawling's journals and formulas. I played along and told her she needed new sources. She threatened to burn down our business and kill you and Kaleb. She gave me forty-eight hours to get what she wanted."

"Then she met with you down by the beach," Stone said.

Dagger was pacing now. The more of the events he relayed, the more pissed off he got. "Correct. She did her usual threatening routine. Only then she upped the stakes and told me she would kill Riley."

"So the problem client is Katarina. That's who you went to meet with when you left me behind," Riley said. For the first time she looked away from the whiteboard she'd been studying and locked eyes on Dagger's.

"Yes. I know what Katarina is capable of, and I didn't want you anywhere near her. I left you in Stone and Kaleb's safekeeping. I knew if something went wrong and I didn't return, they would never let Kat get to you," Dagger said.

The room went silent for a few heartbeats. Riley looked from one man to the next.

"I understand. I'm not saying I agree with how you handled it, but I do understand," Riley said. "What's our next step? Do you agree with me that Anthony Welby is the Anthony Samuels was referring to?"

"Yes, I do. And I think Welby *is* Mr. White. Welby didn't originally intend to have Neal killed. He didn't want Neal to know who he really was, so he called himself Mr. White," Dagger said.

"Even if Welby used a different name, Neal could've easily seen him on TV. He's been on several times over the years. And, he's been cashing in on my mother's death, touting his concerns all over the news." Riley could feel her face starting to flush with color. She balled her hands into fists. Her fingernails dug into the palms of her hands; she kept tightening the pressure to force her focus away from the heat rising inside her.

"He probably disguised his voice when he spoke with Neal."

"Wait a minute," Stone jumped in. "Premier Oil and Gas and Sheridan Enterprises are by all rights competitors. Why on earth would Samuels work with Welby?"

"Samuels told us the board was old-school and refusing the changes he suggested. Welby convinced Samuels he and his company would help take over Sheridan. Samuels believed the two of them would be equal partners and reign supreme over the oil and gas industry," Dagger explained.

"Correct me if I'm wrong, Riley, but Premier is the giant in the industry, although it is currently limited in research capability. Whereas Sheridan has a broader and more extensive research division and is more on the cutting edge. Welby would acquire a seasoned research division, with Claudia as the cherry on top," Dagger surmised.

"And after Welby merged Sheridan into his conglomeration, his next step would be to figure out a way to keep Mom's research," Riley said.

"Exactly. No one was supposed to get hurt, especially Claudia. She would return home safe, after she gave them what they wanted," Dagger said.

"You think Welby was tying up loose ends and sent Eric to kill Neal and then Samuels?" Stone asked.

"Welby has Eric get rid of Samuels, and he keeps both

companies for himself. As for Neal, he sealed his fate when he agreed to spy for Welby."

"I keep circling around. I can only come up with one plausible action for tomorrow's meeting," Kaleb said.

"Which is?" Riley asked.

"How good are you at creating formulas?"

"Not as good as my mother, but I can hold my own. Why?"

"We don't intend to ever give Katarina the formula. However, we must give her something to convince her we're willing to deal," Kaleb said.

"Okay." She squinted one eye, not sure where he was going with all this.

"Let's give her one page," Kaleb said. "The real formula is pages and pages long. We give her three or four lines of genuine formula. Then you, Riley, fabricate enough formula to fill the rest of the one page. One that looks plausible but isn't. Can you do it? Can you devise a formula that will take them some time to discover it's a fraud?" Kaleb asked.

Three sets of eyes fixated at her.

"I like your idea, Kaleb. Regrettably it would take me a great deal of time to come up with a genuine-looking formula that Welby's scientists couldn't easily spot as a fake," Riley said. She stared at the timeline, her arms folded and tapped her chin with an index finger. No one moved or made a sound. "Hmm. I think I can make Kaleb's idea work with a slight twist." She turned away from the whiteboard and focused on the three men. "I'll work on making minuscule changes throughout the entire page. This will render the formula useless; however, it will take Welby's scientists some time to decipher. After all, our goal is to make it appear genuine, and at the same time, lead them down the wrong test tube." She smirked at the guys. "Start brewing the coffee, it's gonna be a long afternoon and evening—not you, Kaleb." She gave Kaleb a wink.

"That's not cute," Kaleb said. He folded his arms and pouted.

"I'm not leaving you out. You can set me up at a computer." Riley patted Kaleb on the back as she walked by.

"And...you can go pick us up dinner in a few hours. You're great at that," Stone teased. He pulled up his shirt sleeves.

"Shit. What's this?" Dagger grabbed Stone's arm and turned it so he read the black marker on it. "Collecting phone numbers on your body now, Stone. What...are you that hard up?"

"I'm not the only one," Stone grabbed Kaleb's arm and pulled up his sleeve, exposing the truth.

"Is this what you numbnuts do when you're on a job?" Dagger was trying hard not to laugh as his two buddies squirmed.

"Traitor," Kaleb said to Stone. "If you really must know, we got these in the line of our mission."

"Uh-huh," Dagger said as he settled in his desk chair and crossed his arms.

"We did. Really. Kaleb's telling the truth…for once," Stone said. For his troubles Kaleb punched him in the shoulder. "We had to play along with a group of sorority girls on campus to get close to the crime scene and find Riley," Stone replied.

"Oh, to be a fly on the wall," Riley giggled, still looking at her computer.

Riley worked for hours. She took a quick break for dinner and to stretch her back and legs. The clock went from one, to two, and on to three in the morning. As the morning wore on, the guys picked spots in the office to doze. Stone snagged the sofa, Kaleb set up a folding cot, and Dagger was in his office chair. His feet were on the desk, arms crossed, chin resting on his chest. Riley would get up to stretch her legs only long enough to refill her non-stop coffee.

She worked and reworked her fake formula. Her goal was to keep her changes as far from the real formula as possible, and at the same time preserve some plausibility that this was her mother's actual work.

She blinked rapidly as she reached the end. It worked. This could really fool a run-of-the-mill scientist for days—maybe even weeks. She was so pumped up on caffeine and adrenaline, she wanted to dance around the shop. Glancing at the time on her computer screen, she couldn't believe it was ten minutes to five in the morning. She yawned, her jaw cracking from the strain. Riley got up, walked over to Dagger, and tapped him softly on the shoulder.

Dagger snapped awake and surveyed the room. "What's wrong?" he asked.

"I've done it!" Riley crowed, doing a happy dance, fists pumping.

Stone and Kaleb startled awake, heads on swivels, scanning for intruders.

"I've created a formula that will have the best scientists scratching their heads."

"Cool!" Kaleb exclaimed.

"I think I did. If we're lucky, it could take Welby's scientists days, maybe weeks, depending on their scope of knowledge. I wish I knew who they were. The second Welby has this formula in his hands, the clock is ticking. We'll have no time to waste. We'll need to find my mother, before the scientists realize the formula is a fabrication."

"Are we ready for tomorrow?" Dagger asked.

"I have to make a copy of Riley's formula on an empty USB, and we're good to go," Kaleb said.

"Let's head back to my place and sleep for a few hours. We're all tired, and Riley's exhausted," Dagger said. "We can sleep until the afternoon, and then plan out the final steps."

Riley yawned again and collapsed on the loveseat, curled up into a ball, and fell asleep.

****

Dagger drove the Range Rover into the parking lot of a deserted dockside diner.

"About seven years ago," Dagger said. "This place was owned by a friendly, outgoing couple, and recognized as one of the top ten eateries in San Diego. Live music played nightly, and the owner was a lead singer. I brought Kat here many times; it was one of my favorite hang-outs. After closing one night, two armed robbers broke in, stole all their money, and shot the wife. Her husband never set foot in the place again, even though he'd received many offers to sell, he couldn't let it go."

Dagger drove around to the back side of the diner and parked. Stone and Kaleb jumped out of the back. Dagger opened the tailgate and started extracting gear. "Two hours to the scheduled meeting." He helped Stone and Kaleb sort their diving gear. "You guys should make it to the old industrial marina with plenty of time left to take up your positions."

They all headed for the water.

"And you're sure you don't want us to follow Katarina?" Kaleb asked, for the fifth time.

"No. I don't want you running the risk that she'll spot you and then shoot you." He turned to Kaleb. "Kaleb will tag her boat with the GPS tags and Stone, you keep a look out."

"Then we take cover under the closest pier and keep track of everyone in Kat's entourage. You're positive you don't need backup on land?" Stone asked.

"We won't. She won't dare harm us when she finds out we've only handed over a sample of Claudia's formula."

"And Katarina won't try to take me with her after I tell her my mother's formula is extremely complicated and I don't have my notes with me," Riley said.

"How are you so certain she's coming in by boat?" Riley asked.

"I'm not *certain*. I do know Katarina, or I thought I did. Add together the choice of meeting place along with her love of the water, and the high probability she's staying on a boat, and it becomes likely she's arriving by boat.

"You're sure Kat won't kidnap Riley and threaten you to bring her Claudia's formula?" Kaleb asked.

"Yes. Katarina wants the money. For that to happen, she needs all the information. My guess is she'll posture and threaten, but only to reach her goal. You two make damn sure her boat is securely tagged. We need to be able to track her," Dagger said.

"Roger that," Stone said. "You and Riley are going to remain at the marina until Katarina leaves. Then we surface and meet up. Let's get going, Kaleb."

Dagger and Riley watched as the guys tugged on the rest of their equipment. The guys walked into the water and quickly slipped beneath the surface.

"You ready to do this?" Dagger asked.

"I'm all set and hopefully one step closer to finding my mother."

"Let's get this party started." Dagger took her hand and walked her back to the SUV.

They drove a few miles before turning onto the road for the industrial marina. He pulled over into a flat sandy spot. "End of the road for the vehicle; we'll need to walk down to the docks. The security fence isn't far from here."

They got out and Dagger grabbed his bag from the backseat, with everything they might need to haul an injured teammate out. "Let's hope this stays packed," Dagger said.

They reached the fence and started climbing. As Dagger swung one leg over the top, he noticed Riley was still standing in the same spot he'd left her.

"Are you coming?" He swung his other leg and started down the other side. As he dropped the last few feet to the ground, Riley scaled the fence up and over and landed on the ground like a ballerina.

He shook his head and stifled a laugh. "Nice moves."

Riley took a bow and walked off to the storage sheds. Once they were out in the open, Dagger pulled his binoculars out and scoured the building tops and cranes. Large piers lined the water's edge. Dagger scanned the area slowly from the vantage point of the sheds. Riley glanced at her phone. The meeting wasn't set to take place for another seventy minutes.

"Katarina's true to form. Here she comes now. I'd say she's on a ship's tender, a good sized one. I count four men with her."

"Where are they?" Riley asked.

"Look out a little to your right, see her?"

The setting sun reflected off the water. Riley placed her hands over her eyebrows, trying to block out the sun. "I don't see anything. Wait, I saw something move."

"That's her." Dagger continued to examine the water though his binoculars.

"Hold on, the meeting isn't scheduled for another hour. What about the guys? Do you think they're ready?"

"Positive. The guys have worked with Katarina in the past. They know her MO. She always arrives at least an hour early. She likes the upper hand in every situation."

Dagger scanned the surrounding water as Katarina's boat drew closer. He saw no other boats in the vicinity. He refocused on her boat and watched as she pulled her binoculars from her bag. She started at the far side and slowly panned the marina. He watched as she inspected where he and Riley stood and knew the instant she spotted the two of them. She halted, dropped the binoculars, and scowled directly at him.

"She's seen us, and she's not the least bit happy we beat her to the punch." He put his binoculars back in their pack and waited.

As they docked, one of Katarina's thugs jumped out and tied off the boat. Katarina started up the dock with three of the men in tow; the last man stayed with the boat. All were packing sidearms; Dagger was sure she was carrying guns and knives.

"You're early," Katarina said in a clipped tone as she approached the sheds.

"As are you," Dagger answered. "Looks like we can finish up our business early and go our separate ways...and still in time for dinner."

"Only if you brought what I asked for," Kat answered. "Where's the data?"

Dagger reached in his jeans pocket and pulled out the USB.

One of the guards pulled a tablet out of his jacket. Kat took it and plugged in the USB. No one spoke as she confirmed the data.

Katarina pulled a pistol from her shoulder holster and aimed it at Riley. "You're playing games with me. This is not the complete formula. It's not possible." Her men leaned away from her ever so slightly, and their hands went into their pockets. "They will kill you both where you stand."

"You're the game player," Dagger said. "You and I both knew we would never bring you the entire formula. Doing so would seal Dr. Rawling's fate. We still don't know if you have Claudia, or if she's even alive."

Katarina pulled her phone out and dialed a number. She said something in Russian, then turned her phone in their direction. Claudia filled the screen.

"Mom! Are you okay?" Riley cried.

"Riley," her mom said, her voice shaking, "whatever they tell you to do, don't—"

Katarina disconnected the call, and the screen went black. "There's your proof. Now give me the rest of the formula."

"Not until we have Claudia," Dagger said.

"You want to go down this road? Keep it up, and I will take *her* with me." Kat wagged the pistol in Riley's direction.

"It would not be in your best interest. Riley's still working on deciphering the formula."

"Even better, I take Riley and the formula. You get nothing," Kat said as she took another step closer to them.

"No, you don't," Riley said. "Neither the key nor the formula are with me. I left them behind for safe keeping. You take me, and I'll give you nothing; let me work on it, and I'll consider trading the formula for my mother's safety."

"I turned Claudia over to the Russians," Kat snapped. "They're getting restless and want to return home. You have one more day, Riley. No more excuses or your mother will come home to you piece by piece." Katarina turned around and headed back to her boat.

Dagger and Riley watched her leave.

When Kat was out of earshot, he said quietly, "You did well."

"Do you think we stalled her long enough for Kaleb to tag her boat?"

"More than enough. They've probably counted the number of bullets they'd need to use to drop Kat's team."

Katarina boarded her tender. She glared in their direction and held up one finger. Then her boat sped away from land.

"I'm sorry for asking—what did you ever see in that viper?" Riley asked.

"I was just thinking the exact same thing. She is nothing like the woman I knew. It appears the woman I thought I loved never existed."

The boat faded into the horizon. Dagger and Riley waited. A few minutes later, Kaleb and Stone surfaced next to the pier.

"She's a pure ball of sunshine," Kaleb said as he yanked off his face mask.

"For a while there, Kaleb and I were close to entering the fray. No way were we going to let that bitch—sorry, Dagger—take Riley," Stone said.

"Be my guest, call her anything you please. I plan to," Dagger replied. "She told us the Russians are holding Claudia."

"She spoke Russian to the person who answered her phone," Riley said.

"Kat probably has a handful of Russians who work for her." Dagger looked at his two partners. "Tell me you got her ride tagged."

"We sure did," Kaleb said. "Let's blow this dive."

Chapter Thirty-One

"You're spinning your wheels, Anthony," Katarina paced the length of the bridge and then stopped and honed in on her computer. "You want the formula and you don't want to harm Claudia. We'll get the formula—eventually. But we have precious little leverage since we can't kill Claudia and Riley has the formula. Then there's Dagger. He'll stall for as long as possible. You and I both know the longer they stall, the more likelihood we have of getting caught. Especially now that they know Claudia is alive and the Russians have her. I say you cut your losses and start a new plan," Katarina said. She watched Anthony Welby on Skype, carefully evaluating his reactions.

"Damn it! I've come too far not to get what I want. However, you're right. This entire situation is becoming a three-ring circus," Anthony said.

"I could put a bullet in the good doctor's head and toss her overboard," offered Katarina.

"No! Claudia is too valuable an asset. There's a deserted Premier ship docked at the main facility. It's scheduled to be refitted next month and no one is on board. Bring Claudia to the ship's conference room in one hour."

"Just what do you hope to accomplish?" Kat asked.

"I intend to get what I want. This way will take a little longer. Nevertheless, it will happen. Who has Claudia seen since her capture?"

"Only two of my men."

"Not you?" he asked.

"No. Why?" Katarina raised an eyebrow. What crazy plan was he brewing up now?

"We're going to let her go, but I want you to stage it as an escape."

"Have you lost your mind? She'll go straight to the police."

"She won't. She'll go right to Riley. And when she hears my ultimatum, she will comply. One hour."

Katarina stared at the black screen. Anthony relished pushing the envelope. She enjoyed taking his contracts for the excitement, but there were times it was better to admit defeat and move on, lest you risk being discovered. This was one of those times.

Kat had no intention of going down in flames with this man. She began devising her own plan.

Katarina located the two men attending to Claudia.

"Take her to this ship and hold her in the conference room. I'll be there shortly." She handed one a slip of paper.

The men blindfolded Claudia and led her to the outboard. Kat watched them leave, then headed for the tender. She planned on mooring it on the far side of the facility, away from the Premier ship for stand-by, in case this asinine plan went south.

****

Riley and Dagger watched as Kaleb worked on bringing the GPS of Kat's tagged boat online.

"There's the boat," Kaleb said, as he pointed to the blinking spot on the screen.

"The tender is anchored out to sea about three miles." Riley estimated.

"Sounds about right. What's the plan?" Kaleb asked.

"We give them a couple hours to head to their bunks, then we head out and see if Claudia is on board," Dagger said.

"Let's eat," Stone said as he walked into Hunters and Seekers with bags full of takeout.

Kaleb left his desk. The blinking spot was still stationary…a few minutes later, it began to move.

Kaleb glanced down at his screen, still chewing the last of his meal. "Son of a bitch. Their boat moved." He yanked out his chair and dropped in it, his fingers flying over the keys.

"Where is it now?" Dagger asked.

"Give me a second. There, I've got it. It's…docked at one of the seaside taverns. Maybe Kat is having a couple drinks."

Everyone gathered around Kaleb and spied over his shoulder.

"Wait. It's moving again," Riley said, pointing at the screen. "It's heading back in the direction it came from."

Riley's phone rang. She ran over to her purse and tugged it out. She squinted as she regarded the screen. "It's an unknown number." She pushed the answer button. "Hello?"

"Riley!" Claudia said.

Riley pushed the speaker button and held the phone out in front of her. The three men moved in closer. "Mom! Are you all right? Riley shrieked. "Where are you?"

"I'm on the corner of Pine and Johnson. I got away from them! Come get me!"

"Are you safe there? Can you hide?" Riley asked.

"I am for now—hurry!" Claudia answered.

"Something doesn't feel right," Dagger said. "If Kat was assigned to Claudia, there's no way in hell Claudia would be able to give her the slip. We could be walking into a trap."

"Maybe it's a trap, but it doesn't matter. Let's move!" urged Riley.

"We are going, but you need to realize what we're up against," Dagger said. Dagger extracted two Glocks from his desk drawer and two magazines. "Riley you're with me. Stone, you and Kaleb head over to my place and make sure it's secure. Head on a swivel. Katarina won't be far, I feel it in my bones." He checked to make sure the magazines were full and shoved one magazine into each Glock. "I'm telling you, this isn't right. If I know Kat, she's in this up to her eyeballs. Make sure you're both armed to the teeth." He shoved one Glock into his back holster and the second into his drop leg holster.

"If you're not at your place in thirty minutes, we're coming to get you," Stone said.

Riley and Dagger drove faster than the law allowed and ten minutes later Riley said, "There! That's her."

Dagger drove past Claudia to get a look around, then pulled a U-turn and headed back in her direction. Riley jumped out of the Range Rover as it slowed. She raced up to her mom and threw her arms around her, squeezing tightly. She pulled back slightly and held her mom's face in her hands. Riley's vision was blurred with tears. Her face was drenched, and the flood only intensified as the reality of this moment sunk in.

"You're alive! You're really alive! I never thought I would see you again. I love you, Mom." Another wave hit, and her tears gushed. She held her mom at arm's length, inspecting every inch. "Are you okay? Did those bastards hurt you?"

"Nothing important. I'm fine. A few bumps and bruises, but fine," Claudia said. Tears streamed down her face and ran down her neck. "I never thought I would see you again, my darling Riley-Girl. How are you? You look exhausted." Claudia threw her arms around Riley, again, holding on.

Dagger jumped out of the Range Rover and threw open the passenger door and back door. "Riley, let's go!"

"We have to go...they could be tracking you. This could be an ambush; get in the car!" Riley pushed her mom into the backseat. As she slammed the door shut her vision skittered around the vicinity. She jumped into the passenger side and Dagger flung her door closed, slid over the hood of the Range Rover, jumped into the driver's seat and sped away, before Riley could clear the tears from her eyes.

Dagger took the first turn, heading away from his house. Riley started to question him when she realized he was taking every precaution to shake a potential tail.

"We only have ten minutes before Stone and Kaleb head out to look for us. Buckle up tight, ladies. This isn't going to be a Sunday drive through the park."

"Mom, meet, Dagger Eastin," Riley said. She gripped the panic bar as Dagger nearly two-wheeled it around the next corner. "If it weren't for him and his partners, I would've never made it through this ordeal in one piece."

Dagger's eyes flashed in Riley's direction and back to the road.

"It's so good to meet you, Dagger. Thank you for helping my girl." Claudia said, as their eyes met in the rear-view mirror.

"It's been my honor, ma'am," Dagger said. He gave Claudia a slight nod.

Riley turned back and looked at her mom. Claudia smiled, but it looked strained and fake. She turned away and watched the scenery careen past. Claudia seemed distant...a bit off...but Riley shrugged the thought away. She'd be off, too, if she experienced what her mom had for the last month.

As they drove into Dagger's driveway, Stone stood squarely in the open garage. His hand was behind his back, as if he were expecting to pull his gun. As he stepped to one side, he tapped his wrist with his index finger. "One more second," Stone said as Dagger and Riley got out of the vehicle. "Place is clear and secured. Any problems?"

"Not yet," Dagger said.

"I brought in two guards from our contractors. The guard that was assigned to Riley was supposed to be on leave for the next week. He requested to be assigned here. I think he feels responsible for the campus mess," Kaleb said.

"Where are we?" Claudia asked. "Why aren't we going to my house?"

"Your house was broken into, Mom. I cleaned it up, but you might find a few things out of place."

Claudia's hand went up to her mouth.

"This is my place, Dr. Rawlings," Dagger said. "It's equipped with a state-of-the-art security system, guards patrolling the grounds. And then there's these two," Dagger pointed at his partners. "Not as good as guard dogs, but they'll do."

His comment brought a tiny smile to Riley's mom's eyes. His concern warmed Riley's heart.

"Let's get inside and talk about getting you settled, Dr. Rawlings," Dagger said, guiding her up the stairs and into the house.

"This is Kaleb and Stone." Riley placed her hand on each of the men as she introduced them.

"It's wonderful to meet you, Dr. Rawlings," Stone said.

"Please, all of you, call me, Claudia."

"Stone's a doctor, Mom. I think it's a good idea to have him give you a quick examination."

"No need," Claudia said.

"These three men own Hunters and Seekers. They were hired by Wayne to salvage your ship and bring it back to port," Riley said.

Her mother flinched at Wayne's name.

"When you called, you said you got away from *them*. Who did you mean?" Dagger asked, jumping into the conversation.

"The two Russian men who held me captive," Claudia said. "Tonight, they drugged me before taking me out of my stateroom. They said they were moving me to a new location. Someone must've screwed up the dosage. Either that, or we rode in the car for a very long time. When I woke up, I was lying in the backseat of the vehicle. I remained still and pretended to be out. One of men said it was going to take a while to get out there and he wanted to get something to eat. The other man agreed, and they pulled into a restaurant. I think it was three or four blocks from where I called you."

"Were they speaking English?" Dagger asked.

"No. Russian. I speak a variety of languages."

"Did they speak to you in Russian?"

"No. English. I never told them I spoke Russian."

"Smart," Kaleb said. He stood guard across the room at the front door. Stone was pacing the main floor, looking out each window and the patio door as he passed.

"And you saw no one else? No one else ever came aboard while you were held there?" Dagger asked.

"There was no one else. I never heard or saw anyone except the two men." Claudia confirmed.

"Claudia, can you tell us what happened that night on the ship?" Dagger asked.

Riley was going to suggest her mom eat something. Then she realized Dagger was questioning her now before anyone or anything had the chance to influence her story by accidentally feeding her any information.

"I'd only just returned to my cabin for the night, when I heard the ship's alarm go off. I grabbed my phone and called Riley. She didn't answer. I left her a brief message. Neal bolted in and told me we must get off the ship immediately. I recall my surprise at seeing him there. I questioned him, and he told me he'd tell me everything, after we were safe."

When Claudia said "Neal," she hesitated.

"I started out the door in front of him and felt a prick to my neck." Claudia rubbed the back of her neck. "That's the last thing I remember until I woke up aboard a strange ship. I'm exhausted. Can we continue this tomorrow?" Claudia asked.

Riley's gaze darted to Dagger. He nodded.

"We can wait until tomorrow, Mom. You'll be safe here. We're all staying here until we get to the bottom of what happened," Riley said. "Tomorrow we'll have to call the police. I'm sure they'll want to interview you right away."

"Why?" Claudia wrinkled her brow and balled her hands in the material of her pants. "We don't need to call them. I wasn't hurt, and it's over." Claudia licked her lips. "I do need to contact Wayne and tell him I'm okay and coming back to work."

"Mom, you can't even begin to know how thrilled I am that you're home and safe. But you're the only witness to what happened on your ship that night," Riley said.

"What do you mean? My entire team was aboard, and the crew, along with Neal. Call Wayne. He'll give you the names of all the people that were on board. You'll see."

"Mom, Wayne was murdered a couple days ago. And everyone on the ship died. Including Neal. Only he didn't die until weeks later. You...are the sole survivor."

Claudia's eyebrows drew close together as she frowned at Riley.

"What are you saying? I don't understand."

"I'm saying—you were all poisoned with carbon monoxide, and the ship was sunk on purpose. Everyone died—including you. You were in the morgue, or should I say there was a woman they claimed was you in the morgue. The people behind this went so far as to jury-rig a DNA test to prove it was you. We only discovered she was an imposter a week ago. We had a funeral for you, and a tribute, and everything."

Claudia's mouth dropped open. She slumped in the chair and closed her eyes.

Dagger was right, Riley thought. Something didn't feel right.

Chapter Thirty-Two

Riley dropped into the loveseat. "I got Mom settled in the first guest room. Something is definitely wrong."

Dagger sat beside her and took her hand. "She must be exhausted. It's likely her memory is foggy, but it could be from the drugs."

Riley deliberately shook her head. "No. I can't help feeling like she knows more than she is saying—I think she's lying to us." She pressed her lips tightly together.

"How so?"

Riley turned and studied Dagger. "Do you really believe the story about her getting away?"

Dagger shrugged his shoulders. "No, it's too easy." He rubbed her hand that was lying on his leg, enveloping her hand in his. "They've come too far to just set her free, no strings attached."

"She flinched at the mention of Wayne's name. Then, when she was talking about the night on the ship, each time Mom referred to Neal, she hesitated. And she was bordering on defensive when you asked her if she'd seen or heard anyone other than the two men."

"I thought the same thing when she answered me. As far as your other two observations, I'm glad you're here. I missed those."

"How do we handle this?" Riley asked.

"I think the best way is to act naturally. Deal with the situation a step at a time," Dagger said and gave her hand a reassuring squeeze. "Give her the facts and be there to support her. You need to keep mental notes on any behavior you notice that is out of the ordinary and tell me as soon as you're able. Your mom is showing a lot of strain and lying to you isn't something she can sustain for much longer. She'll eventually come clean. I'll keep the guys posted."

"Dagger, I need you to know how utterly grateful I am for your help in saving my mom. Something tells me I wouldn't have ever seen her again if it wasn't for you."

Dagger slid his arm around Riley's shoulders and pulled her into him. "Let's get some sleep. No matter what we must confront down the road, your mother is home safe. I intend to keep her that way."

****

Riley and Dagger walked into the kitchen and found Kaleb and Stone chatting with a smiling, charming Claudia. Riley smiled. Here was the mom she knew. Maybe today would be a better day.

Dagger reached over and took Riley's hand. She gazed up at him and smiled. Riley wished she knew if he still secretly had feelings for Kat. One thing was certain; he'd been her anchor since the second her mother phoned, and for that she would be in his debt.

"Good morning," Claudia said. She noticed them holding hands. "I guess I've missed quite a bit while I was gone. I'm looking forward to getting to know you, Dagger. If Riley likes you, you must be an exceptional man."

Stone picked up on the unease in the room. "Riley, Claudia was telling us about your early days in Oahu. How you learned to swim before you learned to walk."

"So I've often been told. Guess I've always been drawn to the water," Riley said, feeling in the spotlight. "Are you feeling better today, Mom?"

"I am. Freedom makes me feel one step closer to normal. I never really understood, until now."

"I got in touch with my friend, the police detective," Kaleb said. "I explained what happened last night. He agreed to come over here alone and interview Claudia."

"I'll feel much more relaxed staying here," Claudia said.

"Thanks, Kaleb," Riley said.

An hour later the detective arrived and Claudia repeated what she'd told Riley and the guys about her kidnapping. Her mother answered every question as briefly as she could and avoided any of the detective's attempts to get her to elaborate.

"Thank you, Dr. Rawlings. Let me know if you recall anything more. We'll put an APB out on the two Russians and keep you updated with our investigation," the police detective said, as he gathered up his things and put them in his briefcase.

"Detective, what'll happen with the woman who was identified as my mother?"

"We'll investigate recent missing person files and retest her DNA."

"Who ran the initial DNA test?" Riley asked.

"It was Proof Positive. They do most of our tests. We'll be investigating how this mix up occurred. Also, it would be in your best interest to allow us to handle the process of letting the public know you're still alive, Dr. Rawlings. Our public relations officer will want to speak with you. I'll give her your contact information, and the two of you can work out the details."

"When do you think the public relations person will contact me?" Claudia asked.

"Today's Sunday. We'll give you another day to get settled in," the police detective said. "So no later than Tuesday morning. You might as well be prepared. You're a high-profile person, coming back from the dead, so to speak. It's going to be big news for a week or so. Staying here with all the security is the best thing for you. The farther away you can keep the cameras and questions, the better off you'll be."

As the detective made his way to the door, Claudia turned to the group. "That went well," Claudia said. "I plan on returning to work on Tuesday."

Riley stared at her mother, dumbfounded. "You're not going into work. You're staying with us until the police find the people responsible for your team's deaths and your kidnapping."

"But, Riley, I need to go in—" Claudia started to explain.

"No, you don't need to be there. You're still in danger." What in the world was her mother thinking? "Dagger and his team can assign you a couple of bodyguards. You can go back to the office after the news of your return dies down, with the understanding these guards will be with you. I'm sure when the board does find out that you're still with us, they'll expect you to take a few days off. They don't even know you're alive; this is going to be a shock to everyone. They've mourned your death, Mother. They held a memorial event. Dedications were made in your name."

Claudia sucked in her breath. "I'll stay hidden only until the news of my return is out. The very next day, I'll be going back to work." Claudia held up her hand as Riley started to speak. "I need to go back to retrieve the last part of my research. I made a copy and hid it before I left for the ship. It's the only copy with my latest results—I didn't have time to update the copy on your father's grave. I'm assuming you made it there and retrieved my research?"

"Yes, we did," Riley answered. "But don't try to derail the conversation! The only way you're going back to work is with guards who will be shadowing you in close proximity and limiting your exposure outside. Once this mess gets ironed out, you can go back to life as usual."

"I suppose I can live with that," Claudia said. "I've been wondering, Riley, how did you do finding the clues I left for you?"

"I dove with Dagger down to the wreck, brought back most of your things, and found the clue in your yellow sweater," Riley said. She was standing over her mom, her hand resting on her mother's shoulder. "I followed the scavenger hunt you created for me all the way to the SSD card." Riley ran through the entire hunt.

As Claudia listened, a myriad of emotions passed over her face. Fear and panic were clear when Riley explained about being attacked while she was on Oahu; happiness when Riley spoke of getting to know Stan, Estelle, and Jill.

"Estelle and Stan were beside themselves when we told them you were dead." Riley watched as a single tear escaped and trickled down her mom's cheek. "You need to phone them tomorrow. They'll be thrilled. I understand why you spend so much time with them. They're wonderful people. We plan on visiting often," Riley told her.

Claudia reached up and patted her daughter's hand. "I knew you'd be able to figure out the clues. You're the only person who would be able to ferret out my hunt."

"We only recently discovered it wasn't you in the morgue because the poor woman's face was mangled," Riley said. "Aunt Fran identified your body and only had your build and hair color to go by. She didn't know about your tattoo."

"I wouldn't put it past Welby to order Eric to kill someone just to play the part," Dagger said. "They arrived on the research ship via helicopter. Eric could have brought the woman's body with him and dropped her on site."

"What's one more death?" Stone said. "After all they murdered everyone on board, except you, Claudia."

"How do you think my DNA test got confirmed?" Claudia asked.

"I think I have a pretty good theory," Kaleb said. "Proof Positive is one of many boards Anthony Welby sits on."

Riley was sitting next to her mother, holding her hand. Instantly, Riley noticed Claudia's hand went from warm and soft to clammy.

"The DNA didn't have to be planted on the woman's body. All Welby would need is a lab tech in his pocket. He gives the tech a sample of Claudia's DNA and voilà, the woman in the morgue is Claudia Rawlings," Stone said.

"Oh my God," Claudia whispered. Her entire body went ramrod stiff. She squeezed Riley's hand so tightly, Riley could feel her rapid pulse.

Riley turned to Claudia, and seeing her ashen face asked, "Mom, are you feeling okay?"

"All those people, my friends, my colleagues—oh, Riley. I killed them!" Claudia began to cry. "They died because I was on that boat; they died to ensure that pig had sole access to my research!"

"Mom, you didn't have anything to do with it; how can you think that? That monster did it. He didn't know who you might be working with, so he decided that killing them was nothing more than insurance. It's not your fault; it just isn't!"

"I'm feeling a bit ill," Claudia's voice came out no more than a whisper. "I need to go lay down for a bit." She gripped the arm of the loveseat and tried to stand, but failed.

"Let me help you to your room, Claudia," Dagger said as he reached down to help her up. Claudia blinked rapidly and acted as though she didn't see him. She started shaking uncontrollably, but with Dagger's help, she managed to stand, although she swayed on her feet.

"Let me help you, Dagger." Stone was immediately by his side. The two men cautiously supported Claudia. "Riley, my medical bag is in the room I stayed in. Please bring it to your mother's room."

Riley fled the room as if she were being chased by a great white shark. By the time she found Stone's medical bag and got to her mom's room, Claudia was lying down with her shoes off and Dagger was covering her with a blanket.

Stone listened to her heart for a few seconds, and then took her blood pressure.

"Do you normally have high blood pressure, Claudia?" Stone asked.

"No," Claudia replied weakly.

"Well, it's extremely high and it's safe to assume it was even higher a few minutes ago. Claudia, are you allergic to any medication?" Stone asked.

"Nothing that I'm aware of," Claudia mumbled.

"I'm going to give you a mild sedative," Stone said. "It's fast working and will help you sleep."

Claudia's lids drifted closed and her body relaxed.

"The sedative should keep her asleep for hours," Stone whispered to Riley.

"Is she doing better?" Kaleb asked when they returned downstairs.

"She was having a panic attack. It causes high blood pressure," Stone said. "I think Claudia will be okay after she sleeps for a few hours. That misplaced guilt could easily have caused her reaction."

"You're right, but there was more to it than just the guilt, as bad as that was," Riley said.

"Really? What?" Dagger replied.

"I was holding her hand. It was warm and soft. The instant Anthony's name came up, though, her hand turned clammy. The tension in her body ratcheted up the more we walked her though the events. She went totally stiff during Kaleb's explanation of DNA and Anthony being on the board of Proof Positive. She squeezed my hand so tight I almost yelped. I could see her pulse in the tendons on her neck. When I looked into her face, there were beads of sweat on her upper lip. The rest you already know. One thing is for certain, Anthony Welby is at the core of her anxiety."

"Makes perfect sense to me. Except I keep tripping up on Claudia getting free from Katarina," Dagger said.

Riley and the men made their way into the living room.

"We need to push Mom into telling the truth. We have no clue what kind of danger we all face," Riley said. "If Mom was telling us the truth about only seeing two Russian men, wouldn't it be reasonable to conclude that those were Kat's men? Perhaps even the

ones we saw at the meeting?" Riley asked.
"Yes, it would make perfect sense," Dagger agreed.

Chapter Thirty-Three

"How's she doing?" Dagger asked as Riley came down the stairs.

"She's still sound asleep in the smaller bedroom. The guys are sharing the other room. Stone's keeping a close eye on her; he doesn't want her waking up and being confused about her surroundings," Riley said.

"I called Vice Admiral Morrison and updated him," Dagger said. "He was a big help to me, and I didn't want him finding out about your mom on the news."

"What did he say?" Riley asked.

"He was thrilled for you and he said again, if we need anything, let him know."

Riley and Dagger were out on the patio grilling steaks when Claudia came out with Stone.

"This is a beautiful place, Dagger. The view is fabulous," Claudia said.

"You're looking more relaxed, Mom. How are you feeling?" Riley asked.

"Better. I'm sorry to fall apart on you; I know I'm not responsible for their deaths, but I suppose I just came to grips with my grief," Claudia said.

"True. Although I think it was more than that," Riley said as she watched her mom. Claudia stared at Riley silently, her face frozen and wary. Her mother's trepidation was palpable.

Riley mentally registered any reaction and every nuance Claudia displayed as she continued to explain. "Every time Kaleb mentioned Anthony, you reacted. Each reaction was more intense, until your body couldn't handle the stress and rebelled."

Claudia recoiled at Anthony's name. She shook her head and as she began to speak, her breath caught in her throat. "I haven't a clue...wh...what you're talking about."

"I'm not sure—" Stone started to speak and stopped short when Dagger shook his head.

"Mom, we want to help you, but you must be honest with us. You're stressed out enough from grief. And this charade you're trying to pull off isn't convincing us in the least and it's stressing you out so much it's affecting your heart." Riley took her mom's hand and led her over to a chair.

Dagger was impressed to see Riley stick to her guns.

"I can't—I can't tell you," Claudia said, looking at her feet.

"You can trust us, Claudia. We'll protect you," Dagger said. "Tell us how you really escaped."

"I can't..." Claudia's voice gave out.

"My opinion," Stone began, "based purely on your visceral reaction to Anthony's name, is that he's somehow scared the living daylights out of you."

"I think you're on to something, Stone. Coercion sounds like a logical explanation," Dagger's voice was low-pitched and soothing. "Is Anthony threatening you, Claudia?"

"No. I don't want to talk about this...I can't." Claudia refused to make eye contact with anyone as she shook her head in quick, choppy motions.

Claudia was getting more agitated by the second. Stone shot Dagger a warning look. They needed to get Claudia to talk soon, or they'd have to let it alone for a while. Dagger didn't want to chance a repeat of last night. He wondered what would frighten this woman so much she couldn't even tell her daughter. He'd seen the love in Claudia's face when she stared at Riley—finally, it dawned on him. She wasn't afraid for herself...she was protecting her daughter.

"Claudia." Dagger paused. "Anthony Welby threatened to hurt Riley if you told anyone of his involvement, didn't he?"

Claudia's panicked stare was all the answer he needed, but then she shook her head wildly, tears gushing down her face. "I must keep her safe," Claudia cried.

Riley hugged her mother tightly and she murmured 'mom' over and over as she rocked back and forth.

"He told me not to tell anyone," Claudia said between sobs. "He said he would kill you. I can't live if something happens to you."

Riley glanced pleadingly into Dagger's eyes. He knew she wanted him to say something to help sooth her mother's agitation.

"Nothing is going to happen to Riley, Claudia. I give you my word. I will protect her with my last breath." Dagger placed his hand gingerly on Claudia's back.

"We all will," Kaleb said, stepping forward with a soft smile. "We're brothers and we stick together, no matter the circumstances. You're no longer a mission or a contract…you and Riley…you're family."

"Kaleb's right, Claudia," Stone said. "No harm will come to you or your daughter. On that you have all our word."

Claudia looked up with uncertain eyes. For a few heartbeats, Dagger could swear even the birds and insects were still.

"Anthony Welby wasn't only involved in what happened," Claudia said. "He was the mastermind behind the entire plan. He sank our ship, killed everyone on board, and kidnapped me. He used Wayne Samuels and Neal like puppets and tossed them aside when he was done with them. I want that sadistic bastard thrown into the deepest, darkest hole for the rest of his natural life."

"Claudia, please tell us what really happened the night you escaped?" Dagger asked. He took a seat on the patio across from Riley and Claudia.

"May I have a glass of water?" Claudia asked as she cleared her throat. Kaleb nodded and went inside. He returned and handed Claudia a glass. She smiled and thanked him.

"I was being kept in a stateroom on a ship. The two Russian men who'd been questioning me during my capture came to my stateroom. They blindfolded me and transported me by water to another ship. I only saw the conference room, but from experience I knew it was a very large vessel." Claudia took a sip of water. "When Anthony Welby entered the room, I couldn't believe he was involved. He told me he wanted my formula…the man is insane. He killed all those innocent people just to kidnap me and get my formula. He said that since I was unwilling to give it to him, he'd taken matters into his own hands. I'm sure I riled him even more when I asked him how that was working out for him. Both because I wasn't cooperating with him and I knew Riley wouldn't have given up my formula."

"So, you poked the bear, did you?" Dagger asked.

"I did. A few times. I was just so angry at him," Claudia said. "He told me my lack of compliance had brought us to this impasse. He assured me he'd still get my formula...and then he said he was letting me go."

"He just let you walk out the door?" Riley asked, confusion etching her features.

"No. There were a few stipulations," Claudia said. She took another sip of water. "The story I told you that night...that was verbatim from Anthony. But what really happened was the two Russians blindfolded me and dropped me off where you picked me up. They even gave me a phone to call you."

"Dagger, you were right," Riley said. "We could've been walking into a trap, if it wasn't for Anthony's obsession with Mom's formula."

"I'm sorry I put you all in harm's way. I guess I didn't think." Claudia looked at Dagger and then Riley. "I would never intentionally put any of you in danger."

Riley took her mom's hand in hers. "We know, Mom. Did Anthony say anything else?"

"He did. He told me I'd be going to work for Premier Oil and Gas."

"What? You work for Sheridan," Riley stated.

"That's exactly what I said. But he said Premier is in the process of buying out Sheridan. I told him that wouldn't happen, Wayne wouldn't allow Sheridan to be taken over. Anthony said, Samuels was no longer a problem. He was gone, and Neal left with him." Claudia's eyes filled with tears. She set the glass down. "I didn't understand what Anthony was saying. Wayne and Anthony were friends. I asked him where Wayne went and how did he manage to buy out Sheridan. And what did Neal have to do with any of this? Anthony laughed at my confusion. He told me Samuels was a means to an end—nothing more. And Neal was nothing more than Anthony's ears and eyes inside Bender's office. Anthony was nearly giddy when he told me Riley was with Neal when he was killed! I remember my vision blurring with red. I wanted to kill this man with my bare hands."

Claudia straightened and squared her shoulders. "Anthony said I was to tell no one of his involvement in my kidnapping. He finished by saying if he even *thought* I'd said anything, Riley's life would be forfeit. She would die in a horrible accident. I told him not to dare threaten my daughter. He told me I misunderstood. He hadn't threatened anybody, he'd just stated a fact." Claudia shook her head. "The man is certifiable. He explained that all I needed to do is go back to work at Sheridan Enterprises and soon he would be acquiring me. And should I decide to quit, my daughter's life would be forfeit."

"That's not going to happen, Claudia," Dagger said.

"Hell no," Kaleb said. "We're taking that dickhead down."

"I assume that's why you're insisting on going back to work, because of Anthony." Dagger said.

"Of course," Claudia agreed.

"Now what do we do?" Riley asked.

"We speed up the process," Dagger said. "Tomorrow Claudia will phone Kaleb's detective friend and let him know she's ready to take the next step."

Riley and Claudia gaped at Dagger in confusion.

"You need to *appear* as if you're living up to Anthony's demands," Stone said. "And you can only do that if you go back to Sheridan."

"That I can do," Claudia said, giving them a brisk nod.

Chapter Thirty-Four

"How was your first day back?" Riley asked, as Claudia and Stone walked into Dagger's house.

"Interesting, unsettling, and long. I received a summons from Anthony. He's going to be at the company tomorrow and demanded my presence at three in Samuels' office—which he has apparently taken over."

"I don't think meeting with Anthony is the best idea," Riley said.

Dagger came into the kitchen, walked over to Riley, and put his arm around her shoulders, drawing her into him. Ever since he'd told Riley about Katarina, he was more at ease, more like himself. However, Riley was still uncertain with regards to her feelings.

"This is expected. Welby is marking his territory," Dagger explained. "Claudia is his primary asset, so he wants to be sure she's falling into line. It's happening a little quicker than we thought which is probably for the best."

"I don't think she should be alone with him. Maybe I should go," Riley said.

"You can't go with her. You do, and he'll know we suspect him of something. She needs to do this on her own," Dagger said. He turned and focused on Claudia. "Do you think you can handle this?"

"I want Riley safe. I want my life back, and I want it parasite-free," Claudia said.

Kaleb handed out glasses filled with red wine. "Here's to no more suckerfish," he said with a snicker.

****

Claudia held her head high as she exited the elevator on the floor of Wayne's office and walked into the fire. She opened the door to his office, blinked with incredulity, and examined the unfamiliar surroundings. The takeover wasn't even official and already the office was entirely redecorated. Not a trace of Wayne Samuels existed.

Anthony was on the phone and motioned for her to sit in the *one* chair in front of his desk. He was attempting to intimidate her, treating her like a child called to the principal's office. He ended his call and focused on her. Her heart thrashed in her ears. Claudia centered on her breathing. She wasn't going to allow this monster to fill her with panic any longer.

"Another few days and this company will be all mine," Anthony said.

"What about the board?" Claudia asked.

"I have no need for them. This will be a privately held company. What I do need is for you to come to work every day. I want you close, so that I can keep an eye on you. Make sure you stay in line and finish your formula. I have something you must see, Claudia."

He pushed a couple buttons on his phone and then placed it on his desk facing her. Claudia's image appeared as the video started.

"This project is mine, Wayne," Claudia on the video said.

"I realize that. I want us to work together. Think of how much more we can gain," Wayne Samuels said.

"Even if it means sinking a ship and vanishing?" Claudia asked.

The screen faded to black.

She was absolutely baffled as to what she saw. Claudia recognized her lab in the background, but she and Wayne never had this conversation. Was there no end to Anthony's treachery? "What is this?" she asked. "It's a fake."

"This is a snippet of the video proving you and Wayne were the ones behind the sinking of the research vessel and the deaths of the crew and passengers." He sneered.

"Have you lost your mind? Wayne and I never had that conversation."

"The video proves otherwise." His voice dripped with sarcasm.

"That video is fabricated. I would never do such a thing. And I know of a couple forensic scientists that could prove it's a forgery."

"I'm sure you do. Nevertheless, this video will be seen worldwide before you have a chance to dispute its contents. But then, your reputation would be totally destroyed. Then there's the matter of any scientist you contact experiencing a fatal mishap. Let me paint a picture for you—you wanted ownership of your formula. Wayne wanted in on it. So he suggested you get rid of anyone with any knowledge of your research."

"What are you talking about? The company doesn't own this project, I do."

"That's not what the world will think. They'll believe you and Wayne murdered the passengers, sunk the ship, and faked your kidnapping. All to keep you both clear of suspicion." His eyes were mere slits, reminding her of the snake he was.

Claudia shook her head and blinked rapidly a few times. She rubbed the bridge of her nose and gawked at him. *This man really is certifiable*, she thought. "Wayne is dead. Your story is flawed," Claudia replied.

"On the contrary. You, Claudia, are a greedy and spiteful woman. Wayne provided a service, and when he was no longer of value, you rid yourself of him. You'd no intention of sharing your wealth with the man."

"So—that's what everything boils down to for you. Money," she bit out.

"The one with the most money rules the world."

She couldn't help herself. She laughed. This man was insane.

For the life of her, she couldn't recall what she'd found interesting about him. To think, she once called Anthony a friend, a man she dated, and enjoyed having long conversations with. It was all a façade, she realized that now.

Anthony's nostrils flared. He slammed his fists down on the desk and bared his teeth at her like a wild animal. "Don't you dare laugh at me! You're a complete idiot, Claudia. You don't know it yet, but your life is over. You belong to *me* now."

"No. I. Don't." She challenged him with a steely stare.

He glared at her. His eyes protruded from his fire-engine-red face as he sucked in a breath. "You have two days to conform. This is only a snippet of the video. The rest of it proves everything I've said. There will be no doubt you are the person behind the entire plan. I'm leaving on my boat tomorrow. You are to meet me there Sunday night at exactly six in the evening, with your formula and research." He threw a slip of paper at her. "Those are the coordinates."

"And what if I don't?"

"If you don't, you will be very sorry—as will Riley."

Claudia jumped up and leaned so close that she was nose-to-nose with Anthony. "Riley has nothing to do with this," she screamed. "You leave her out of it."

"There are more ways to hurt you than physical. I'll take the one thing in this world that means the most to you and make you watch while I kill her." Anthony smirked at his threat.

Claudia reared back like a cobra preparing to strike. Her eyes fixed on his as she silently cursed herself for the day she allowed Anthony Welby into her life.

Without another word, she turned and headed for the door.

"Two days. Sunday night at six, Claudia. Otherwise this video goes directly to the news, and you can kiss your little girl farewell."

****

Dagger's doorbell rang and he headed to see who it was.

"It's Claudia," Stone said, inspecting the security monitor. "She's early. Why is she ringing the bell? We gave her a key."

Dagger threw open the door, noticed the dark sedan in front of the house and the bodyguard a few feet behind Claudia. She was flushed, antsy, and on edge.

"Claudia, why didn't you use your key?" Dagger asked. "Welby could have—"

"Believe me. I'm totally safe. At least for the next two days. He'll be out of town and won't have any interest in me for the next forty-eight hours, give or take," Claudia said as she walked in the house. "Sorry, I left all my stuff in my office."

She'd moved into the main room and was pacing jerkily, reminding Dagger of a junkie needing her next fix. Everyone gathered in the room and left her a good deal of space.

"Mom, what's wrong?" Riley asked as she came in from the patio. "Can I get you something?"

Claudia continued to pace, acting as if she'd not heard Riley and oblivious to the world around her.

"What did Welby tell you?" Dagger asked.

She spun around and pinned him with her wide eyes. "Everything. He told me everything!"

"Claudia, maybe you should rest for a bit. The last thing we want is for you to have another attack," Stone said.

"I'm fine. Really, I am. Just pissed off! The arrogant son-of-a-bitch!"

Eyebrows shot skyward around the room.

"Tell us everything that happened at your meeting," Riley said. "But could you please take a seat? You're making us all dizzy."

Claudia stopped and looked around the room. "That man is undeniably insane. Truly, he is. He's already taking over the company and the deal isn't done…the company isn't his yet."

"Tell us what he said," Dagger said.

"I know his endgame. He plans to take me down, in every possible way." She dropped into the nearest seat. "He's created a video which makes me appear to be the mastermind behind the sinking of the ship, the staging of my kidnapping, and Wayne's murder."

"What?" Kaleb asked.

"He has a video. He showed me a snippet of it. I'm talking to Wayne and I admit everything."

"Did you and Wayne ever have such a conversation?" Dagger asked.

"Never…The man said—he *owned me*," Claudia said, her voice rising with disbelief.

"I bet that went over well," Riley mumbled, attempting to lighten the mood.

Claudia smiled. "I think that was the point when I literally got up in his face."

"Go Claudia," Kaleb cheered.

"He's the most egotistical, despicable, asinine bastard I've ever had the misfortune to know. He actually thinks living is all about having the most money."

"So what did he want from you?" Dagger asked with a slight chuckle. It was good to see Claudia taking back her life.

"He wants me to meet him Sunday evening at six on his boat." She yanked the slip of paper from her pocket and handed it to Dagger. "These are the coordinates. I'm to bring my research and formula with me. If I don't, he said he would kill Riley and make me watch."

Dagger's hands clenched. "When hell freezes over."

"This is good," Stone said. Dagger glared at his partner. "What I mean is, now we know his plan and we can make one of our own."

"Claudia, why haven't you investigated the possibility of a buyer for your bio-fuel?" Kaleb asked.

"It requires more testing on a larger level on a larger,

undistributed algae bed ideally. To do that, I'd need more time and more resources."

"Sounds like you need a backer with deep pockets," Stone said.

"A backer would be ideal. With one caveat, it must be someone with morals that can stand up to the prospect of dollar signs. I would rather my discovery never come to light than fall into the hands of someone who only wants it *purely* for profit. Prime example—someone like Anthony Welby."

"So far, you've only dealt with the Waynes and Anthonys of the industry," Dagger said.

"Yes. Believe me, I'm not naïve. I realize most companies only see the bottom line. However, I refuse to be the person who triggers the pillaging and destruction of our oceans," Claudia said.

"We have twenty-four hours to work out a plan," Dagger said.

Chapter Thirty-Five

They were all gathered at the table finishing breakfast. Dagger's phone beeped. He pulled it from his pants pocket and read the message. "Claudia, your ride will be here in thirty minutes."

"Geez, if I didn't know any better, I'd say you all couldn't wait to be rid of me," Claudia huffed and got up from the table.

Riley, Dagger, Stone, and Kaleb looked at one another.

"Kinda feel like we just kicked a puppy," Kaleb said.

"I heard that," Claudia said from halfway up the stairs.

Everyone chuckled.

Fifteen minutes later Dagger's phone beeped again. He read the text and entered a reply. "He'll be here in ten. Let's shuffle the cars around and clear a space for him in the garage."

Riley and Claudia were sitting in the main room when the guys came in from the garage.

"Good morning ladies. It's wonderful to see you again, Claudia."

"Henry? Don't tell me you're the person the guys called in to babysit me?" Claudia narrowed her eyes. "Why didn't you tell me you were going to ask Admiral Morrison? He's much too busy a man to be watching over me."

"I confided in Admiral Morrison a while back with regards to this mission. He insisted we keep him updated and call on him if we needed help. We need help. There's no one else we can trust, and no one will think to look for you at the admiral's," Dagger said.

"I'm honored to help. And please call me Henry."

"I don't know if I can do that," Dagger said.

"It's an order, Commander. Outside of any professional event, I'm Henry, got it?"

"Yes, sir," all three men answered, their backbones stiffening as if coming to attention.

"Okay. My understanding is I keep Claudia out of sight at my house until you come to retrieve her."

"Yes, sir," Dagger said. "I meant to ask, is your staff still on duty?"

"I gave most of my staff two days off. The only people left are my security personnel, lead housekeeper, and chef. I can't cook worth a damn," Admiral Morrison snorted. "Not to worry. They have top security clearances."

"I'll run up and get Claudia's bags," Stone said.

Stone returned with a suitcase in each hand and headed for the garage. Kaleb grabbed the door for him, and everyone followed him out.

"Mom lie down in the back seat," Riley said. "We don't want anyone to see you leave and follow you."

"Ready, Claudia?" Morrison asked. "Don't worry about a thing, Claudia is in good hands. You get this done and stay safe. Personally, I can't wait to see Anthony Welby behind bars. I always thought he was an arrogant pissant," Morrison huffed. "It's a beautiful day, Claudia. I hope you brought your swimsuit. My lanai is fully glass enclosed and camouflaged with greenery on three sides. My security is top-notch, so we'll be able to enjoy ourselves." Morrison smiled at Claudia as he escorted her out to the garage.

"You boys promise me you'll be extra careful. I could lose my formula and my freedom. What I can't lose is my daughter," Claudia said. She examined the three men's faces. "You guys take care of her."

They said goodbye and Riley hugged her mom. Then they loaded Claudia and her bags into the admiral's glacier-blue Bentley. Stone pushed the button on the wall and the garage door rose. Admiral Morrison gave them a thumbs-up and drove away.

"I guess it does pay to work your way up to the top levels," Kaleb said as he shook his head. "That's one sweet ride."

"I'm sure it helps that he's single," Riley said.

"How long has he been divorced?" Stone asked.

"He hasn't. Admiral Morrison is single—as in never married."

"And he's smitten with your mother," Dagger said. "He's been very worried about her. I think he's texted me every day to check on her."

"So why haven't they ever gotten together?" Kaleb asked.

"I don't know—timing?" Riley shrugged her shoulders. "Admiral Morrison is a private man. You must be in his position. I think the times they've run into one another the past few years, either one or the other has been involved with other people or tied up with work."

"Well, Dagger—we might have to start calling you Cupid," Stone said.

Riley laughed so hard she snorted.

Dagger shot him a glance. "I dare ya."

Dagger sat on his patio, his feet resting on a hassock. Riley walked out and dropped down next to him.

"You really think we can pull this off?" she asked.

"It's all about the timing. We've contacted every source we have between the three of us. Welby's boat has been anchored in the same spot since last night. His chopper took off from there early this morning…Are you sure you want to do this?" Dagger asked her.

Riley lifted her head and focused squarely on Dagger's eyes. "I don't have a choice. Anthony isn't getting close to my mother or her formula."

"You're an extraordinary woman, Riley Rawlings." Dagger cupped her chin and gave her a quick kiss.

Stone pulled open the sliding glass door leading out to the patio. "Riley, Eddy's here."

She followed Stone back into the house. A short stocky man with expertly-styled flaming red hair stood in the kitchen emptying cases on the counter.

"Nice to meet you, Eddy." Riley extended her hand.

"You're a real beauty," Eddy said, taking her hand in both of his and kissing her cheek.

"Stick to your job and don't get any ideas, Eddy," Dagger said as he walked in.

"Ooohhh," Eddy replied in a sing-song voice. "This is a first. I must compliment you, Dagger. You, my friend, have excellent taste." He gave Riley an animated smile. "Have a seat, my lady, and let's get started.

"Kaleb and I are running back to the shop and picking up a few more things. Stone will stay here with you," said Dagger as he grabbed his keys and headed for the garage door.

"What? You don't trust me to be alone with this lovely lady?" Eddy feigned hurt.

"I do…but why tempt you?" Dagger joked and winked at Riley, then headed out the door. Kaleb chuckled and slapped Eddy on his shoulder as he followed Dagger out.

"I studied the pictures you sent me. Your mother is stunning. I know where you get your wonderful features. It took me some time to get the eyes spot on, but I did it. I have to say what worries me most is your hair." Eddy ran his hands through Riley's thick, straight hair as he spoke.

"Why my hair? Aren't I wearing a wig?" Riley pulled her hair up onto her head.

"Yes, you are." He opened his tall case sitting on the counter and carefully pulled out the Styrofoam head with a wig resting on it.

"My goodness. I could swear its mom's hair. It's perfect." Riley gently ran her hands over the wig.

"I'm worried about the thickness and length of your hair. Even with my supersonic hair gel, I'm not sure I can get it plastered close enough to your head. I'll put a bald cap over your hair and tack it in place with some glue. However, it still may not be enough to give the illusion of your mom's correct head shape." Eddy said. "Worst case scenario, I might have to do a tad bit of thinning and cut a few inches of length off."

Riley's neck was stiff. She didn't understand how actors put up with this routine every day.

"There. What do you think? I took off only enough length to get the right look." Eddy handed her a mirror.

"It looks good. You saved me a trip to the stylist." She glanced down at the hair on the floor.

Eddy took the hand mirror from Riley and pulled out the table mirror from the wig box. "Now comes the magic."

Eddy pulled two pictures out of his briefcase, one of Riley's face, the other Claudia's. He'd drawn lines and made measurements on the photos. It fascinated her. He grabbed a bottle and squirted a generous amount into his hand. Rubbing the contents all through Riley's hair, he slicked her hair back and up, pushing it snug against her skull. Grasping the next bottle, he picked up the wig, and spread a thin line of glue all over the inside edges. Studying the pictures of Claudia, he pinpointed an exact spot on Riley's head, placed a small section down, and drew the rest of the wig over her head. Her mother's hair was sable brown, much lighter than Riley's, and stopped at her shoulders. Riley's hair was naturally straight; her mom's hair had a natural wave.

Riley looked similar to her mom, with subtle differences. Claudia's cheeks were fuller and her nose slightly wider. Her eyes were a light hazel and her complexion lighter. Riley had her dad's bronze complexion and deep chocolate eyes. Her eyes were so dark at first glance, her pupils appeared blended into her irises. Her lips were a tad fuller than Claudia's.

"I initially planned on making you a complete silicone mask, but I think we can get around it." He took out four silicone pieces. Two were three inches long and looked like a narrow 'D' and the other two were smaller and narrower.

Eddy rubbed a cleaning solution over her face and allowed it to dry. He placed glue on the back of one of the larger pieces, glanced at the pictures, and placed the piece on her cheek. He repeated the process on her other cheek, along with gluing the smaller pieces along the length of her nose. He opened a jar and spread what looked like soft clay on the edges of the prosthetics and blended the clay onto her skin.

Eddy stood back and studied his creation. Finally, he walked to the other end of the table, picked up a huge black case, and set it down next to the mirror.

She had never seen so much makeup. It rivaled the makeup department store counters.

Flipping through several jars, he pulled out his choice along with a sponge and brush. "Close your eyes, doll. Don't open them until I tell you to."

Riley sat quietly while Eddy applied her makeup.

"Okay, open your eyes. Don't move," he said as he quickly and expertly dropped a colored contact lens in each eye. "Close your eyes and then blink a couple times—perfect. Have a gander."

Riley picked up her mirror. "Oh, my gosh. I'm my mother! You are a genius, Eddy."

"I am, aren't I. And...I was right." Eddy crossed his arms over his chest as he admired his work. "Once I lightened your complexion, put in your cheek and nose prosthetics, you don't even notice the slight difference in your lips. Especially with the light-colored lipstick. Take this." He put the lipstick in her hand. "Make sure to reapply this right before you 'go on.'" He grinned and winked at her. "I'm also leaving you this bottle of makeup removal compound. When you want to remove your bald cap and prosthetics, put the compound around the edges."

"Thank you, Eddy."

"Go and change into your mom's clothes. Make sure to choose a long-sleeved top, otherwise we'll have to put the makeup I applied to your face on your exposed arms. I need to see the complete package."

"How's it going?" Stone asked as he walked in from outside.

"Riley could be mistaken for Claudia's twin," Eddy said. "She's upstairs getting changed."

"Want a beer?" Stone asked.

"I wouldn't turn one down," Eddy said.

Riley walked down the stairs and into the main room where the two guys were relaxing. Stone was taking a drink from his bottle when he saw her.

"Holy crap." Stone coughed, choking on the beer. "Riley?"

"What do you think?" She turned modeling the long-sleeve button-down blouse with an abstract design of jade and royal blue, a pair of Claudia's deck shoes.

"Wow... If I didn't know any better, I'd swear I was staring at Claudia. Outstanding job, Eddy," Stone said.

"Why, thank you." Eddy made a mock toast with his bottle.

The door to the garage opened and Dagger and Kaleb walked in.

"Whoa!" Kaleb said. He walked closer to Riley, gawking at her. "You even made her look older with the little lines around her eyes...I mean, ahh—shit!" Kaleb's face flushed crimson as everyone cracked up at his embarrassment.

"Just don't be an idiot and repeat that to Claudia," Dagger said, as he slapped his friend on the back. "You are an artist, Eddy, truly."

"You guys are gonna make me blush," Eddy said. He got up and started packing up his supplies. "My work here is done."

"Let us pay you today, Eddy. We put you out by calling at the last minute. We're lucky you were available," Dagger said.

"I'll bill you same as always. It was my pleasure. You guys are my number one clients. I'll get out of your way."

"Thank you so much." Riley walked over to Eddy and kissed him on the cheek. Stone and Kaleb carried out Eddy's supplies. Dagger leaned against the kitchen counter and eyed Riley.

"Not many people get this chance," he said. As his eyes traveled over her body, an electrifying caress followed.

"What do you mean?" Riley's brows drew together as she picked up the mirror. She peered into it trying to figure out what Dagger was referring to.

"I already knew that you'd get even more dazzling as you age. How could you not? Like mother, like daughter."

Chapter Thirty-Six

"This was the best you could do?" Kaleb asked, snickering at the rickety boat.

Riley, Dagger, and Kaleb stood on the dock looking at the twenty-six-foot motor boat. The aft deck was open and lined on three sides with built-in benches. The cuddy cabin was at the bow, the top half of the cabin walls contained glass, except for a small section that housed the head. The steering station was at the rear of the cabin, built in next to the head. Riley could tell this boat had seen better days.

"I'd like to see you do better," Stone said. "This little gem is on loan from a friend—so don't blow it up. Or if you rather, the three of you could arrive in *our* boat. Maybe the bad guys won't notice 'Salvage Hunter' written in big bold letters across the stern."

"Smartass," Kaleb said.

"Knock it off guys," Dagger said, as he dropped his gear into the boat. "You better head out, Stone. We'll wait here until you give us the go-ahead. Don't push your luck. If the place is crawling with security, forget it."

"And if I do?" Kaleb asked. "What happens if sleaze-bag Welby has additional ammunition tucked away in his home office?"

"It's not worth risking your life, Stone," Riley said.

"You're taking a huge risk, Riley," Stone said as he gathered up his things. "I'm not going to be the one who screws it up. I'll secure anything I come across. You guys be careful."

"See ya on the flip side," Kaleb said.

Stone pushed a tiny ear piece into his ear. "Testing, one, two, three."

"Gotcha loud and clear." Kaleb gave his partner the thumbs-up. Stone returned the gesture and headed for the parking lot.

"We're going to head back to the office and wait for Stone's call," Dagger said.

"I'll stay here and watch the so-called boat." Kaleb smirked.

"I count three guards outside Welby's," Stone's whispered voice filled the office as it came through the office phone's speaker.

"How about inside?" Dagger asked.

"There was one. He came out a few minutes ago and took dinner orders, then he took off. I think they'll all take a break when their food shows up. I'm good to go. You should be, too. Watch your six."

"Right back atcha." Dagger said. "Ready?" He looked over at Riley.

"Yes. I want this entire fiasco over. Mom's life is on shaky ground until we get the evidence to put Anthony away." Riley marveled at the way these three guys went from joking and ragging on one another one second and then flipped a switch and became a cohesive team. She hoped she didn't muck up this entire plan.

Dagger took Riley's hand and they walked down to the docks. Kaleb was typing away on his tablet.

"Guess you heard Stone is breaching Welby's estate," Kaleb said without glancing up.

"You ready to get this done, or are you too busy writing the next great novel?" Dagger asked.

Kaleb shook his head and made a face that reminded Riley of a mom embarrassed by her teenager. "Funny…Stone will activate his mic after he gets inside Welby's office." Kaleb focused his attention on them. "Come aboard. Let's get this game started." He reached out and offered his hand to Riley.

Dagger untied the bow and stern lines and threw them into the boat, then got into the boat and pulled in the bumpers. "This boat does go faster than four knots, doesn't it?"

Kaleb's half-lidded eyes sliced in Dagger's direction. One side of his mouth quirked up. "How do I do that? Is it this stick marked 'throttle'?" Kaleb asked in a flat voice.

"Jackass," Dagger mumbled.

He sat down next to Riley. She was laughing.

"Traitor," he teased as he gave her a light bump with his shoulder.

"What are you talking about?" she asked, the picture of innocence.

Dagger shook his head. "I'm pretty sure Claudia would never act like that."

"How 'bout I really freak you out?" Riley winked at him a couple of times and puckered her lips making kissing sounds.

"Not in front of the child." He chuckled and snaked his arm around her waist and tugged her closer.

Kaleb cleared the jetty and pushed the throttle forward. They increased speed and headed out to sea. The only sound was the purring of the engine.

"We're approximately fifteen miles away," Kaleb said a while later. "Seas are pretty calm. I don't think we should get any closer than a mile. We don't want to call attention to ourselves while you're slipping out of the boat."

Dagger got up and walked over to his equipment. He tugged on his wet suit and slid his goggles on top of his head; then he strapped on his weight belt and attached his knife. Next, he checked his oxygen tank and meter and hauled on the tank. His Glock, suppressor, and leg drop holster went inside his dry bag.

"Take this." Kaleb handed him a small gray plastic box. "It's your earpiece. Turn it on and put it in as soon as you're on board. It's sound activated. I'll relay any news from Stone to you and vice versa."

"Sounds good." Dagger took the box and shoved it into the dry bag. "How far out are we?"

"Three miles."

"I'll get out at one mile."

"I'm going to swing wide and approach at an angle," Kaleb said. "Less eyes to spot you."

"Gotcha." Dagger walked over to Riley. She stood as he got close. "Don't take any chances. I should be on board fifteen minutes after you."

She nodded. "Be careful. I don't want you getting hurt."

"Dagger, you're up. Do you want me to slow down, old man?" Kaleb joked.

"Who you calling old man? No, just keep it steady and don't run me over, junior."

Dagger got on the last bit of his equipment as the boat slowed slightly. Sitting on the gunwale, he gave Kaleb a thumbs-up. Placing one hand on his mouthpiece and the other on the front of his mask, he winked at Riley and fell back into the ocean.

Riley turned around, eyes scouring the surface of the water. Dagger popped up and gave them the 'okay' sign. She released her breath and her heart started to beat again.

"Is he good?" Kaleb asked, never looking back.

"Yes."

"Don't worry so much, Riley. Dagger's done this same maneuver a thousand times. He'll be fine." Kaleb throttled down, and they crept over the water. "Don't want our friends thinking we're in a hurry."

Anthony Welby's one-hundred-foot luxury motor yacht came into view. Riley raised her hands to her forehead, blocking out the sun as she took in the site of the magnificent ship. Suddenly, she experienced a heaviness in her stomach. Was she really going through with this plan? She pushed the thought out of her mind.

Kaleb whistled. "Now that's a beauty," Kaleb said. "Too bad it's soon to be dry-docked."

"We can only hope," Riley said.

Kaleb peered at his watch. "We're an hour early. What are you going to say if they ask why?"

"I know what to say. Don't worry so much, Kaleb." She gave him a crafty grin when his eyes darted to her.

"Cute. I think you've been spending too much time around my good friend, Dagger. You're starting to sound like a smartass."

"Thank you."

He chuckled and shook his head. Reaching under the wheel, he tugged out a green ball cap with a company name on it and shoved it on his head. "Welcome to First Class Water Taxi."

She laughed at the absurdity of it. "Seriously?"

"Hey. I didn't name the company. All kidding aside, you really are good for him, Riley. I haven't seen him this happy in years. So don't do anything dumb on board."

"Aww thanks, Kaleb. I'll try my best."

They were yards away from the yacht when two men appeared on the aft deck.

"Oh, goodie. A welcoming committee." Kaleb pulled alongside the deck and threw a rope to the bigger man standing there.

The man snatched it and hauled the boat in, barely allowing Kaleb enough time to toss the bumpers over the side. Riley stepped on the gunwale of her boat and placed one foot on the stairs of the yacht. She was stopped in her tracks as a thug who could be Mr. Clean's clone stepped squarely in her path.

"Dr. Rawlings?" Mr. Clean asked in a deep voice.

"Yes. I have an appointment with Mr. Welby." Riley did her best to act put out.

"You're an hour early."

"I realize as much. Do you know how difficult it is to secure a water taxi on such short notice this time of year?" Without allowing the man to answer she continued, "I had to agree to leave earlier than I planned or else I'd be on stand-by until the next boat was free. Would you prefer me to be late?"

Riley crossed her arms over her chest and glared at Mr. Clean, who looked to his left, as if imploring his partner to help him out. The only response he received was a shoulder shrug and questioning gawk.

"Right this way," Mr. Clean said as he stepped aside.

He eyed Kaleb. Kaleb ignored him; he just whistled and turned away. Then he nabbed a book and settled into the cushioned bench, putting his feet up and pretended to read.

The trio walked to the door and disappeared.

****

Kaleb glanced down at his watch. Dagger should be close by now.

He reached into his pocket and slipped his earpiece into his ear. "How's it going, Stone?"

It took a minute for Stone to reply.

"You caught me at a bad time. Thought I was going to have to put a man down. He got lucky, nature called," Stone said. "I'm in Welby's office. Hold on."

There was shuffling and colorful language. "Problem?"

"The dumbass guard is right outside the door, talking on his phone."

"We can't wait all day. You're gonna have to move it."

"Yeah, yeah," Stone replied in a loud whisper.

Kaleb waited for Stone.

"Cocky bastard."

"The guard?"

"No, Welby. The nimrod left his computer on. It was asleep."

"Well, that makes things easier. Place the SSD card in."

"Then what?"

"I'll walk you through it."

"Kaleb," Dagger's voice sounded on his hand-held radio. The radio was disguised as a phone.

"Hold on, Stone. I hear you, Dagger. What's your status?"

"I'm aboard. Are we on schedule?"

"Roger. Riley was escorted away. Stone's downloading Welby's computer as we speak."

"Roger. Any idea where they were heading?"

"Nope. They weren't exactly thrilled she's here early."

"Okay. I'll find a spot and keep a lookout."

"Roger, Dagger." Kaleb switched back to his earpiece. "How ya doing, Stone?"

"I think it's about half done."

"Let me know when it's finished, and I'll walk you through hiding our tracks. Did you find anything else?"

"No. The place is spotless. My guess is everything is on the computer."

"I'll bet there's a badass of a decryption code I'm going to have to deal with."

"And you'll enjoy every minute. Everything is downloaded."

****

Mr. Clean walked Riley up two decks. He stopped. Punched in a code and opened a door. "You can wait in here. Don't touch anything. This is where Mr. Welby will soon be meeting you."

She walked in and was surprised to see a large desk. Mr. Clean made her life easier by walking her right into Anthony's office. "Mind if I use the head?" she asked.

"Go ahead." The guard pushed the door back against the wall. "I'll be right here." He stood in the open doorway to the suite.

Great, Riley thought.

This was not going to be as simple as she'd hoped. She went into the bathroom, closed the door, and did a quick inspection to make certain she wasn't being watched. Once she was sure it was clear, she opened her mother's purse and extracted the tiny bug. She practiced with it for a few minutes, placing it in different positions between her fingers.

Thank goodness the bug would activate as soon as it was attached to a solid surface. It was going to be a challenge securing it close enough to the desk with the guard watching her every move.

Surely he would notice if she had to fiddle around to turn it on.

Riley glimpsed the mirror and froze when her mother looked back. No wonder the guys had acted a bit uncomfortable. She did, just looking in the mirror.

She reapplied the lipstick Eddy gave her and placed the bug at the first joint between her middle and ring finger. She flushed the toilet and quickly turned the water on and off. She closed her eyes, took a few deep breaths, and then headed back into the suite.

Mr. Clean hadn't moved an inch. Riley wandered around the room aimlessly, steering clear of the desk. He remained mute, and yet she felt his stare burning into her back. She walked toward the bookcase behind the desk and caught the subtle alertness of her babysitter.

"Mind?" she asked, as she pointed to a row of books.

He squinted at her, undecided. Finally he nodded, but still suspicious, he grumbled unintelligibly.

Riley smiled her thanks and pretended to be engrossed with the titles. She moved closer to the desk but stopped when she perceived his energy bristle and yanked out a book.

Time was quickly running out. Closing the book, she slid it back into its place, turning at the same time and stumbling forward. As she did so, she reached up to catch herself and pressed the bug as far back into the bookcase as possible, attaching it to the bottom side of the waist-high shelf.

Finding her footing, she stopped and brushed her hands down her blouse. Riley was tempted to turn to see what the guard was doing, yet fought the urge. Instead, she pulled a book from the shelf above, opened it and started to skim through it, something she knew her mother would have done. A few minutes later, she coughed, patted her chest, and coughed again. Slipping the book back into place she turned to the guard.

"Is it possible to get a drink?" She coughed.

Mr. Clean studied her.

There was a buzz and the guard yanked what looked like a pager from his pocket. "Mr. Welby is running late. He said to make you comfortable. Come with me," Mr. Clean said, walking her to a lounge area.

"Help yourself," he said nodding to the dining room.

An impressive buffet ran one wall of the dining area. Riley fixed a cup of coffee. At the same time, Mr. Clean's radio squawked.

"Yeah," he answered. "What? Shit. I'll be right there." He snapped the radio back on his belt. An alarm started to scream. That was her signal Dagger was on board.

"What's going on?" Riley asked.

"Nothing that concerns you. Stay put. I'll be right back." He hurried away.

That was Riley's cue. She headed back in the direction of the stern. Right before she opened the hatch leading to the companionway, she spotted a guard standing at the top of the stairs.

Her escape route was blocked.

Chapter Thirty-Seven

Anthony would see right through her disguise as soon as she spoke. Unable to reach the boat by returning the way she'd come, she needed to find another way off this yacht. Where was Dagger's diversion?

Every direction Riley turned was peppered with guards. The only vacant avenue was up to the next deck. With no other option, she entered the companionway and climbed up to the bridge.

Three of the crew milled about. She bypassed the bridge and continued up to the top deck. She peered out the small porthole, inspecting the half of the deck she could see.

Not seeing anyone, Riley cracked the hatch open. Twilight had fallen, making it difficult to verify the deck was indeed deserted but from as far as she could tell, the deck was empty. She stepped out and ran to the nearest gunwale. She glanced over the side in pursuit of a ladder—no luck, and the water was so far away. Tiptoeing around the deck, Riley hunted for the easiest way down to the water.

There was a thump that sounded like someone jumping onto the deck, making Riley halt midstride. She listened for any sound out of place, fixed like a statue for minutes. The wind picked up, the yacht bobbed between the growing waves, and she was met with only the sound of the water lapping against the side of the vessel. To say she was spooked was an understatement. She twitched at every trivial sound.

Focus. You're running out of time. She could swear she heard Dagger's voice in her head.

She was bent over the gunwale to get a better view when all at once her feet left the deck. Riley reached out blindly, grappling for the rail to keep herself from being thrown off the yacht. The distance was too far. An arm coiled around her waist and wrenched her back, tearing her hands away from the rail. Her attacker slid her arm right up under Riley's breasts, strangling Riley across her chest. A faint feeling filled Riley. An icy fist clenched her heart and she struggle just to take in one more breath.

"Well, well, well, Dr. Rawlings. I don't believe you were given free run of the yacht. It's quite rude to leave before the evening's festivities even get started."

The sound of this woman's voice was seared clear down to the deepest depths of Riley's soul. Nevertheless, she remained silent, biting her tongue, fully aware that her false identity was the only thing keeping her alive.

Riley remained mute. Her feet were barely tickling the deck, and the attacker continuously tightened her death grip around Riley's chest. And yet these were nothing in comparison to the razor-sharp blade of the knife pressed flat against her throat.

"What, no snappy comeback? Oh, I'm sorry. We haven't been properly introduced. My name is Katarina Petrin. You were my guest aboard my ship for those many weeks. Anthony believes he can frighten you into giving up your formula. I'm not as gullible...I've studied you, Claudia."

Riley couldn't begin to imagine what type of hell Katarina and Anthony had put her mom through during her incarceration.

"I know you'd rather die than allow any of your work to fall into the wrong hands. That's why I'm here." Katarina leaned in, breathing the next words into her ear. "You're leaving with me. My new buyer will pay triple the amount for you than Anthony has offered."

Katarina stepped forward, forcing Riley to move with her. Her body began to tingle due to lack of circulation. She felt like a ragdoll being dragged round the deck. *Dagger where are you, where are you?* These words looped through Riley's mind. He would come, but if he did, he, too, would be in danger.

They were halfway to the stairwell when the door flew open. Dagger filled the hatchway, backlit. His relaxed stance was belied by the business end of a Glock reflecting in the last of the day's light and pointed directly at Katarina. Water glistened off his black wet suit. He looked every inch the warrior.

"Drop the knife and move away from her, Katarina," Dagger

threatened, his baritone filling the space. "Step away, and I'll let you leave."

"Let me? You'll—let—*me*—leave?!" Condescension dripped from every one of Katarina's words. "Claudia, you must be paying him well to shadow you here. Tell me, is your daughter his bonus?"

Riley remained frozen and mute in Katarina's steely grip.

"Where's your tongue now?" Katarina pressed the knife harder against Riley's throat. Riley held her breath. One exhale could slice her open.

"I'm not going to repeat myself again, Katarina. Let her go," Dagger commanded. Every muscle of his outstretched arm was taught. Riley could barely see the movement in his chest as he breathed in and out. He looked every bit like a marble sculpture of Zeus. Any moment he could throw a thunderbolt and end this standoff.

This woman was insane. She was rambling and making no sense. Dagger had to keep the upper hand. Money was the only thing Kat held more sacred than killing. He'd faced down this same situation so many times, he'd lost count. Except never before had he experienced the sensation currently flooding his system. He was fighting two fronts at once. Katarina, he understood. The mental battle, the adrenalin coursing through his every cell was something he'd never felt. The feral terror of the knife at Riley's throat filled his vision. It was only due to the years of missions that held Dagger in one piece.

"Oh, I'm leaving, Dagger. And I'm taking Dr. Rawlings with me. Tell him to stand down, Claudia. Don't test me," Katarina snarled.

Katarina lightly sliced the surface of Riley's skin. Riley gasped at the pain. With the knife still against Riley's neck, Katarina grabbed Riley's wig and yanked back so violently, both the wig and the bald cap ripped away. Riley shrieked in pain, as small patches of skin tore from her head. Her straight, cocoa-brown hair tumbled around her shoulders.

"Riley Rawlings. Isn't this a surprise. Seems the game has changed. I thought I held the queen, when really all I've got is a pawn. And a bleeding one at that," Kat growled.

"Step away from Riley, Katarina." Dagger had no intention of losing Riley. He took a step toward the women.

"Ohhh…do you have feelings for this little vixen?" Kat rubbed the spine of her blade down Riley's neck and chest, a red trail left behind. "I am disappointed in you, Dagger. Do you think you can shoot me before I slice Riley's neck wide open?"

"Don't make the mistake of doubting my conviction." It took every ounce of willpower for Dagger to look away from the knife and focus only on Kat's eyes. "I won't hesitate to shoot you."

"You would shoot your own fiancée?" Kat swung her hair back.

"You're not my fiancée anymore, Katarina. You never were. I was engaged to an illusion, someone who never existed. Someone who never had feelings for me. It's over. Put the fucking knife down and walk….a…way." His sight never swayed from hers. He was watching for her tell. She may not be the woman she pretended to be. However, he'd been on enough missions with her to recognize her tell…He waited.

Katarina's eyes shot from one side of the deck to the other. He could see she was searching for solutions and exits.

"Don't even think of trying anything stupid," Dagger warned.

Kat threw him a sardonic grin. Dagger knew Kat's ability to work a situation to her advantage. And he knew she wanted to take Riley with her for leverage. If Kat decided she couldn't escape with Riley in tow, she wouldn't hesitate to kill her. He watched. He would know what she decided the very instant Kat knew. He'd have a nanosecond to decide on his shot.

Kat took a step backward. Dagger couldn't help himself, he locked eyes with Riley and gave a subtle head shake. She wanted to fight.

No, Riley. Don't move. Don't even twitch, he thought as hard as he could.

She was in the grips of a cornered wild animal. Katarina would lash out if Riley made any sudden movements. Riley needed to trust in him now.

Kat took another backward step, butting up to the gunwale. She flung Riley out of her grip and attempted to push her over the edge of the gunwale and overboard.

Riley ducked down closer to the deck, before Katarina could reclaim her death grip on her. Katarina stood still for just a half second. She glanced at Dagger, flashing a look he knew so well. The look signaled Kat was about to play her final hand. Dagger aimed his Glock and shot.

The bullet found its target and struck Kat's shoulder, pushing her against the top of the gunwale. Trying to stop her plunge over the side, Katarina frantically reached for Riley. Riley jerked away and sprawled out flat on the deck as Katarina toppled over the gunwale, screeching Dagger's name, and fell into the sea below.

Dagger ran to Riley. "Riley, you're bleeding. Put pressure on your neck," Dagger said. A light flashed on his wristband.

"What's that?" Riley asked, pointing to the blinking light.

"Our radar has triggered. There's an inbound vehicle," Dagger said. "Can you walk?"

"Yes," Riley answered, as she wiped away the blood oozing from one of the places on her head.

"We need to hightail it off this bucket of bolts, yesterday."

They headed back down the companionway. As they reached the second deck, two deckhands came up from below.

Dagger and Riley ducked into the first empty stateroom and listened as the men stood at the end of the companionway talking.

"How did those dumb asses lose Dr. Rawlings?" one of the men asked.

"Guess she left the area when all hands were called to the fire," the second man said.

"She can't get very far. Besides her water taxi is still docked."

"And her driver is still on the taxi?"

"Yeah, he's still reading a book."

"Search this deck. Meet me up top when you're done." One of the men started up the stairs.

The remaining deckhand stood in the passageway observing one end and then the other. He turned to his left and walked down to the first room, opened the door, and walked in. Dagger stayed put. A few seconds later, the man came out and continued to the next room.

Dagger waited until the deckhand turned the corner. Then he cracked open the door. Turning back to Riley, he signaled for them to leave. They hurried from the room into the companionway and down to the lower deck.

Dagger motioned for Riley to stay put. He walked out onto the deck and glanced around. When he was sure they were alone, he went back to where he'd left Riley. "It's clear, we need to go…quickly and now."

As they raced to the boat, Kaleb jumped up and started the

engine and Dagger helped Riley aboard. He leapt on board behind her as the boat drifted away from the yacht.

"Quick, get in the head," Dagger said, holding the door open for Riley.

"Why?"

"If anyone sees the boat leave, they'll only see Kaleb. They'll think he's heading out for another call."

Riley stepped inside the head. The tiny room was made even smaller as Dagger stepped in behind her and shut the door behind him. She was standing with her back to him, every taut muscle pressed firmly against her. She peered in the mirror directly at Dagger. He'd shot the woman he once planned to spend his life with, and not one iota of remorse or regret showed on his face.

"Is she dead?" Riley asked.

"I doubt it, it was only a flesh wound, and she's been trained to drop from high places." Dagger shrugged.

Riley exhaled.

"Forget it, Riley." Dagger grabbed her shoulders and turned her around to face him. "I took the shot I needed to take to get her off the ship. I was prepared to take the kill shot, if it came down to that. Kat is a cat. She's got nine lives, lands on her feet. She's not done hunting us."

"You would've sacrificed yourself to save me. When you looked me straight in the eyes the last time…I saw," she said.

"If I had to." Dagger's gaze was wandering over her. That sizzling feeling, like he was actually touching her enveloped her once again.

"Don't do that, ever." She tried to make it a demand.

"I can't swear to that when it comes to you."

"Even if it means you could get shot, captured, or worse?" Anger and fear intermingled and rose to the surface. Her heart raced and beads of sweat appeared on her upper lip.

"Yes." Dagger reached up and wiped away the sweat along with the three streaks of blood on her face.

"No…I couldn't live with myself." She grabbed hold of his arms and gave him a strong shake. His predatorial glare burned into her. "No!" Even though Dagger didn't answer. She knew she'd lost this battle. He'd do it again and again.

A single knock sounded on the door behind Dagger.

"We're clear of the yacht." Kaleb's voice was muffled by the door.

Dagger reached behind him, opened the door, and stepped out. "What about the incoming?" he asked, walking a few steps behind Kaleb.

"It's a helicopter. It will be overhead in seven minutes, so stay inside the cabin. I've changed course, and we're heading inland." Kaleb hopped up the few stairs to the steering station. "Once the chopper passes over, I'll get us back on course. I plan on skirting land as close as possible. We should be able to get close with this little boat: it will make it difficult for Welby and his goons to pinpoint us if we mingle with the recreational boaters."

"When Anthony realizes *Claudia* has disappeared, he's going to go after her," Riley said.

"She's fine, Riley. We knew it would be his next move, except he has to find her first," Dagger said. "As soon as Kaleb gets the information we need, we'll go directly to the authorities."

The distinct thrum of helicopter blades passed over them, off their distant starboard side.

"There's Welby," Kaleb said, reading Premier Oil and Gas printed on the undercarriage of the chopper.

"How did Stone's mission go?"

"He was in and out. Retrieved everything we asked for. Not a snag. Last I spoke to him, he was heading to the office."

Chapter Thirty-Eight

"Good see you all back in one piece," Stone said as Riley, Dagger, and Kaleb entered Hunters and Seekers. "Damn, I spoke too soon." Stone set his cup down and walked over to Riley. "What happened?" He peeled one corner of the tape free from her neck.

"Riley tried to stop a knife," Kaleb said.

"Ouch. Get up on the counter where I can see better." Stone picked up his medical bag and placed it on the counter next to Riley. "Where did *this* blood come from?" He noticed the three streaks on her head. Stone gently drew Riley's hair back and saw the three spots, each the size of dimes, on her hairline. "Someone ripped the wig off you."

"And the bald cap," Dagger growled.

"Holy hell. You've been put through the ringer." Stone closely examined her wounds. "Did Eddy glue the back of your wig too?"

"One spot, right here." Riley lifted her hair and showed Stone the injury on her hairline at the base of her skull.

"I could try and suture them up. They're not deep but painful all the same, I imagine." Stone looked over each spot once again. "I think the best course of action is to keep salve on them and bandage them for a few days."

"Whatever you say, Doc," Riley gave Stone a tired smile.

"I need to clean you up," Stone said. He wet a cloth with solution and carefully cleaned all the wounds. Then he took the last of the tape from her neck and cleaned the wound.

Riley winced at the sting.

"This going to require sutures. Do you want me to take you over to the hospital to get them done?"

"Won't you do it?" she asked.

"I can. I just want you to have the best possible outcome and the smallest scar."

"I trust you, Stone. I want you to do them." Dagger stood next to her the entire time, holding her hand.

"You need to keep your neck dry for a couple days. It's okay to get the spots on your head wet. I'll give you some waterproof bandages for your neck so you can shower," Stone said.

"And I'll help wash your hair and face for you," Dagger said as he helped Riley to sit up.

"That would be great. If you don't mind." Riley was touched at his suggestion, especially since it was offered in front of his partners. It suddenly dawned on her…She had a deep love for this man. She'd been in love with him for a while, and it had only intensified with each passing day. Even when he had distanced himself, she couldn't fight what she was feeling. This was an entirely new sensation. But did Dagger feel the same for her? She knew there was something there. He'd saved her life and said he'd do it over and over. Was it only because saving people was drummed into him?

"You head to the shower and let me know when you're ready." Riley walked into the dressing area and left the door cracked open. She headed for the bath, then remembered she'd forgotten to get the bandage, so she headed back for the kitchen. She stopped short behind the door when she heard Kaleb.

"You got it bad, bro," Kaleb said.

"Don't start with me. It's been a long hellish day, and the night isn't going to be a cake walk," Dagger said.

"You've got it wrong. Riley has become a part of our 'family.' Hell, I love her—"

Dagger whipped around and glared at his friend.

Kaleb shook his outstretched hands in front of him and continued. "As a little sister. I'd protect her with my life, because she's like my sister and she's important to you."

"I gotta admit," Stone said, "I feel the same way."

"Good. Because I want her around—at least for as long as she'll put up with me." Dagger visibly relaxed. He picked up Riley's bag and started for the bathroom. "Thanks, Stone."

Riley hightailed it into the bathroom on tippy-toes.

"See you soon, Romeo," Kaleb said.

Dagger rolled his eyes skyward and shook his head. "You just couldn't leave it alone."

****

"Time to get up sleepy heads," Stone said. He relocked the door behind him. The aroma of coffee and fresh baked goods wafted in.

Stone, Kaleb, Riley, and Dagger had been exhausted and fallen asleep at the boatshed hours earlier. Dagger was sprawled out on the sofa. Due to his size, he'd claimed most of the cushions. Nevertheless, Riley had managed to stake her spot, wedged between the back of the sofa and tucked in beside him. Her head was on his chest, one arm wrapped around him and her body was covered with a blanket. She was fast asleep. Dagger did no more than yawn when he heard Stone moving around. But when he caught the aromatic scent of breakfast, like a scent hound, he was ready for the hunt.

"Shit on a shingle…tell me it's a dream and not morning yet." Kaleb mumbled and threw a pillow over his head. He'd worked for hours, until his eyes got blurry and Dagger forced him to rest. Kaleb had thrown a futon on the floor only feet from the sofa and fell into it. For a few precious hours they regenerated.

"What time is it?" Kaleb's muffled question sounded through the pillow.

"Eight-thirty. I brought breakfast," Stone said.

Kaleb sat up, his pillow cast aside, as the scent of food triggered his primal instincts. Riley stirred and stretched like a cat waking from her nap.

"Morning," Dagger said as she looked up at him with her sleepy eyes. *She's alluring when she's asleep,* Dagger thought as his gaze caressed her face.

"Morning, mmm…something smells heavenly," Riley said as she sat up. She looked in the direction of the kitchen. Stone held up his cup of coffee and a cinnamon roll.

"Come get it while it's hot and there's still some to get," Stone cocked his head at Kaleb standing beside him and Riley giggled.

"What?" Kaleb gave an innocent look, his mouth full of blueberry scone.

Dagger and Riley joined them. For a few minutes, they all enjoyed their breakfast in peace and quiet.

"What's your status, Kaleb?" Dagger asked.

"'Bout that. I've got bad news. Stone's trip over to Welby's place was a bust. The only information on that computer deals with his legit businesses. I couldn't find anything that would help us."

"That sucks," Dagger said. "What about his system onboard his ship?"

"I did all I could last night. I left the program running. It's going to take time to break into Welby's computer files."

"Looks like it's finished to me," Stone said between gulps of coffee as he stared at Kaleb's screens.

Kaleb walked over to his computer. "Well, I'll be damned. I'm getting to be a pro at this. It only took me two attempts." He set his coffee and half-eaten bagel down, rubbed his hands together, and scrolled through his findings.

Stone leaned on the back of his chair.

"What?" Riley asked. "Did you find anything we can use against Anthony?" She'd wedged her way between Stone and Kaleb to get a better view, their sibling-like interaction not lost on Dagger. The guys really did feel protective of her. He'd never seen them like this with any other woman.

"How about his day-by-day reports regarding Claudia's capture," Kaleb gave her a Cheshire Cat smile as they did a high five.

"Are you serious?" The excitement in Riley's voice was contagious.

"That's not all. There's a video of Claudia's interrogation and the voice recordings Anthony pieced together to make her look guilty. Hours and hours of audio surveillance of Wayne's office and spreadsheets containing payouts to everyone involved, including Eric's payment for locating and 'staging' the Jane Doe, whose name happens to be Sandy Coats," Kaleb continued. "The pay-off of the tech at the genetics lab is here. Everything we need to bring this asshole down. We've got Anthony Welby by the short hairs."

"Fantastic," Dagger crowed and slapped Kaleb on his back.

"Wait...what the hell is this?" Kaleb said, as he frantically punched at the keyboard. "Bloody, hell—no you don't. Son of a bitch."

"What's happening?" Riley asked. Panic filling her voice, she grabbed a hold of Kaleb's shirt.

Dagger joined Stone glancing over Kaleb's shoulder. The three of them stared unbelieving as the strange symbols ate up Kaleb's screen like some sick game of Pac-Man.

Kaleb continued to curse a blue streak and fight with his

keyboard. Without warning the screen went blank. "It's gone," Kaleb said in a mournful tone.

"What do you mean—gone?" Stone asked.

"Gone. As in no longer there," Kaleb groaned.

"How can that be?" Riley asked. "Admiral Morrison swore up and down that was the most high-tech bug. He said it wasn't traceable."

"And it wasn't. We just got screwed by an old-fashioned virus. It must have triggered when the information redirected to my computer. Welby, that devious bastard, had his system set up to work only on a dedicated computer IP address. It would only load on his computer on board the ship. If the files get rerouted to another IP address, the virus wipes the download."

A slew of inventive words spilled from Kaleb's lips. "That's why I didn't find anything on his home system. If he attempted to access those files at his home, the same thing would've happened to him. Kinda brilliant in its simplicity." His elbow was on the desk and he was leaning his forehead into his palm. His head slid down his arm, as if it were too much for his hand to hold.

"Now what?" Riley sagged against Dagger. "We know about everything Anthony did, but we still have no proof. We can't let him get away with this."

"We won't," Dagger said. "Let's get everything we need packed up in our vehicles and head over to my place. We're going to lock my place down and rework everything from the day the SDPD called us to search the wreck. We'll find something."

****

They had spent the last forty-eight hours combing through every notation on the whiteboard, every electronic file the guys had written, all the SDPD files, and every step they'd taken to get to this point. Riley couldn't look at one more piece of evidence, in any form. She stretched and stood up. "I need to clear my head and get some fresh air." She walked toward the patio door.

"Want some company?" Dagger asked, glancing up from his computer.

"No thanks. I'll only be a few minutes." She stepped out, leaving the slider open a bit to give the men some fresh air.

She leaned against the rail and gazed out over the ocean, watching the sun move lower in the sky. A multitude of pinks, purples, blues, and oranges played over the water. The trees framed the beach.

She closed her eyes and took in a couple deep breaths. When she opened her eyes, there was a figure standing at the edge of the trees. The position of the sun made it impossible for her to get a clear view, but she could tell the person was facing her direction. A shudder tumbled down her back as the person started toward her.

"Dagger." She looked back over her should and called his name in a low tone.

"What's wrong?" Dagger asked. Without a sound he materialized directly behind her.

"We're being watched, and someone is coming this way." Riley stared at the figure.

Dagger raised his hand to shelter his eyes from the sun and stepped directly in front of Riley. "It's Katarina," he said. "You stay here. I'm going to see what the hell she wants."

"I'm coming with you." He knew her tone, but the last thing he needed was for Riley to be put in danger.

"No, you're not. It could be a trap. Please go inside," Dagger urged.

"No. I'm staying put. I won't go with you, but I refuse to hide."

Without making eye contact with Riley, Dagger stepped off the patio and headed for Katarina.

"What the hell are you doing here, Katarina? The bullet through your shoulder wasn't clear enough to you?"

"I got your message. I wouldn't be here if I had another choice. I need you to do something for me," Katarina said. She'd always been a pro at hiding her feelings—that had been beaten into Dagger's heart. All the same, she was nervous, and he could see it.

Dagger guffawed. "Lady, you've got some brass balls. What on God's green earth makes you think I'd lift one digit for you?"

"Because if you help me, you help yourself."

"Spit it out. You have one minute." Dagger glanced down at his dive watch.

"Anthony put out a hit on me."

"I don't see a problem so far." Dagger folded his arms.

"I'm sure you don't." Kat shrugged. "We had a little tiff over money and patent rights, and nobody cheats me. I'll be damned if he's going to come out smelling like a sweet spring morning." Kat slipped her hand into her jacket pocket.

"I'm gonna stop you right there. If I see anything that even resembles a weapon come out of your pocket, Kaleb's gonna drill a hole right through your head."

Katarina's hand stilled as she studied Dagger's cabin. She caught the glint of an M24 Sniper Weapon Systems barrel in the second-floor window. She slowly raised her empty hand and equally slowly slipped her other hand from her pocket and held up a jumpdrive. "Believe it or not, we have something in common. We both want to throw Anthony in the stockade. I need to send a worldwide message—screw with me, and pay the price." She handed the jumpdrive to Dagger. "This has everything you need to put him behind bars for life."

Dagger didn't move. "You want me to do your dirty work for you."

"No. I could mail it to the police, FBI, or hell, even the CIA. Consider it my way of saying…I'm sorry."

"They would come after you," Dagger said.

"Not with what I'm giving you. All I ask is that you wait twenty-four hours. Give me enough time to get out of the country and to go into hiding until Welby and his contract are out of action."

"Under one condition," he said, taking the jumpdrive. "I don't want to see you ever again. You stay away from me and mine."

"You mean Riley." She peered around Dagger and looked up at the patio. The petite Amazon warrior remained standing her guard.

"And everyone else. I'm dead serious, Katarina. Next time we won't be talking."

Katarina turned and started to walk away but stopped and turned back. "I want you to know, Dagger, that what I did back then wasn't personal. I was a sleeper agent. I did what I was trained to do. If it makes you sleep better, I sincerely enjoyed our time together."

"Goodbye, Katarina."

Chapter Thirty-Nine

When the team was through assessing all the files on the drive, everyone sat in silence, trying to digest what they had read.

"Katarina copied Welby's files, what a very bad girl," Kaleb said, shaking his head.

"Except for the redacted sections that included her." Stone pointed out.

"Are you surprised? She only gave us this to save her own skin. At least it gives us what we need," Dagger said.

"Now comes the important question," Riley said. "What do we do with this?"

"What do you mean?" Stone asked.

"Anthony Welby is an extremely powerful and internationally known business tycoon. If we hand our information off to the wrong people, it could disappear forever, leaving Mom dangling on the line as the guilty party, responsible for everything Anthony choreographed," Riley said.

"Okay. So we take our findings to the most powerful and honest person we know," Dagger said. "Make a copy of everything, Kaleb. We have someone to visit tomorrow."

Hours later Dagger entered the bedroom and found Riley sitting on the bed, staring out the window.

"I thought you loved her," Riley said without turning around. "I figured out a woman was behind your sudden disappearance. You refused to give me even a clue as to what you were up to. You were aloof and moody. So...I thought she was the one you loved." Riley continued to stare out the window. "Dagger, I saw you that day on the beach with her...she kissed you. I was so confused. A myriad of scenarios kept running through my mind. And when Katarina called, and you put your phone on speaker...the things she said, the fact that you wouldn't even look at me...it broke my heart. I was convinced at that moment that I was no more than a mission to you."

What a complete jackass I've been. He thought. "I told you...I did, or thought I loved her, once, a long time ago. There's nothing between us now." He walked around to where Riley was sitting and knelt in front of her. She was looking down at her hands. He couldn't read her. She looked sad and something more, he just wasn't sure what it was.

"I wanted so badly to believe. But you kept sneaking off, and Kaleb and Stone were covering for you." Riley lifted her head and stared into his face, like she was searching for something.

"That's not what was going on. I need to explain, if you'll let me." When Riley didn't say anything, he continued. "I realize I should've told you what I was doing. I handled it badly...believe me, Stone and Kaleb were livid with me and how I was treating you." Riley tried to smile, but it didn't reach her eyes. "I kept sending you mixed messages, and I'm deeply sorry. I guess if I'm honest with myself, I did what I did because of my truly poor decisions in the past. I was embarrassed of my past and terrified something bad would happen to you because of it." Dagger took her hands in his.

"You saved me, Dagger. On the ship when you shot Katarina and later when you told me you'd do it again and again, I willed myself to believe you...and I do. You already explained. I know now in my soul, Kat is no longer in your life."

"I never dreamed I would tell anyone what I'm about to tell you. Kat used me. She made me out for the fool. I need you to know my history with her. We can't put her behind us until you know how I got to this point." He got up off the floor and sat next to her on the bed. The time had come to shed light on his history, both the good and bad of it.

"I wanted to be a salvage diver. Not only a diver, but the best diver. My team was top-notch, we were known throughout the Navy. When I was thirty-one, my team was helicoptered out to a ship anchored directly above one of the most important discoveries of the time. The Navy brought in a civilian contractor to assist. The company sent out their marine archaeologist, who was a specialist in Russian vessels. Her name was Katarina Petrin.

"The mission was long, and Kat and I spent a great deal of time together. When we got back to land, we started dating. We worked more missions together, and two years later we were engaged. I thought I'd found the one. We had the same hobbies, liked the same things, enjoyed being with each other. Thinking back, there was a big red flag when Kat didn't want to move in with me after we got engaged. She spent all her time at my place but wasn't willing to give up her apartment. At the time I didn't think anything of it.

"Shortly after I proposed, my team was deployed for three months. When I returned, the shit hit the fan. Katarina was taken into custody, suspected of passing government secrets to the Soviet Union. I couldn't believe it. She'd come to this country at the age of four. Her parents were killed; her aunt and uncle took her in. She became an American citizen at fifteen. Kat was brilliant, even as a child. She did her internship with a government agency and was hired immediately by a top marine archaeology company. Kat did most of her work with the Coast Guard and Navy. I could not believe that this woman, whom I knew and loved, was a sleeper agent for Russia."

Riley had turned toward him. She chewed on her bottom lip and hung on his every word.

"That wasn't the worst of it. She dragged me into her mess. For a time, the government thought I was a spy, too. They investigated and questioned me. I teetered on losing everything I'd worked for, but I was eventually cleared. Kat admitted to being activated four months after we started dating."

"Oh, Dagger. How awful! What happened to Katarina?" Tears dammed up in Riley's eyes, but not one broke loose. She made a small wince and looked down at their joined hands, but never moved hers. His gaze followed hers. He was gripping her hands so tightly they had turned white…instantly he released her. Gently, he brought her hands to his lips and kissed them.

"Kat was placed in government custody. Everyone thought she'd been put away for life, but the CIA can do crazy things. That day at Hunters and Seekers when I left to take a message, it was a text from her. Kat had been offered a new opportunity to work as an agent for the US. She agreed and got out. Kat has a handler. Even so, I think now it's safe to say, she's her own boss."

"Then why did you meet with her?" Riley's face wrinkled from her eye brows to the corners of her lips.

"Because she threatened to kill you. I discovered my feelings for you when she threatened to kill you." Dagger knew he was laying his heart on the line once again. He might come away from this emotionally obliterated. But he had to risk it for the chance of sharing his life with this amazing woman.

"That first phone call. She described what you were wearing, and I knew Katarina Petrin had you in her sights...that's a deadly place to be. Riley, I haven't been involved with anyone for six years. I wasn't willing to put myself out there; I'd been betrayed and was nearly branded a traitor because I thought I was in love. I wasn't willing to trust my judgment ever again; the risks were too high. I only dated casually. If the woman started to get serious, I found a way to end it."

Riley sat there stunned, scarcely breathing. Willing him to go on.

"That's how I lived my life. Until the day a stunning, strong woman walked into Wayne Samuels's office on one of the worst days of her life and gave me the *you-don't-impress-me-in-the-least* look. At that moment, I knew you were someone worth taking a risk for. I could see you were a person of substance, one who would fight ferociously for the people she loved."

Riley threw her arms around him, hugging him tight. "I didn't feel fearless that day. I was terrified. And you threw me even further off-balance."

Dagger pulled her to him and drew her lips to his. Their kiss set a blaze within him. Stoked a need he'd never known he could feel, until this woman invaded his life and tore down his defenses.

He pulled away and looked at her. "You're ravishing when you're off-balance."

"I need to take a shower and wash the dirt of the day off," Riley said.

Dagger was confused. Riley could see it in the slight tilt of his head and the questioning look in his eye. "Remember, you can't get your stitches on your neck wet," he said.

"Stone said I could today. But if you're concerned you can keep them dry for me." She rose from the bed and peeled off her top and her shorts.

Now he was the one off-balance, although he recovered quickly. "For you, anything." Dagger stripped and followed her as she made her way into the bathroom and turned on the shower and got in.

Dagger moved in, brushing against her as he closed the glass door. She picked up the soap and soaped his arms and chest, slowly working her way southward. He reached for the shower wall and pressed his palms against it, allowing her to take the lead. She paid special attention to certain areas, causing Dagger to throw his head back and moan.

Then she moved down each of his legs, reveling in the feel of them. She outlined his taut, steely thighs with her soapy hands and moved to his backside sliding them up and down his impressive buttocks, feeling them flex in her palms.

"My turn," Dagger said as he soaped his hands.

He turned her toward the wall and rubbed his soapy hands along her shoulder blades, over her back, and started lazy circles on her buttocks, as he leaned down and nibbled an earlobe. Within seconds, goosebumps rose over her body. He moved his hands up to her breasts, and Riley thought her legs might give out.

Dagger rinsed her off and turned off the water. Taking her by the hand, he led her out of the shower and wrapped her in a towel. "I need you out of the shower, where I don't have to worry about the wrong parts of you getting wet."

Dagger lifted Riley into his arms. He carried her back into the bedroom, gently placed her on the bed, and dimmed the lights in the room. This man had caused her to doubt herself and him. But he'd also forced her to take a hard look at herself, her life, and what the she wanted. She'd gone through hell thinking her mother was dead. Dagger really did stand right beside her every step of the way—even when she wasn't aware of it at the time. The tenderness on his face nearly brought her to tears.

Dagger dropped his towel and stretched over her without his body touching hers and bent close to claim her mouth. Their tongues danced together. His taste was all man, spicy, hot, and intoxicating, intermingled with the clean scent of his soap.

One hand softly caressed her breasts. He teased her thighs apart while raining hot kisses on her face. He stared deeply into her eyes as he found his mark and drove himself inside her; a ragged gasp ripped from her. He slowly withdrew and then plunged again, going deeper with each thrust. Riley grasped his waist and tried to keep him inside her, but he was too strong.

Dagger groaned but didn't break eye contact. He kept his movements smooth and steady. She smiled slowly and continued to tug him down on her. Sheathed within her, he lowered himself down until every inch of their bodies melted together. Dagger picked up her rhythm and gradually increased the speed and intensity.

Riley's body was on the ragged edge. She tried to hold on, but every muscle inside her gripped Dagger. Together they hung on the precipice; Riley was completely unwilling to let the feeling end, but her body betrayed her, and her orgasm tore through her like a wildfire.

She cried out in ecstasy.

He remained on top of her, and she could feel his heart thudding madly. He tried to lift his weight off her, but she clenched her legs around him and forced him to stay put.

"Keep that up, and I'm going to demand a repeat performance," he breathed into her neck.

"You're not going anywhere," she teased.

He lifted himself up to his elbows and studied her with an inquisitive look. He smoothed her hair away from her face and placed a light kiss on her forehead. "I'm afraid I'll hurt you."

One side of her mouth quirked up. Her rich eyes glinted, giving her an impish appearance. She pushed at him. He rolled off her taking her with him until she sat atop, straddling his waist. She rubbed her soft body against him. Her one motion brought his entire body to life, and he grew hard instantly. She found her target and excruciatingly slowly lowered herself, burying him inside her. She rocked her hips slowly, remaining fully seated on him all the while; her muscles stroked him. He fought his urge to take control. She started this situation, and he was going to allow her to finish it— even if it killed him.

"Holy hell, woman. What are you doing to me?" he asked, panting. He gasped as she made slow, rhythmic circles with her hips, all the while kneading him. He sucked in a sharp breath.

"Relax," she breathed.

"That's hard at the moment."

"Why, yes...yes, it is." Her breasts rose and fell. Her body shimmered. She was a petite woman and her body soft in all the right places. His Amazon warrior…His nymph. She was perfect for him.

"Ga-ww-d, Dr. Rawlings, you surely got a wicked streak. You're going to be even more of a handful than I could've ever imagined."

Dagger felt the instant Riley started her climb up to ecstasy. The heat of her penetrated every cell of his body. He wanted the feel of her imprinted in him for all eternity. He fought to let her lead him there until his body couldn't bear it. He thrusted over and over. Riley started her release, and he was right there with her.

Finally spent, Riley lay next to him. They kissed and caressed without a word between them. Dagger turned on his side and snugged Riley against him. She was the missing puzzle piece of his heart and soul. The hole in his universe he believed would never be filled. He grabbed a handful of blankets and covered them. The desolate feeling that had taken residence in his heart melted away.

Chapter Forty

"Good morning, sir," Dagger said, standing in the massive entrance of Admiral Morrison's house.

"What did I tell you—it's Henry, Dagger," Admiral Morrison said. "Come on in. We're having breakfast on the lanai. Join us." He waved them into his house.

"Thank you for having us over," Dagger said as he glanced at the team.

"Cook has already set places for you and is preparing your meals as we speak."

Dagger stepped aside, allowing Riley to enter first, followed by Kaleb and Stone.

"This matter must be extremely important for you to bring the entire team." Admiral Morrison led them through the house, to a large glass-enclosed veranda, full of greenery and palm trees. A stone-lined pool filled one side, irregularly shaped, with two waterfalls.

Riley ran to her mother as Claudia stood up from the table. They threw their arms around one another.

Claudia pulled away and studied her daughter up and down, zeroing in on the large dressing on her neck. "Oh my God! What happened to you?"

"I'm fine, Mom. Just a little scratch. Stone sutured it up for me."

"What? A little scratch wouldn't require stitches," Claudia said.

"Don't worry. I'm okay."

Claudia examined her for a bit longer. "I'm so glad you're all here. You had me worried sick."

"Tell us what you discovered," Morrison said.

"Kaleb has all the details," Dagger said, giving his buddy a nod.

Kaleb cleared his throat, as five sets of eyes focused on him. He sucked in a breath and explained what they'd uncovered.

"Thank you," Claudia said. "A huge weight has lifted off my shoulders. I was convinced I would soon be going to prison. Henry is my rock," Claudia said. Morrison reached over and took her hand. Claudia smiled back at him. "He has complete faith in you boys. He kept assuring me you would find something."

"It wouldn't have happened without your daughter's help," Dagger said. "She's fearless—especially when it comes to protecting you."

"Looks like you can wrap this mess up once and for all," Morrison said.

"That's where it gets sticky," Riley said.

"How so?" Morrison asked.

"Anthony is known, revered, and buys off people. The man associates with ambassadors, mega-millionaires, dictators, and monarchs," Riley said. "If we take our information to the wrong person, it could disappear into the ether, never to been seen again."

"I see." Morrison nodded his understanding. "And you're hoping I might know someone powerful enough to keep that from happening."

"Exactly," Dagger said.

"Son, you've come to the right person. How high would you like to go? The Secretary of Defense or the Vice President?"

Their collective jaws dropped open.

"You have a personal relationship with the Secretary of Defense *and* the Vice President?" Riley asked.

"We go way back. The SOD and I are friends from middle school. The VP and I were roommates at the Naval Academy."

"I'd say either one would be more than we dreamed of," Dagger said. "You know them. We'll leave the decision up to you."

"Let me make a call. I'll be damned if I'm going to sit back and watch you take the fall, Claudia." The admiral stood and went to retrieve a phone.

Dagger, Stone, and Kaleb all rose.

"Sit down and relax. You've done all the hard work. I'm only carrying the ball the last yard. I shouldn't be long." Morrison winked at Claudia and left the room.

Admiral Morrison returned a few minutes later. "I put together a three-way conference call. We came to the conclusion the Secretary of Defense was the appropriate position to handle this, based on the assumption Anthony planned to sell Claudia's formula to foreign buyers. I conveyed this was a personal favor to me. Claudia, I needed to fill them in on the overview to justify this level of authority."

Riley's eyes widened. "Mom, you told Henry about your research?"

"I did, yes," Claudia said.

"But in all these years, you never told anyone, not even me. Why now?"

"I should've confided in you, Riley. I kept you in the dark because I believed it would keep you safe. If you knew nothing, there would be no reason for anyone to bother you. I was wrong and I'm sorry." Claudia reached over and cupped her hand on the side of Riley's face. "I've had plenty of time to think, both while I was held captive and during my stay here with Henry. Now that I'm safe and with someone who truly cares what happens to me, I decided to confide in him, because I trust him, and realized I needed someone to talk to about my work. I told him if it came down to keeping you safe or exposing my formula, there wasn't a choice to be made. I would give away everything: my work, my freedom, and my life, if it meant you were safe."

Admiral Morrison reached out and covered Claudia's fist that lay on the table. "I promise, I only told my friends enough to justify their getting involved." Morrison focused on Claudia, as if she were the only person in the room. "Though both men realize you are a private citizen and your research is your own, it doesn't mean they aren't interested in talking with you at some point in the future."

"Thank you," Claudia said.

"The order to arrest Welby was issued and should be executed soon. I'll keep you up to date as I hear," the admiral said. "The Secretary of Defense will be contacting the Coast Guard and most likely the FBI, but it will be Hunters and Seekers who will get the credit for breaking this case wide open and handing over all the information needed to prosecute Anthony Welby."

"Thank you, sir," Dagger said. "Claudia, if you're ready, we can take you back to your house. Riley and I will stay with you until it's safe."

"That won't be necessary, Dagger," Morrison said. "I have

asked Claudia to stay until the dust has settled. She'll be quite safe here."

****

It was a beautiful, crisp autumn morning when Anthony Welby was escorted out of his office at Sheridan Enterprises. Handcuffed, he walked from the building flanked by the SDPD, Coast Guard, and two FBI agents. His scowl turned into full-blown rage when he saw Riley, Dagger, Stone, and Kaleb, who were all leaning against Dagger's Range Rover.

"You!" Anthony bellowed. The cords of his neck protruded, and his nostrils flared. "The four of you are responsible for this farce. This means nothing. My attorneys will have me out before lunch. You have no idea who you're dealing with." Spittle dribbled from the corners of his mouth. "Riley, you will rue the day you hired these imbeciles. I will see to it. Claudia sunk her ship. She killed Wayne and all the others—I have the proof."

"I'm sure you do—*Mr. White*," Riley said. "Yes, we know all about your relationship with Neal and your employee, Eric. Mr. White, you were the man in charge. We know that, and now so does the SDPD, Coast Guard, and FBI."

"Don't forget who issued the arrest warrant," Dagger said.

"That's right…you might've heard of him. The Secretary of Defense." Riley pressed her lips together to keep from breaking out in laughter.

A tic started in Anthony's eye. He tripped over one of the officer's feet but continued his rant. His voice went up an octave. The police tossed him into the backseat of their vehicle and drove away.

"Well, that shook him up." Stone chuckled.

Riley snickered. "I can't wait to see his face when he finds out who helped us."

Chapter Forty-One

*T*wo months later...

"I lost the bet," Kaleb said, walking in from Dagger's garage with another moving box.

"Yeah, you did," Stone said following Kaleb and bumping him with his carton.

"Should I hazard to ask what you guys were betting on?" Riley asked as she pushed a crate against the wall to keep the two men from tripping.

"You don't want to know," Dagger said, bringing up the rear. His hands were full of bags.

"Now it sounds intriguing. Spill it," she said.

The guys carried the boxes into the master bedroom and returned to the main room.

"I bet Stone that Dagger would ask you to join our team before he asked you to move in," Kaleb said.

"You really should learn to filter yourself," Dagger said as he rolled his eyes.

"He never asked me to work with you guys," Riley said.

"Exactly," Kaleb said. "We've doubled our contracts since word got out that Hunters and Seekers was the driving force at putting Welby in prison. We could really use you, Riley. We were a great team."

"I swear to God. Keep it up and I'm going to punch you," Dagger said.

"Why haven't you asked me to work with you, Dagger?" Riley asked as she looked over at him.

Dagger stuck his hands in his pockets, looked down at his feet, and kicked the closest box. He reminded Riley of a young boy who got caught picking on his sister.

"You went back to teaching. You seem to be happy there, and I didn't want to put you in the position of having to tell us no," Dagger said as he pinned his two friends with his icy stare.

"I went back to work for some normalcy and to fill my days."

"What are you saying? You don't adore teaching anymore?" Dagger blinked his eyes and shook his head once as if trying to clear the fog in his brain.

"Ahhh...." Riley sighed. "It's not that I don't like teaching. I've come to realize I don't relish normalcy."

All three of the men were stunned into silence. Finally, Stone chimed in, "Well, ma'am, you've come to the right place."

"Riley Rawlings, would you like to become the fourth partner in Hunters and Seekers?" Dagger asked.

"I thought you'd never ask." Her laughter was so full of happiness, all three men joined in.

"There's one more little detail I want to ask you about, while you're saying yes," Dagger said. "And I should do it now, before one of my overly chatty buddies blurts it out."

Riley squinted her eyes and studied each of the men. Their grins reminded her of boys caught taking their parent's vehicle out for an illegal joy ride.

"*O—kaay.*" Riley had no idea what these three men were brewing up. She folded her arms over her chest, preparing to scold someone. Her mouth fell open as Dagger stepped directly in front of her and dropped to one knee.

"I planned to wait until tonight, but...Riley Rawlings, would you do me the honor of becoming my wife?" Dagger held out a gorgeous, teardrop diamond ring, the band encrusted with square, deep ocean-blue sapphires. It was the most exquisite ring she'd ever seen.

"Yes—" She dropped to her knees and kissed him. "This is the perfect time." She mumbled between kisses.

"Okay, get a room," Kaleb said. He ran over to the kitchen, pulled out four long-stemmed glasses, grabbed a bottle of champagne, and popped the cork. "We need to make a toast," Kaleb said filling the glasses. Dagger picked up two glasses and handed one to his fiancée. Stone and Kaleb joined them. Kaleb looked at his buddy.

Stone took the hint. "Riley Rawlings, you may be marrying Dagger, but you need to understand, you're not just gaining a husband, you're gaining two brothers." Stone smiled as he looked from one person to the next. "We will support both of you and protect from any and all threats. You are our chosen family...we love you, both."

Tears trickled down Riley's cheeks and dripped onto her top. She glanced from one man to the next. Understanding dawned on her. Two of the most considerate, caring, funny, and dependable men she had ever had the great fortune to know were becoming part of her family.

"Shit...look what you did, Stone!" Kaleb's neck and face mottled bright crimson.

Riley handed Dagger her glass, hugged Kaleb, and kissed him on the cheek. She turned to Stone and did the same. She put an arm through each of the guys arms. "Thank you. You two are the brothers I always wanted. I'll be here for you." She smiled at them and then Dagger. A wetness shimmered in his eyes as he raised his glass to Riley.

There was a knock on the door. Kaleb walked over and opened it to find Claudia and Admiral Morrison.

"Please come in," Dagger said, standing behind Kaleb.

"We have some news and wanted to share with all of you." Morrison turned and nodded at Claudia.

"Anthony's team of attorneys decided to settle out of court with regards to stealing my formula and kidnapping me. Guess they didn't want the information plastered all over the news," Claudia said. "He'll remain in prison throughout the trial for multiple wrongful deaths. The rumor is he'll be found guilty and sentenced to life in prison with no chance of parole. It will most likely take years to get to that point."

"Claudia didn't mention the best part," Morrison beamed at Claudia. "The settlement is enough money to support her research for years. She'll be able to do anything she wants with it." Morrison shook his head once and wrapped his arm around Claudia's shoulder. "I'm so proud of her."

"I always have been," Riley kissed her mom on the cheek.

"Wonderful news, Claudia." Stone hugged her. "Open another bottle of champagne, Kaleb."

Congratulations, cheering, hugging, and shaking hands spread throughout the group.

"Does this mean you're going out on your own?" Riley asked.

"Yes. I'm finally going to start my own research company." Claudia beamed.

"Fantastic. It's about time, Mom. You'll love being your own boss. When do you plan to move forward?"

"When Henry and I return from our honeymoon," Claudia said.

"What?" Riley grabbed her mom by the hands and spun her around in circles. Her mother once told her she'd never remarry; Riley couldn't be happier for her.

"I'm thrilled for the two of you. I always thought you'd be the perfect match if you could only get your timing right." Riley hugged her mom and then the Admiral as the men gave their congratulations.

Morrison took Claudia's hand and brought it to his lips. She leaned in and kissed him.

"I know this is short notice, although we don't want to wait any longer than we have to. Do you think your Dean will let you take a few weeks' vacation? We're going to Oahu for the ceremony and honeymoon. We'll be holding the ceremony on one of the more secluded beaches. Estelle and Stan want to help plan it," Claudia said.

"Charlie is going to be my best man, so we'll be coordinating the event with the powers that be. Security will be tight," Morrison said.

"The Secretary of Defense is your best man. How awesome," Kaleb said.

"The VP may attend, too, if he can work it out."

"Wow! We wouldn't miss it for anything," Riley said.

"And getting off work won't be a problem," Dagger chimed in. "Starting the week after next, Riley will have a new position. She's agreed to join our misfit group and become a partner at Hunters and Seekers."

"Riley! I'm ecstatic for all of you." Claudia said.

"It gets better." Dagger's face lit up with a beaming smile. "She just agreed to become *my* partner—forever." He wrapped his arms around Riley, lifted her off the ground and spun in a circle.

Claudia's eyes widened, and a huge grin creased her face. "I'm stunned and beyond happy for the two of you."

Morrison smiled. "Since the day she met you, she's been wishing the two of you would take the next step. Congratulations."

"Thank you, sir—Henry," Dagger stuttered.

"Call me Henry, son. After all, I'm going to be your father-in-law." Henry slapped Dagger on the back. "Say, I've got a great idea. What do you say we hold a double wedding?" He glanced at Claudia.

"I'd love it, but what do the two of you think?" Claudia asked.

Riley gazed up at Dagger.

"As long as you marry me, I don't care about the details. I'll go around the world just to hear you say yes again," Dagger said, answering the question in her eyes.

"We would love to," Riley exclaimed.

"When you walked into Samuels's office that day, chin held high, even with the weight of your immense sorrow and loss, I knew you were someone special. The last thing I could've imagined was you agreeing to become my wife. You've turned my world upside down, Riley Rawlings. And I can't even begin to explain how insanely elated you've made me. I do know life with you will never be boring."

Riley laughed and leapt into Dagger's open arms. "I love you, Dagger Eastin, and I can't wait to begin our next adventure."

About the Author

Author photograph by Samantha Panzera

Joanne writes romantic suspense, paranormal, supernatural suspense, and contemporary romance. She loves to submerge herself in the world of her characters, to live and breathe their lives, and marvel at their decisions and predicaments. She enjoys a wide variety of books including paranormal, suspense, thriller, and of course romance.

Joanne was born and raised in Sherburne, New York, a quaint village surrounded by dairy farms and rolling hills. From the moment she could read she wanted to explore the world. During her college years she slowly crept across the country, stopping along the way in Oklahoma, California, and finally Washington State, which she now proudly calls home. She lives with her husband and Dobermans, in their home located on the Olympic Peninsula with a panoramic view of the Olympic Mountains.

Joanne is a PAN member of Romance Writers of America, (RWA), Kiss of Death, (KOD), Greater Seattle Romance Writers Chapter, (GSRWA), Sisters In Crime (SIC), and Fantasy, Futuristic & Paranormal, (FFPRWA). She served as President of Peninsula Romance Writers, Debbie Macomber's home chapter.

Books by Joanne:

Chasing Victory, The Winters Sisters, Book One
Payton's Pursuit, The Winters Sisters, Book Two
Willow's Discovery, The Winters Sisters, Book Three
Corralling Kenzie, The Winters Sisters, Book Four

P.I.-I Love You, Miss Demeanor, P.I., Book One
Christmas Reflections, Forever Christmas In Glenville, Book One
Christmas Ivy, Forever Christmas In Glenville, Book Two
Forever Christmas In Glenville Collection
Love's Always Paws-Able, Love, Take Two Collection, Book 1
Building Up to Love, Love, Take Two Collection, Book 2
Uncharted Love, Love, Take Two Collection, Book 3
Love, Take Two Collection

Made in the USA
Middletown, DE
17 March 2019